PEACE MAKER

VERDANT STRING

MICHELLE DIENER

ECLIPSE

ABOUT PEACE MAKER

Fliss knows all about her ancestors, the Travelers, who were forced to land on Fjern thousands of years ago, but when it comes to the Gyr—the enhanced warriors who protect the people of Fjern from the monsters that inhabit the planet—she's in the dark, even though she is one herself. There's plenty of ceremony and arcane tradition set up around who receives the gyra—the nanotech that makes the warriors the super-protectors that they are—but Fliss doesn't care about any of that, she just wants to brush off the dust of the tiny mining settlement she's been protecting all her life and leave the combative relationship she has with her father far behind her.

When the Gyr who offered her a way out of her old life dies in spectacular fashion, though, she comes to the attention of a host of powerful people, both the Gyr and the administrators from the institution that controls them, alike. Fliss is about to find out more about the Gyr—and herself—than she ever dreamed of.

Gyr leader, Hannu Kardenian, thought he was being called to investigate the strange death of a fellow warrior, but what he finds instead is a woman who breaks every rule he's ever lived by. Everything about her sets his own gyra on fire, and when she comes to the attention of Gyr Command—the institution that mandates the Gyr's very existence—he is determined to make sure she never ends up in their clutches, even if he has to upend the very structure of Fjern itself.

1
———————

HANNU KARDENIAN AND TWO MEMBERS OF HIS TEAM——HARD, STERN warriors in full battle gear——stood no more than ten lengths from where Fliss leaned against the wall.

They were talking quietly to the senior members of Dakar's team.

Discussing Dakar's death.

Discussing her.

Fliss's ears buzzed with what they were saying.

It made her twitchy.

Kardenian cut his gaze to her, a slight frown creasing his brow.

He was handsome. Beautiful, even.

His dark hair was cut short, his light gray eyes almost silver as they narrowed, watching her.

"I tell you, she isn't Gyr," Rinald, one of Dakar's lieutenants, was saying urgently. "She can't shift."

It came to Fliss, sudden and shocking as a light going on in a pitch dark room, that Rinald believed what he had just said. He wasn't trying to lie.

He didn't know what she was.

And he thought she couldn't hear him.

It struck her with a deep certainty.

And then another thought hit.

Could it be that they *all* thought that?

The earnest way Vanesh was backing Rinald up, she suddenly thought maybe he didn't know, either. That none of Dakar's team did.

Maybe Dakar had never told them.

The epiphany made her legs weak, and she slid down the wall to sit on the ice-cold stone of the floor.

Meli, the last of the three, looked over at her as she did, her gaze suspicious.

Fliss ignored her and bent her head, resting it on her knees as she came to grips with her new perspective.

Maybe they hadn't been treating her like a freak. At least, not at first.

When she'd arrived over six weeks ago, she'd thought they were trying to offend her. But that could well have been all in her head, baggage from before.

Her past with her father, and everything that had happened up until Dakar had found her, continued to mess with her perceptions.

But now her realization cleared the way before her, burning away misunderstandings like mist in the summer morning sun.

All this time, the Gyr in the gyratta had thought she was Fjerna.

A strangled laugh escaped her throat, and she pressed her lips hard against her knees to cut it off.

Dakar had known what she was.

He'd given her a chance at a new life.

But she had thought everyone in his team had known what he knew. That everyone in Gyr Command must know.

She had been wrong.

She thought back now to what she'd perceived as disrespectful slights, mainly whispers behind her back that she'd been easily able to hear. She'd thought she'd been meant to hear them.

Perhaps she hadn't.

Not that that changed what had been said.

She thought back to how Dakar had kept her isolated from the others, kept her from making connections with them, and saw now it wasn't just possessiveness, it had been a deliberate strategy to hide what she was.

She struggled to think why he would do that, when that light that had switched on in her head earlier stuttered and then flared up even brighter.

He'd wanted them to think he had managed to get his control back on his own. That she had nothing to do with it.

The truth of it slammed into her with such force she closed her eyes and gripped her knees even tighter.

The question then was, what had they thought she was doing on the team?

The insinuation had been that she was Dakar's lover.

She'd been insulted when she'd heard them muttering about her presence among them. Her lack of a role.

A lifetime of growing up with her father, with his bitter disappointment and disrespect of her, had colored her expectations.

She'd thought Dakar's team were just doing what so many had done to her her whole life. In fact, she'd thought they'd gone a step further, because she had always thought they knew she was like them, that she could hear them whispering about her.

But what if Dakar had outright lied to them? Not just about what she was, but about why she was there?

No wonder he didn't want her talking to them, becoming friendly with them.

His whole web of lies would have been exposed.

She slowly raised her head, found Meli was still looking at her.

What a waste.

Meli could have been an ally. Instead, she was part of the whisper campaign.

Part of the chorus against her.

Now that Dakar was dead, had killed himself in spectacular fashion right in front of her, they wanted it to be her fault.

That's what they were trying to tell Kardenian's team right now.

But she didn't have to put up with it, she suddenly realized.

She knew what they did not.

Dakar's team wouldn't want to believe their leader had been a liar and a creep, for all she had once seen him as her savior, but Hannu Kardenian would surely be more circumspect.

More even-handed.

She had only met him for the first time this afternoon, but she had a bone-deep sense that he was trustworthy.

She knew it in the way she often knew things. And she didn't doubt it for a moment.

She sharpened her gaze on the huddle of warriors. "I can hear every word you say," she said quietly, making no effort to raise her voice. "I have always been able to. Every whisper, every lie, every nasty remark. I heard every syllable. Because I am Gyr. Dakar knew it, and I'm beginning to realize he hid it from you. Lied to you. But that doesn't excuse the disrespect. You can all go fuck yourselves."

She pushed back to her feet in an easy move, using just the muscles in her legs, no arms to steady herself or give herself a boost.

Meli had gone still at her words, her eyes wide, and Fliss saw a flash of . . . something. Some spike of emotion before she glanced over at Rinald, looking for guidance.

Kardenian had turned her way as she spoke, eyes narrowed even more.

Fliss ignored him, dusting the seat of her pants and walking away toward her room.

It was the worst one in the compound. The smallest, with windows set high, so she couldn't see out.

Dakar had told her that was because she'd come in last, and she had, in truth, never minded.

When she'd first arrived it had felt safe. It was hers, and she was very aware she was the last in.

By a long way.

Everyone had made sure she knew it. How close-knit and established the team was.

It had still been better than her life before.

She reached the door and lifted a hand to open it.

"You're not registered. How can you be Gyr?" Kardenian was behind her.

He was fast. Quiet.

A true Gyr.

She'd sensed him moving, though. Something inside her had jumped in anticipation as he'd come after her.

A feeling of . . . possibilities.

She said nothing, simply pushed her door open, turned, and put out her hand and offered it to him.

After a moment, he gripped it with his own.

"Don't touch her!" Rinald's voice cracked with concern and panic as he came jogging down the passage after them.

"Why not?" Kardenian kept a hold of her hand as he looked slowly over his shoulder at what turned out to be the whole group, all crowded in the passageway behind him.

"Dakar said . . ." Rinald trailed off, as if for the first time wondering why Dakar had forbidden something like that.

"Because it would have told you she was as Gyr as you are," Kardenian said. His voice was calm, and it sent a shiver through her.

She liked the sound of it.

There was a beat of silence and Kardenian released his grip slowly, as if he didn't want to let her go.

"Explain." Vanesh pushed forward. "Why didn't you say?"

Fliss leaned against the doorjamb. "Because I thought you knew. Dakar did, and I thought he'd told you."

"So all those times . . ." Meli's color was high on her cheeks. "You really did hear us?"

Fliss said nothing, just held her gaze, then turned her focus on Rinald, then Vanesh.

Meli blew out a breath. "We thought . . ."

When her voice faded, there was silence. A very uncomfortable silence.

Not for Fliss, though. For them.

"What *did* you think?" Kardenian asked.

"That Dakar had fallen for her. That he was breaking the rules by bringing her into the compound." Rinald spoke in low, bitter tones.

She was used to those tones.

"No one can enter the gyratta unless they are Gyr." Pen spoke for the first time. She was one of Kardenian's. A long, lithe woman with dark hair and dark eyes, similar to Fliss's own coloring. "Surely you wondered how she got in if she wasn't one of you?"

"I've taken everything you've told us about this situation as total bullshit since you tried to convince us she isn't Gyr, even though she was inside the gyratta." Delasio's deep voice resonated with Fliss, made her feel . . . safe. He was also one of Kardenian's, a big man whose dark skin was pulled taut over muscles that looked like cut stone.

"Dakar said he'd found a way to fool the sensors. He said——"

"A lot of things that obviously need to be reexamined." Vanesh cut Rinald off, as if aware that they were starting to dig themselves a hole.

Like admitting to believing a breach had taken place, which they had not reported.

Kardenian finally stepped away from her, half-turning to face the crowd. "I think we may need to start again, don't you?" His voice was soft.

Pen flicked him a look.

Fliss caught the slight widening of surprise in her eyes, and she wondered if it was because of the statement itself or the tone behind it.

Kardenian was annoyed, maybe even angry, with Dakar's team.

"I don't know what to say." Rinald looked a little sick. "Everything I thought was true turns out to be a lie."

"Well, let's start with what brought me and my team here." Kardenian looked straight at Fliss. "Did you kill Dakar?"

Fliss shook her head. She refused to wear that. "He killed himself."

"Why would he do that?" Vanesh sounded utterly furious.

"Because he tried to kill *me*," Fliss told him, jabbing her finger to her chest. "And his gyra refused to allow it. They lifted his knife to his throat with his own hand and sliced it when he wouldn't obey."

The silence that came with her words took on actual weight, and suddenly done with the lot of them, Fliss took a step back into her room, and closed the door in their faces.

2

EXTRAORDINARY.

Hannu Kardenian stared at the closed door for a beat and then turned to face the crowd behind him.

His hand still tingled where it had touched Fliss Belaire's.

His gyra had surged within him the moment they'd made contact, his heart jumping, his chest tightening in a way he had never experienced before.

He thought about what she claimed about Dakar's death.

He had never heard of someone's gyra making the choice to kill them.

It was almost impossible to believe.

And not comfortable, either. Not comfortable at all.

Since he'd received his own gyra at the age of seventeen, he had always felt at one with them. Others, he knew, did not have the same experience. They spoke of a distance, a feeling of being apart, like two personalities in one body.

If gyra could work against their host, could choose to end their warrior's life, then Gyr Command needed to know about it.

Or maybe they already did.

Han was under no illusions that no one would hear about something as explosive as that if Gyr Command could prevent it.

"You said Belaire is new here. When did she arrive?" Han focused on Vanesh, the only senior member of Dakar's team who he thought would give him straight facts, without embellishment.

"She's been here less than two months. Dakar took a sabbatical that ended up lasting almost half a year. When he returned, he brought her with him."

"He was looking for something." Meli was staring at the closed door, too. She had had some of the nastier things to say about Fliss Belaire when Han and his team had arrived, but the truth seemed to have deflated her.

"Like what?" Pen was watching her with a hard, focused stare. She had told Han she did not like the vibe in this place one bit.

Han could only agree.

"I think he was looking for *her*. Whatever she is." Meli tossed her head, tipping it toward the room.

"She's Gyr. There is no doubt." Han didn't understand the spike in his temper. He didn't usually let himself get needled by others.

"She may be Gyr but she can't shift," Rinald stated baldly. "No question about it."

"You tested her, did you?" Delasio asked. His wry tone was well-deserved. Testing happened in training, and Rinald had no place doing it to anyone.

"Dakar had to save her ass, because she insisted on going out with us the first week she got here. A largarti came out of a tunnel when we were walking through the gorge and attacked. She didn't so much as waiver, let alone shift."

"*Did* she insist on going out with us?" Vanesh mused. "Or did Dakar insist? Because I don't remember her being very enthusiastic about it."

There was silence for a moment.

"She says Dakar knew all about her. If he knew she was Gyr but couldn't shift, why would he have brought her along?" Meli wondered.

Good question. Han flicked a quick look at the door again. One he would find answers to.

But not now.

"Gyr Command is bringing in a new recruit." He glanced at Pen and she nodded.

"Dakar's body is ready to move out of the gyratta."

The new recruit couldn't step inside until Dakar's gyra had been transferred from his lifeless body into the recruit's, so there was a small hut beside the entrance of every gyratta compound to induct new warriors.

Han still couldn't believe Dakar's team had somehow believed their leader had managed to get Fliss Belaire in and out without her being one of them.

"How did Dakar explain getting Belaire inside if he told you she wasn't Gyr?" He put the question to Rinald, who had been only too eager to offer the information earlier, before Vanesh had cut him off.

"He said he held her tight against him, her back to his front, and curled over her, so no part of her was exposed as they crossed under the arch." Rinald looked a little lost. "I never saw him do it, though."

"Did any of you see him do it? See her come or go from the gyratta?" Han asked.

There was a long silence where no one met his gaze. Dakar must have made sure no one was around when she went out, and he guessed his team played along so they wouldn't have to report it.

"And why? Did he offer an explanation as to why he would break protocol like that?" Pen asked.

And it truly was a massive breach of protocol, Han thought. And nonsensical. The arch scan didn't work like that.

"He did not." Rinald's lips formed a tight line.

"We were so glad to have him back, looking much better than he had before he left." Meli leaned back against the wall and blew out a breath. "He was much more in control. We didn't want to pry."

"In control?" Delasio picked up what Han also thought was the most important part of that statement. "He was Spiraling?"

The three members of Dakar's team exchanged a look.

Vanesh cleared his throat. "I don't think he was as far gone as that. But he did have . . . issues."

That Gyr Command had left this compound in the control of a Spiraling leader beggared belief. He must have hid it well, because they would surely not have turned a blind eye to it.

It didn't serve their purpose.

Han didn't like what he was hearing here. Not one bit.

"And if she's telling the truth?" Meli asked. "If Dakar's gyra did turn on him and kill him, to stop him killing her? Is it safe for them to be passed on to a new recruit?"

Han wondered the same.

He would have to speak to Gyr Command about it before the ceremony.

With a last look at the door, he moved down the passage, forcing the others back against the wall to make way for him.

This was an out-of-the-way part of the compound, a forgotten corner that now he knew a little more about the situation, he guessed Dakar had set up on purpose, to keep anyone from interacting with Fliss. Touching her.

They would have felt her gyra immediately.

So strong.

That's what he'd sensed from her.

Strong and . . . wild.

He didn't know why he felt that, but it was like no other touch reception he'd encountered before.

And she definitely wasn't registered. He had double-checked.

It wasn't completely unheard of.

Occasionally a Gyr went missing and met a bad end.

Whoever came across the body first received the gyra without the pomp and ceremony he and Gyr Command were about to enact in the Transfer.

He'd read a few first-hand accounts of tiny silver balls rolling toward hikers or remote villagers, and those balls simply sinking into their skin as they picked them up. He'd even served through his training with a woman who, as a medic, had gone to help a Gyr who'd been mortally wounded by a zuby, and his gyra had slid into her at the moment of his death.

Some of the newly-made Gyr didn't even realize what had happened until they started to shift when danger approached.

Gyr Command had to accept them, obviously, and send them for training, but it was more than possible that Fliss Belaire had been even more in the dark, if she couldn't shift.

How would she know what had happened to her? Gyr Command kept as much about the gyra a secret as possible.

The silver balls were not commonly discussed.

Only, Dakar *had* known.

He reached the dead man's office and stepped in, aware Delasio and Pen had followed him. They took up guard positions outside the door and he let them. He didn't think they'd get any more out of Dakar's senior officers.

This compound had held a team of seven.

Six now that Dakar was gone.

And that wasn't counting Fliss Belaire.

Although obviously it should.

He touched the comm console and waited for Teranimo to answer.

"What?" The chief scientist at Vallent's Gyr Command snapped the question, coming into the frame with a scowl.

"The dead team leader," Han said without preamble. "His own gyra killed him. Slit his throat."

Teranimo was silent for an astonished beat. "Why?"

"Because he was about to kill another Gyr. She said his gyra fought to stop him, and when he wouldn't obey, they lifted his hand and sliced his throat."

Teranimo suddenly disappeared with a shout, and then peered into the console, eyes a little wide. "Missed the chair when I tried to sit down," he explained. "I've never heard of one Gyr trying to kill another."

"Now we know what could happen." Han was fiercely glad that Dakar's gyra had refused to allow him to harm Fliss Belaire. He rubbed the fingers that had touched her together. Clenched his hand. "There is some talk about him being in the grip of a Spiral."

"I want to see his gyra. When is Errol arriving for the Transfer?"

Pen, obviously listening in, turned from the doorway and held up a single finger.

"In an hour."

"Hah. I won't get there in time. I'll have to make him wait for me." He lifted a comm screen and jabbed at it. "The Gyr he tried to kill, she didn't fight him herself?"

Good question, Han thought. He lifted his shoulders. "Don't know. She can't shift, though."

"She can't shift?" Teranimo was suddenly extremely interested. "And she was still allowed to remain Gyr? Fithsu Gyr Command allowed it?"

"That's what the other Gyr here say. I don't think Fithsu Gyr Command know, because she isn't registered."

"You sure she *is* Gyr?" Teranimo asked.

"I touched her myself."

And he wanted to go back and touch her again.

Han looked down at the fist he'd made and realized he was aching to do it.

If this was how Dakar felt, he suddenly understood some of his actions.

"What is it?" Teranimo asked, voice sharp.

"Nothing. You want me to stall Errol?"

"He's already stalled. I sent him a message. He won't act without me." Teranimo shed his lab coat and picked something up from the side of his desk. "See you in two hours."

3

FLISS LAY ON HER BED, LISTENING TO THEM DISCUSS DAKAR AND HER, and then heard them leave.

Not all of them, though.

"If you're Gyr, you can hear me." Rinald's voice was low but she could hear him just fine. "Don't go thinking there's a place for you here with Dakar dead. We want you gone."

Someone else was out there with him. She could hear the rustle of their clothing, and if she were to guess, it was Meli.

She curled over on her side, arms wrapped around her, and listened to them walk away.

She hadn't had time to think beyond Dakar's death, but now she had a moment of quiet, she knew she couldn't stay.

Rinald was right. There was no place for her here.

She didn't want there to be.

Dakar had brought her here, and she had thought it would be the start of a new, hopeful phase of her life.

But that hope had begun to ebb over the last few weeks and had ended with the slash of Dakar's knife across his throat, as he screamed obscenities at her.

She flinched as the memory assailed her, almost able to feel the spittle from his mouth on her face again, see the light gleaming strangely from his eyes as they bulged in fury.

She had been able to do nothing but stand in shock and watch the light in those same eyes die as he slid down the wall, knife still clutched in his fist, dripping with his own blood.

The knife meant for her.

He had tried to kill her once before.

She shivered and burrowed into the mattress.

He'd tightened his hands around her throat, then staggered back, eyes wild with surprise at his actions.

He'd apologized that time, but she hadn't trusted him again.

She'd started to avoid him as much as possible, but she understood that he needed her presence like an addict needed their fix.

Needed her, and hated her for that need.

She wondered whether to ask Hannu Kardenian where she could go, what possibilities there were for her. But that would mean more of the same——a gyratta compound where she was bound by strange, arcane rules, many of which made no sense to her.

To be free would be good.

She had the strength and intelligence to make a place for herself in a city like Fithsu or Vallent, and both were not that far from here.

In fact, this gyratta was designated as the Fithsu compound, even though it was an hour by ground crawler to the outskirts of the city from here.

She had learned from Kardenian's questions earlier that she was not listed as an official member of the compound's team, and that meant she had no obligation to sign out or resign.

They already knew Dakar had killed himself. Or his gyra had. There was no doubt from the blood evidence, the angle of the cut, that it had been done by his own hand.

There was no charge she had to answer to.

She had the credits Dakar had given her for her six weeks on the team——she wasn't sure now if they were from his personal savings or taken from the compound's budget——but they were more than she'd ever had before, and surely enough to pay for a place to stay until she got established.

She rolled off the bed, landing silently on her feet, and began to pack.

She had very little; the few clothes she'd owned before Dakar had rescued her and now her new combat leathers and sparring outfits.

The gyratta clothing items were probably considered compound property, but they'd been made for her and wouldn't fit anyone else here. She was sure no one would even consider disputing her right to them.

When she was packed, her bag was a lot heavier than it had been when she'd first arrived less than two months ago.

She had not flourished here, but she was better off.

Still, she shivered again, remembering the spray of blood from the slice of the knife, the murderous intent in Dakar's eyes, and wished she had never met him.

She had been about to escape her father anyway when he'd arrived in her small, isolated community. After her mother's death, she'd been ready, bags secretly packed and waiting for an opportunity.

Dakar had provided one, but another would have come along, or she would have made one for herself.

She regretted not listening to her warning bells when it came to Dakar.

Nothing good had ever come of that.

But here she was, alive, if traumatized and shaken. Ready to make her own way.

She slung her pack over her shoulder and walked out, down the empty corridor.

Everyone was somewhere else, it seemed.

She moved through the common rooms, out to the dusty space in front of the gyratta where the ground and air crawlers were parked.

She felt a twinge, a quick spike of longing to see Hannu Kardenian one more time and tell him goodbye, but the open gate beckoned and she headed toward it.

It was late afternoon, and no one was standing guard.

They almost never did.

Only Gyr could come in and out, and usually someone stood sentinel on the rare occasion when they expected guests like Kardenian and his team, as a gesture of welcome.

She walked under the arch and felt the sweep of the scanner, enjoyed the buzz as it tickled her blood.

She'd made a few adjustments to the scan since she'd been here, tweaking the sweep so it no longer tried to interfere with her gyra in a bad way. She paused, wondering whether she should change it back before she left, but her gyra insisted that what was good for them was good for the gyra of all other Gyr.

She stepped clear of it, but thrust back a hand, brushing her fingers against the invisible curtain as a final goodbye to this place.

It had contained more horror than help, but it had not been all bad.

She had been able to finally find some calm here, especially in the first month, before Dakar began to sink deeper into his Spiral.

She had been among peers at last. And her gyra had loved that part of it. Had wanted connections she had been unable to forge, but the possibilities alone had buoyed her.

She had felt the same blood-tickling fizz inside her when Kardenian and his two colleagues had arrived, and even now, as she made her way to the road, she controlled an urge to turn back and ask if she could join them.

Maybe one day, she told her gyra. *Maybe after we've had a little time to ourselves.*

She looked over at the small hut to one side of the entrance, the Transfer Ceremony hut.

She hadn't needed a ceremony, herself, but she had heard of them, and had always wanted to see one.

Another thing to experience in the future, after she'd found her feet.

She reached the dusty strip of road that wound through the hills in both directions and considered her options. Fithsu lay to the south, Vallent to the north.

Maybe she would let fate decide.

Whichever direction the first ground crawler that came past was going, she would ask for a ride.

Fithsu was closer. Only an hour drive. It would take much longer to walk, but she decided to start heading that way rather than stand around near the compound.

If she was making a break, she might as well go.

She settled her bag over both shoulders, tightened the straps and began walking.

There was no real danger from zubys or largarti on the open road. They tended to avoid the crawlers, and without people and livestock in abundance, like in the towns and villages, there was not much to tempt them.

That didn't mean there wasn't a chance, but it was slim.

She didn't have her own cutter. Not a proper one, like the warriors used. She had used a practice one in the training room with Dakar, but he had never presented her with her own.

Now she knew he'd never declared her officially on the team, she understood why.

Cutters were assigned only to Gyr and there was probably a central list, accounting for each one.

She had a knife, though. It was short, but still something, and she had herself.

Her gyra. Her wits.

That's all she'd ever had before the compound, so it suited her.

She remembered the fuss Dakar had made about 'saving' her when he'd forced her out on a reconnaissance mission her first week in the compound. They'd gone to clear largarti from a gorge near the village of Erduan, one of the satellite communities around Fithsu. When the largarti had exploded out of its burrow, she had been astonished at the way Dakar had leaped in front of her and despatched the beast as if she couldn't have avoided it easily.

Now she wondered if he had jumped in early to prevent her from reacting, all to keep up the fiction that she was Fjerna to his team.

She sighed.

She had so wanted it to be different.

Better.

Fairer.

The roar of a ground crawler came from behind the curve of a hill, changing pitch as it negotiated the slope and then gearing up as it crested the rise.

She walked into the middle of the road and held up her hand.

The vehicle was coming from Fithsu, going in the direction of Vallent.

Looked like she was going north.

4

TERENCE ERROL WAS A SELF-IMPORTANT ASSHOLE.

Han had always known it, but now he got to see it in every petty, passive-aggressive detail.

The senior Gyr Command administrator was not well liked, and that had everything to do with his personality, and not his position.

Han remembered Helen Vaniga, his predecessor, with some fondness.

She had at least been sensitive to the high emotion of a gyra transfer, the feeling of life and death for the new warrior-in-waiting.

There was always a chance the gyra would reject the recruit, would refuse to transfer.

And even if they did transfer, if after the month allowed for melding mind to gyra, the recruit was later unable to shift, they had the agony of having felt the gyra within them, and then having them removed.

He knew some never recovered from that.

No part of this ceremony was without risk.

But Errol liked to center himself in the proceedings, when he was the one person with the least to lose.

He postured now, angry that Teranimo had ordered him to wait.

It was more the indignity of having to obey the chief scientist, Han thought, than the inconvenience of it.

The whining suddenly became too much.

"This is not about you." Han spoke before he could think twice about it.

Errol's mouth shut with a snap, eyes wide.

He'd already started, Han thought wryly, he might as well finish. "This is about preserving Dakar's gyra, and keeping everyone safe. It does neither you, nor your position, any honor to have a tantrum about waiting a short hour."

Errol's mouth formed a thin line, and he shot Han a poisonous look.

The recruit, a young man from the Provinces called Ralin, looked like he was trying to keep a straight face, although Han didn't know if it was shock and horror, or laughter, he was trying to keep under control.

The sound of an air crawler shattered the silence that had followed his statement, and everyone in the room, from Dakar's senior lieutenants, to Delasio and Pen, turned toward the door in relief.

A minute later, Teranimo strode into the hut.

He looked as if he hadn't slept for days, and that he'd spent the travel time tugging at his hair.

"Tell me everything again," he demanded of Han as he moved straight to Dakar's shrouded body.

"He killed himself," Han said. He drew back the thin cloth covering Dakar's body. "Every Gyr who has seen him agrees." He looked around the room, and every Gyr, even those who would have loved to have placed the blame on Fliss Belaire, gave a nod of agreement.

"But?"

"But the woman in the room with him claims he tried to kill her, and his gyra fought to prevent him doing so. When he would not submit, they cut his throat."

Han saw the recruit swallow at that.

These were the gyra that were going to be passed on to him.

If they had killed Dakar, they could kill him.

Which is why Teranimo needed to be here.

"And the woman in question is Gyr?" Teranimo looked around the room, as if expecting her to be here.

"She is, but even though Dakar brought her to the gyratta, he never registered her as part of his team."

Errol made an explosive sound at that and shot Han an accusing look. "I had not heard this."

"I only just found out myself. I only arrived . . ." Han looked at his wrist unit, "four hours ago."

Errol looked like he wanted to argue, and Han knew he would have been wise to keep his thoughts to himself earlier.

"Well, who is this Gyr?" Teranimo looked around at the gathered crowd and fixed his gaze on Meli. "You?"

"She's not here." Vanesh spoke up.

"Well, fetch her." Teranimo turned away, moving to Dakar's body to make a closer study.

He held a gyra-na in his hand, one of the precious two that were all that was left on Fjern.

Han had been present when the third one had failed and had stopped working, and now, every time he was part of a transfer ceremony, he held his breath, wondering what would happen when the other two broke.

They would have to let the gyra decide for themselves, then. And they couldn't compel the older Gyr to give their gyra up when they reached fifty.

He knew Gyr Command feared the day.

In the two thousand years since the Travelers, their ancestors, had landed on Fjern, they had not been able to create a new version of the ancient device.

When they were gone, they were gone.

"I'll get her." Pen pushed away from the wall when none of Dakar's team offered. She glanced at him as she left the room, and Han gave her a subtle nod.

They had already spoken about offering Fliss a place in their own gyratta on the outskirts of Vallent.

The hostility in this one made it unsuitable for her to stay.

Pen could make the offer while she escorted her out of the compound to the ceremonial hut.

And Pen could also observe how the arch reacted as Fliss passed through.

While they waited, Teranimo moved around Dakar's body, crouching down near his neck to get a closer look.

"He was in a Spiral?" His gaze snapped to Vanesh.

The senior lieutenant squirmed uncomfortably against the wall of the hut. "He was . . . not himself."

"He was either in a Spiral, or he was not. He's dead. There is no one to protect now." Teranimo held Vanesh's gaze.

But that wasn't true, Han thought. There could be consequences for Vanesh, Meli, and Rinald for not reporting Dakar's downward spin.

Serious consequences.

"He was finding it harder to come down after a shift," Meli spoke up when Vanesh said nothing. "It was decided he needed a break. He had been Gyr for twenty-seven years, and had never taken a holiday. He packed a bag and went the day after we suggested it, and he was gone for six months."

"And when he came back?" Errol spoke up——even he could sense something was amiss.

"He was better. Definitely better." Rinald sounded sincere.

"He *was* better," Vanesh agreed, reluctantly. "But he started to take risks. Go off on his own, sometimes for days. He told us he was looking for nests of largarti. Then he'd come back, still shifted."

"How long did it take him to come back to himself?" Teranimo asked.

Vanesh shrugged.

"He would go find Fliss. Then he'd come out of his room, calm as you please," Meli said. "This morning, when he died, he hauled her into his room, still in full shift."

"So he came back to himself, out of his shift, and then tried to kill her?" Teranimo sounded like he was just trying to get the facts right, but Han knew better.

He was as close to losing his temper as Han had ever seen him.

"Well, he's not in shift, is he?" Rinald said, pointing to Dakar's body. "So that's what must have happened."

"That is what must have happened," Teranimo agreed. "But he came into the compound in full shift? You saw him, no longer in combat, but still in shift?"

There was silence.

"And then he grabbed a member of your team, dragged her into a room, still in shift?"

More silence.

"We should have intervened." Vanesh spoke for the first time, voice hesitant.

"I find it interesting that since we arrived, you've been trying to point the finger of blame for Dakar's death at Fliss Belaire, but could that be because your own actions wouldn't stand up to scrutiny?" Delasio's voice was soft.

He had obviously taken a liking to Fliss. Or a deep dislike of Dakar's senior team.

"She was unshifted, dragged into a room by a Gyr in a Spiral, and you did nothing to help her?" Errol finally spoke up. Han wondered what had taken him so long.

"Had he done it before?"

Teranimo's question seemed to shake Vanesh.

"Maybe a few times."

"How many is a few?" Han asked. He felt a growing anger for the way this team had treated Fliss Belaire.

"Every time we came back from a mission," Meli said. "But he never harmed her, and he came out calm."

"How do you know he never harmed her?" Han asked. "Did you ask her?"

There was more silence.

"She didn't seem injured." Rinald's voice trailed off as he remembered that Fliss was Gyr. She could take a lot of harm and look none the worse for it.

"At the time, we didn't know she was Gyr," Meli whispered, suddenly working it out along with Rinald.

"This is all very interesting." Errol pushed off from the hut's wall and looked down at Dakar's body. "But what I need to know is, can we go ahead with this transfer or not?"

Han flicked a glance at the recruit, forgotten in the corner, and felt for the boy.

He would have been expecting the greatest day of his life.

Now he couldn't help but have doubts over what he was getting into.

"I need to speak to Belaire first." Teranimo looked around, as if hopeful she might have arrived while he wasn't looking.

Han wondered what was taking Pen so long to come back with her, when the hut's door opened and Pen stepped inside.

"I can't find her anywhere, and her things are gone."

Han caught just the briefest guilty shuffle from Meli, and turned to her.

"What do you know?"

She couldn't hold his gaze and looked away.

He swung his attention to Rinald, and the lieutenant looked back with a touch of bravado.

"We told her she had no place here without Dakar. We told her to go." He cut his gaze from Han's face and looked at Errol. "We didn't think she'd take us to mean right away. We thought she might leave with Kardenian's team."

"How long ago was this?" Han asked, but he guessed it had been after he, Pen, and Delasio had left Fliss's door.

"Two hours." Rinald lifted his shoulders.

Han pushed past him and stepped out, walking toward the arch.

He lifted the cover flap that protected the screen built into the side of it, and studied the data.

She had left an hour and a half ago.

He found the scan results interesting. She scanned higher than most Gyr, as if she contained more gyra, and then there was a tiny blip, as if she had put her hand back through the screen.

Everything about her seemed mysterious.

"Where did Belaire come from, originally?" He turned to the others who'd followed him out, dropping the flap down. He didn't understand why, but he didn't want Errol and Teranimo to see her scan.

"You think she's headed home?" Vanesh asked. "I don't know that she ever said where she's from. Neither did Dakar."

"What kind of lead does she have?" Teranimo asked.

"She left an hour and a half ago." Theoretically, she had every right to leave, but she was Gyr, and that came with responsibilities.

She was not a free agent under the rules that governed everyone who lived on Fjern.

If you were Gyr, you lived in a gyratta, you protected the Fjerna, and you obeyed the rules of Gyr Command.

But that was for recruits like himself, like the youngster behind him, who had signed up for it. Who accepted their gyra knowing what was in their future.

If Fliss was one of the few who'd received their gyra from a fallen warrior, out of their own control, she had not agreed to those terms.

"And there is no record of her in Gyr Command?" Teranimo lifted a screen from the bag he had slung across his chest, and tapped at it. "Fliss Belaire?"

"No." Errol frowned. "I've never heard that name."

"You said Dakar was away for six months," Teranimo turned to Vanesh. "You have no idea where he went?"

"I found some suspicious comms on his unit that might be relevant," Delasio said. "He obviously traveled around for many months, staying a few weeks at a time in each place, but then, three months ago, he engaged in some back and forth that looks very off."

Han recalled Delasio had tried to talk to him about it, just before Vanesh and his fellow officers had grabbed him to point the finger of blame at Fliss. "Remind me what you found again."

"He was corresponding with someone in what looked like a rough code for years." Delasio pulled out a device and tapped at the screen. "On one occasion, though, Dakar slipped up and referred to his friend as Ralf Bellini. They were corresponding sporadically until three months ago, when there was a lot of back and forth, and then nothing, ever again."

"Ralf Bellini. That name I *do* vaguely recall." Errol frowned.

"That's because Ralf Bellini was Gyr. Missing these past twenty-six years." Teranimo lifted his head, and Han thought he saw a greedy, excited, almost covetous look flash across the scientist's face.

"So you're saying comms blew up because he was invited to visit, and then ended because Dakar went to see him in person?" Pen asked.

Errol looked extremely unhappy. "Dakar should have reported it if he knew where Ralf Bellini was. We didn't know if he was dead or hiding from Gyr Command."

"Maybe it was the other way around," Delasio said. "When the comms stopped, Dakar decided to use the last of his time off to go see what had happened to his friend."

Errol seemed to come to the end of his patience, slapping a hand against his thigh. "Well, if the Gyr we need to talk to is gone, and we can't question her right away, let's get on with the transfer."

Teranimo turned and walked into the hut with almost indecent haste, and Han thought it very telling he was so eager to do as Errol requested, when earlier he had been so adamant he needed Fliss's input first.

The Gyr Command scientist didn't care about Dakar's gyra anymore. He was far more interested in hunting down the mystery that was Fliss Belaire.

Han followed him in, senses sharpened, watching him carefully.

Teranimo had the gyra-na out again, but this time he'd activated it, and when all the lights within it flared blue, he placed it on Dakar's naked chest.

Han always found the slow blossom of the silver ball above the box fascinating, as the gyra-na drew the gyra out of the blood and gathered them into one unit.

Nothing happened this time, though.

"Is it broken?" Errol asked, voice tight.

"I don't think so." Teranimo didn't look unhappy. He didn't look annoyed. He looked . . . excited.

"Then what?" Errol snapped.

"I think the gyra have already transferred."

"Transferred to who?" Errol's voice was high with outrage.

"It has to be the only person in the room with him when he died," Vanesh said. "Fliss Belaire."

That's why the arch scan read so high.

Han tried to keep his expression neutral, but he was shocked to his core.

Fliss was already Gyr, and Dakar's gyra had moved to her on his death anyway.

He had never heard of that happening.

But Teranimo had.

He could see it on the scientist's face.

Han did not understand why his gyra prickled under his skin in warning at Teranimo's expression, but he would listen to them.

They hadn't let him down yet.

5

ENID QUINN——PROSPECTOR, LONG-HAULER, AND TRADER——DIDN'T
try to hide her curiosity.

"So you're from the Fithsu Gyratta?" She changed gear on the
crawler, speeding up after pulling away from the road after picking
Fliss up.

Her voice was deep and throaty, and Fliss liked her immediately.
Liked the way her white curls framed her face, and the steady, kind
hazel of her eyes.

She nodded. "I was. I'm going to take a break, spend some time in
Vallent."

Enid's eyebrows rose. "I didn't know the Gyr could do that,
although I suppose there's no reason why you can't. Everyone
deserves a break now and then."

Fliss looked over at her, wondering what she meant, because
she'd met Dakar when he was taking a break, but then her eye caught
on a pile of circuit boards lying in the well between the seats.

She picked the top one up.

Her gyra connected and found the problem. Fixed it.

"This one is good to go, now." She extended the board to Enid.
"Where would you like it?"

Enid's eyebrows climbed again. "You just held it in your hand."

"That's how the gyra work." Fliss smiled. "They love to do it."

"I hadn't heard that." Enid slowed the crawler, setting it in auto, and took the board, leaning back to grab a thin, flat device, and slid the circuit board into a slot.

The screen lit up.

Enid looked at it for a beat and then switched it off, leaned back and put the device away. "Well, thank you for that, you saved me a trip to get it repaired, and the money I'd have to pay those crooks at the repair shop."

"Call it payment for the ride," Fliss said. "Although I can pay you in credits. I have some."

"Lots, way I hear it. Don't begrudge you it, mind, you risking your life to beat back the zubys and the largartis and god knows what else, but I thought you lot were swimming in it."

"I've only been working in a gyratta for less than two months," Fliss explained. "I haven't had time to build up much in the way of savings. But I think I have enough to rent a place in Vallent until I can find a job." She had worked a lot harder at home than she had at the compound——which had felt like a long holiday to Fliss——but her father had never so much as handed her a single credit for her work.

She had kept the few credits that had been slipped to her from time to time for fixing electronics, hiding them in preparation for the day she ran.

She had made twenty times her meagre savings in the weeks she'd hung around the gyratta, taking it easy.

So Enid was right. The Gyr did earn a good amount.

Enid said nothing, lapsing into a quiet contemplation that was soothing rather than awkward.

Fliss picked up the next circuit board on the pile and let her gyra play.

Four of them were not revivable, but the rest were in working order when she was done.

"You really do enjoy doing that," Enid said. "I've been watching you."

Fliss lifted her shoulders. "I don't do anything, my gyra do it all. But they enjoy it, so I enjoy it."

"I don't think I really understand what you mean, but you've just paid for your ride two times over, way I see it. I'm glad I'm the one came along just when you were needing a lift."

"I couldn't choose between Fithsu or Vallent, so I decided to go in the direction of whoever came along first. But Vallent is bigger than Fithsu, isn't it, and further away?"

"An eight hour crawler journey from here," Enid confirmed. "Fithsu is only an hour and a half by crawler from your compound. Much quicker by air crawler, though. Couldn't someone have given you a lift?"

"Maybe." It was possible, but she hadn't thought to ask. Fliss gave her a crooked grin. "I didn't wait around to find out. I just wanted to go."

Enid watched her, eyes seeming to see too much, then her gaze swung to the road and she gave a grunt of surprise.

A zuby stood right in the middle of it.

It looked pissed off, but that's how they always looked, as far as Fliss was concerned. And she had seen her share.

"If I ram it, it could seriously mess up my rig. Put us out of commission." Enid looked over at her, as if asking what to do.

"Don't ram it. That'll just upset it. And it can take a lot of damage before it goes down. We don't want that." Fliss bent to get her knife from her bag. "Stop here and wait. I'll get rid of it."

"You sure?" Enid bit her lip.

Fliss smiled at her. "I'm Gyr, Enid. It's what we do. What we're for."

Enid pulled the crawler to a stop, but didn't turn off the engine.

Fliss was glad of that as she climbed down from the high-set door and jumped the last few steps to the ground. The engine noise would disturb the zuby, make it more anxious.

Help it choose to go elsewhere.

The crawler's wheels were double Fliss's own height, but this zuby was maybe half again taller than that, and would definitely do some damage to the rig.

She walked quietly forward, letting her gyra take in the situation, trusting them and herself to find the perfect solution.

The zuby watched her come, a low, aggressive rumble vibrating from its throat.

Its big head swung back and forth as it stood firmly in the center of the road, its small, beady eyes gleaming in the late afternoon light.

It bared its teeth, long, slightly orange-tinged, and almost too many for its wide mouth.

When she was close enough to know she'd catch it if it ran, she sped up, letting herself almost fly across the ground.

It went still, surprised at her aggression, then reared back as she leaped at it.

She managed to land exactly where she'd aimed——its flank—— her boot getting a good grip on its scaly, rough skin, and she used that to boost herself up onto its back.

As soon as she landed, it began to do the funny little dance zuby always did when they were threatened, a back and forth high on their toes, which she'd always found amusing to watch.

She kept her balance despite the jerking and ran up the length of its spine, jumping the last, too-steep-to-get-a-grip part on the back of its neck, and coming to a crouch on its head.

"Listen," she whispered as she placed her hand on its skull.

It went suddenly, instantly still.

"Go back to where it's safe. Hurry." She sent the suggestion in a hard push, and it reared again and leaped off the road, running toward the left.

She jumped, flinging herself off its head and somersaulting backward, spooking it a little as it caught her movement out of the corner of its eye and giving it even more incentive to move.

She landed lightly, stood with hands on her hips watching it disappear between the rocky outcrops, and then turned and jogged back to the crawler.

As soon as she was settled back in her seat, she glanced over at Enid Quinn, and found her staring back.

"Never seen a Gyr wrangle a zuby before?" Fliss asked.

She had thought the Gyr in the more populated lowlands would have had more of an audience when they fought the raveners, but, at least in Dakar's compound, they had gone out alone, much like it had been for her, at home on the high escarpment.

"No. I thought it would be more . . ."

Fliss leaned back against the window. "Bloody?"

"Yeah."

"Sometimes it is. Seems to be the way they do things around here, but where I come from, I was the only Gyr, and I don't have a proper cutter. So I had to come up with another way. And it doesn't seem right to kill them, when we're the ones who are the late-comers, so to speak." She was very much alone in this view, she knew, but she voiced it anyway. "Since our ancestors crashed here, we've taken over. I feel sorry for the raveners, being killed just for living on their own planet and doing what they naturally do."

"Bet that goes down well in the gyratta," Enid said, with a cackle in her voice.

"Well, in the one I just left, I didn't raise it. Not after I went on the first hunt with them." She thought of the largarti Dakar had killed that day, and shook her head. So unnecessary.

He'd seen how she dealt with the largarti and the zuby and even the carranda on the escarpment. He'd been intrigued, but told her that wasn't how the other Gyr were trained.

He didn't tell her not to do it when she got to the compound, but now she knew he had no plans to allow her to be part of the team.

He'd just allowed her out once, 'rescued' her, and never invited her along again.

"Forgive my asking, and tell me to mind my own if it's not something you talk about, but aren't you suppose to . . . change . . . when you do that. Shift, or something?"

"Most Gyr shift," Fliss agreed. She had been brought up with her father screaming that it was the only way to be a Gyr. That she should

be able to shift. That she was a failure——to him, to all Gyr——
because she did not. "Not all, though."

She couldn't shift for a good purpose.

Dakar had helped her see that, and then he'd turned around and
lost his mind over it.

It still confused her. And saddened her.

"Well, this has been one learning experience after another," Enid
said, cheerful as she accelerated away. "Can't say I'm sorry I decided
to head home to Vallent early, even though it meant some night
driving."

"When will we get into town?" Fliss asked, wondering where she
would find a place to stay. She already felt intimidated and nervous
about doing that.

About being a stranger in a strange place.

Again.

"Early hours of the morning," Enid said. "But I've got a spare
room you can use to catch a few hours' sleep before you head on your
way. As I said before, those circuits would have cost me a lot to have
fixed. It's more than fair."

"Thank you." The relief of not having to worry about a room
swamped her, and exhaustion dragged at her. Fliss knew it was the
last two days worth of events catching up with her.

Dakar's death. The shouting and finger-pointing. The arrival of
Kardenian's team. Having her welcome at the compound revoked.

"Wake me if there's another ravener," she murmured to Enid, and
then closed her eyes and slept.

6

HAN OFFERED THE RECRUIT, RALIN, A RIDE TO VALLENT.

He couldn't come back with the team to their gyratta, not without gyra, but the Gyr Command offices in the small city would organize an air crawler to get him home, or offer him a place to stay for a while, in case new gyra became available.

Whatever happened, he would be next in line for them.

He could have gone with Teranimo or Errol, but he agreed to Han's offer the moment it was made.

"Do you really think the gyra went to someone who was already Gyr?" he asked after they'd lifted off and the purr of the engines was less intense.

"Yes," Pen said. She never prevaricated, she said what she thought. Han respected that.

"How?" Ralin sounded so innocent. "Why?"

"Because they thought her worthy." Han shrugged.

"But when you already have gyra, surely you can't accept more." Ralin looked lost.

"The gyra in her probably called to the gyra in Dakar's body, and they answered," Delasio said. "They like to be useful, like to be in a Gyr. And Dakar was dead."

"But the gyra-na . . ." Ralin looked confused. "It's what makes them leave, doesn't it?"

Pen shrugged. "On a dead body, the gyra-na forces the gyra out, or maybe it's just they are drawn to a live body, and the gyra-na is a way to get one. But on a live body . . ." She shook her head. "I've never seen the gyra-na used on a live body, but every time a gyra-na has broken, it's been trying to get gyra out of a living Gyr. Every time."

"Is that true?" Ralin turned to Han.

"It's certainly true that the one time I saw a gyra-na malfunction and break, it was trying to extract the gyra from a non-shifting Gyr."

"What happened?" Ralin looked a little pale under the warm brown of his skin.

"The Gyr in question was put to other duties." Han felt like a liar as he said that, because although that was what he'd been told, he didn't believe it.

He'd asked after Lucille Defoe many times, requested a meeting with her, requested a comms link to call her, and he had been denied every time.

They had either killed her and taken her gyra that way, or they were doing something to her and didn't want other Gyr to know about it.

Because maybe, just maybe, that would be the last thread to snap.

Everything about the way Gyr Command was set up, from the lists of Gyr, to the Transfer ceremonies, to the gyratta compounds, was designed to keep them in check. They were useful——indispensable——against the raveners that roamed the world that their ancestors, the Travelers, had crashed onto. But the Fjerna, the normal men and women who had not been given gyra, who were not part of the protective force created to help their little population of explorers survive, had been afraid of their rescuers from almost the very beginning.

It was clear to Han that a great deal of thought had gone into the structure, the culture, and the ceremonies of the Gyr.

And mostly it was to keep them in check.

He could even understand it.

The Gyr were stronger, faster and more intelligent. They could become monsters themselves to fight the raveners they protected the rest of their people against.

But they were separated into compounds far apart, and the transfer of the gyra was very firmly in Gyr Command's hands.

There had been a few uprisings from the Gyr over the two thousand years since the *Cercatore,* their ancestral ship, had crash landed onto Fjern, but each time, they had been brought back into the fold.

A revolution wouldn't change things, because even if they could break free, they were too few to do anything but form a separate community and leave the Fjerna to the raveners.

What Han wanted was to break down the rules that controlled them, pull down the rigid structures that kept them in their place.

He wondered whether the scientists who had created the gyra, and chosen a small unit of soldiers to absorb them, had thought about the long-term consequences of their invention.

Whether they understood that two thousand years later the nanotech would still be working, passed on in very controlled circumstances, to a group still tasked with their original purpose—— to make whatever new home the Travelers found for themselves less hostile.

Watching the gyra-na break when they tried to pull the gyra from Lucille Defoe had started the journey for him.

Lucille's gyra would not leave her, and rather than be forced out, they had destroyed the machine that tried to make them.

After that, he had never seen Lucille again.

He had sworn he would find her. That he would make sure she was all right.

And now he swore that Fliss Belaire would not suffer the same fate.

Because while he'd always got on with Teranimo, the look on the scientist's face was avaricious when he'd worked out, along with Han, what had happened to Dakar's gyra.

If the source of Fliss's gyra was Ralf Bellini, and if the transfer had happened a second time with her team leader, then she was indeed a Gyr of interest.

"How did Fliss Belaire leave the Fithsu Gyratta?" Delasio suddenly asked. "Did she take an air crawler?"

Han had assumed she had, had not considered anything else, because the Fithsu Gyratta was so far from town, isolated in the middle of ravener territory. He thought back to the line of ground and air crawlers parked in front of the compound, and realized none had been missing.

"She wouldn't have ... walked ... would she?" Pen frowned.

"It's possible she walked to Fithsu, intending to take transportation from there." He wanted to turn the air crawler around and follow the road to Fithsu to find her. She would possibly already be in the small town by now. She'd left the compound nearly five hours ago, and she could have picked up a lift the closer to Fithsu she'd gotten.

"Any of you know someone in Fithsu?" he asked. He would not contact the Gyr Command offices there. He knew Teranimo would have already been in touch with them and ordered them to be on the look-out for her.

He was interested in a more unofficial search.

"I know someone," Ralin said, surprising them all.

Han took the details, grunting in recognition of the name. A medic who'd been part of Gyr Command for years before she'd retired.

Ralin's father had worked with her, it seemed, and the families kept in touch.

He'd contact her, ask her to keep an eye out.

He wanted to find Fliss before Gyr Command did, but he reminded himself she was not helpless. Even if she couldn't shift, she had two sets of gyra within her.

She would be a match for anyone Gyr Command sent after her.

"Will they hunt her?" Ralin asked.

He'd picked up on their worry, Han realized. The recruit hadn't even flinched at the thought that a Gyr *would* be hunted, like an enemy.

"Yes," Han said. "But Gyr stand with Gyr."

"I'm not Gyr," Ralin said. "Not yet."

"When you are," Pen told him, "you will understand."

7

Fliss woke up with a stream of sunlight shining right on her face.

She blinked, shielding her eyes, and then swung her legs over the side of the narrow cot and leaned forward, out of the direct stream of sunlight, and took in the tiny room.

She had stumbled in here just before dawn, and had only taken in the most basic of details.

It was a narrow space, perhaps a workroom or a large storage closet at one time, turned into a spare room for Enid's fellow long-haulers who passed through Vallent and were in need of a bed for the night.

She yawned, stretched, and felt remarkably good.

She'd slept well. Better than in the compound, where she'd always been on edge, her gyra alert for an attack.

It had been a hostile environment; she could see that now she was out of it.

She was very glad to have left.

She stood up and took a step toward the narrow window. Enid's house was built into the Vallent City wall. Her room poked just over the top of the wall itself, and had a view out over the large fields that lay outside the wall's protection.

Enid had told her last night she lived on the edge of the city because there was no room within for her massive long-haul crawler.

As the city expanded, more and more things were being forced outside the walls.

From the house next door, a woman called to her domesticated hanne, housed in a well-secured coop.

Her mother had kept hanne for eggs in Fliss's home village as well.

The squawks and fluttering of wings as the woman emptied their feed into a trough was a familiar, comforting sound.

Her mother had done this very thing, every day, until she had been too ill to leave her bed.

Fliss wondered why the coop was so well-built when it was inside the wall. In her experience, people didn't spend the kind of credits such a sturdy structure would have cost for no good reason. But surely the raveners could not get over the massive, thick wall.

With a last look over the brown and green fields, the forests beyond, and the blue mountain peaks in the distance, she turned and went to find the bathroom.

After she'd showered, she rummaged through her bag, undecided about her clothes. Wearing the Gyr practice uniform would give her respect and probably open many doors for her in Vallent, but she was hesitant about riding on the Fithsu Gyratta's reputation, given how little she'd done there.

In the end, she pulled on the clothes she'd owned before Dakar found her. The outfit was Provinces-style, with tight leggings and a tunic, all handmade and undyed, the sage green of the rincel fiber edged with hand embroidery in white thread, done by her mother.

"That color sure does suit you," Enid said, looking up from her seat at the kitchen table as Fliss carefully made her way down the narrow staircase. "With that dark hair of yours, and those dark eyes."

"My mother made it," Fliss said, flustered. Only a handful of people had ever told her she looked good, and none of them had been sincere, like Enid.

Or so she'd thought at the time.

Enid took a closer look at her clothes, reaching forward to take Fliss's hand and look at the flowers embroidered on the cuff.

"She's good, your mother. Talented. What's her name?"

"Kath Sinclaire. She's dead now." Fliss hadn't told anyone her mother was dead since she'd followed Dakar out of the tiny settlement where her father held sway.

"Recently?" Enid asked, eyes knowing and kind.

Fliss nodded, suddenly unable to say any more. She looked around the room instead, and saw Enid had set out food on the table.

"Sit you down and have a bite."

Fliss did so, remembering she hadn't eaten since breakfast the day before.

Her gyra could keep her alive for a long time on very little, but it was better to keep her strength up.

They ate for a while in silence, sipping the hot oloa tea that came from the east sector and that Fliss had never tasted before she got to the Fithsu Gyratta. It was so good, and she couldn't help but compare it to the weak, salty, marsh flower tea she'd drunk at home.

That Enid had a whole jar of it, that it was available outside the compound, cheered Fliss immensely.

"Thank you for being so welcoming." She lowered her cup and held Enid's gaze. "I'm very grateful."

Enid rubbed the back of her neck, uncomfortable. "I told you, you already paid me back twice over. What I'm sorry for is I don't have a bigger place or I'd offer you a room for as long as you need one. But I was wondering, have you heard of the Travelers' Trust?"

Fliss shook her head.

"They're a council-run place in all the big cities, and they offer a place to stay for people wanting to relocate. You get a small set of rooms in the building for two months, free, and then you can stay longer for a small rent, unless they need the space for new travelers."

Fliss wondered if her father had known about the Travelers' Trust.

"How long have they been going for?" she asked Enid.

"Long as I've been alive," Enid said, with what Fliss thought was a sharp, considering gleam in her eye. "And that's a long time."

So he would have known.

All those times he'd told her she'd be living on the streets if she left, all lies. Because he was from this world.

She sighed.

Enid poured Fliss more oloa tea and leaned back in her chair.

"I'm friends with Eloisa, who's in charge of the Trust here in Vallent, and I'll be happy to introduce you, get you set up." Enid stood, brushing crumbs from her shirt. "You won't be looking for work for long, being Gyr, but it's a nice place, the Trust, so you might want to stay for a while, if they have the room. And you'll meet others looking to settle here. So you should make some friends."

Fliss thought of Kardenian and the two Gyr with him and felt a pang. She and her gyra had both thought they would make good friends.

She was still a little sorry she hadn't waited and asked them if she could go with them.

But no.

Asking another favor, putting herself at the mercy of someone else's kindness, was something she could no longer swallow.

That probably meant she shouldn't have accepted either the lift or the bed for the night from Enid, but somehow, that hadn't felt the same.

Besides, she'd fixed Enid's circuits and cleared the road of a zuby for her.

It had not been a one-sided exchange.

Now that she was free, it never would be again.

FLISS ENJOYED the walk into town with Enid.

It was a good twenty minutes to get to the center, but there was plenty to see on the way.

"I only saw Fithsu from an air crawler when I joined the gyratta," she told Enid. "It's better to see the houses and gardens from the street. And there are a lot more here in Vallent than in Fithsu."

"You come from a much smaller place?" Enid asked.

"Tiny," Fliss said. "A group of prospectors who live along a river out in the Provinces. Up high on the escarpment."

Some of the dwellings where she'd lived were little more than shacks. A world apart from the fine-crafted buildings and landscaped gardens on either side of the street she was walking down now.

Not to say that many of the homes made by the prospectors were worse than these. Some had been delightful, all the more beautiful for their inventiveness, but some had been nothing more than tents.

Her village had a temporary feel, whereas here, she sensed permanence in the stone walls and large glass windows.

"I don't understand why people obviously spend money securing their homes as if they expect a ravener attack, but then they all have large windows." Windows any self-respecting ravener could run straight through.

"It's the isilo," Enid said. "The bigger raveners like the zuby and the largarti can't get over the wall, the Gyr make sure of that, but the isilo can sometimes get in. They're smaller, faster, and there's a lot more of them."

"I've heard of them, never seen one."

Isilo didn't like the escarpment, with its cold winds and open fields. They preferred the warmer climes of the lowlands, nearer the coast, or the far north, like here, with its dark forests and mountains.

"They're about the same size as a person when they lift up," Enid said. "Sharp teeth in a long, narrow snout, and very sharp claws. They take children, if they can." She sounded grim. "But mostly, they take hanne and other livestock."

"How do they come into the city?" Fliss asked.

"They swim in."

"Swim in?" Fliss was puzzled.

"Down the river. It's at the north end of Vallent."

"I didn't know there was a river here. Is it big?" The river that ran through her home village of Leverta only ever got hip deep, although it was wide.

"No, it's narrow, deep, and fast. Not like the ones you'd be familiar with in the Provinces." Enid paused and cocked her head. "Your settlement, are they sifting the river sands for caltine?"

Fliss nodded. "It's the only thing worth enough to look for in such small quantities. Most prospectors get paid enough for a single large piece to survive for another month up there, so they stick by it, hoping for a big break."

"And you were protecting them from the raveners?"

She nodded. "My father runs a store up there. He charged a subscription fee from the prospectors for my services." And kept all of it for himself.

She wondered what he'd done about that when she left.

Perhaps her father had gone back to protecting the settlement himself.

He'd made out to their small community that he came with her often, but less and less people believed that, as the years went by.

Before she was born, he'd done the protecting for real. Then he'd pretended for years, going out and killing raveners by whatever means he could.

He still had his cutter from his days in a Gyr compound, but he had never allowed Fliss to so much as touch it.

Her first time out in the bush, alone——because her father said she needed to learn——had been when she was six years old.

Her mother had never forgiven him, and Fliss didn't think they'd ever spoken directly to each other again after that.

For some reason, she hadn't told Dakar that story.

He thought she persuaded the raveners to leave instead of killing them because she'd been working alone, and had no weapon.

She did it because she had developed her methods as a child.

The idea of killing the raveners had never occurred to six year-old her.

"Anyone going to be coming after you?" Enid asked the question casually, but there was something in her tone, a shaky edge of rage, that made Fliss wonder what had happened to Enid when she was younger.

"My father might be a bit . . . disappointed to no longer have my services, which made him a good living, but he's a little . . ." She thought of how to describe it. "A little off-side with Gyr Command. They would like a word with him, and I don't think he'd risk them finding him to have that word, even to bring me back."

She hadn't understood that until Dakar had shown up in the small river-side community.

Her father's fear at the sight of his old friend from his days in a gyratta had been a revelation.

She had planned to run anyway, with her mother no longer in need of her care, but seeing the tremble in her father's hands when Dakar had walked into the store had lifted her hopes even higher.

She could run, and he would not chase after her.

He was the one stuck now, not her.

"Anyway," she looked over at Enid and smiled. "Don't forget, I'm Gyr. It would be hard for him to take me back against my will."

Enid didn't nod in agreement, she looked straight at Fliss. "That may be true, but the kind of people I'm thinking about, they don't always come at you straight. They sneak. They hide. They lie. No one is completely impervious. So you watch your back. And call me if you need help. If I'm here, I'll give it to you."

Touched, Fliss could only nod, and they both lapsed into an easy silence for the rest of the way.

When they reached the busy heart of Vallent, there were fewer houses with gardens and more tall buildings and tight-packed stores and little restaurants. Some had tables out on the pavement, although now the season had shifted from summer to the cool of autumn, there were few people sitting outside.

The council hall stood at the far end of an open square.

Fliss had admired Fithsu's from the air, and thought this one looked similar.

46

"Is the open square in front for big meetings?" Fliss asked.

"In theory." Enid gave a wry smile. "Most of the arguing goes on in the chambers, though. And the council hasn't made any decisions the townsfolk don't like for some time."

She led the way to a large, four story building one street over from the hall.

It had a slim, bright blue door, and flowers in pots on either side.

A man was sitting in the sunshine on the steps leading up to it.

He looked young, and his clothing was, if not the same as her own, a slightly more modern version of it.

They nodded to him as they stepped around him and walked up to the door.

Enid's friend, Eloisa, was happy to see her, and was only too pleased to give Fliss a place at the Trust.

"A Gyr Command recruit?" she asked, beaming at Fliss. "We have a young man from Tynida staying with us, Leven, and he's meeting up with a friend from back home today who's a Gyr Command recruit, too."

"Fliss isn't a recruit," Enid corrected. "She's Gyr. Saved my hide last night when a zuby decided to stand on the road and block my way."

"Then . . ." Eloisa looked confused. "Why don't you stay at the Vallent Gyratta? They'd be happy to have you."

Fliss shook her head, but she felt a lurch of nerves in her gut. She hadn't realized how structured the system was.

It seemed, if you were Gyr, you lived in the gyratta.

She didn't even know who ran the gyratta in Vallent. Dakar had never spoken about the system, other compounds, or any part of the Gyr hierarchy with her.

Whatever she knew, she'd picked up in passing in the dining room.

"She's taking a break." Enid spoke up for her again. "No reason why a Gyr shouldn't take a break, is there?"

Eloisa looked shocked, and then thoughtful. "No. Everyone deserves a break." Her hand had paused over a row of keys when she had heard Fliss was Gyr, but now she plucked a set off its hook and handed it over. "Will you be looking for work, or are you just on holiday?"

Fliss didn't think being on holiday was quite in the spirit of the Travelers' Trust, from what she understood from Enid, and anyway, she had to work, or starve.

She shook her head. "I need a job. But it doesn't have to be anything permanent. I'm happy to try a couple of new things."

"She's very good with electronics," Enid put in. "Fixed some things for me, good as new."

"Oh?" Eloisa seemed flustered by that. "I thought you'd be more inclined to . . ." She fluttered her hands.

"Kill raveners?" Fliss asked, amused.

Eloisa gave a laugh. "Well, yes. You Gyr famously *are* good at that."

She led the way up to the third floor, to a plain wooden door in a line of four more. Fliss unlocked it with the keys Eloisa had given her, and stepped into a small living area. Off to the side was an even smaller bedroom, with a tiny bathroom attached.

The living room had big double doors out to a balcony with just enough room for a single chair.

"There's no kitchen, I'm afraid, you'll have to eat out, or use the communal kitchen below, but we have a list of recommendations downstairs of where is good."

She and Enid left Fliss to settle in and went down to Eloisa's office for tea, with an invitation to Fliss to join them when she was unpacked.

It took only a few minutes to put her things away, but Fliss walked carefully around the space, enjoying the idea that this was her place.

Everything was clean and functional. The small, neutral haven that she needed for now.

You need your own kind, her gyra whispered to her, still giddy at being with so many Gyr at Fithsu Gyratta.

Maybe she did.

But she also needed to understand what would be expected of her if she chose to go back to a gyratta.

And she didn't trust anyone to tell it to her straight.

She would find the answers herself.

She knew she would be happier in the company of other Gyr, but she wouldn't do it if it meant any kind of servitude.

Her father had cured her of that.

8

———

"SHE'S NOT IN FITHSU." HAN LEANED BACK IN HIS CHAIR AND LOOKED over every member of his team.

There were eight of them, including himself.

Fliss, when he found her, would make nine, and that would be resisted by some of the gyratta. They'd want her to make up their own numbers, but Han would not be accommodating.

Not this time.

"The retired medic in Fithsu looked everywhere?" Pen asked.

Han nodded. "She'll keep an eye out, but if Fliss was there, she found a lift almost immediately and left straight away."

"And Vanesh is sure she didn't take a crawler?" Delasio's contempt for the Fithsu Gyratta came across loud and clear.

"So he says." Han lifted his shoulders. Given the lies they'd been told so far, Del's skepticism was not unfounded. "Although he did mention she wore clothing from the Provinces when not in uniform. So that at least gives us a starting point."

"Why're you so keen on her, boss?" Minette was leaning against the wall beside the door, her tight curls piled high on her head, her muscular body relaxed.

Han hesitated. "She's different. And Teranimo looked . . ."

"Hungry," Pen offered. "Hungry and obsessed."

There was a moment of silence.

"You think they'll do something to her? Like Lucille Defoe?" Barnes, red-haired, freckled, built as wide as a mining ground crawler, pushed off the wall he was sharing with Minette and scowled.

"I can't be sure, but I'm not taking the chance." Han was telling the truth, but he was also aware he was lying. He thought about it, and then decided to come clean, because he was putting everyone here in Gyr Command's sights. "But also . . ." He tried to find the right words.

"He has *feelings* for her." Pen interrupted his awkward silence again. "He got the Look when he saw her."

"The Look?" Ranuk spoke as if awed, and Han flicked him an obscene gesture.

"For real, boss? You want to . . ." Jayna waggled her brows. "For real?"

"Very romantic," Ellen said, and sent him a dirty grin. "Very . . . swoony."

Han couldn't help the laugh that burst out of him. "I'm just trying to be upfront. Because finding her, bringing her here, is going to piss Gyr Command off. Teranimo wants to study her, that's obvious, and he won't take it well if we become a road block to that." He sighed. "I want everyone to be clear about my reasons. I don't want to see another Lucille Defoe situation, but also, when I touched her . . ." Even before that, he admitted to himself. Right from the first time he'd laid eyes on her, all curled in on herself, her long, dark hair swinging over high cheekbones and her delicate fingers gripping her arms. "I wanted to keep doing it."

They were silent for a beat, all humor gone.

"You're serious, serious," Pen murmured. "You think your gyra connected?"

It was the myth they all wanted to believe but didn't dare to.

The stories of Gyr in the early days, couples connected in unbreakable bonds, tight units of two who were a team in every way.

A special partner for every Gyr.

The gyrbar.

But Gyr Command had taken control of who got the gyra, and where the Gyr would be stationed.

And there had not been a gyrbar for a long, long time.

"If it's true," Delasio cleared his throat, "all the more reason to find her. And find her fast."

"She can't have disappeared. Did she go home?" Barnes asked.

"If she did, it doesn't help us, because we don't know where she came from, except for the clue about Provinces clothing." Pen crossed her arms over her chest.

"Meli said she thought Dakar went looking for her, but I'm inclined to believe Delasio's theory. That he was corresponding with Ralf Bellini and when the correspondence stopped, Dakar took off to go looking for him." Han thought about it. "And that means he knew where to start looking."

"We could try to break the code they corresponded in," Delasio said. "It might give us a clue to where Bellini was based. It has to be somewhere in the Provinces, but that still leaves a massive amount of ground to cover."

"But if Dakar went searching for Bellini, why did he come back with Fliss?" Minette looked skeptical. "And why hide her away?"

"He was up to something, all right." Han leaned back in his chair. "I want to find out from Fliss what it was."

"We're acting under the assumption that Ralf Bellini is dead, though, right?" Jayna said. "So how was he corresponding with Dakar? How did Fliss get her gyra?"

"What if he died recently?" Ellen asked. "Ralf's in correspondence with Dakar, who doesn't report him to Gyr Command, and then Dakar stops getting comms all of a sudden, and he goes looking for his old friend in some desolate Provinces outpost. Finds his . . . what? Step-daughter? Niece? Random member of Bellini's community who was present when he died, or stumbled across his body? She's now a newly-made Gyr, and Dakar decides to take her back to Fithsu Gyratta with him?"

"Could be," Han conceded. But there was something about Fliss. She hadn't felt newly-made to him. Not at all.

"And then you're saying Dakar goes mad, gets into a Spiral, and tries to kill his new Gyr. And his gyra refuse, and kill him rather than let him do it?" Ranuk shook his head in disbelief.

"It's the only explanation that accords with the evidence." Han looked over at Pen and Delasio, and they nodded in agreement. "And when Fliss told me about it, I believed her."

Again, Pen and Delasio nodded.

"And then, on top of that, when Dakar died, his gyra immediately transferred to her?" Barnes sounded just as skeptical.

"They weren't inside Dakar anymore, that's for sure," Delasio stated.

"I didn't say anything, because I didn't want to draw attention to it, but her arch signature when she left the Fithsu Gyratta was high. Very high." Han wasn't sorry about hiding that, although it became irrelevant after they discovered Dakar's gyra were gone.

"Like carrying two sets of gyra high?" Minette finally pushed off the wall and stood straight. "That's crazy."

Han had never heard of such a thing, either, but . . . "It wasn't crazy to Teranimo. If you'd seen his face———"

"Hungry and obsessed," Pen said again, in agreement. "He's heard of someone getting two sets of gyra before, or suspects it's possible at the very least."

"So, what next?" Jayna's voice was soft.

"If you want out, tell me now." Han let his gaze linger on each one, but all he got back were sneers.

"For a gyrbar? You can be sure I am in," Delasio said.

Everyone else simply nodded.

Han accepted their loyalty in silence and stood. "As Barnes said before, she can't have disappeared. She either made it to Fithsu and got a lift out to somewhere else, or she headed this way, to Vallent."

"I'll take an air crawler, go ask some questions in Fithsu," Barnes said.

"I'll come along," Minette said, and when Barnes extended his arm to her, in a parody of the manners from the early days of settlement, she gave a laugh, tucked her hand in the crook of his elbow and let him lead her out the room.

"We'll let you know," she shouted over her shoulder as they disappeared.

"I'll head for Vallent. And maybe I'll stop at Gyr Command and find out what Teranimo is up to." Han couldn't stay here. He had to hunt.

"Want us to hold the fort?" Pen asked.

"Five of you should be enough, given it's getting colder. The raveners are out less now. If you need me, call and I'll come back immediately."

He shouldn't leave, not on so personal a mission, but this was more important than protocol. More important than the dictates of Gyr Command.

This was destiny.

9

Fliss liked Vallent.

The town was large, far larger than any she had seen before, although she understood it was smaller than Fjern's capital, Nasnere.

Still, it was a major center, and she enjoyed wandering the well-maintained streets.

Everything was built with local stone, but property owners used door color, flower boxes, hanging baskets, and architectural design to differentiate themselves from their neighbors.

She found a shop selling sweet treats and bought some, spending far longer than she probably should have choosing what to get.

They had never had anything like this at home. Occasionally, one of the Gyr in the Fithsu Gyratta had made a dessert, and she hoped these would be as good.

She found a blue ceramic bowl, the shade shifting from light to dark in concentric rings, glossy and smooth, and could not resist buying it for her little apartment, as well as some red, green, and yellow fruit to put in it.

She had never bought something like this for herself.

See, she told her gyra, *this is what we needed. Some fun and freedom.*

By the time the sun had set, she was very pleased with her day.

She sat in her armchair, her blue bowl on the low table in front of her, looking out the window at the lights along the busy street.

She was comfortable and happy, and seriously considered staying in her rooms, eating the fruit she had bought, and getting an early night, although the scent of cooking food and the murmur of voices from the street below tempted her to explore a little more.

As she sat, conflicted, she heard the scuffle of feet outside her door before someone knocked politely.

She wondered whether it could be Enid, but her new friend had headed home hours ago.

She opened the door to find the young traveler from the Provinces, who she'd passed on the Trust's steps that morning, standing in her doorway.

"Good evening." He seemed nervous. "I'm Leven. I saw you earlier. Eloisa told me you've come to stay at the Trust, and I should show you a good place to eat." He paused. "Have you had dinner already?" He smiled at her with hopeful anticipation.

Fliss glanced back at her armchair and her pretty bowl, and forced herself to be sociable. She shook her head. "I was just wondering where to go. I'm Fliss."

"Fliss." He said her name carefully. "I eat most nights at a place five minutes from here. I told Eloisa I'd be happy to take you along."

She grabbed her jacket from its hook near the door and stepped out to join him in the passage, carefully locking up behind her.

"You're from the Provinces, like me?" Leven asked as they took the stairs. He was still in the Provinces-style clothing she'd seen him in this morning, and she could hear the slight twang in his accent that pinned him as from the escarpment.

"Yes. Although I'm from a prospecting site, not one of the more established villages." She followed him out of the front door and down the steps, taking a deep breath.

The air was cool, but it smelled good. Someone laughed from across the street, and she smiled in response.

Maybe Leven had done her a favor, after all.

"I'm from Evernia, have you heard of it?" Leven glanced at her as they crossed the road. He was tall and thin, head and shoulders taller than herself. She guessed he was two or three years younger than her, as well.

Fliss nodded. "It's over a day's drive by ground crawler from where I grew up, but a lot of the prospectors who end up at the river start off in Evernia, at the Pit."

"We get a lot of people moving through," Leven agreed. "My parents both work at the Pit, although there's a lot of farming that goes on around there, as well."

"Do you have a gyratta out there?" Fliss asked. She had never thought about gyrattas before she'd joined one herself. She had grown up thinking a lone Gyr was how every settlement did things.

"A small one. Only four Gyr." Leven stopped when they reached a building set on a corner. It was well-lit inside, and through the window Fliss could see people sitting on benches, eating and drinking at long wooden tables in a room with a roaring fire. "My friend Ralin, who's also from Evernia, put himself forward as a Gyr recruit and was accepted. He's next in line for the gyra."

"I think Eloisa mentioned that. He's here in Vallent?" She wondered why. Surely the main Gyr Command office was in Nasnere?

"There was a possibility of a gyra transfer near here that didn't work out. I suppose he can't tell me the details, but they're letting him wait here in Vallent for a while."

A Gyr would have to die for their gyra to come available. That seemed a little ghoulish to Fliss. She would not like to sit around waiting for someone to be killed in order to receive gyra.

But Gyr were killed, no matter how fast and strong their gyra helped them to be, because raveners were unpredictable, and sometimes there was nothing you could do, no way out of a situation.

The Gyr who lived to a ripe old age were few, or so her father had told her.

Those who passed the age of fifty were made to give their gyra back. She had been told that, as well.

Dakar had been close to that age.

The countdown had started for him on the forceable removal of his gyra, but he never had to go through that. His gyra had killed him, themselves.

Leven opened a door beside the big window, and Fliss stumbled as she stepped through it.

The recruit, Leven's friend, could he have been expecting the transfer of Dakar's gyra? Is *that* why he was so close to the Fithsu Gyratta?

She heard a roaring in her ears.

Why had she not considered it before now?

Transfer ceremonies were not something she'd ever experienced. She didn't know how long after a Gyr's death the transfer took place, but if it was soon, then that would make sense.

She was stunned that she had simply not thought about it.

Her naivety in this world was showing.

"Are you all right?" Leven was looking at her with alarm. "You seem . . ." He trailed off, looking uncertain.

"I'm fine." She forced herself to smile. "I only got into Vallent just before dawn this morning, and I was suddenly hit with a wave of fatigue."

"A meal should help." Leven steered them to the end of table that had two places free and grabbed two menus from a stand in the middle of the room. "I always have the same thing when I come here, but each time, I'm sure I'll choose something different."

Fliss forced herself to read the choices and order a dish, and then let Leven chatter on about his plans in the big city, and how wonderful it was to be someplace other than Evernia and the Pit, while she reeled at her mistake.

She had completely forgotten about Dakar's gyra.

They were her gyra now, but she had been so traumatized by Dakar's death, and then upset by the reaction of his team, the arrival of Kardenian and his team, and then the order to leave, she genuinely had not thought about them again at all.

It had happened so fast. She had crouched over Dakar to see if there was a way to save him, and the gyra had bloomed, silver and beautiful, tiny teardrops above where her hand rested against his skin, and they had rolled down and slid into her fingertips.

Would anyone believe that?

She bent her head over the stew that she'd ordered, and tried to calm herself.

Now that she was aware of the implications, she felt panicked. Because Gyr Command would have to know by now the gyra had gone to her.

They had brought a recruit out to receive them, and had wasted their time.

She accepted a drink from the server and took a cautious sip, mainly because Leven seemed so insistent on her trying it.

Too insistent.

It was tart and dry, and she liked it. It had alcohol in it, but not much——certainly less than the hard water they drank up in Leverta.

Besides, she'd worked out early on her gyra dealt with the alcohol, mostly.

She could drink any prospector she'd ever met under the table.

"Not too strong for you?" Leven asked.

"No, I like it." She saw a flash of satisfaction in his eyes, and hoped that she misunderstood.

She seldom did, though.

Between her and her gyra, she was very good at reading body language.

She might have considered being blunt with him about his chances of getting her drunk and more inclined to sleep with him, but she had to live in the same building as him, so she said nothing, sipping her drink as she ate, and letting him talk as she tried to think of the possible outcomes of her being chosen by Dakar's gyra.

Would they want them back?

Inside her, her gyra told her forcefully that was not going to happen. Dakar's gyra were indistinguishable from hers, now. They were going nowhere.

She relaxed at that.

She had plenty of gyra already, and Dakar's gyra had not made a significant impact on her, which was partly why she'd forgotten all about them, but they had chosen her, and they had killed Dakar to save her.

She felt attached to them.

No one had asked her about them at the gyratta, and she had been ordered to leave, so technically, she decided by the time she'd finished her meal, she really had done nothing wrong that she could see.

If she had broken some rule of Gyr Command, well, that was inadvertent. She had never been inducted into Gyr training, and that was on Dakar, not her.

"You were right," she told Leven. "I really do feel a lot better after that meal."

When the server came around, they paid for their dinner and then walked back out onto the street.

The atmosphere inside the restaurant had been cozy and pleasant, the gentle murmur of conversation, the dim lighting, and smell of good food.

"Your friend from Evernia, the Gyr recruit, he couldn't join you tonight?" Fliss asked, turning in the direction of the Trust.

"Ralin's eating with some of the senior people at Gyr Command tonight." Leven turned with her. He had had two large glasses of the drink he'd insisted she try, and he swayed, just a little. "We might meet up later."

"Well, thanks for bringing me along. It's a good place. If you want to go find your friend, that's fine with me. I'm headed back to get an early night." She inclined her head politely and started walking.

She had had to deal with men who hoped for a chance with her since she was young. Men who had tried to soften her up with alcohol. With insincere compliments. Even with gifts.

Not that Leverta was short of women——it wasn't. There were just as many women as men prospecting the river.

She'd always assumed it was because she was Gyr.

They wanted to say they'd slept with the settlement's protector.

She'd only ever chosen those who kept their mouths shut and hadn't tried too hard.

And she certainly didn't oblige boys who pretended to be welcoming, using it as an angle to try to bed her.

"Ralin will look for me at the Trust. I'll walk back with you." Leven caught up with her, and she slowed her step out of courtesy.

They walked in silence for a bit.

The air was even colder now, and she could smell the river she had only glimpsed at from a distance earlier today.

"You never said what your plans are in Vallent," Leven said.

"I haven't decided yet. I'll look for work, see what's available that suits me." She shrugged. "I'm just enjoying being in a big town and everything it has to offer."

"What did you do before?" Leven stumbled a little on the stone-paved road. There were no ground crawlers allowed in town and aside from a few other people going about their business, they had the road to themselves.

"My father owned a store that supplied the prospectors with goods and food," she said, carefully neutral.

It occurred to her that if he told his friend Ralin who she was, Gyr Command would probably know five minutes later. And while she had convinced herself she had done nothing wrong, she wasn't interested in an argument over it with Gyr Command.

Not yet, anyway.

Not while she was spreading her wings for the first time in her life.

"You worked for him?"

"Yes." There was no lie in that. "But it was time to see a bit more of the world."

"Us Provincials need to stick together," he said, and gave a delicate burp. "They don't know danger here like we do. Not with a fully-staffed gyratta and these big stone houses. They look down on us."

"I've only been treated well so far, and I like everyone I've met here," Fliss said, aware her voice had gone a little cooler.

"That's because you're a beautiful woman. Who's going to be rude to *you*?" Leven said. "It's harder being a boy from the Pit."

Fliss wondered if that was true.

She didn't know enough about Vallent yet to say, either way.

They had reached the steps of the Trust when someone behind them gave a shout, and she turned to see two people running toward them.

"What's wrong?" she called.

"An isilo. It's just come ashore. Get inside." The man's voice was hoarse, and he and his companion reached a door she assumed was their own, and disappeared behind it.

"An isilo?" Leven gripped the door handle and inserted his key in the lock, hands shaking.

Enid had said the isilo sometimes came into town by way of the river. She had also said they liked to take children.

"Is the gyratta close?" she asked Leven.

Fithsu Gyratta had been almost too far from Fithsu to be of any use in an immediate emergency, but the logic had been that most of the raveners were in the countryside around the town, and it was more efficient for the Gyr to patrol the surrounding area and stop the raveners before they reached the town at all.

She didn't know how it worked here.

"Five minutes out of town, Ralin says." Leven had the door open. "Let's get inside."

"Good idea," Fliss told him. She waited until he was through, and then pushed it closed.

He made a muffled sound of surprise from behind it, but she was already running toward the river.

She could hear shouting as she got closer, and then a woman screamed, the sound setting off something visceral within her.

She increased her pace, sprinting the last few blocks to come out on a wide promenade beside the fast-flowing water.

There were lights to her left——what looked like a pier or dock ——and she could see two bodies lying on the ground near it.

A creature she assumed was an isilo was standing, head cocked, looking at them.

It took a step forward, head low, moving with stealth, and she was sure in that moment that it was going to eat them.

They may already be dead, but she did not want to take a chance they weren't.

She whistled.

She had many years to practice it.

It had brought her the attention of every ravener she'd ever encountered.

It did not disappoint on this occasion, either.

The isilo turned its head toward her, and she started walking toward it, slowly.

She didn't want to run at it, in case it spooked and darted off.

Once it was loose in the city center, there was plenty of damage it could do.

"Stay away from it," a man shouted at her from the side.

She turned to see where he was and noticed a man hanging from the awning bracket of a cafe facing the river.

"I'm Gyr," she called to him. "Stay where you are."

"Thank the Stars for that." A woman standing in a window on the second floor of another building leaned out of it, hands cupped on either side of her mouth, and shouted up the street: "The Gyr have arrived."

People behind the isilo scrambled back and away, and Fliss approved, both of their courage in trying to battle it themselves, and their understanding that they would just be in the way now that she was here.

"Quiet now," she warned, because while the woman's shout had had the right effect, it had also disturbed the creature.

Its attention was straying from Fliss, the movement and noise of the townspeople getting to safety had unsettled it.

"Look at me," she crooned to it.

It was about a quarter of the size of a zuby, and it looked quick.

The zubys were vicious when they were riled, and if they got their teeth into you, there was no surviving it, gyra or no, but they weren't that fast and they were often nervous of things smaller than them because they couldn't see very well.

An isilo would be harder to get her hands on in order to make a suggestion.

And she had been interacting with zuby, largarti, and carranda since she was a child. She had come to know them. She had never dealt with an isilo.

"That's right. Come now." She kept moving forward, her voice gentle, her pace steady.

She knew the moment the creature locked onto her as prey.

She felt the familiar shiver of fear that ran through her before a confrontation——her gyra warning her it would be better to run, that she wasn't safe.

That's the point, she told them.

They very seldom agreed.

They had always been firmly of the opinion that her life was the most important, and everyone else could fend for themselves.

The isilo went still, hunching down, its hind legs bunching, its long forearms with their wicked claws tucking in to its chest.

It hissed, but quietly, and then darted forward, leaping at her in long, airborne hops, rather than running.

She wished the lights on the promenade were better, the glow of the solar lanterns cast a gentle, romantic illumination of the stone paving and glittered off the water, but she'd have preferred something brighter, to help her with her timing.

She would have to jump.

She sped up, racing straight for the creature, and leaped into the air.

She got lucky, because as she jumped, she startled it, and it whipped back its head.

As she reached it, flying past, she managed to stretch out an arm, snagging its neck. She tightened her grip and swung herself onto its back, her free hand going to the top of its head.

"Stop."

It didn't like that. And it didn't stop.

It bellowed in surprise and panic, trying to fling her off.

The problem was, unlike the other raveners, her weight was a real concern for it, whereas most of the big ones hardly felt her when she landed on their backs.

"Water." She didn't know how fast the isilo were in water, but at least that would confine it to the river, rather than being loose on the street.

It was screeching now, as if she was stabbing it, rather than simply riding it, and whether in obedience to her command, or out of dumb luck, it ran straight for the water and flung itself in.

The river was freezing.

Water closed over her head, but she hung on to the isilo, which dived down, its long tail whipping back and forth to power it through the current.

"Burrow," she thought at it, forcefully, because she was worried it would turn and bite her if she let go of its neck.

What had her mother warned her about, when her father had ranted about her unGyr-like methods of dealing with the raveners?

Be careful getting on a monster's back, because it's difficult to get off.

It was certainly difficult now.

The isilo angled immediately to the left, to the far bank, and swam against the current where its flow was less strong.

Fliss hung on, but she didn't have long to wait before it reached the city wall.

There was a metal grate across the water, attached to the arch created in the wall to let the river flow in.

The isilo dived down and Fliss kept hold.

There were lights overhead, shining into the water——an attempt by the locals to see what was going on at this entry point into their otherwise secure city, she guessed. It was easy to see the bottom of the grate had been bent upward.

"Burrow." Fliss let go moments after she gave the command again.

The isilo wriggled underneath the grate and then swam away, twisting left and right as it went, as if under attack.

She swam forward, using her strength to bend the grate back down, but it was weakened now, and would have to be replaced.

She pushed herself up to the surface, facing back the way she'd come, and let the current take her back.

When she reached the surface, she was in the middle of the river, close to where she'd gone in, and she swam toward the side.

As she pulled herself up onto promenade, a man put a hand out to help her, and she accepted it, more to be friendly than because she needed it.

"Thanks."

"Never saw anything like it." The man stepped back to avoid the gush of water coming off her. "How did you swim from the grate to here so quickly?"

She squeezed the hem of her tunic. "Have you felt how cold the water is? No one would want to hang around in there any longer than necessary."

He grinned at that answer, then frowned. "Where's your cutter? You didn't lose it in the river, did you?"

"I'm not with the Vallent Gyratta," she said, her teeth suddenly chattering as the cold night air met the even colder water that soaked her clothes. "I'm from the Provinces, on a journey to see a bit more of the world, so I don't have a cutter."

"You didn't shift, either."

"No. I'm one of the few non-shifting Gyr."

"Oh?" He blinked at her. "I suppose I had heard rumors there were some, but I didn't realize you dealt with raveners."

"What else would we do?" she asked.

He didn't have an answer and shrugged.

"Are those people all right? The ones lying near the dock?"

The man had turned in that direction, and she did the same, shivering as she walked.

"I don't know. They were taken away the moment you got the ravener in the water."

"Good." She squeezed her sleeve and water poured off it. "The grate was bent up. It'll need to be replaced."

He gave a nod. "That's what they usually do when they get in, no matter how often those grates are reinforced."

She shrugged. "I'm going to go have a hot shower and change. I'm glad I was able to help."

She stopped at the road she'd come out of when she'd run toward the isilo, and the man gaped at her.

"You're not coming to talk to the council leaders? They're all there." He waved in the direction of the pier.

She shook her head. "I'm freezing. And in the Provinces, we Gyr don't usually stand on ceremony."

He grinned in response to that. "Fair enough. Thanks again. I'm Marcus. I own the cafe on the waterfront."

He was the one who'd been hanging off the awning bracket, she realized.

"Fliss." She nodded, then her whole body was gripped with a shiver, and she hunched her shoulders. "I'm sure I'll see you around, Marcus."

She turned away, and Marcus did the same, striding away from her, voice raised as he called to the others by the pier.

It felt like it took a lot longer to get back to the Trust than it had to run to the river, but her reward was a hot shower at the end of it.

No one was around, not even Leven was waiting for her to get back, which was a relief.

She locked her door behind her and dripped all the way to her bathroom.

10

Han looked down at his empty plate and wondered when he could escape the dinner he'd been invited to at Vallent Gyr Command. He'd agreed because Ralin would be present, and he wanted to support the new recruit, but conversation had been surprisingly lacking.

Han looked around and saw Teranimo was staring at the wall beside the door, as if completely lost in his own world.

Errol was making conversation with Ralin, and the recruit was trying to answer politely.

Han had spent the afternoon looking through Gyr Command records, trying to trace Ralf Bellini's movements, and had encountered nothing but obstruction.

It was as if Gyr Command was deliberately blocking his investigation.

Errol had refused to give him access to some databases, and Teranimo had refused to help him altogether, citing too much work.

It was part of a pattern he'd noticed for at least the last year. Subtle moves that served to put the Gyr on the outside, asking for permission, instead of including the Gyr as decision-makers.

At first he thought he was imagining it, or that it was down to certain individual administrators, but more and more, it seemed to be a deliberate choice.

The absolute refusal to give him any indication of what had happened to Lucille Defoe was the final clue.

They were freezing the Gyr out. Making them supplicants, rather than the equal partners that they were.

"I just got word there's an isilo come ashore out of the river." The woman who burst into the small dining room looked straight at Han.

He rose, reaching for his cutter. "Where?" he asked, moving as fast as he could with the woman, who was not someone he recognized, trying to keep pace with him.

Behind him, Teranimo, Errol, and Ralin rose as well, but he didn't wait for them or look back.

"Middle of the promenade. Near the pier." She reached out as if to grab his arm, then thought better of it. "I think it's been dealt with, but one of the town councilors said to let you know."

"Dealt with?" All his people were at the gyratta or in Fithsu. Han assumed her information was inaccurate. He stepped into the street and ran, cutter in hand, his gyra buzzing in his veins in anticipation of a shift.

He heard shouting when he was about a minute away, but it was quiet by the time he reached the river, and he feared the worst.

A group of people huddled near the pier, which he did not understand at all.

Why were they not trying to hide or get to safety?

Someone looked up——he recognized her as one of the Vallent town councilors——and she waved to him. "Kardenian?"

"Yes." He slowed as he approached the small crowd. "Where's the isilo?"

"The other Gyr dealt with it." A burly man waved his hand toward a street a little way down the promenade.

"The other Gyr?" Han's gyra prickled in anticipation beneath his skin.

"The woman. Fliss." The man smiled. "No cutter, no shifting. And still ..."

Han didn't like the sound of admiration in his voice. It sounded too . . . proprietary. "And still?" he asked.

"She ran straight for it, man." The young teenager who spoke up shook his head. "Like, straight for it, like she wasn't even a little bit afraid."

"And then she sort of swung onto its back and rode it into the river." A woman beside him spoke quietly. "They disappeared under the water, and she seemed to . . ." she shrugged, as if struggling for the words ". . . send it on its way."

"If Randal and Carrie live, it's thanks to her." The councilor glanced toward the pier, and Han saw evidence of blood on the ground. "It was going to eat them."

"Where is she?" He couldn't believe Fliss was right here. Had probably been right here all day, while he'd been sitting in Gyr Command, looking for clues to where she might have originally come from.

"She went home." The burly man spoke up again. "She was freezing after having to swim in the river."

"And where is home for her?" Han asked, anticipation rising.

Everyone shook their heads.

No one knew.

That was all right, he thought as he walked back to Gyr Command.

Vallent wasn't that big. He would find her.

And at the very least, now he knew where she was.

THE KNOCKING PULLED her from sleep, and Fliss rose from her bed and stood, listening for a moment, unsure if she wanted to respond.

If it was Gyr Command knocking on her door at . . . she glanced at her wrist unit . . . two in the morning, that was not a good sign.

"Fliss?"

The sound of Enid's voice relaxed her, and she made her way to her little entrance hall and leaned against the doorjamb as she opened up and peered out.

"Sorry to wake you." Enid looked . . . unhappy, and when she glanced at the white-haired man accompanying her, Fliss was left in no doubt who she was unhappy with.

"What's wrong?" she asked.

"Can we come in?"

Fliss stepped back, pulling the door wide, and then followed her two guests in.

"I didn't want to come, but Jackson here was insistent." Enid sighed and sank into a chair. "I'm really sorry about this."

"I'm here to offer her a job, Ennie, not ask for a favor." Jackson's voice held an edge. He looked straight at Fliss for the first time. "I heard you're Gyr."

The old man hadn't sat down. He looked slightly unkempt, his bushy hair sticking up as if he'd just rolled out of bed.

"You heard right." Looking at Enid's tight lips, she had a feeling he hadn't heard about it from Enid, though.

"A few of the people out by the river earlier came into the tavern where I was drinking and told me how you dealt with that isilo." He glanced down at Enid and his expression softened. "I am sorry to wake you, but I need a Gyr to accompany me on a transport job, and I was told there were none available to protect me tomorrow. When I heard you weren't part of the gyratta, suddenly the business that I was going to have to cancel looked like it might be able to go ahead, if you're up for a two day trip."

"What kind of trip?" She leaned against the wall, trying to judge the situation.

"I need to go up into the foothills on a hauling job, but there's no Gyr available to go out with me. The gyratta told me I have to wait at least a few days, and the job's tomorrow, or not at all."

"I know you want some work, and I didn't want to not bring Jackson to you with the offer, in case you would be interested." Enid leaned forward in her chair.

Fliss had the impression her new friend wasn't sure she was doing the right thing, but didn't want to be responsible for Fliss missing out.

Fair enough.

She could say no if she didn't like it.

Jackson glanced at his wrist unit. "If I don't let them know I can do it in the next hour, the shipment will go to someone else."

"What's the shipment?" Fliss wasn't aware the Gyr acted as personal bodyguards to transporters, but then she hadn't been told a lot. People had definitely come and gone from Fithsu Gyratta on individual or two-team missions, not just the big group round-ups.

Maybe this was what they'd been doing.

"Rilmite," Jackson said. "From a mine up in the Palqua Hills."

She hadn't heard of rilmite, but she hadn't exactly had the best education. She'd tried to catch up while she'd lived at the gyratta, with more time on her hands and access to online information and books. Rilmite hadn't come up, though.

"So you need a Gyr to keep the raveners away on your journey to and from the mine? How much does it pay?"

He flicked a look at Enid, as if looking for help, but she pretended not to notice, her focus on Fliss's new blue bowl.

"What's the going rate?" he asked. "First time I've had to hire a Gyr privately."

She thought of the money Dakar had given her, divided it to come up with a daily rate, and then doubled it. "Two hundred credits a day, no matter how little or how much of the day I work," she said.

He seemed to relax. "That's fine. That's doable for me." He waved a hand. "Enid'll tell you where to find me. Be ready to go at six this morning."

He let himself out, moving with purpose.

"You should have doubled it," Enid said when the door closed behind him.

"I'll know for next time." Fliss smiled.

She moved to her armchair and took a seat. "You seemed a little worried about me taking the job. What's making you nervous?"

"Not exactly nervous." Enid sighed and leaned back in her chair.

"It should be fine. I've known Jackson for years, but he's acting strange. He heard from my neighbor that I'd given someone a lift into town, put it together with the story of you getting rid of that isilo, and came knocking on my door fit to wake the dead, desperate to find out if you were still staying with me." She moved, a little agitated. "He seems a mite too invested in this job. It's not something he's done before, that I know of, and I haven't heard of any mine up in the Palqua Hills. I mean, there are mines up there, but they usually deal with the transporters in Renardo, because it's closer to them, and Renardo has a nice straight road all the way to Nasnere."

Fliss wanted to see Nasnere.

Fjern's capital city, the place where the Travelers had landed and established themselves.

"You been there?" she asked Enid.

"A couple of times." Enid slid her hands down her thighs to rest them on her knees. "It's worth a look, I can tell you that."

That sounded like high praise, coming from Enid.

"What kind of territory will we be traveling through to get to these foothills?"

"Nice open fields to start, then some dense forest, but as you get closer to the Palqua Hills, it's good ravener territory, lots of rocky outcrops, so there'll be work for you to do."

"He wouldn't need me if there wasn't." Fliss knew he wouldn't be spending the money, otherwise.

"You sure you're up for going to work in four hours?" Enid asked. "You can't have had more than a couple hours sleep, on top of a busy day."

A busy day. Fliss gave a chuckle. "It was actually a really great day until the end. And it was more the swim in that freezing river than the isilo."

Enid shook her head. "I've seen you deal with a zuby, so I'm sure that isilo didn't have a chance, but I'm sorry you're not going to have more time to settle in."

Fliss lifted a shoulder. "There'll be time afterward. It's only two days, and the credits will give me a buffer."

"Jackson says it's only two days, but I think he's lying." Enid rose to her feet. "I can't see why a Palqua mine would want rilmite coming to Vallent. It's the wrong direction. My guess is his contract is to take the shipment to Renardo, and he doesn't want to admit that, in case you don't want to be away for the three day round trip it will take. Three days at least."

Fliss thought about it. Didn't like it.

More because she didn't like being lied to than the extra day on the road.

But she'd made it clear the cost of her time was per day, so she'd come out of it well ahead.

She sighed. "It's fine. And even though I obviously asked for too little, the money is good. It'll keep me in oloa tea and pretty bowls for quite some time." She ran her fingertips along the edge of her bowl.

"One word of advice." Enid took a step back, and Fliss stood to join her.

"What's that?"

"If Jackson has broken circuit boards in his crawler, charge extra for fixing them, and pretend it's more complicated than it obviously is for you."

Fliss grinned. "Good advice."

She yawned. She'd be able to catch another three hours before she had to get up, pack, and find Jackson.

"Where's Jackson's place? You said he lives near you?" Fliss guessed he'd need a field like Enid's to park his crawler if it was hauling ore.

"Two houses down," Enid confirmed. "Don't let him give you any trouble. Walk away if you don't like it."

More good advice, Fliss thought as she closed the door behind Enid and went back to bed.

She should have done that sooner when it came to Dakar. She wouldn't make that mistake again.

11

"WHAT DO YOU MEAN, SHE'S GONE?" HAN STARED DOWN ELOISA, frustration making him a little less polite than usual.

It was just after midday, and he had finally run Fliss to ground. Or so he'd thought.

The Travelers' Trust administrator narrowed her eyes at him. "Exactly what I said. She left me a note early this morning saying she was offered a job that would take her out of town for two days."

"What job?"

Eloisa threw up her hands. "I don't know. She didn't say."

"I need to find her urgently." Han glanced up as someone came through the front door into the wide reception area.

A young man, dressed Province-style.

Eloisa followed his gaze. "Leven, have you seen Fliss today? Do you know where she went?"

"I didn't know Fliss had gone at all. I was up and out early on a job. Is she all right after what happened last night?" Leven glanced at the stairs that led to the apartments above, as if eyeing an escape.

Han's gyra perked up, and he turned the full focus of his attention on the youngster.

"What happened last night?" he asked softly.

Leven blinked at him. "The isilo attack." He looked at Eloisa as if for help. "I showed her that place to eat, just like you asked me to, and on our way home we heard the shouting about the isilo attack. I got into the building, to keep out of the way, but Fliss ran off. I don't know where to but I think she headed straight for it."

"Well, she is Gyr," Eloisa said. "That's probably perfectly normal for her."

Leven gaped at her. "Gyr?" His voice came out an octave higher than it had before. "Gyr?"

"She didn't mention it?" Han wondered why.

Leven shook his head, dumbfounded.

"Who else might she have told about her plans?" Han turned back to Eloisa.

She hesitated, but then seemed to come to a decision. "Enid Quinn. Out on the edge of town. A long-hauler. She gave Fliss a lift to Vallent and she helped get her settled here at the Trust. If anyone knows, it's probably her."

At last. An actual lead.

"Let me know if she comes back, Eloisa."

He didn't wait to hear her answer, though. He was already striding out the door.

As the big, heavy ground crawler rumbled up the slopes of the Palqua Hills, Fliss had to get two raveners off the road.

Jackson seemed to want them killed, but she had simply looked him in the eye, saying nothing when he remonstrated with her, and he eventually ran out of steam.

"You wanted them gone, and they're gone. Why do you want them dead?"

He looked away from her, fiddling with the controls of the crawler. "Just insurance, in case they decide to come back," he mumbled in the end. "Never been this far north into the hills before. I didn't know it would be so dangerous."

Her gyra told her he was lying, and she believed them.

"I'm going to go sit up on the roof," she said, opening the window on her side, and hopping up onto her seat.

She reached up and out, got a grip on the roof racks and pulled herself up.

Once she was on the big, wide roof, she leaned back down through the window. "Slow down if you see anything and I'll jump off and deal with it."

He looked like he wanted to object, but that would have been crazy, as she was doing exactly what he'd hired her to do.

She felt safer up here, even though he was just an old man and no threat to her whatsoever.

But something was wrong, and she knew she was safer doing things on her own terms, keeping herself unpredictable.

They had driven through the day, and while it was early evening now, full darkness was still an hour away.

She stood up on the roof, her gyra keeping her perfectly balanced, and saw two lights illuminating the dusk up ahead.

When they got close enough that even Jackson was able to see them, he stopped the crawler and leaned out the window. "Climb on in, that's the entrance to the mine up ahead. There's no danger of raveners inside the fence."

Just then, a largarti scuttled across the ground crawler's headlights.

Jackson gave a sharp cry.

"It's fine." She jumped down and landed beside his door, a move that startled him——he jerked and she noticed his hands held a white-knuckled grip on the wheel. "I'll go sort that out and wait for you here. When do you think you'll be back out?"

"Leave it, it's gone." He looked out into the darkness, but the largarti ran back across the lights, keeping its body high and its legs wide, which they only did when they felt threatened.

"Clearly not." She watched the beast, wondering what had it so riled. "It's not going to let us pass. Something's disturbed it."

At that moment, it charged the crawler, and Fliss ran straight for it, jumping high and landing on one of its bent upper legs, then up onto the flat carapace covering its head.

"Away," she ordered, hand over the area where its brain was.

She could have jumped off it as it obeyed, but she wanted to find out why Jackson was so desperate to get her back in the crawler and take her into the mine.

The largarti scuttled right, carrying her with it as it moved into the scrub that was its natural habitat.

"Go to your burrow." She considered jumping off now, out of sight, but the creature was so disturbed, she wanted to see where the burrow was, so she hung on as it raced through the bush.

When it began to lower itself, Fliss leaped to safety, and it disappeared into a deep fissure in the ground.

She could hear chittering sounds.

It had a clutch.

That explained the aggression.

Then she felt the earth vibrate beneath her feet and heard a rumbling sound.

Someone was setting deep level charges.

She didn't know a lot about life outside her village, although she was working to change that, but she did know mining.

Every prospector who came up to Leverta had tried their hand at several mining careers before they ended up panning for caltine in the river.

She knew the rules, she knew the barriers to entry, she knew the fine letter of the law.

She'd had to listen to the bitter complaints about the provisions that restricted activity and the gleeful boasts of those who'd managed to circumvent them.

From the rumble of the earth, it sounded like someone was circumventing those rules now, because it was for sure illegal to set charges near largarti burrows.

That could get a lot of people living in the area killed.

She jogged toward the sound, wondering what Jackson had done when she'd been carried off by a ravener.

He might still be waiting for her out on the road, or maybe he'd driven into the mine.

The bush got thicker as she moved forward and she slowed.

Her gyra were telling her there was danger here, picking up tiny noises and clues and processing them in a way that she could not, and she heeded them, moving silently.

A quiet cough sounded to her right, and she went still, then began working her way back, moving around what she guessed was a guard, and coming up behind him.

He was nervous.

He should be, this close to a largarti burrow. He held a large weapon in his hand that was completely foreign to her.

Weapons were another thing she knew well.

With only her to keep the raveners at bay, the prospectors all bought an array of heavy weaponry for protection.

Whatever this guard held in his arms like a baby, it was nothing like any weapon she'd ever seen before.

She ghosted past the man, who appeared to be wearing a bulky type of battle gear. She could see padding on his chest and on his forearms, and she didn't know if someone who wasn't Gyr could have spotted him in the growing dark at all.

He seemed to melt into the gloaming.

She took even more care as she moved closer to what was clearly the mine.

Where there was one guard, there would be more.

She expected a fence of some kind, in fact Jackson had mentioned one, but what they'd set up was actually a series of beacons on poles, transmitting a frequency from point to point which she guessed was supposed to deter the raveners.

It might actually work some of the time.

The raveners didn't like very low or very high frequency sounds, and this was as high as she'd ever sensed.

But it wouldn't stop them if they were hurt, hungry or enraged, and might actually make things worse.

That might be why the guard was outside the 'fence', not inside it.

Either that or he was watching for her.

She put her hand on one of the beacons and her gyra leaped inside her, hungry to learn something new.

And it was new, all right.

It was like nothing she, or her gyra, had ever encountered, just like the weapon.

But her gyra were clever, and they mastered it quickly enough.

They shut down the pole she was touching, and the one beside it, and she walked through the gap without setting off any alarms.

Before she moved on, she turned and reset it, just in case someone felt the need to come check on a malfunction.

The sound of shouting came from up ahead of her, and then another deep boom shook the ground, and she heard a ravener shriek in rage to the west.

They were playing a dangerous game out here.

And if all they had was a few guards and the transmitters, they didn't have enough to cope.

It made her wonder if Jackson had brought her up here on even more false pretenses than she'd started to imagine.

Like to offer her a job dealing with the ravener problem on this mine site.

The more she saw of the operation, the more likely that scenario seemed.

Maybe Jackson knew what was going on up here and when he'd heard about her after the isilo attack, had gotten in touch with the mine manager to see if they were looking for an unaffiliated Gyr.

Maybe he *was* contracted to haul ore, although Enid had already said that was suspect, but saw a chance to bring them a Gyr who wasn't tied to a gyratta.

She had not considered how tempting a prize she would make to some people when she'd decided to leave the compound.

She hadn't understood a lot about how the system worked.

Hadn't realized she would be a useful commodity.

But they couldn't force her to patrol for raveners for them.

Why hadn't Jackson simply said there was a job up here for her as a Gyr?

The only answer she could come up with was he had guessed she would have declined.

It still made no sense to her, and she had found that most things had a logical explanation.

Whoever Jackson was working for, they would be operating on what they thought was a logical plan.

She just didn't have all the facts yet.

She slowed her steps again as she approached another guard, this one more relaxed than the one outside the frequency perimeter. The woman had holstered her weapon in a large thigh holster and was eating a nutrient bar.

The comm unit clipped to the guard's shoulder squawked and she swore softly as it gave her a start.

She spoke into it, and Fliss went completely still in shock.

The woman was not speaking Fjerna.

And Fjerna was the only language on Fjern.

Everyone on the planet had arrived together on the *Cercatore*, and they still used a version of the language their ancestors had spoken on that massive explorer ship.

The people of Fjern had spread out somewhat from the early days of settlement, when the shock of the raveners had kept them huddled together, but even those who'd taken to exploring uninhabited lands still spoke the mother tongue.

So what could explain this?

Strange weapons. Strange tech. Strange language.

Fliss felt a skitter of fear run down her spine.

Aliens?

Aliens would explain the sheer madness of depth charges near largarti burrows.

But it didn't explain where Jackson fit in.

How had he become entangled in this?

And yet, if they were aliens, they looked just like her. Or near enough, what she could see of them in the dark, with their padded battle gear.

She could see the glimmer of a cluster of lights to her left, and angled carefully in that direction, moving between the bushes, alert for more guards.

She passed two more, both with weapons holstered.

They seemed bored.

Then the ravener who'd screamed earlier, a tarinac, if she guessed the roar correctly, either crashed through or brushed up against the barrier near the road she'd come in on with Jackson, and the guards began to run in that direction as someone barked orders at them through their comms unit in that strange language.

Although, now she heard it again, there were some familiar words.

It was like someone had taken Fjerna, and twisted it around.

She stopped dead in her tracks.

They had always known they were not the only Travelers.

There had been a massive fleet of ships.

Some had been destined for planets they already knew would support them and allow them to thrive. But there were too many Travelers and they needed to spread their risk, so others, like her own ancestors, had gone deeper into the unknown, arming themselves with special soldier units gifted with gyra, giving themselves the best possible chance to survive.

Could these be fellow Travelers, who had managed to fly the heavens again, and had found Fjern?

She was sure if other Travelers had found her planet and had openly made landing, even those in Leverta would have heard of it.

It would be at least a topic of conversation in Vallent.

But it wasn't.

Which meant this was either being kept secret by Fjern's administrators or no one knew they were here.

Other than Jackson, obviously.

And now, her.

12

An intermittent high-pitched buzz preceded each roar of the tarinac, and Fliss guessed she was hearing the sound the strange weapons made when they were activated.

They seemed to be a lot less effective than a cutter, but then, the Fjerna had had two thousand years to work out what worked on a ravener and what didn't.

From what she'd read in the history books, the projectile weapons the Travelers had used when they'd first arrived on Fjern had done little more than enrage the hostile monsters they had found on what was to become their new home.

A sharp blade was better, but as they had managed to improve their tech from barely none at all after the *Cercatore* had been forced to land to what they had today, the swords they'd switched to at the start had gone through many upgrades.

Nowadays, a cutter was a curved metal blade with an arc of plasma along the edge. It went through the carapace or hide of every ravener known on Fjern.

It would be nice to have if things went wrong, Fliss acknowledged.

Certainly, whatever these people were using was not up to the job.

She finally got within sight of the tarinac, its long neck and arrow head easily visible over the dense bush, even in the growing dark.

It swung its neck down and she could smell the throat-catching stench of its poison spray on the air.

She turned away, facing back the way she'd come to take a deep gulp of fresh air, and then she held her breath as she moved up wind.

The guards that had gone to meet it were coughing, and she heard a shout of concern from one of them.

Someone had probably gone down.

Tarinac venom was lethal if you inhaled enough of it.

She got clear of the vapor, walking slowly to allow her gyra to deal with the small amount she'd been exposed to.

She approached the tarinac from the east, slowing to a stop just within the bushes as three guards seemed to shoot bright streams of light from their weapons at it. The beams lit up the shadowy dusk, illuminating a fourth person lying still on the ground.

The tarinac gave a bellow, and one of the three shooters got a face full of venom and went down next to one of the tarinac's massive feet.

She could not watch them be crushed.

She let out a cry, a warble she had perfected over the years, and the tarinac swung to face her, the others forgotten.

She ran at it as it dipped its head, teeth bared, and before it could expel more venom, she got her hands on its head.

"Pack," she told it. "Find the safety of pack."

She jumped back as it whipped its head up, but it didn't want to find the safety of its pack, she could see.

It wanted to fight.

An adolescent with a taste of the mating frenzy.

She sighed.

They would fight anything in the first year of leaving their mothers' side and wandering around, looking for a bachelor pack.

Another stream of light hit its side, and she turned to face the two remaining guards with a scowl.

"Stop that right now, unless you want to get a face full of venom, and for your friends who are already down to die."

Both seemed startled by her admonishment, but they tipped the barrels of their weapons skyward.

One less problem to worry about. She was just glad they seemed to understand Fjerna.

She turned back to the tarinac.

It looked undecided, and she would need a little more persuasion to get it going.

She jumped high enough to grab the long, matted hair of the mane that sat around its shoulders, and used it to swing herself up onto its back.

She scrabbled up its long neck. "Go find a mate." She only mouthed it, and in truth, she didn't need to speak any of her suggestions aloud, although she found they were stronger if she did.

Eventually it turned away, moving through the bushes, and unwilling to get carried too far, she somersaulted from its head, and landed in a crouch on the ground.

Then she ran back toward the guards.

They were standing over their fallen colleagues, and she could see they were worried.

"Jackson, the long-hauler I came with, will have some anti-venom in his crawler."

They nodded, but hadn't spoken so far. It did seem as if they understood her, though.

One of them spoke their strange language into the little comms unit attached on their shoulder, and a squawk of sound came back in reply.

She wondered whether she should disappear back into the bush, now she had saved them from the tarinac and told them about the anti-venom, but a sound behind her made her turn, her gyra urging caution, to find two other guards walking toward her, weapons pointed right at her.

Their behavior was clearly threatening.

"This is the thanks I get for saving you and your friends?" she asked the two soldiers standing over the fallen.

Both ducked their heads, and she guessed from that they understood her well enough, and they didn't want to look her in the eye.

"Come." One of the guards pointing his weapon at her said, and tilted his head west. The word was accented but it was in Fjerna.

She moved as he directed, toward the gate where she'd left Jackson, feeling calm enough.

She didn't know for sure what was going on, and it could well be they had no plans to harm her.

Even if they did, she was difficult to hurt.

But she was very afraid they would not want her running free, knowing, as she did, that they were here. They wouldn't want to risk scrutiny, not with the way they were running things up here.

And she had no plans to be a prisoner again.

13

Fliss could just make out Jackson, standing outside a long, narrow building in the last of the daylight, pacing as if nervous.

He looked up as she got closer, and his gaze flicked over her shoulder to the two soldiers herding her forward with their weapons trained on her.

"Hey. What's this? No one said nothing about taking her prisoner."

His angry shout drew a man out from the door behind him, and when Fliss got a look at him, she knew this was the boss.

He was not wearing the bulky, padded uniform of the others, but instead a sleek black outfit that was extremely well-fitted.

He watched her with interest as she walked toward him.

She flicked her gaze over him, as well, then focused on Jackson.

"You have some explaining to do," she said.

The long-hauler sputtered, hands waving in front of him. "Maybe there was a little bit of lying in the offer I gave you, but only because I couldn't tell you the truth without spilling secrets I had no right to spill. No one said they were going to take you prisoner." He turned to the boss man. "Why are they pointing those things at her, Heldar?"

"Well now, we don't know what we're dealing with, do we? So it's best to be careful." Heldar dipped his head in greeting to her, but Fliss did not respond.

She was never going along to get along again.

The man seemed to realize she wasn't going to give him what he was looking for, and his eyes narrowed.

Before he could speak, the two guards who'd survived the tarinac attack appeared, each with a fallen soldier over their shoulder.

"They'll need your tarinac anti-venom," Fliss told Jackson. "I don't think they have much longer."

"They told me earlier they needed it and I fetched it from my crawler. It's here." He patted his pockets and took out two ampules with fitted syringes.

"Administer it," Heldar ordered, and Jackson sent him a dirty look, but moved forward to where the two soldiers were laying their friends down on the dusty ground.

He jabbed each of them in the arm and depressed the plunger, then straightened and shuffled back.

"How long does it take to work?" One of the soldiers spoke up, their language slow and thickly accented.

"It's instant." Jackson shrugged. "You either get it in time, or you don't."

"This place is truly a nightmare," Heldar said with feeling. "How many monsters are out to eat you here, anyway?"

"The problems you're having are because of the depth charges and the high frequency fence," Fliss said. "It bothers the raveners."

"What would you know about the depth charges and the fence?" Heldar asked, his focus sharpening on her.

Fliss frowned at him. "The ground is literally rumbling beneath our feet, that's how I know about the depth charges. And the fence attracts the largarti. They use high frequencies to communicate with each other." That was a lie, but she doubted they'd be able to contradict her, and she wasn't going to let them know she understood their strange fence.

Jackson must have told them something about the Gyr that made them want her, but she didn't know how much the old man had shared, or how much he knew, come to that.

Heldar studied her for a beat, then looked at the guards still standing over their friends, one of whom was now groaning.

The other was still ominously still.

"Report," he said.

"She did something to the monster," one of the guards said. He was a tall, bulky man, made even bulkier by his padded uniform. "It ran away."

"Something? What something?" Heldar sounded impatient.

The guard shrugged. "It was too dark to see. Something to its head."

"She climbed onto its back and then up onto its head," the other soldier chipped in, her voice a little husky, which told Fliss she had probably breathed in a little vapor herself. "Why don't you ask her?"

"Because I'm asking you for a truthful report. She could tell me anything."

"She's Gyr." Jackson's tone was scornful. "Of course she got rid of it. Getting rid of raveners is what they *do*." He shook his head and looked over at Fliss. "They were looking for solutions to their ravener problem, and when I heard about you, freelancing outside a gyratta, I thought you might be interested, but I couldn't tell you the truth in front of Ennie. This is a secret project."

"And here I am, under armed guard." Fliss would not forgive him for this. Neither would Enid, and from the way Jackson's eyes were darting from the guards to herself to Heldar, he knew it.

And feared it.

Good.

"Evlar isn't coming out of it." The soldier was crouched down beside her friend, and had got her arm around his shoulders, lifting his head slightly off the ground.

His lips were blue, and Fliss could see he was nearly dead.

As Jackson said, either the anti-venom kicked in, or you were too far gone.

The other guard who'd been unconscious was curled on her side now, coughing, and she'd be okay, although it would take her a few days, at least, to recover.

"We can't afford to lose any more people." Heldar sounded very annoyed, and Fliss noticed none of the soldiers standing around him particularly liked his tone. "How do you get rid of the monsters?" He turned on Fliss. "Teach my people and I'll let you go."

She studied him, astonished. "I can't teach someone who isn't Gyr." She flicked her gaze back to Jackson. "What did you tell him, that he believes it's even possible?"

"I told him we have Gyr to deal with the raveners. That you're stronger and faster than the rest of us." Jackson looked completely at a loss. "She's right. It's not something that can be taught. You're either Gyr, or you aren't."

Heldar didn't look like he believed a word of it. "Everything can be taught."

"If you had cutters, maybe I could show you a few things," Fliss admitted. "But why would I do so under duress? I'm not inclined to do anything for you at all."

"Cutters?" He seemed confused by the word. "What are they?"

"A type of weapon. I don't have one, though."

"Then what did you use?" Heldar's hands clenched.

"This," Fliss lifted her jacket, to show her knife in its sheath at her hip.

"Bring it." Heldar pointed to one of the guards still holding their weapon on her, and he stepped up to her, pulled the knife out of its sheath, and held it out to Heldar.

It was long-bladed, the hilt perfect for her grip, and Heldar lifted it up to catch the light attached to the building behind him.

His lip curled. "That's it?"

"Their skin is thick. A sharp, bladed weapon works best. Certainly what you're using doesn't work." She looked over at the guards.

"It's true. Laz fire doesn't do anything to them," the bulky man said.

"That's *not* true." The woman shook her head. She was still

90

crouched beside her dying friend. "It does do something. It makes them angrier."

The man she was holding suddenly went completely limp, and Fliss could see he was gone.

The woman gave a cry, a sound that said this was more than a battlefield colleague's death to her.

She gently set him down and then stood, face like stone. She began to talk, her voice low and angry, the language still strange and twisty to Fliss's ear, as if understanding it was just out of her reach.

Heldar answered her sharply, and clearly issued an order to the two guards holding their weapons on Fliss, but they refused to obey him, if Fliss was reading their body language correctly.

The woman walked over to the other guard who'd survived, helped her to her feet, and the bulky guard joined her, taking his fellow soldier's other side. They supported her weight as they drew her away, disappearing behind the building in front of them.

Fliss could see the two soldiers who were left eyeing the body at their feet.

Heldar spoke to them in short, choppy sentences, and one of the guards handed over his weapon to Heldar and lifted the body up, his actions gentle and respectful.

There seemed to be a big disconnect between the ground troops and the leader here.

After the guard disappeared with his dead team mate, there was a moment of silence.

"What to do with you," Heldar said at last, looking her over unpleasantly. "Chilm says you saved her and Dragmar, and lured the monster away from stepping on Jardern. You also told them about the anti-venom. My people owe you, and I don't like that. Not when I'm getting plenty of push-back from them already."

Jackson made a sound of disgust and began to back away. "You told me you were looking for help with the raveners. I found you someone who can help. Since I brought her here, she's done exactly that, has saved your people, and now you're saying that's a problem?"

"I'm just trying to understand," Heldar's accent was stronger than it had been, as if he was struggling to express himself in Fjerna. "You told me you had someone who is part of a special group of fighters who deal with the monsters for you. Genetically modified, was my understanding. I had heard they don't look like everyone else. They're almost monsters themselves." He looked back at Fliss. "But there's nothing about her that's any different to any of my people. She's actually shorter than Chilm, and her super special weapon is this." He brandished her knife.

"And still, I got rid of the tarinac." Fliss shrugged, her gaze fixed on Heldar.

She would really like her knife back before she escaped, but that wasn't looking likely.

"So maybe you've got training my people don't have. I just need to work out how to make you share it. In a way, it's better you don't seem to be actually important, which is what Jackson here made out." He glanced at the long-hauler, who was still moving backward. "Over-hyping the solution won't get you more credits, it will get you punished."

"More credits?" Jackson asked, outraged. "I haven't seen a single credit since the first time your people stopped me on the road and gave me some to get you supplies in Vallent, promising to give me a lot more of them later. You're the one who's overhyped what he could do."

"It will be hard for them to give you Fjern credits," Fliss said. "How can they, when they're aliens?"

Heldar went very still, and slowly turned back to her. "Now why would you say a thing like that?"

"You don't speak Fjerna as your mother tongue." She glanced at Jackson, who was gaping at her. "Who on Fjern doesn't speak Fjerna?" She pointed at the guard, still covering her with his weapon. "Your weapons are nothing like I've ever seen before, and you don't understand the raveners at all. Not at all. No one on Fjern has that luxury. In other words, you can't be from Fjern."

"Well." Heldar rocked back on his heels. "You pick things up quickly. That's unfortunate."

"Given you look exactly like us, my guess is your ancestors were the same as ours, part of the Travelers, and the planet you landed on was a gentler place than Fjern. One that allowed you to progress faster and learn to fly the heavens again. But it looks like you're here to take what you can, not negotiate in good faith. You're stealing from us."

As she finished speaking, Jackson spun around and ran, moving quickly for a man of his age.

Heldar lifted the weapon in his hand and pointed it at Jackson's back. A stream of light flowed out with a buzz and hit him.

Now was the time.

Fliss moved, darting around the only guard left and keeping him as a shield between her and Heldar, then diving for the bushes, just as light flickered over her head. She rolled and came to her feet among the thickets.

As soon as she had cover, she accelerated, moving as silently as she could.

She could hear shouting behind her and wondered if Heldar had killed Jackson, or simply injured him.

She felt a pang of regret for the old man, but her gyra did not. He had endangered her, and it seemed as if he'd done so purely out of greed. He'd lied and he'd kept this very illegal operation secret.

She hoped he was alive and able to recover, but she didn't feel obligated to go back for him.

She ran for the fence and there was no one behind her by the time she reached it.

She had some time.

She put her hand against one of the poles, and her gyra shut it all down, tripping the circuits and killing the frequency transmitters.

She sensed them dying one by one as the message from her gyra traveled along the line that encircled the mine.

She needed the raveners to run free inside the mine area. It would slow the aliens down, making it difficult for them to work while she went for help.

It offended her that fellow Travelers had chosen this course of action, when they could have arrived openly.

They would have been welcomed.

The very thought of their existence was exciting, and she knew she wouldn't be the only person on Fjern who felt that way.

Whatever mineral they needed, the people of Fjern would have happily provided it to them.

But if Fjern let this go, more would come, she was sure of it.

And her planet would be seen as an easy target.

She lifted her hand off the pole and ran back into the bush, heading down the hill toward Vallent.

Heldar called her planet a nightmare.

Well then, he could leave.

14

NOT FOR THE FIRST TIME, AS HE FLEW FAST AND LOW TOWARD THE Palqua Hills, Han wondered if he should have waited for one of his team to come with him.

The time it would have taken for Pen or any of the others to get to Vallent had seemed too long to him.

He forced himself to admit he also wanted some time alone with Fliss.

He kept second-guessing the feeling he'd had when he'd taken her hand.

His gyra leaped in his blood just at the thought of it, but he was more than just his gyra.

He was nervous to jump to any conclusions about her being his gyrbar, the mythical partner——the lover, fighter, friend who resonated perfectly, gyra to gyra.

He had left the fields and woods behind him some time ago, and the landscape was changing as the sun set and the sky darkened, the slopes getting steeper, the bush more dense.

He had a description of Jackson's ground crawler from Enid Quinn, and while the sun still shone, he'd been able to see deep tracks, most likely made by a vehicle in the damp soil, as clear as an informal path in the wilderness could be.

He slowed the air crawler as the ground levelled out a little onto a small plateau, before the mountains rose up in earnest.

He caught a glimpse of a crawler parked near a gate as he flew overhead, and then saw lights shining from a number of low buildings.

He banked the crawler, looking for a good place to land, and something hit him from the side, an explosion of light that temporarily blinded him.

The angled rotor blades on the four corners of the crawler shut off, and just as the crawler began to fall, the emergency power kicked in.

It would give him two minutes at most before he would have to land, but it meant he wouldn't crash.

He headed down the hill, getting as far from the place he was attacked as he could, and touched down in a small clearing only moments before the engines shut off for good.

For a moment he sat in silence, stunned at the turn of events.

Then he leaned back, picked up the small bag he'd packed to go chasing after Fliss, and clambered out.

If she was back there, he had no choice but to return. At least this time he would know to expect trouble.

A sound behind him had his gyra flaring, and he turned slowly.

Fliss stood, watching him from the shadows.

He took a step toward her, relief that she was safe roaring through him.

"What happened?" she asked.

"Someone shot the air crawler." He stopped when he saw her tense at his approach.

He wanted to slice Dakar's throat himself if the Gyr leader was the cause of this wariness in her.

"The aliens," she said. "They'll be coming to find you." She paused. "Well, as they're already coming for me, I suppose they probably saw where you came down."

"Aliens?" Han wondered if he'd heard her right.

A shout came from the bushes a little way up the hill.

Fliss turned to face down the hill and started moving.

When she looked over her shoulder and gestured impatiently for him to follow her, he grinned and ran to catch up.

It was a long trip back to Vallent on foot, but somehow, that didn't feel like much of a problem.

"I DON'T KNOW if Jackson is dead or alive." Fliss leaned back from the stream where she'd just scooped up some water to drink, and watched Hannu Kardenian flick water from his hands.

"He took you into that situation. He can fend for himself." Kardenian's voice was flat.

"That's what my gyra say." She shrugged. "I could see on his face how horrified he was when he realized how out of his depth he was. I felt sorry for him."

"You're sure they're aliens?" He leaned back on his heels, his light eyes glittering in the reflected moonlight off the water.

All three moons were out tonight, and two were nearly full.

"As sure as I can be without seeing the ship they came in." She didn't blame him for his caution. It was a big claim to make.

"And Jackson said they stopped him on the road, and made a deal with him to get them supplies in exchange for credits?"

She nodded. "And then, apparently, he offered up my services, without telling me about the deal. Although . . ." She thought back to what had been said just before she'd escaped. "Heldar said something right before he shot Jackson, something about the Gyr being genetically altered, almost monsters themselves. He was dismissive of me, because I looked the same as him and his people. Like he thought Jackson had tried to trick him. The way he said it, I don't think he got the information about the Gyr shift from Jackson. But obviously, whoever told him that either lied or he misunderstood. He thought Gyr were permanently in a shift state."

Kardenian was silent for so long, she rose to her feet.

Eventually, he rose up beside her, standing close.

She liked the way he smelled.

Her gyra wanted her to touch him, and she clenched her hands to stop herself reaching out.

They had run for at least an hour, and had left their pursuers far behind them.

"I don't like it." Kardenian looked back the way they'd come. "If someone on Fjern is helping them in secret, that's a problem." He looked back at her. "I have to admit, at first I thought . . ." He trailed off, and she could see him considering whether to keep talking.

She stayed silent, waiting for him to make his decision.

Eventually, he sighed and continued. "I thought it was Gyr Command shooting at me. Trying to stop me from reaching you."

Whatever she'd expected him to say, that was not it.

She realized she was gaping.

"Gyr Command?"

"They were a little too interested in you after they heard what Vanesh and the others had to say. And when they worked out Dakar's gyra had chosen you, even though you were already Gyr, that interest became a little too keen, in my opinion."

"I was brought up to be suspicious of Gyr Command." Fliss recalled the rants and the drunken diatribes about the evils of the system from her father. "But I never took the warnings seriously."

She had too little respect for her father to believe him.

Kardenian turned fully to face her, giving her all his attention.

She shivered a little under the blast of it.

"I started out my life as a Gyr trusting them, but a few things have happened to change that. The most serious is the disappearance of Lucille Defoe, a Gyr who couldn't shift." Kardenian tilted his head north, as if listening.

Fliss did the same, but she heard nothing but the sigh of the wind and the gurgle of the stream at her feet.

"You were worried they were going to do the same to me?"

He lifted his wide, heavy shoulders. "I was."

And so he'd come looking for her.

This was what they needed, her gyra told her. Friends and allies.

"Thank you."

He suddenly grinned at her and held out his hand, as if expecting her to take it. "My pleasure."

Aware she didn't know all the traditions and norms of Gyr life, she tentatively raised her own hand and clasped his.

Her gyra hummed.

They had done the same when she and Kardenian had touched outside her room in the Fithsu Gyratta, but she had been too upset to register just how strange the feeling was.

She raised her eyes, and saw deep in his own that he had known this would happen.

"What do you know of the Gyr?" he asked, voice a little thick.

"Not much," she admitted, her own voice husky.

Even when they were discussed, she didn't listen. When she realized she could never please her father, never be the type of Gyr he said she should be, she had tuned him out.

It had made life a lot more bearable.

"There is——"

He cut off as a humming sound reached them.

It didn't sound like any crawler she'd heard before, but they *were* dealing with aliens.

"What is that?" she murmured.

"Some kind of air crawler?" His voice was just as quiet. "We need to find cover."

There was plenty around.

The stream was crowded along its banks with trees and bushes, and Kardenian jumped across it and waited for her at the edge of a line of trees.

Fliss leaped after him and followed as he led them into very dense undergrowth.

No crawler would be able to see them from the air in here.

The ship whined overhead just as she ducked under the heavy

branches of a ranst tree and Kardenian reached out for her and tucked her close against his side.

For a moment, it was as if her brain shut down.

She stood, pressed tight along his length, and tried to understand what was happening.

We are home, her gyra told her.

A crackle of light up ahead and the roar of a tarinac jerked her back to reality, but she couldn't help looking up at him.

Kardenian was staring down at her. He lifted a hand and brushed his thumb along her cheekbone.

"I heard that," he said, awestruck. "We are home, too."

15

THE SHIP THAT THEY'D HIDDEN FROM SEEMED TO HOVER ABOVE, disconcertingly accurate in its positioning.

Han knew that he should move, at least draw his cutter, but he could not.

Not right away.

He closed his eyes against the sensations coursing through him, and then found he *could* move a little, lifting his free arm to curl around Fliss's shoulders and draw her even closer.

The sound of her gyra's words still rang in his head, a thousand bells of harmony. *We are home.*

He had not known what to expect of a gyrbar.

Only a few writings on the phenomenon had survived the first hundred years of their people's settlement on Fjern——the original days of trying to settle a planet where almost every living thing on it was trying to kill them.

Han suspected if the Gyr Command of today had any idea it was more than a myth, they'd make sure even those few mentions were made inaccessible, because the gyrbar posed a significant danger to Gyr Command, and to the Fjerna in general.

Fliss now came before they did.

He was no longer theirs, but hers.

Yes, his gyra said, in enthusiastic agreement. *That is how it should be.*

The tarinac he had heard screaming and bellowing a moment earlier crashed through the bushes close to where they hid, and the crackle of light from overhead came again, accompanied by a pained, panicked shriek from the massive beast.

They were using a ravener to flush him and Fliss out, he realized. Somehow, they knew they were here, and they were herding the tarinac in their direction by hurting it.

"How do they know where we are?" Fliss asked what he was thinking.

"Some tech we don't have, perhaps."

Han had not disbelieved her when she'd said she thought the people they were dealing with were aliens——descendants of Travelers who'd settled another planet in the Great Migration——but he'd thought it was possible she was mistaken.

She had grown up isolated on the escarpment, buried deep in the Provinces, seemingly without any interaction with the outside world. Now he realized she had got it exactly right.

The weapon they were using on the tarinac was nothing he'd ever seen before.

"They're herding it very close." Han tightened his grip on her.

"It's wrong to hurt it like that," Fliss said, and he could hear an edge in her voice.

The sound of the vessel overhead grew louder, as if it was just above them, and Han could see the massive legs of the tarinac moving toward them. Unlike the usual, ponderous steps, these were jerky, agitated.

Enraged.

Fliss pulled away from him, and he tightened his hold automatically, before letting her go.

"I want to try something." She looked upward, at where the strange air crawler hovered above the treetops, but before she could tell him what, the white light from above stabbed down, hitting the branches above them.

The tree shuddered, and long, delicate fingers of white crackled down the trunk.

Their time had run out.

They had no choice but to run straight toward the tarinac.

The air crawler above seemed to lower even further, and Fliss looked up again, and then, instead of swerving away from the ravener, she ran straight at it, a strange warble coming from her throat.

The tarinac instantly lowered its arrow-shaped head but before it could expel its venom, Fliss reached it, jumping up onto its nose and placing her hands on the space between its eyes.

He had drawn his cutter when they'd been forced to run, the familiar sensation of his shift coming over him, the stretch of his clothing as it accommodated his form, and when he slowed, working out the best approach, he was fully transformed.

He wasn't needed, though. It was over in a moment. Fliss shouted something, as if speaking to the tarinac, then dropped back down and raced back to him.

They must have been visible between the trees, because light flashed down again, like lightning, narrowly missing them both and filling the air with a strange, throat-catching smell.

In the strange, sudden quiet that followed, the tarinac flung its head upward, curving its neck in a typical fighting tactic.

It connected with the air crawler hovering above.

The pilot had come down too low, and the hit reverberated.

The tarinac roared as it struck the vessel——Han didn't know if it was from pain at the hard contact, or in triumph——but the crawler tumbled out of the sky, bouncing off trunks and branches, and when it landed, the tarinac clumped over to it and slammed a foot on it, over and over again, the stamping accompanied by the shriek of metal being torn and crushed.

He slowly shifted back, his gyra a tickle in his blood as he watched the defeat of their enemy.

He turned his head to Fliss. "What did you do?"

She seemed slightly embarrassed, almost defensive. "Told it to attack."

She looked over at the tarinac as it slammed its foot against the air crawler a few more times, and then began to retreat, the low, throaty rumble of a male in extreme rage audible as it shouldered its way through the bush.

"It listened to you." He kept his tone neutral.

She sent him a tentative smile. "They don't always, especially if they've been stirred up, but sometimes I'm only helping them do what they already want to do."

"Helping them?" He could hear the strain in his own voice.

"Giving them a picture of what to do. It hadn't thought of hitting the air crawler out of the sky." She jerked as a bang came from inside the downed vessel. "Do you think anyone's alive in there?"

"Let's see." He still held his cutter, and he activated the plasma and concentrated on shifting as he approached.

Fliss moved close beside him, but stopped to scoop up a long piece of wood that had been snapped off when the air crawler was slammed from the sky.

"Heldar took my knife," she said, sounding angry about it.

Before he could reply, the bang sounded again.

Someone was inside, trying to get out.

They weren't going to. Not without tools and probably a plasma torch.

Han looked at his cutter, which had a plasma arc running down its blade. It might be able to cut into the metal, but he thought it would probably struggle.

It was designed to cut into ravener skin, not metal hulls.

He turned to Fliss, saw she was backing away, gesturing to him to join her.

He kept his shift, just in case, and came to stand beside her.

He towered over her in his shifted state, and she crooked a finger for him to bend closer.

"They've probably already called for help," she whispered into his ear as he obliged. "Let's go."

He nodded and slowly shifted back. She was right that it was better if whoever was still alive inside didn't hear them.

They may think they'd been killed in the attack or by the ravener, and it would certainly give them more time to escape if the aliens had to spend some time looking for their bodies.

Fliss waited until he was completely out of his shift, and then began to jog away.

He fell into step with her as she used the path the tarinac had cleared for them as the way out of the dense forest.

"Where did you learn that trick with the tarinac," he asked.

"I had to clear the village where I lived of raveners from a very young age," she said, glancing across at him, and again he sensed her unease. "I didn't have the strength to fight them, and I certainly didn't have a cutter, so I learned to suggest to them that they should go elsewhere."

"How young?" he asked, struck at the notion, because every theory they had about her and when she got her gyra was premised on the fact that she had only recently received them.

Certainly, if he and his team were correct in their reading of Dakar's actions, Ralf Bellini had only died three months ago.

"I was six," she said.

"Ralf Bellini died when you were six?" He almost stopped, he was so surprised.

She glanced across at him, baffled. "Why do you think my father is dead?" She shook her head. "He's still very much alive."

16

She had only taken a few more steps when she realized Kardenian had stopped.

She slowed, looking behind her to see what was wrong, and then he was suddenly beside her, moving so fast she barely tracked him until his hands were gripping her shoulders.

"If Ralf Bellini is alive," he asked, voice rough, "how are you Gyr?"

She blinked up at him in surprise, and then realisation struck. "You thought I was Gyr because my father died and his gyra chose me?" She lifted her hands and placed them over his.

She didn't understand her compulsion to do it, but she knew it felt good, touching his skin.

Maybe that was a good enough reason.

She certainly had made the decision to suit herself since her mother had died and she no longer felt obligated to stay in Leverta under her father's control. Why shouldn't she do what felt good? Especially as Kardenian didn't seem to mind.

Quite the contrary, if she read the way his nostrils flared as their hands touched.

"Yes. It's the only explanation on how you *could* become Gyr." He flexed his fingers on her shoulders, and then lifted them, twining them through her own.

"I was born Gyr," she said. Nerves and a faint need to apologize rose in her. Every acrimonious conversation she'd had with her father made it difficult to feel anything else.

"Born?" He stumbled back.

She glanced behind him, aware they should be running, that more of Heldar's people would be after them before long, but she and her gyra both realized this had to be dealt with now.

"My father ran from Gyr Command and came to live in Leverta. He met my mother and they lived together. I was born a year later." She fixed her gaze on his. "I was not a normal baby, apparently." She tried to smile.

Her mother always said it with humor and love, but her father used it as a cudgel.

Ralf Bellini had ideas on how a Gyr baby should be, and she had never obliged.

"Maybe your ideas on how she should be are wrong, then," her mother had said, first gently, and then increasingly sharply through the years.

"You were born Gyr." Kardenian stepped very close, unlinking their hands and placing his palms on either side of her face, staring at her as if he were drinking her in. "Ralf Bellini is your biological father."

He sounded astonished.

The sound of another alien air crawler rose behind them, and Fliss stepped back. "I think we should discuss this later."

Kardenian seemed to pull himself out of a fugue state, and he turned back to look.

"Let's talk while we run."

She didn't wait to answer, running again through the dense bush of the foothills.

When they reached the base of the mountains, they'd have pockets of forest to hide in, but a lot of open ground, as well.

It would be difficult to find cover and whatever was after them was big. Much bigger than the small crawler that the tarinac had smashed out of the air.

Fliss looked upward and couldn't see it, although it sounded like it was almost directly above them.

Clouds had moved overhead, covering the sky and blocking the light of all three moons

The sound of two crashes came from up ahead, and she slowed, wondering whether they'd thrown something down.

Kardenian slowed as well, moving silently over the ground.

Her gyra approved.

She pointed right, indicating that they should skirt around whatever it was that had landed just beyond the bushes and he nodded in agreement.

He followed her as she picked a way through the undergrowth, careful to be as silent as he was.

A stream of white light flickered out of the darkness, a moment before her gyra could warn her.

She dove for the ground, but she was too late.

She felt the bite of pain in her shoulder, and landed badly as she went down, rolling away and fetching up against a tree trunk.

"They can see us, somehow," she managed to croak to Kardenian. "Be careful."

He hadn't made a sound as she'd taken the hit——the controlled, battle-focused Gyr that he was.

She approved of that, too.

But he did shift.

She watched him gain head and shoulders in height, his muscles bulking up even more until he was massive.

She panted through the pain, her gyra screaming in shock inside her.

Calm, she told them. *Think.*

They settled a little, and then Kardenian looked back at her, a brief moment where she saw the rage, the utter pitilessness on his face.

His cutter was already out, the plasma dancing along the blade, and without any sound at all he turned back to face their enemy and raced forward, dodging right and then left as the streams of light came at him.

The shooter on the left stopped shooting when he realized Kardenian was almost on him, and Fliss could hear him trying to back up and then run.

He only got out half a scream before she guessed his head was separated from his shoulders.

She'd heard the second shooter moving toward her while Kardenian went after the first, and she didn't bother to try and hide.

She was still lightheaded with the pain, and besides, they had a way of seeing in the darkness. They had done it when they set the tarinac on her and Kardenian, and they had done it again now.

"How do you see us in the dark?" she asked softly into the shadows.

The shooter stopped abruptly, surprised.

"You can see me?"

"Yes," she lied. She could barely see him at all, but she could hear him, knew exactly where he was.

"Heat signatures," he said.

She didn't know what that meant, but she needed to keep him talking, and get him to come closer. "And you were dropped from the air crawler?" she asked. "You flew down?"

He responded in his own language, and she guessed there were no good Fjerna terms to described how he'd jumped from the sky from such a height.

She would like to know how to do that.

She had a feeling it would be fun.

Something flashed as he spoke, and it looked like a wrist unit on his arm that suddenly lit up.

He said something in his language, the sound of his voice making it clear he'd turned away, and then turned back to her.

Kardenian was here.

Her gyra sensed him, standing just behind her attacker.

"Your language is similar in many ways to ours," she said to the alien, to keep his attention. "What did you say just then?"

He paused. "I can see from the heat signatures that my partner killed the man who was with you. I was reminding him we were supposed to keep you both alive."

He expected her to react to his statement that Kardenian was dead. To be upset.

He thought his partner was behind him, not Kardenian.

Maybe the flash of light from his wrist she'd seen moments earlier was a warning to him that someone was coming up behind him, but hubris, or over-confidence, had him convinced it was his partner.

That they had been the victors in this confrontation.

Wait, Fliss said to Kardenian in her head. Her gyra had spoken to him before——she hoped they would be able to again. That it wasn't based on physical contact but something else.

The clouds that had blocked the moonlight up until now parted at that moment, and she saw Kardenian, cutter raised, standing directly behind the alien. Waiting to separate the soldier's head from his body.

"Why?" She let her voice catch a little. "What do you want from us?"

The soldier opened his mouth to answer her, but then hesitated, as if he finally sensed something was wrong.

As he turned, Kardenian swung, and the soldier slumped sideways, head coming to rest a little distance from his body.

Kardenian stood over him, still radiating fury, as if two deaths weren't enough. He wanted to kill them all.

Fliss slowly rose up from where she'd lain against the tree, her shoulder tingling as her gyra repaired it. The pain of it still pounded at her, and it was hard to move.

Her gyra were very upset. More than they'd ever been when she'd been injured in the past. She had the sense some of them had been injured themselves by the blast.

This wasn't just their inbuilt protectiveness of her, they were harmed, as well.

Their view seemed the same as Kardenian's. They wished there were more aliens to kill.

They did not feel even slightly sorry for the death of the man in front of her.

Looking at the body, in contrast, Fliss felt a pang of regret. This was a person who could have been a huge asset to Fjern. A person who had stories to tell of other planets, of what had happened to the other Travelers who'd started the journey from their original, long-forgotten home into uncharted space, along with Fliss's own ancestors.

It was a waste, but the dead soldier, his friend, and the people with them had set this course. It was their decision to be violent.

What they seemed not to realize was that the whole of Fjern was violent, too.

Fliss's ancestors had been shocked with how unfriendly the environment on Fjern was, but they had adapted and they had survived.

They had thrived.

When she finally managed to stand straight, Kardenian moved toward her, stepping over the soldier he'd killed as if he weren't there in order to reach her.

He was still in shift, as if he couldn't let go of his form, just in case there was a chance of more people to kill.

"Where are you hurt?" His shifted voice was deeper, rougher.

"Shoulder. It's healing." She tried to keep her voice light, somehow knowing that her pain did not sit well with him.

He ran a gentle, massive hand along her shoulder and down her arm.

"They can see us from the heat we give off," she said, putting her hands on his chest. "We aren't safe hiding under foliage."

He sighed, and slowly shifted back. "Then we need to move. To get back to Vallent."

"The soldier called it a heat signature." She tilted her head. "They can't see an actual picture of us on their wrist units, I don't think, because he thought whoever was coming up behind him was his partner. He just assumed his friend had killed you, not the other way around. So it must be something less precise."

"Like a blob of light," Kardenian said. "I thought I caught a glimpse of that just before I killed the other one."

"Maybe," she agreed. "That is interesting tech." She moved away from him and crouched beside the fallen soldier. Took off his wrist unit. "Can you get the other one?"

Kardenian looked up at the sky, and Fliss remembered the air crawler that had dropped the men off.

She couldn't hear it, but it might be coming back around.

Would be, she acknowledged. At the very least to fetch the soldiers.

Kardenian was suddenly gone, and while he retrieved the other unit, she held the one she'd taken in both hands and let her gyra probe it.

They didn't understand it, and so she pulled out a thin metal strip she carried with her to fiddle with electronics, and pried the back of the unit open.

There were two circuits stacked one behind the other inside, and one of them contained a homing beacon.

Her gyra disabled it. They could work out the rest when they were safe and had time.

Finally, she could hear the faint throb of the returning air crawler.

"Karden——"

He was suddenly there.

She took the wrist unit he held out, opened it up, and disabled its homing beacon, too.

Then pocketed both units.

"Let's go, Fliss." Kardenian was looking up at the sky with a frown.

"Ready." She liked the way he said her name. But before she joined him, she picked up the weapon the soldier had used on her.

She wanted to study it, as well.

They ran together, abreast where they could, switching to single file when the way was too dense.

The nerves she'd felt about admitting her heritage had evaporated.

He had reacted strongly, but she didn't think it was in disgust or disappointment.

More in wonder and surprise.

She would find out why that was when they had time to talk.

Right now, though, the air crawler was hovering over the site where the two soldiers lay dead, and so it would have to wait.

What she needed to think about was a way to become invisible to tech that could detect the heat of their bodies.

And she needed to do it soon, before the air crawler realized what had happened to its people, and came looking for them.

17

SHE WAS GYR-BORN.

Han could hardly get his head around it.

If it was true, and he had no doubt that it was, then she was the first Gyr-born he had ever heard of.

All recruits were told that if they became Gyr, they would not be able to have children. The gyra affected their fertility.

Individual Gyr had to give up their gyra to become parents.

In fact, that was how Gyr Command was able to keep the Gyr population young, healthy and fit.

Those who wanted children enough, left. Passed on their gyra to younger recruits.

It was an extension of their function, or so that mythology went. The focus was on their job——protecting the Fjerna——and children had no place in that.

But somehow Ralf Bellini had run from Gyr Command, and had fathered Fliss.

The other thing that was speculated about, when Gyr gave themselves time to think of such impossibilities, was that if it ever *was* possible to have children, what would a Gyr-born be like?

What would gyra do to a baby?

The talk always veered into the realm of fear and fantasy.

That a Gyr-born might not be quite normal. Might be . . . damaged in some way.

That the risk of allowing gyra free rein *in utero* could potentially result in any number of mutations.

Fliss felt very right to him. To his gyra, too.

Fliss spoke of her father in a way that told Han she disliked him. They clearly were not close, and Han wondered how a Gyr who had helped create something as amazing as a Gyr-born could let their relationship deteriorate in that way.

There was still a lot to discuss, but behind them he could hear the large air crawler that had come back to pick up its soldiers.

He'd looked back a few times, and could just make it out, hovering more or less where he'd fought them.

They would be worried the homing beacons had stopped working, and they would go down soon enough and discover the headless bodies of their colleagues.

Han didn't think they would react well to that, but he did not regret what he'd done.

They had been dead the moment they had hurt Fliss.

But as soon as the air crawler came after them, the aliens would be able to see two blobs of heat running for Vallent.

They could be tracked in the dark with that tech and they would be easy to find.

"We need to find a yinalla herd."

Fliss looked over at him, frowning a little. Then gave him a massive smile. "To hide our heat signatures."

He nodded.

Not only would it keep them safe, Fliss was still favoring her shoulder, and he wanted to give her time to rest and recover.

Whatever they had hit her with was still hurting her, and he wanted to smash their weapons until they were tiny pieces of rubbish lying on the ground.

He glanced at the one Fliss had taken from the dead soldier and realized that if he'd been thinking more clearly, he would have taken the one from the first soldier he'd killed, as well.

The aliens couldn't have an unlimited supply of them, which meant every weapon that was taken was one less available to hurt the Gyr and the Fjerna.

It was also always better to know more about your enemy than they did about you.

The sound of the air crawler faded to nothing.

"Do you think they've landed?" Fliss asked.

"I do." Which meant they'd find their dead friends shortly.

They really needed to find that herd of yinalla as soon as possible.

If it were Han's people lying dead, he would come after whoever had killed them with a vengeance. These were aliens, but they were also descended from the same Travelers as the Fjerna. Han had a feeling they would behave in similar ways.

He kept his eye out for the narrow trails through the bush that yinalla often made, and though he took them down a few he thought had potential, both times they came out on the banks of a small river, not into one of the big clearings where yinalla liked to herd together to spend the night.

The sound of the air crawler started up again, far behind them in the distance, but getting closer.

They had just run out of time.

He grabbed Fliss's hand and jumped into the water with her.

"You think this will help dull our body heat, because it's so cold?" She was shorter than he was by a head, and the water came up to her neck.

"Don't know, but it's the best we've got."

She murmured her agreement, and he kept a hold on her as he let the current carry him, his eyes on the banks to see if he could spot a herd.

If the yinalla used this river often to drink, they might have made an open area where they could all sleep together near it.

"There." Fliss had let him pull her along, but now she tried to stand on the riverbed and found herself too short. Water closed over her head and she was completely submerged.

He kept his grip on her, putting his own feet down to stop them both and she fetched up flush against him.

He put his arms around her, lifting her up out of the water.

She wiped a hand across her eyes, pushing her long dark hair back, and pointed, although he'd already seen them.

A sleeping herd of yinalla lay curled up near the bank, their numbers so large the herd extended further into the trees.

A few had woken with the noise he and Fliss had made, but after a moment of silence, the animals tucked their heads back down.

Holding Fliss tight against him, Han walked carefully through the water, aware of the air crawler moving closer and closer, aware, too, that any loud noise or fast movement might cause the whole herd to run.

He found a foothold on the bank, and lifted Fliss.

She pulled herself up, then turned, hand outstretched for him.

He took it, and he felt her strength as she carefully hauled him up.

"Curl up," she whispered, mimicking the shape of a yinalla.

He copied the grouping closest to them, curving his body around her own.

She lifted her head and rested it on his shoulder just as the air crawler flew overhead.

A few of the yinalla snorted awake, the big matriarch at the center of the herd struggling to her feet to work out what was going on.

Han could just make out the curve of her single white horn as she raised her head to the sky.

The air crawler kept going, moving away toward Vallent, and the matriarch eventually settled down again.

"Should we keep going?" Fliss whispered.

"No." They needed rest, and her shoulder needed a little more time to heal. His gyra were sure of it, and he could only guess that her gyra had communicated that to his own.

Besides, he didn't want to move. He was closer to her than he had been before, and he felt a lightheaded buzz.

His clothes were wet and cold, but his gyra worked to keep him warm, and between Fliss and himself, they would generate some body heat.

"Thank you for coming to look for me," she murmured against his jacket. "They would have taken me, otherwise."

He didn't answer that. It was maybe too soon to tell her he would always come for her.

She didn't seem to understand what was happening between them, and that was all right. He had time to tell her.

As long as she was happy lying curled in his arms, he was not going anywhere.

18

THEY SNUCK AWAY BEFORE THE HERD WOKE.

It wasn't that the yinalla weren't dangerous——every animal on Fjern was dangerous——but they weren't in the same category as the raveners.

Still, over a hundred enraged yinalla was not something any Gyr wanted to take on if they didn't have to.

Their long legs and curved horns were white, their bodies a mottled brown and cream, which made them almost invisible as the sun rose through the trees and the dappled light fell all around.

Fliss had never been so close to the creatures, and never in a herd of this size.

They preferred the higher ground, the thicker forests, and they were seldom seen on the escarpment.

While she was in the Fithsu Gyratta, she'd heard it mentioned that they had a wicked bite that had some poison in it, and she was relieved when they managed to slip back into the river and let it carry them away without disturbing even one of the sleeping beasts.

It felt like her clothes had only just dried when she forced herself to follow Hannu back into the water, and she had to swallow a gasp as the cold hit her.

He held out his hand to her, and she took it, bemused at his behavior. No one had ever extended a hand to her before, other than her mother.

Certainly not Dakar and the Fithsu Gyratta.

And never her father.

But Hannu Kardenian had done it over and over again since they'd been on the run together.

And her gyra urged her to get even closer if she could.

When they were far enough away from the yinalla, he tugged her to the bank and they scrambled up it.

She wrung out her hair and then her jacket and shirt. When she glanced up, she found him watching her, his gray eyes warm with a heat that made her blush.

"How's your shoulder?" he asked after too long a pause.

"Fine." Her voice was a little rough, and she cleared her throat. It really was fine. The gyra that had been damaged must have recovered as well, because she no longer sensed shock and outrage from them.

They were all more or less back to normal.

That was good to know, if they were going to go up against the soldiers again. They could survive a hit, except . . .

"They said they didn't want us dead," she said, suddenly remembering her full conversation with the soldier before Kardenian had killed him. "So the weapon they used on me either doesn't kill at all, or it has levels of potency."

She wanted to lift it off her back and study it, but they really didn't have time right now.

As if reading her mind, Kardenian squinted up at the sky, slowly lightening with the dawn. "If we run, we should be in Vallent by tonight," he said, and then his gaze moved from the sky back to her, as if he couldn't help himself.

She nodded. She was hungry and cold, but running would sort out the latter, and there was nothing she could do about the former.

The scream of a carranda sounded off to the right.

She did not feel like dealing with the chief monster of all the monsters, and neither did Hannu, if his grimace was anything to go on.

"Let's avoid that," she said.

"Agreed." He suddenly grinned at her, the smile transforming what was a harshly handsome face into one that made her heart trip in her chest. "Let's go before it scents us." He started to jog into the trees.

She followed, slowly at first as her body warmed up, then faster as the sound of the carranda crashing through vegetation got louder.

It had definitely caught their scent, but they eventually left it behind, moving fast through thinning woods, down the gently sloping hill toward wide open fields.

There was no cover out here, but she hadn't heard the air crawler since last night.

"Do you think they're afraid to come too close to Vallent?" she asked as they both slowed before reaching the tree line.

"If they're here in secret, then yes. But I'd have thought stopping us from getting to Vallent and raising the alarm would be worth a little risk to them." Hannu stopped at the last tree, his gaze scanning the open ground in front of them.

"I did bring down their fence," Fliss remembered, as they both started a gentle jog forward. "They might be battling the raveners as well. I don't know how many air crawlers they have, but if it's just the one left, they might have more important priorities, like saving their own people."

"They had a fence around the mine?" Hannu glanced at her. "I didn't see it."

"It was a circle of thin metal poles. They pulsed a high frequency from transmitter to transmitter in a relay, to discourage the raveners."

"How did you bring it down?" Kardenian asked. He didn't break his stride, and she admired the way he moved; efficient and fast.

"I created a command to shut down the circuit," she said. "The message jumped from pole to pole, and switched each one off as it jumped."

"Where did you learn electronics?" he asked, leaping over a narrow water channel and then waiting for her on the other side.

She laughed as she jumped. "I didn't learn electronics. My gyra do all the work."

She thought he looked at her strangely, but they didn't have time for chatting.

Now they were in the open, and nothing seemed to be waiting for them, they upped their pace, racing for the forest in the far distance, their next area of cover.

She knew her face had taken on a grim demeanor, the result of the cold night, no food and her injury taking its toll.

She could keep up with Kardenian, but it was an effort.

She knew the moment he realized she was struggling, because he slowed his pace.

"You need to tell me when you need a break," he said.

"I never need a break," she told him. She had been told that since she was tiny——her father screaming at her to go faster, be stronger, jump higher.

Her father's disdain had pushed her, but she, or rather her gyra, had made him pay.

She could never recall the moment when he had been completely outmanoeuvred by her gyra without wanting to smile, but she suppressed it.

"Everyone needs a break," he said.

She slowed her run and then began to walk, hands on her hips, catching her breath.

Hannu Kardenian was the leader of a gyratta. A Gyr in his prime.

"My father used to tell me Gyr never take breaks."

"Your father lied."

She burst out laughing. "I worked that out. Especially when Dakar arrived. It was quite a revelation talking to him."

Her father had hated it. Hated the long talks she'd had with Dakar, walking out along the river, learning everything Dakar was willing to tell her about the Gyr and life outside of Leverta.

"Why would he even say something like that?" Hannu wondered.

"So he could scream at me a little more, tell me I was no proper Gyr if I was so weak as to need a rest." She leaned back her head, looked up at the sky as she said it. She had never shared anything like this with another person. "If I couldn't shift, I had to make up for it by being a *machine*."

"He was Gyr, he must have rested."

She lifted a shoulder. "I was too young to see that. And I needed more rest than he did, then."

"How old were you when he started training you?" Kardenian sounded surprised.

Of course, recruits usually became Gyr when they were eighteen or so. He would be thinking of that age range.

"Since I could walk," she said. "I think I told you before, I got sent out to hunt raveners when I was six."

Kardenian said nothing for a long time. "I remember you saying that, but I don't think I really understood. Your father took you out hunting raveners with him when you were six?" There was a strange tone to his voice.

"No. He sent me out alone to hunt raveners when I was six."

He stopped dead, turned to face her. "Why?"

"He hated me."

"How could a Gyr hate his own daughter, a Gyr-born?" He sounded absolutely astonished.

"Because when I was three, I took his gyra away from him." She couldn't suppress the smile this time——the memory still had the power to make her happy.

But Hannu wasn't smiling.

He stared at her in shock.

"He could hurt me a lot more as a Gyr than as a Fjerna," she explained. "And I was only very little. My gyra decided to even the playing field."

19

He could hurt me more as a Gyr.

Han tried to shake the rage that had risen in him at those words.

If Ralf Bellini was still alive, as Fliss said, then he had better hope Han never ran into him.

"Did Dakar know all this?" he asked when the silence between them had stretched out way too long.

She watched him with a strangely blank face, and he had the terrible suspicion she was waiting for him to disappoint her.

He never would, he vowed. *Never.*

"I told him," she said, and started walking again.

And the bastard had not contacted Gyr Command. Had not done anything.

"You trusted him?" Han asked.

She made a gesture with her hands, as if to say *sort of.* "He was the first Gyr I met since I took my father's gyra, and my gyra were happy to interact with someone just like me. So I started out wanting to give him the benefit of the doubt."

"And then?" Because Dakar had ended their relationship trying to kill her with a knife.

"I realized quickly enough he had a problem. He was in what I now know is called a Spiral." She glanced at him. "It was only when I overheard Dakar and my father arguing that I realized he had come to Leverta because he thought I could cure him." She sighed. "I don't know if my father suggested to him that non-shifting Gyr existed as a way to help shifting Gyr find their balance when they ran into problems, or if he came to that conclusion on his own."

"Is it likely your father told him something like that?" Han wondered.

"Maybe if he thought he could lure Dakar up to Leverta with that story, and then get me to take Dakar's gyra and give them to him." She shrugged. "He certainly never told me he thought the reason I couldn't shift was as a safety valve for other Gyr. He acted as if I was a failure for not being able to shift."

"Did he ask you to take Dakar's gyra?"

Fliss shook her head. "I left before he could, but he was definitely working himself up to ask me for something. Dakar circumvented him. He offered me a place in his gyratta, and as I had no desire for my father to have the strength of a Gyr again, I would never have done what he wanted. If I even could." She gave a wry smile. "I had planned to leave anyway, because my mother had passed away a month before, after a long illness, and I had only stayed because of her. The thought of living in a compound with a whole team of Gyr, rather than going out on my own, was very exciting. I went with Dakar very willingly."

"He believed the part about you being able to slow his Spiral." Han suddenly realized this explained everything about Dakar's behavior.

"Yes. He held my hand when he couldn't get out of his shift, and my gyra were able to calm his enough that he came down from a battle high." She rubbed her jaw, and Han had the sick feeling maybe she was remembering being hit there. "But he kept trying to see if I'd cured him, pushing himself into situations someone in a Spiral shouldn't have. Every time I helped him out of a shift, he would counter it with extreme behavior. He wanted to believe I could cure him. And when I finally told him that at best, I could keep him from getting worse, he tried to kill me in a rage."

"And his gyra wouldn't let him." Of everything that had happened, Dakar's gyra refusing to let him kill Fliss had been the most shocking, but now he knew her gyra had been interacting with Dakar's regularly, helping them, he could understand how it had happened.

Fliss gave a lopsided smile. "No. We were friends by then, his gyra and I. They refused to harm me. I never thought they'd kill him, though." She rubbed her arm, and he guessed her gyra, and Dakar's, were buzzing in her veins. She looked over at him. "You know what gyra are like. Very protective."

Actually, he didn't.

His gyra always tried to keep him safe, but he wouldn't say they were particularly protective.

Maybe it was because her gyra had been with her since before she was born.

"I can run again," she said. "We can slow down when we reach the next forest."

She started running straight away, and he had no choice but to follow.

She was right. It would be better to get under cover, even if that didn't mean much with the tech their enemies had access to.

There was no sign of them, though, and that was a good thing.

It was just raveners they'd have to deal with, and they were Gyr, they could handle that.

THE BUZZ in the air was clear as soon as they crested a rise about an hour out of Vallent.

It was a Fjern air crawler, though, not an alien one. The difference was in the hum.

Fliss wanted to relax at the sound, give a little cheer, as she was beginning to flag in earnest, and even Hannu looked a little worse for wear.

They had been running since dawn, with very little rest, and no food at all.

At least there had been plenty of streams to drink from.

"Wait," Hannu ordered, putting out his arm to stop her moving forward. "Hide. I'll flag them. If I don't call to you, stay put until we're gone and then get to the Vallent Gyratta any way you can."

"In case it's Gyr Command?" She didn't want to believe she was in true danger from them, but Hannu did. He was sure they'd done something to his non-shifting Gyr friend, and he didn't want to take the chance the same would happen to her.

He took her hand, gave a quick squeeze of reassurance. "If it's them, I'll lead them away. Don't go back to your place in Vallent, they'll have worked out where you're staying by now, after the isilo attack. My team will help you if I'm not at the gyratta."

She looked directly at him, something she hadn't done a lot of as they'd run side by side.

"All right." It was a leap of faith, but her gyra told her there was no risk of him proving false, and she was more than inclined to believe them.

"Thank you." He took her agreement the way it was intended, as a show of trust.

The buzz got louder and she dropped to the ground and rolled under the closest bush.

Hannu moved away, jogging forward to put a bit of space between them and making it easier for her to observe what was going on.

Then he stopped, standing still and looking upward as the sound of the air crawler enveloped them and the grasses blew wildly in the downdraft of the four rotors.

He did not move as the air crawler landed.

Whoever was piloting it did not turn the engine off, as if expecting Hannu to run over and clamber aboard for a quick take-off.

When he didn't approach, someone clambered out and ran toward him.

Pen. She recognized the woman from the Fithsu Gyratta.

She got close to Hannu and they put their heads together, their words impossible to hear over the sound of the blades.

Hannu didn't so much as look her way, and after conferring with Pen for less than a minute, he gave a nod and ran with her toward the air crawler.

The sound of the engine grew even louder and they lifted off.

Fliss lay still as it seemed to hover in place for a minute or more, and then it rose higher, higher, and then banked toward Vallent.

Guess she wasn't getting a lift home, after all.

20

HAN LOOKED ACROSS AT TERANIMO, SITTING ON THE OPPOSITE BENCH inside the air crawler, and silently cursed.

He felt sick at the idea of leaving Fliss behind, but he refused to expose her to the scientist.

Pen was right, the scientist had not looked safe when he'd worked out what had happened to Dakar's gyra.

"What are you doing here?" he asked. He had to tamp down his anger at Teranimo's interference, and he was worried he might not manage to keep things polite.

Teranimo frowned at him. "Delasio said your comms had cut off suspiciously, and no amount of hailing could raise you, so your team wanted to come looking for you. I thought I could help, in case you were injured."

Teranimo was a medical tech as well as a scientist. Han had forgotten that. Still, he eyed the scientist in silence.

Someone was helping the aliens out at the mine, someone had told them about the Gyr and their shift.

"Is there something going on here that I don't understand?"

Han thought he detected a hint of hurt feelings in the scientist's tone.

"I was shot down," he said eventually. "By aliens."

There was absolute silence at his words.

"By . . . aliens?" Pen asked.

Teranimo gaped at him. "Where?"

"A mine they've created up in the Palqua Hills." He tapped his fingers against his thigh, wondering how much to say.

Teranimo watched him, too intelligent not to start making connections. "You think *I'm* involved?"

He didn't raise his voice, but again, Han thought he heard a hint of hurt there.

"Someone is. They knew about the Gyr, about our shift. After they shot me down, they came looking for me. The two soldiers who tried to take me said they had orders to bring me back alive. They've riled up the raveners around the mine they've established and now they need help getting them under control. Someone had told them about us. Someone from Fjern knows they're there, and hasn't said anything, unless you've heard a group of our fellow descendants from another ship of Travelers is stripping us of some of our mineral wealth?"

"No." Teranimo's tone was short. "They look like us?"

Han nodded. "Different tech, though. Different type of air crawler altogether. No blades. They can track us using something called a heat signature on their wrist unit. When I took cover, they came straight for me in the pitch dark, following the heat my body was giving off."

For the first time, Teranimo looked like he was taking Han seriously. "That's . . . brilliant," he said.

"How do you know about their tech?" Delasio asked, turning from the pilot's chair.

"I had a short conversation with them before I cut their heads off," Han said.

Teranimo grimaced. "Did you have to? To have been able to question them——"

"I was over a day's run from Vallent, with no air crawler, and with their friends still hunting me. Yes, I had to." He rubbed his forehead.

"Besides, there are plenty more of them."

"What weapons did they have?" Pen asked.

"A long black tube with a handle, that spits white lightning." He decided to pretend he had been hit, so that they would understand the danger, without bringing Fliss into it. "It hurts, but because they weren't trying to kill me, I think they had it on a lower setting."

"You were hit?" Teranimo asked.

"Shoulder." Han tapped it. "Took me overnight to fully recover."

"If they can find you using your body heat, how did you hide from them?" Pen asked.

"I found some yinalla and curled up to rest on the edge of their herd. They couldn't tell my heat signature apart."

"That's . . . also brilliant," Teranimo smiled at him, then looked out of the window as Vallent came into view. "You're sure someone is helping them?"

"No question."

"Maybe they have Gyr, too, so that's how they knew about us." Pen was usually more cynical, but she obviously didn't want to believe a fellow Fjerna was actively working against his or her own.

"They called us monsters, and came at me with no idea that I was faster and stronger. Hence my cutting their heads off, even with their lightning weapons."

Pen leaned back, shaking her head. "This is bad."

"What made you go out on a patrol that far into the mountains?" Teranimo asked. There was something in his voice, like he was waiting in tense anticipation for Han's answer.

"After the isilo attack two nights ago, I thought I'd see what was going on, given they so rarely come into the city. I saw some ground crawler tracks going up into the foothills and I followed them from the air." Han shrugged. "What's going on in that mine might well be why we had an isilo attack. They're using depth charges. They've got angry raveners all around them."

"Shit." Delasio whistled from the front as he brought the air crawler down beside Gyr Command.

Teranimo hadn't taken his eyes off Han since he'd asked the question, and Han stared blandly back at him.

"I'm not your enemy." Teranimo's voice was low. "I don't know why you think I am, but I know you went out there looking for Fliss Belaire."

There was silence as Delasio switched off the engine.

"And if she's out there, she has to be in more danger from these aliens than any danger you think I, or Gyr Command, pose to her." Teranimo suddenly looked tired.

Han leaned forward. "I have two words for you," he said. "Lucille Defoe."

It was as if he'd struck Teranimo.

The scientist flinched back.

"I thought so," Han said, grim, as he stood. "Until I see Lucille Defoe alive and well, neither you nor anyone from Gyr Command will come anywhere near Fliss Belaire."

"You all believe this?" Teranimo asked, looking from Han, to Pen, to Delasio. "You believe we can't be trusted?"

They all nodded.

"I . . ." He shook his head.

"I'll come with you into Gyr Command to tell Errol what I saw up in the Hills." He looked over at Pen. "Then I'll make my own way back to the gyratta."

He waited for Teranimo to get out of the air crawler, gave a tiny shake of his head when Pen began to do the same.

He leaned back through the door.

"I had Fliss hide near where you picked me up," he said, speaking so softly only another Gyr would hear. "Go fetch her and take her to the gyratta."

Pen gave a nod.

Han closed the door, and as he joined Teranimo, the air crawler lifted off.

"Where are they going?" Teranimo turned as they banked out toward the Hills.

"Just to do a sweep for raveners."

"You're lying. They've gone back for Fliss Belaire, haven't they?"

Han didn't respond, and Teranimo shook his head.

"We need to sort this out, Han. I don't want to be at odds with you."

"And yet, here we are," Han murmured. He hadn't meant to show his hand so soon, but Teranimo had challenged him about Fliss.

"I have deciphered the code Dakar and Ralf Bellini used in the correspondence between them that Delasio found." Teranimo's wild curls blew in the fresh breeze, and he looked . . . exhausted and energized at the same time.

Like a man with a compulsion.

Han had forgotten about the coded messages, and was angry at himself for that, although Delasio had included the information in his report before they knew the truth about Fliss.

"You may know it already, but she's Gyr-born. Ralf is very clear about that in his messages to Dakar."

Han said nothing, dread pooling in his gut.

If Teranimo knew, then at least the more senior people in Gyr Command knew, too.

"You know, her father told Dakar that he thought non-shifting Gyr were the gyras' way of dealing with the Spiral. That they were a safety valve for others." He tugged at his curly hair. "I had never considered that, and it seems he was right, from what Dakar's team said about Dakar's behavior with Fliss." He shook his head. "What a breakthrough, if true."

Fliss thought that if her father had told Dakar that, it was to entice him to visit, so he could steal his gyra.

Han wondered if Ralf Bellini had actually believed it to be true, even though he was using it as a lure.

It hadn't softened his attitude to his daughter, if so.

Just like Gyr Command.

They had had centuries to understand the reason for non-shifting Gyr, Han thought bitterly. They had not even tried. They'd simply removed the non-shifters' gyra and found someone new to pass them on to.

They hadn't questioned what they were doing for a moment.

Lucille Defoe was a case in point.

Teranimo sighed in the face of his silence. "I wish you would trust me." He put a hand on Han's arm, gripping tight. "Don't raise Lucille Defoe with Errol."

Han glanced at him. Gave a nod. He wouldn't have even raised it with Teranimo if he hadn't called Han on his reasons for going up into the Hills.

Errol must have heard the air crawler, because he came out to meet them, and the conversation was suddenly over.

"What's going on?"

"It seems we have a problem," Teranimo said. "We have some interlopers on Fjern, and someone is helping them run a mine in the Hills."

Han studied Errol as Teranimo told him the news.

Did he look surprised enough?

It was hard to tell.

Truth be told, Han would guess Errol as the betrayer long before Teranimo, but while Vallent might be geographically closer to the Palqua Hills than Renardo, it didn't have the same clear route to Nasnere, and Nasnere was the seat of government. If anyone was helping the aliens, they were probably from the capital.

The sound of the air crawler faded to nothing, and before Han followed Teranimo and Errol into the building he looked up in the direction it had gone.

Hopefully they would find Fliss and get her to the gyratta.

Leaving her had been a physical wrench, and he didn't want to ever have to do that again.

21

THE SOUND OF THE AIR CRAWLER RETURNING GENERATED MIXED feelings for Fliss.

Hannu was either coming back for her, or the enemies he suspected were embedded in Gyr Command had worked out she was out here, and had come back around to scoop her up.

It was hard to decide which was more likely.

She had taken things slower since he had gone, aware that she was not at peak fitness.

If she came across a ravener out here——and that was more than likely——she needed a little in reserve to take it on.

Now, with the throb of the approaching air crawler, she had to choose whether to sprint for the stand of trees a little way ahead, or simply stand and wait for them to come.

She just didn't have the necessary energy to go any faster, she decided. And that would leave her far short of the trees.

Might as well stand and wait than be caught running like a frightened fazzy with a ravener on its bushy tail.

She stood much like Hannu had, a hand on her hip, watching the air crawler circle and then narrowing her eyes against the down-draught as it came in to land.

Pen clambered out and gestured to her, and she hefted her alien weapon a little higher on her shoulder and complied.

There was a moment of awkwardness as she approached, with Pen seeming as ill at ease as Fliss was in her greeting.

"That the weapon Han was telling us about?" Pen asked, looking for a distraction.

Fliss lifted it off her shoulder as she pulled herself into the crawler, and set it across her lap. When Pen settled opposite her, she held it out to her to look over.

"Where's Hannu?" she asked. She was disappointed not to find him inside, but she realized he would have jumped out to greet her if he'd been in the air crawler, not Pen.

"At Gyr Command, telling them about the aliens. Teranimo, the Gyr Command scientist, was with us in the crawler when we flew out the first time. Han didn't want him to know about you."

Fliss nodded. "He said."

"Didn't work," Delasio said from the front. He was flying the crawler, but he leaned back a little and looked over his shoulder at her, gave her a sweet, welcoming smile. "Teranimo had already worked out why Han went out to the Hills."

"So what now?"

"We'll go back to the gyratta. Take it from there." Pen lifted the weapon, giving it a thorough once-over. "They won't lay so much as a finger on you."

She sounded implacable.

Fliss wondered why they were so determined to protect her, but she let it go for now.

The air crawler lifted off, and just as they banked south, she saw a carranda running on the far side of the stand of trees she'd been making for.

It was moving fast, drawn by the sound of the air crawler, no doubt.

"Good timing," she said to Pen.

Pen glanced out the window, saw the carranda and frowned.

"Ever seen one move that fast?"

"A few times." But not often. Fliss looked beyond it, but couldn't see anything else.

"Do you think the aliens are driving them down from the Hills?" Delasio asked.

"They're certainly not being cautious with the noise they're making at the mine, and their weapons only antagonize the raveners."

"So it's not deliberate?" Pen asked.

"I don't think they know enough about the raveners for it to be deliberate. More like they're blundering around, arrogantly thinking they can set up camp here without any attempt to understand the environment." Fliss recalled what Heldar had said about his crew. "They've lost quite a few people because of it. Jackson, the long-hauler who took me up there under false pretences, was bringing me to them as a solution to their ravener problem."

"You?" Pen asked, surprised.

"As I don't belong to a gyratta, he thought once he got me there they could persuade me to work for them."

"But you don't shift," Delasio said.

She gave a wry smile. "That hasn't stopped me from dealing with raveners since I was very young."

They didn't seem to have a response to that, and Fliss leaned against the window, too tired to engage any more.

Pen handed her a couple of energy bars and a bottle of water, and she realized just how hungry and thirsty she was.

When the bars were gone, Pen handed Fliss some more and she ate in silence, looking out the window as Vallent came up on her side of the air crawler.

Delasio kept going, swinging around the walled city and heading west.

The gyratta was set a little way beyond the town, its walls the same dark reddish brown as Vallent's, the layout similar to the Fithsu Gyratta, although this one seemed to have a garden inside the inner courtyard, as well as a training area.

The air crawler landed outside the gate, and Fliss followed Pen out to stand in front of the arch.

"I never knew you were from the Vallent Gyratta when you came to investigate Dakar's death," she said. If she had known, she would have been more inclined to approach them about staying here.

She had assumed they were from Nasnere. Sent from the capital city.

"We planned to invite you to come back with us after the Transfer ceremony," Delasio told her as they headed inside. "But by then, you'd already left."

They stepped under the arch, and Fliss felt the fizz of the scan.

It was out of sync, the same as the Fithsu Gyratta arch had been.

She stood under it, letting the scan hum through her, and her gyra tweaked the frequency.

When it was right, she moved through.

"What was that about?" Pen had walked through and had turned, watching her strangely.

"Couldn't you feel the scan was off-kilter?" Fliss asked.

"Off-kilter?" Delasio shook his head. "Feels the same way it always does."

Fliss shrugged. "The oscillation was off."

Pen walked back toward her, stepped under the arch, and stood outside the gate for a moment, then walked back through.

"Well?" Delasio asked her.

"It . . . actually does feel better. The fizz is pleasant, rather than putting my teeth on edge." Pen slid her a look. "How did you change it?"

"My gyra synchronized with the frequency of the arch. I did it for the Fithsu Gyratta, as well. When it's off like that, it damages our gyra."

Delasio tried it again, as well, moving back under the arch, stepping outside and then inside again. "You say it was damaging our gyra every time we stepped through?"

"That's what my gyra tell me." Fliss couldn't explain it more than that.

"My gyra . . . agree." Delasio's face was the picture of surprise. "I think they were so used to it, they didn't register the harm until it was gone."

"It's probably because you've been in and out of gyratta since you became Gyr. The Fithsu Gyratta was the first one I'd ever been inside," Fliss said. "I knew it was wrong immediately."

"Maybe that's it." Pen put out a hand, trailed it through the scan, as if testing it again. Then she stepped firmly away. "Well, come on inside. We'll find you a room and see what we can do about getting you some clothes."

"I have things in my apartment in the Travelers' Trust," Fliss said.

"I'll see if I can catch Han before he leaves Gyr Command. He can fetch them for you," Delasio said, moving to the right and disappearing through a door.

They all called him Han, not Hannu or Kardenian, Fliss noted. She liked their informality.

Liked them.

Her gyra agreed. This was a place for them to thrive, it told her.

She had wanted more time on her own, to find her feet, but events had overtaken her.

And this was not a bad second prize, she admitted.

She followed Pen through the building.

The bedroom she was taken to had a transparent door out into the courtyard garden, and a small bathroom off to the side.

"This is lovely," she said. "Thank you." It was, in truth, leagues ahead of what she'd had in Fithsu.

"I'll leave you to have a shower and settle in," Pen said. "I'll leave some spare clothes for you to change into on the bed while you're in the bathroom, so you don't have to get back into what you're wearing."

"Thank you."

She waited for Pen to close the door behind her and eyed the bed with longing.

But she did need a shower, so she dragged herself into the bathroom and scrubbed under the hot spray.

When she came out, she saw Pen had left a set of comfortable stretchy pants and a top for her, and she pulled them on and fell onto the bed.

She had hardly slept in three days, and her gyra were urging her to rest.

She lay on the bed, closed her eyes, and went under.

22

Han took a loaner air crawler from Gyr Command back to the gyratta.

Delasio had contacted him to let him know they had Fliss safe inside the gyratta walls, and he could barely stand to make small talk with Errol and Teranimo while he knew she was waiting for him.

He'd slipped out as quickly as he could and went to the Travelers' Trust to get Fliss's things.

"She'll be staying at the gyratta from now on," he told Eloisa.

She'd eyed him suspiciously. "She said she was taking a break from being Gyr for a while."

"Did she?" He wondered again at what her life had been like. Narrow, most probably. Ralf Bellini would not have wanted his daughter wandering Fjern, not when everything about her screamed unique. Whether to protect her, or just himself, he would have tried to keep her tied as close to him as he could. "I'll get her to stop by and tell you herself why she's changed her mind, but for now, I'll take her things while I'm here."

Eloisa had led him up to Fliss's room and had packed her things for him. She'd handed him a bag and a blue bowl with fruit in it.

"She bought this yesterday, and seemed very pleased with it."

He'd taken it and stored it carefully in the air crawler, flying the short distance to the gyratta as fast as the little ship would go.

When he set down, he gathered Fliss's things and walked under the arch into the gyratta.

He paused a step beyond it.

"Feels different, doesn't it?" Pen stood beside the door into the building, leaning back against the wall.

"Yes. I can't quite put my finger on why."

"Fliss." Pen pushed off from the wall, walked over and lifted her hand, letting the arch play across her palm. "She said the oscillation was off. Her gyra fixed it. She said she did the same at Fithsu."

"I never noticed before."

"No. None of us had. She guessed it was because Fithsu was the first gyratta she entered, but we've been exposed to the gyratta arch since we were made Gyr. She could tell straight away something was wrong."

"You'd have thought Gyr Command would be monitoring that."

"Yes." Pen shared a glance with him. "You would."

He wondered if his quest to find Lucille Defoe had poisoned Pen against Gyr Command, to the point where she was speculating that they were deliberately harming them, but it wasn't a difficult conclusion to draw.

Gyr Command was supposed to be maintaining the arches, supposed to be keeping their gyra healthy.

It was one of the main reasons for Gyr Command's existence.

If something was wrong with the arch scan, why were they finding it out from Fliss?

"Where is she?" he asked, impatience riding him.

"Fast asleep." Pen turned back to the door and held it open for him as he carried the bowl and Fliss's bag inside. "She was running low on energy, inhaled the energy bars I gave her, had a shower and then when I went to call her as you landed, I found her absolutely out for the count."

"I don't think she's slept properly since directly after Dakar's death. And the last two days have been one incident after the other."

"Got some info for us, boss?" Delasio was waiting in the passageway.

Han looked down at the bowl and bag in his hands, but if Fliss was asleep, it was better that he left her alone.

He gave a nod and walked into the big common area.

His whole team was present, with Minette and Barnes back from Fithsu, and the others sitting on the long couches, looking up at him with interest.

He set Fliss's things down on a table and turned to Pen and Delasio. "No problem finding her out in the fields, then?"

Pen gave a snort. "She was suspicious at first, but she stood her ground, waiting for us to land. When she didn't see you, she hefted that weapon she took off the aliens in a way that told me she'd use it if she felt threatened."

Han grinned. "Fair enough. I'd told her that Gyr Command might not be friendly if they caught up to her."

"Forget Gyr Command, there was a carranda right there," Delasio said. "Running toward us faster than I've ever seen one move before."

Kardenian stilled. "Did you see any reason for its interest?"

"Maybe it caught Fliss's scent, then was disturbed by the air crawler." Pen shrugged. "As Del says, it was moving very fast."

"Good thing you got to her before it reached her." Jayna leaned back in her seat and crossed her ankles, hands behind her head.

Having seen her deal with the tarinac near the alien mine, Han wasn't so sure it would have been a big problem. "She would probably have handled it. Told it to head back home, or something."

Ranuk gave him a strange look, then after a beat, he frowned. "Are you being serious?"

"She doesn't have a cutter, and she doesn't shift. But she's been the Gyr protecting her community for a long time. She came up with other ways to deal with raveners."

"How long has she been Gyr?" Pen asked. "When she said the Fithsu Gyratta was her first, I had the sense she meant she had been Gyr for a long time before that, but how can that be? Didn't Ralf Bellini just die?"

Han wondered if he should wait for Fliss to be here for this conversation, but looking around the room, at the confusion and interest, he decided he'd better address it now. "Fliss didn't get her gyra from Ralf Bellini. Or rather she did, but not the way we thought——him dying and her coming across his body. Ralf Bellini is Fliss's biological father. She got her gyra from him because she's Gyr-born."

The genuine shock on his team's faces was probably an echo of his own when she'd told him.

"I've never heard of one," Delasio said at last. "Are you sure about it? She didn't just get her gyra very young? Too young to remember getting the gyra and so she thinks she's Gyr-born?"

"No." Han shook his head. "Her father is still very much alive."

Another shocked silence.

"How can that be?" Ellen's voice was a whisper. "I thought Gyr-born was a myth."

"Or a horror story," Barnes said.

"Which is why I'm telling you this about her now, while she's asleep." Han did not want her to hear the darkest myths about Gyr-born. "She honestly doesn't realize how unusual being Gyr-born is. Her father told her it wasn't unique at all, and that she wasn't Gyr enough. He spent her whole life comparing her to a totally mythical group of Gyr-born he knew damn well didn't exist. Her lack of shifting ability made him sure she was somehow defective as a Gyr, and she's lived with the burden of that for a long time."

There was more silence. He could see the horror, and the pity, on his team's faces.

Han cleared his throat. "There's more. And I'm telling you this because if Fliss talks about it——and she doesn't seem reluctant to do so——I don't want you to react in a way that might hurt her."

"More?" Ellen choked.

"Her father's . . . disappointment . . . in her lack of shift meant he was physically and mentally abusive. I don't understand why he would behave that way, but Ralf Bellini seems like someone who should never have been given gyra to begin with." Although there were probably many like him, Han admitted. Mistakes were definitely made when recruits were chosen. "Anyway, in order to protect her, her gyra drew his gyra out of him to make him less able to hurt her, when she was three."

"They . . . drew his gyra out of him?" Ranuk almost whispered the words, and his horror was clear. "They can do that?"

"Hers can." Han needed to get past this with them. Get them to understand, or he would be in the position of standing between his team and someone he thought very likely was his gyrbar. "She was very young, and perhaps being Gyr-born has something to do with it. Her gyra saw a logical way to protect her, and they did."

"That makes sense." Minette spoke for the first time. "It *is* logical."

"Just like Dakar's gyra making him slice his own throat is logical from her gyra's perspective when he was trying to kill her." Pen was watching Han with thoughtful eyes. "Can her gyra speak to ours? Command ours?"

He thought about the words he had heard, the definite communication he'd gotten from her, and tipped his head from side to side. "I don't know about command, but I think there is some communicative ability."

"So she could take our gyra? Slice our throats?" Barnes verbalized what they were all worrying about, Han could see.

"Only if you try to hurt her or kill her. It seems to always have been in self-defence." Han smiled at them, and for the first time, it wasn't a friendly smile. "But don't worry about her gyra. If you do either one of those things, I'll be dealing with you myself."

"Shit." Ranuk eyed him. "She really is your gyrbar?"

"I . . . think so." Knew so, but he was going to be cautious here. And he knew Fliss was still working out what was going on.

"Let's move away from threats of death and losing our gyra for a moment." Ellen grimaced. "I'm more interested in her telling the raveners to go home. What do you mean by that?"

"Her father sent her out to clear the raveners from their area when she was six."

"With no weapon?" Ellen gaped at him, shook her head, and then waved her hand for him to continue.

"With no weapon, no training. He didn't even go with her. He hated her for taking his gyra."

"She thinks he was trying to kill her?" Delasio asked, and his voice was even deeper than usual.

"She never said that, but it seems obvious to me." Han really would like to meet Ralf Bellini one day. "He wanted her dead, and then to find her body, take back his gyra and her own. She had the last laugh, though." He shook his head at the picture in his head. "She was tiny, with no weapons, so when she found the raveners, she used her gyra to ask them to leave."

Jayna's laugh exploded out of her, and she put a hand over her mouth. "I don't know whether to laugh or cry."

Neither did Han.

"And it worked?" Barnes sounded very skeptical.

"We were being hunted by the aliens in an air crawler without blades to keep it up. I don't know how they make it fly, but it could hover very low, and it was herding a tarinac right at us. They could see us with tech that shows our body heat, and they were shooting the tarinac with the white lightning weapon they have, and it was headed our way. Fliss ran to the tarinac, put her hands on its head, and encouraged it to smash the air crawler out of the sky."

"It was flying that low?" Minette asked.

"It was. And the tarinac did it. Smashed the air crawler into the ground and then jumped on it."

Pen gave a low chuckle at that. "Didn't like being hit with lightning, I gather."

"No." Han grinned. "Fliss said she just gave it a suggestion on how to deal with what was bothering it. It already wanted to attack the air crawler, she just helped show it how."

"That's how she dealt with the isilo the other night, too." Ellen was nodding her head. "I've had a few people from Vallent get in touch with me, and most are saying she rode the isilo, ordered it to go. It didn't make sense to me, but now, hearing this, I can see what they meant."

"Well, shit." Ranuk was shaking his head. "She's a bit more than we were expecting, isn't she?"

Barnes gave a laugh at that, and Han saw smiles all around. He relaxed a little.

"Two things. Yes, she is even more unique than we thought." He held up one finger. "But two," he lifted the other, "Teranimo knows something is going on. He was acting strangely, and when I threw Lucille Defoe's name at him, he got even stranger, and asked me to keep quiet about my problem with her disappearance until he got back to me."

"What do you think's going on there?" Pen asked.

"I don't know. But this alien issue is probably going to take priority. Errol wants us to go into the Hills and round them up."

"Pen and Delasio told us a bit about it, but explain a bit more. Aliens?" Jayna looked almost amused.

"Fellow Traveler descendants, is my guess," Han said. "They look like us, but they have different tech, speak a different language, and they know nothing whatsoever about Gyr and raveners."

"You're serious." Minette stood, suddenly agitated. "Real aliens?"

"As real as it gets."

Pen walked out the room, and came back a moment later holding the weapon Fliss had taken off her attacker.

"This is the weapon they were using, Fliss said."

Han nodded. "Let's go outside, and you can shoot it at something in the training courtyard."

They all trooped out, and Pen aimed at the target they used for knife work practice.

She hefted it in her arms, touched something, and white lightning shot out, hit the target, and encased it in white light.

When it shut off, there was a scent of smoldering wood in the air.

"Shit," Barnes breathed, impressed.

"It hurts," Fliss said from behind them, and they all spun to look at her.

She was wearing stretchy leggings and a loose shirt, and he could see her eyes were still sleepy, her hair mussed.

"You were hit?" Ellen asked.

"My shoulder." Fliss tapped it.

"I thought you were the one who was hit?" Pen said to him.

He shook his head. "I couldn't say it was Fliss who'd taken the hit, but I still wanted Teranimo to understand the aliens' weapons weren't harmless, so I told him it was me, so I could describe the harm done."

He couldn't help walking over to her, his hand coming to rest on the shoulder that had been hit. "All right?" His finger brushed the side of her neck, and she lifted her hand suddenly, gripping his forearm.

For a moment, he thought she was going to shove his arm away, but instead she slid her hand down and let it rest just at his wrist, the tips of her fingers touching the skin of his inner arm.

He stood still, taking comfort in her touch, and in her need to touch, which seemed to be as strong as his own.

When he finally focused his attention back on the training area, he found all his team watching him, eyes bright with interest.

Fliss cleared her throat. "The food and the sleep did me good." She glanced back toward the open doors to the common room. "Thank you for bringing my bowl."

He didn't know why he felt a gut punch at that. All he could do was nod in reply.

"Did either of you speak to the aliens?" Ranuk asked.

"I was taken prisoner by them," Fliss said, and Han felt a lurch of fear again at the thought of her in their hands, weapons pointed at her. "They've learned Fjerna. They speak it with a thick accent, and they don't always get the grammatical structure right, but they're understandable. Their own language sounds to my ear like a twisted, upside-down version of Fjerna. I think we probably started with the same root language, but over thousands of years they have morphed into something distinctly different from each other."

"But they look like us, Han says?" Jayna gripped her upper arms with her hands.

"Just like us." Fliss nodded. "But they don't have Gyr in their society, I don't think. They didn't understand what Jackson or the other ally they have among the Fjerna told them, and they blunder around, antagonizing the raveners and then are surprised when they attack."

"They have another ally?" Delasio aimed his question at Han, and Han nodded.

"I told Errol and Teranimo about it. I made it clear there was someone who'd helped them. How else could they set up a whole mine in the Hills? Jackson only met them on the road between Vallent and Renardo. They were looking for ways to get supplies. I don't know if whoever helped them initially got cold feet, or suddenly had an attack of conscience, but if they were looking for outside help from a total stranger, they must have been desperate."

"They might have killed whoever helped them," Fliss said. "Or when the traitor came to check out the mine, a ravener got them."

They were silent for a moment while they thought that through.

"Might be an idea to find out if someone in power from Nasnere has gone missing recently," Pen said.

Han nodded. "I'll mention it to Errol. He's contacting Nasnere, and between him and Teranimo, they're going to make a big fuss, reaching out to everyone in the capital they know. Errol wants us to go out there early tomorrow and shut it down, but he wants to wait until he hears back from Nasnere before he officially sends us."

Barnes cracked his knuckles. "I am very much looking forward to that."

Fliss let go of his arm and shoved a hand in her pocket. "We should be prepared for them, if we do go. I have their wrist units." She held them up on her palm.

"We don't have a tech person on the team," Minette said, although she walked closer to peer down at the items Fliss was holding out.

"I'm more interested in the weapon," Ellen admitted.

"What do they mean you don't have a tech person?" Fliss turned to look at Han. "We're all naturally tech people."

He had wondered at her insistence on taking the circuit boards, and her explanation of how she'd shut down the aliens' fence.

"Your gyra interact with electronics?" he asked.

She stared at him for a beat, and he could see fear and confusion in her eyes.

"Am I different in this way, too?"

He reached out and took her free hand. "Some Gyr are good at electronics. We don't know why some have the knack and others don't. You're even more valuable to the team because of it."

She gave a tentative nod.

The others were taking turns to look over the weapon and learn how to use it.

"See, it doesn't matter either way to us," he told her, nodding toward the rest of the team. "We are focused on raveners, so our gyra are, too. You have lived with your gyra a lot longer than we have lived with ours. It makes sense there'll be some differences."

"My gyra are prickling under my skin where we are touching." She looked up at him. "It feels like . . . a bubbling brook or a chorus of birds at dawn. Energized and happy."

Her words sparked the excitement of his own gyra, and he had to force himself not to pull her closer.

"What is happening between us?" she asked, keeping her voice very low. Her gaze was still on his hand where it held hers.

"I'm not completely sure," he admitted. "But I think it has to do with our gyra. The first Gyr called it the gyrbar."

She lifted her gaze to his. "Gyrbar?"

"The perfect partner. Where everything is in sync."

She narrowed her eyes, her hand still warm and relaxed in his. "Where can I find out about it?"

"There're a few mentions in the archives, but not many." It made him wonder if Gyr Command had tried to limit Gyr finding their gyrbar in the early days, or if it was genuinely a rare occurrence. "I don't know if they would help. If the stories are true, then you and I would be the first gyrbar since those texts were written, thousands of years ago."

Her expression was solemn. "You think it's because I'm Gyr-born?"

He lifted his shoulders. "Maybe."

"It feels good," she told him, her gaze sweeping away, as if she were too shy to look him in the eye anymore.

"It does." His voice caught on the words.

She gave his hand a squeeze and stepped back, letting go. "I'll go work on the circuits."

She turned and headed back indoors.

Han's gyra buzzed inside him, wanting to follow. But it was time to give her space.

He'd told her everything he knew, and she needed to think about it.

She likes us, his gyra told him. *We make her happy.*

That was more than enough for now.

23

"Hello, hello."

The two women who she hadn't been introduced to yet walked into the common room and pulled up chairs, one to Fliss's right, the other opposite her.

"Hello." Fliss suddenly felt shy. She had not had this welcome at Fithsu, and she didn't want to go down the same, isolating route that had been her path there.

"I'm Ellen, this is Jayna." The curvy, dark-haired woman who sat opposite indicated the leaner woman on her right, whose ginger hair seemed to gleam in the light coming through the open doors.

"Fliss," Fliss said. "Pleased to meet you."

"So you were in Vallent the whole time, and got rid of an isilo, too?" Ellen slid a lock of hair behind her ear. "More than one of my Vallent friends has been in touch to recount the tale."

"Did the two people who were bitten by the isilo make it?" Fliss asked.

Ellen lifted her shoulders. "Don't know. I can ask around."

"So how do you do it? Give the raveners like that isilo orders?" Jayna asked, leaning forward on her elbows.

The question wasn't antagonistic——she sounded genuinely interested——and Fliss decided to give these people the benefit of the doubt until she was proven wrong.

"I told it to find its burrow."

There was a beat of surprised silence from both women.

"You're . . . serious." Ellen tilted her head. "How does that work?"

"I use my gyra to transmit into their heads. I've got a good grip on what works with the big raveners, but I'd never had to deal with an isilo until the other night. It took a couple of tries to get on its wavelength. Even then, I'm not sure if my riding its back was what sent it on its way, or the orders I was giving it."

"So you don't ever kill them?" Jayna frowned.

"How could I kill them without a cutter?" Fliss lifted a shoulder. "I was very young when I started, as well, so I had to improvise. And besides, the raveners are just being themselves. If I can keep people safe without killing them, it's a fairer outcome."

There was another silence.

Fliss wondered if she should have spoken up about her lack of interest in killing raveners so early on. Waiting until they liked her better might have been wise.

"What I want to know is how you got Dakar's gyra." The words came from behind her, and Fliss turned to see the man she'd heard someone call Ranuk standing in the doorway.

Perspiration had caused strands of his tussled, curly hair to stick to his high forehead. He had a bottle of water in his hand, and he gulped some down before sliding into a seat near Ellen. His light brown eyes shone with curiosity as he focused on Fliss.

Like Hannu, Delasio, and the giant everyone called Barnes, Ranuk was big.

Did shifting change their body shape, Fliss wondered, or did Gyr Command choose them that way from the beginning?

She eyed the women, and they were definitely taller than average, but like herself, not overly so.

She couldn't shift though, and she assumed they could.

Silence settled, and she realized she hadn't said anything in response to Ranuk's statement.

"I didn't intend to take Dakar's gyra." Fliss lifted her hand and looked at her fingertips. "When I touched him, to see if he was still alive, they chose to transfer across to me."

"Did they form a ball, like they do with the gyra-na?" Ellen asked.

Fliss frowned. "I've never seen how they look when they're transferred using the gyra-na. But no, they formed four small teardrops and slid into my fingertips."

"Why?" Ranuk asked.

"They liked me." It was as simple as that, for her. "They protected me by killing their host, and I was happy to accept them."

"That's like nothing I have ever heard when it comes to gyra." Ranuk leaned back in his chair.

"What have you heard?" She felt a frisson of nerves along her arms and down her spine.

"The gyra are neutral," Jayna said. "They don't like or dislike. They are simply tiny robots, whose job is to keep us safe and give us as much advantage against the raveners as they can."

"Maybe that is so with your gyra." Fliss spoke hesitantly, because she was aware now that she was very much not like others of her kind. "It might be because my gyra have been with me since before I was born that our relationship is different."

Ellen gave a slow nod. "That makes sense, but since then, you've had your father's gyra and Dakar's gyra added in."

That was true. She blinked. "In the beginning, they feel a little different, but not for long." She thought about it. "They are very quick to learn, and both times, they chose to come to me after a conversation with my own gyra. It was never me forcing them in."

"Will your gyra talk to mine?" Ranuk asked, and held out his hand.

She asked them, heard the interest and curiosity in them.

"Yes."

She reached over the table, and touched his fingers with hers. She could feel the hum of her gyra, like bubbles tickling against her skin, as they exchanged information with Ranuk's.

With a grunt, he pulled back, his eyes wide as he stared at her.

"I didn't think I'd feel anything," he said eventually.

"What did you feel?" Jayna had half pulled back her chair, as if she was going to stand, but instead perched herself at the edge of her seat.

"I felt welcome, and interest, and curiosity, and . . ." He glanced beyond her, tilting his head up, and she knew without a doubt that Hannu had come to stand behind her. "Peace."

"Is that why Dakar dragged you off with him when he was in the grip of his Spiral, to get some peace?" The big giant with the red hair, Barnes, asked, moving into her line of sight from the right.

"Yes," she said. "My gyra helped his, so he could shift back. He thought that the reason some Gyr can't shift was so they could be a safety valve for those who can." She decided adding her father's possible role in leading Dakar to that belief wasn't useful to this discussion. Dakar had believed it, and that was why he'd done what he had. "He saw me as the antidote to the Spiral, a way to help Gyr reset their gyra when they find it hard to return to normal after shifting."

"Why did he try to kill you, then?" Minette asked. She had come in behind Barnes, and she moved around the table and sat between Ellen and Jayna.

"He resented needing me. He used the help I could give him to shift back, but then he'd be angry, with me, with himself, with the world in general, that there was a problem with his gyra in the first place. He'd go out, push the limits, when he should have been resting, and then, when he was desperate, he'd have to come to me again. That last time . . ." She bowed her head and she felt Hannu's hands slide onto her shoulders.

She drew in a deep breath. "That last time, he seemed to lose all sanity. He was raging that if he couldn't shift back, it was because that's how it should be. That his gyra were only doing what was right."

"The final stage of a Spiral." Delasio sounded incredibly sad.

Fliss looked up at him. "I had never seen anyone in a Spiral before. I tried to soothe him, but that seemed to enrage him even more. He took out a knife, grabbed hold of me, and brought me close. I could see in his eyes he was gone, an absolute shell of who he'd been."

She didn't say what happened next.

Everyone here knew that part of the story.

"So what happens now?" Minette tapped the table with her fingertips. "I don't want to live with the threat of a hostile Gyr Command hanging over us. And I think other Gyr need to know about Fliss. They need to know a Gyr-born exists."

Fliss hadn't thought about anything further than finding her place right here in this gyratta.

The thought of finding a place among all the Gyr on Fjern was daunting.

"One step at a time," Hannu said. "We'll probably have to deal with the aliens tomorrow. That might be a good thing, because if we're successful, we'll have to take them to Nasnere. There's two gyratta there. We'll be in a good position to speak to the others. Slowly spread the word."

"And Gyr Command?" Ranuk asked.

"They've never openly come out and definitively held a stance on Gyr-born. They've made out it's a theoretical issue, as Gyr can't have children." Han's hands squeezed her shoulders, and then he stepped back. "Let's hear what they have to say when the reality of a Gyr-born is right in front of them."

Fliss wanted to protest that she didn't want to be dangled in front of Gyr Command like some kind of challenge, but when she looked around the room, all she could see was determination and . . . maybe hope.

She kept her mouth shut.

This was her place now. She could feel it herself, and her gyra were ecstatic to be among Gyr.

"Fliss?" Han's voice held a question. "You don't like the idea?"

How had he picked that up?

She thought about her resolve to never go along to get along again.

"It's just I never thought I'd be so controversial, just for being myself."

"Not controversial," he said. "What you are is the future."

24

MAKING DINNER WAS INTERESTING.

Other than Hannu, who had left to take a comm from Gyr Command just as they were starting to make it, everyone pitched in.

Fliss was thrilled when her offer to make a dish from the Provinces was accepted with alacrity.

Ellen was from the far east, not the central Provinces as Fliss was, and Barnes came from the coastal west. Everyone else except Delasio was from one of the northern towns, and Hannu and Minette were from Nasnere itself.

Although there was a wide variety of foods throughout the Provinces, there was one thing that everyone on the escarpment had in abundance.

Risnick.

There was an art to making it well, otherwise it was hard and chewy, and Fliss's mother had made sure her daughter knew the trick of it.

"We always buy some when it comes available at the market, and eventually someone tries to make it, but not with much success," Ellen said, watching Fliss as she carefully sliced it at the correct angle.

"This is different to the Fithsu Gyratta." Fliss put the thin slices in salted water to rest. "They rostered us on, two per meal, and we had to follow a menu that had already been decided."

"They did that at my old gyratta in Renardo," Delasio said, peering into the risnick bowl. He was from the far south, from Catharta, and he hadn't had risnick before that was cooked properly.

"Sometimes, if Vanesh had time at Fithsu, he'd make a dessert to go with the meal." She had tried to compliment him on it, but she had the feeling he thought she was being insincere.

"Han does that sometimes. And Minette. It must be a Nasnere thing. I think Vanesh is from Nasnere, too, isn't he?" Jayna asked.

"Vanesh? Yes." Minette leaned against the table. "He was in my training group. Not a bad guy, but Pen tells me he didn't treat you very well."

Fliss shrugged. "He thought I was Fjerna. That Dakar had somehow snuck me into the gyratta."

Barnes made a sound. "How did he think Dakar had done that? And why didn't he report him, if that's what he believed?"

"He tried to put as little emphasis on that point as possible when we were questioning him," Pen said from where she was stirring something on the stove. "He knew full well the implications."

"If they thought you were Fjerna, how did they think you could go out on duty?" Ranuk asked. He was slicing vegetables and dropping them into a bowl of marinade.

"They didn't take me on call-outs, except one time." Fliss still couldn't believe how that had ended. "Dakar deliberately antagonized some largarti near their burrows, and one came out to attack. Before I could even move, Dakar intercepted it, acting like he was saving me. Then he never took me out with them again."

"He wanted to show them that you couldn't shift," Pen said. "That's what they kept saying to us when we questioned them. That you couldn't be Gyr, because you couldn't shift."

"My father told me that Gyr who couldn't shift were cast aside and their gyra taken. It was one of the ways he kept me in Leverta ——the fear that someone would force my gyra from me. But then Dakar arrived, and convinced me my father was lying to keep me trapped. It was easy to believe that, but it was Dakar who was lying and for once, my father was telling me the truth, wasn't he?"

There was a small silence, even Ranuk's chopping stopped.

"They might try. But has Han told you about Lucille Defoe?" Pen asked.

Fliss gave a nod.

"They couldn't take her gyra. The gyra-na broke instead."

"But she's also never been seen again," Fliss said. That was not a reassuring alternative.

"No." Jayna slid something into an oven and closed the door, her face flushed with the heat. "But we won't let it go. It cannot be allowed to stand."

Fliss hoped for her sake, and for Lucille Defoe's, that she was right.

SHE ATE around a table with the others.

Hannu——or she should think of him as Han, as that's what everyone called him——joined them just as they were putting the food on the table.

"What's the word?" Delasio asked.

"Nothing yet, but most likely we go first thing tomorrow. Nasnere is in a panic about it, especially the information that someone knows the aliens are here and hasn't said anything. They don't know who to trust. Teranimo thinks they'll inform the Renardo Gyratta about it, as well, and the Renardo team will probably send a few Gyr to meet us before we attack."

"Who'll stay here?" Pen asked.

Fliss hadn't thought about that, but of course at least two would have to stay, in case of a ravener attack.

"We'll choose the usual way."

Fliss wondered what that way was, but didn't want to ask.

She accepted the praise for her risnick, which Ellen claimed was the best she'd ever tasted, and even Delasio, who had clearly had some bad risnick experiences in the past, claimed he finally saw the point of the dish.

After dinner, she chased down a box full of old or broken electronics and withdrew to her room, realizing she hadn't had such a lot of people interested in her before, ever.

She needed a little breather.

Especially from Han, whose gaze rested on her often.

She was exquisitely sensitive to every look, every moment of focus.

She shivered suddenly, set down the screen she'd been working on, and slowly lifted her eyes.

Han was standing in front of the glass doors on the garden side of her room, hand raised to knock.

He paused, and she gestured him in.

"I was going to come looking for you," she said as he stepped inside.

"Oh?"

She lifted the screen she'd been working on. "My gyra have worked out how to connect the heat signature circuits to some of the older screens."

He came over and looked over her shoulder, and she lifted the screen, touched a button, and three blobs of orange light bloomed in front of them.

One on its own, two standing close together.

"I just passed Barnes coming here," Han said, pointing to the lone figure, "and I heard Pen and Delasio talking."

"One of the circuits didn't work, and I think it's because I got it wet." She reached over the desk and lifted an old remote starter for a ground crawler. "But the second circuit stacked inside the wrist unit seems to be a comm link, and my gyra tell me it runs on simple code. We think we can interfere with their technology by sending a command for it to reset itself. The command will transmit when someone presses the button."

"Just the heat signature screen is a significant advantage for us." Han lifted it thoughtfully, turning in a slow arc.

Fliss could see the brief bloom of orange light as he moved it, catching those in the team who were close by.

"Dakar didn't use your ability with electronics?" he asked as he set it down.

She shook her head. "I didn't tell him. I didn't realize it was unusual."

"Your father didn't tell you?"

She thought about it. "I don't recall ever making a big thing of it. He knew I could fix things, but I don't know if he understood how easy it was for me. If something broke, I repaired it without necessarily mentioning it." She wondered if her father was stuck with broken equipment now, suddenly realizing that they didn't magically keep going.

Han was quiet for a beat, and then he pulled up a chair and sat down. "I came to speak to you about Gyr Command. I could see over dinner that things were moving faster than you're comfortable with. I want you to know neither I nor the team will ask you to do anything you don't want to do."

"I think it's the idea of being a cause." She wanted personal connections, not to be a rallying cry. "But if something has happened to Lucille Defoe, and if there is a chance they want to do the same to me, then of course I will do what I can to stop them."

He nodded, and impulsively she reached out to him.

He had initiated touching her a few times, but she had been more wary, forcing herself not to do what she wanted to do.

She took his hand, and he went very still, his eyes meeting hers, shocking in their intensity.

She brought his hand closer to her chest, cradled it in both of her own. "When we touch, my gyra rejoice," she told him.

"Mine, too." His voice was deeper, rough, and he leaned closer, sliding his free hand along her arm to cup the back of her neck.

Then he touched his lips to hers.

She had thought about kissing him, but the reality of it was a jolt. She gasped, her lips parting against his, and he leaned closer, deepening the embrace.

Overwhelmed by sensation, she pulled back, feeling dazed, and they stared at each other for a long beat.

He seemed about to say something, but suddenly his wrist unit chimed, an annoying chirp that she had heard before at the Fithsu Gyratta.

"Raveners," she said.

He swore quietly under his breath. "I'm on duty."

"I'll go with you." She wanted to work with him. Felt a need to do it.

His eyes widened in surprised. "Are you sure?"

"Yes."

"All right." He turned back to the door. "Do you have a fighting uniform?"

She nodded toward the bag from the Travelers' Trust he had brought for her.

"Meet me outside by the air crawlers."

He stepped out and she flicked the blinds shut for privacy, changing swiftly.

She had only worn the uniform once, but it was a good fit, the fabric capable of stretching into a shift that wasn't going to happen with her. It gave her a wide range of movement, though, and the matte black fabric made her almost impossible to see in the darkness.

She braided her hair as she jogged through the building to the front, throwing her head back in enjoyment as she ran under the arch, like a ray of sunshine across her cheek on an icy day.

Han was waiting for her beside an air crawler, a large, powerful figure in the shadows.

She didn't understand what was happening, why she felt a frisson of nerves and excitement every time she looked at him.

It doesn't need understanding, her gyra said. *It just is.*

Maybe that was true.

But she had never been one to blindly accept. She would be a beaten down version of herself, she would be her father's pet, if that had been her personality.

Her gyra were forced to agree.

Han swung into the crawler as she reached it, and leaned over to open her door.

She pulled herself inside, and as soon as she was strapped in, he lifted off.

"What's the trouble?" she asked.

"A zuby, very close to the city walls."

Han dipped the air crawler down as they approached the city, banking left.

The zuby was easily audible in the distance, its massive bellow a deep thrum of sound.

Han aimed the air crawler toward the noise, and when they were close enough to see the beast, which was trying to climb the wall, and getting close to succeeding, he buzzed overhead to distract it, and then moved away from the city, hoping to catch its interest and draw it off.

That worked a little.

It dropped off the wall and turned in their direction but then it came to a stop.

Han landed, and he started to shift before he was even out of the air crawler.

Fliss saw the flash of the plasma arc as he lifted his cutter.

"I forgot you don't have one." Han had moved to the front of the crawler, his shifted face a strange mix of himself, and some feral creature, with a sharper nose, longer ears, sharper teeth. "Take mine."

He tried to hand it to her, but she shook her head.

"I've never had one. Besides, I have other ways." She glanced at him. "Do you want to do this my way, or your way?"

"Let's try your way." As he spoke, the zuby, which was still staring at them, went up on its toes and did its little back and forth dance.

Fliss used the moment to run at it, zigzagging right, then left, keeping it confused.

She ran past it, jumped, and used its hind leg to boost herself onto its hind quarters.

She glanced over at the air crawler, saw Han, massive in his shifted form, standing still, watching her.

She ran up the zuby's back, and it made a sudden sound of pain and panic.

There was a gash along its spine, which she noticed almost at the same moment as it bellowed. She was running on the open wound, unintentionally hurting it, and she jumped again, trying to reach the top of its head.

She didn't make it.

She had had to jump too soon, and where she landed was too acute an angle to gain a hold. She slipped back down, landing hard on the wound.

It screamed at her, rearing back, trying to buck her off, then tried to fling itself to the side, out of its mind with pain, and she flipped as she dived off it, landing on the rough ground, crouching low and keeping still.

It shook itself, a whole body shudder, and turned back to the wall, pressing itself up against it.

"What happened?" Han was suddenly beside her.

"It's badly injured. Looks as if something scraped along its spine. I hurt it when I was running along its back."

Han swore softly. "This is the aliens' mess coming back to bite us."

"Yes. I don't know what they did to it, but I can only think it was them." She looked over at the zuby. It was shaking, moving restlessly. She suddenly had an idea. "Can you throw me?"

"Throw you?" He stared down at her from his shifted height.

"Up onto its head." She did not want this animal hurt any more than it had already been hurt.

He sighed. "I don't want to, but my gyra say yes."

She touched his arm. "Thank you. It's going to start climbing that wall again soon."

She jogged forward, moving at an angle to make it harder for the zuby to track her, and Han easily caught up. She slowed, and then walked carefully along its side, so it would have to turn its head to see them.

"Toss me up," she said, turning to look at Han over her shoulder.

He grimaced, looking very unhappy about it, but he went down on one knee and she climbed up, balancing.

His massive hands curled around her shins, and then he stood and launched her upward in a single movement.

She flew, getting high enough to reach the zuby's head, where she grabbed the looser, softer skin above its eye to swing herself up.

She crouched on its head as it shivered again and rubbed up against the wall.

She could hear the stone and reinforced steel in the high wall groan beneath its onslaught.

"Hush," she told it. "Calm."

It stilled, but it continued to lean against the wall as if huddling for comfort.

"Not safe here," she told it. She could have ordered it to go to its cave, but given its injuries, she was sure it would have gone there if it could have. They naturally went into their rock caves if they were hurt.

She thought of the rocky terrain on the road between Vallent and Fithsu, where she and Enid Quinn had encountered a zuby, and projected that into the zuby's mind. Where there was room for one zuby, there would be room for another.

It turned in that direction, quivering.

"Go."

It took off, slamming back against the wall first, and using it as a pushing-off point in its race across the open fields.

Fliss flung herself off it. She always enjoyed the height, the fun of the somersault, the skill at landing lightly.

"Where did you send it?" Han asked.

He was standing right beside her. He'd moved so quietly, she hadn't even heard him.

This is a clever Gyr, her gyra told her. *Worthy. Very worthy.*

"I think its cave has been damaged or destroyed. I sent it to the rocky gorges between Vallent and Fithsu. There was a zuby on the road the night I left the gyratta to come to Vallent, so I think there has to be burrows out that way. It was the best I could think of."

166

Han slowly shifted back, and just as he reached normal form, his wrist unit burbled.

"It's dealt with," he said into it.

"Do I need to send clean-up?" a woman asked.

"No. We chased it off, we didn't kill it." Han cut the comm.

"Who was that?" Fliss asked.

"One of the monitors at Gyr Command." He shrugged. "Hetta, I think." He was looking after the zuby.

She wanted to get closer to him, but she knew if she did that, it would bind her tighter.

Close doesn't mean controlled, her gyra said. *It just means close.*

Maybe. Maybe the head games and her long history with her father were intruding yet again, skewing her view so that she couldn't see the truth.

Or maybe her gyra were just saying what she wanted to hear.

"You're nervous."

She realized Han had gone quiet beside her, and she glanced across, saw he was watching her.

"I'm fighting myself," she told him. "I imagined living in a city, pleasing no one but myself, living normally, without any attention or fuss."

How different things had turned out.

"How is that fighting yourself?" he asked.

She sighed. "Because for all I want to be on my own, when I touch you, I want to keep doing it. When you're standing beside me, like now, I think it's a waste of time that we aren't kissing."

"I can remedy that." His voice was low as he pulled her close. She didn't resist him at all. Instead she rested against him, running her hands up his back and tipping back her head, giving him access to her throat, to the sensitive skin below her ear.

He kissed his way up to her eyes and then to her lips, and she sighed as he kissed her mouth, opening for him so their tongues touched.

A rustle in the low bushes made them both go still.

"Waronga?" she whispered.

167

"I think so."

They backed away slowly, and she heard the faint buzz as the plasma arc on Han's cutter activated.

With a low grunt, something launched at them, and Han moved so fast she barely caught the slash of his blade.

The faint stink of waronga blood scented the air.

Before she could say anything, Han's wrist unit gave a ping.

"It's Errol." He glanced down. "We're cleared to go tomorrow morning."

She started walking back to the air crawler, and he came up beside her, draped an arm over her shoulder, pulled her close, and kissed the side of her temple.

"Wouldn't want to waste any time," he told her.

She was still smiling when he lifted off to take them back home.

25

Han let Delasio pilot the big air crawler they used for transporting the team while he coordinated with the Renardo Gyratta.

Jayna and Barnes had lost the draw, so they had to remain at the compound, holding the line.

He organized with Taque, the leader of the Renardo team, to meet them north west of the mine, and go in on foot.

Han had had to persuade Taque that whatever weapon had taken down his air crawler could just as easily take down Taque's own.

He glanced at Fliss. She was sitting opposite him, calm and collected in her battle gear.

He knew the moment she felt his gaze on her. She went still and then lifted her head.

"Show them what you were working on last night," he said.

She looked a little nervous about that but gave a nod, shifting the alien weapon she had brought with her off her lap.

He had offered her a cutter again, but she had declined, even though the alien weapon did not seem to do much more than annoy the raveners.

"Their weapons have to work against the aliens themselves," Fliss had explained to him. "They wouldn't consider it a weapon unless it did."

When this was all over, he would give her some training on a cutter. Even if she had other ways of dealing with the raveners, he'd feel happier if he knew she had a way to defend herself.

She bent down and pulled the screen from the bag at her feet and switched it on. Everyone crowded around and looked at the blob of orange that was him, sitting opposite them.

"It's not as specific as I thought it would be." Pen studied the screen intently. "That's how you were able to hide among the yinalla and they couldn't tell you were right there?"

Minette whistled. "You hid in a herd of yinalla? They're vicious."

"They were asleep, so it wasn't that dangerous," Fliss said. She switched off the screen, put it back in the bag, and pulled out the remote starter.

"What does that do?" Pen took it from her cautiously.

"I hope it will disrupt their tech by resetting it. I didn't have any way to test it, though, so it might not work."

"So if it does work, we'll be able to see them on that screen, but their equipment will be down?" Ellen gave a slow, wicked smile.

Fliss gave a tight nod as if embarrassed, rather than take her due at the impressive results she'd managed.

She was careful not to make herself the center of attention, and when she was, she was uncomfortable in the role.

Han guessed it was from years of keeping out of her father's way, and wondered again how Ralf Bellini could have so twisted what should have been a close relationship.

"I need to tell you about the aliens' armor," she said, looking around at everyone. "I've never seen that kind before. It looks hard and bulky although it's similar to ours in that it's difficult to see in the dark. And they have little comms units clipped to their left shoulder."

"My cutter went through their armor," Han said. "But it did take a bit of effort." He remembered the rage he'd been in at seeing Fliss hurt. "Maybe quite a lot of effort."

"They riled you up, did they?" Ellen asked.

He grunted in answer, and Fliss suddenly looked up at him and gave him a tiny smile.

She knew, he realized. She knew that he had been riled because she had been hurt.

"And you say they speak a weird version of Fjerna?" Ranuk asked.

"It only sounds a bit like Fjerna when you listen to them speak for a while," Fliss said. "Like they've taken Fjerna and twisted it around a bit. Some words sounded familiar but not quite the same."

"Their air crawlers don't use blades. I don't know how they fly, but it's quieter than our air vessels. And they can jump out of them at a very low altitude and land safely. I asked the soldier how but he didn't seem to have the words to describe it in Fjerna."

"You had a chat to him?" Ranuk asked.

Since last night, when he'd taken Fliss's hand, Ranuk had been different. Less edgy in his movements, a little quieter.

Han hadn't known what to think of the interaction at the time. He trusted Ranuk, had not thought Fliss was in any danger from him, but he'd felt his gyra watching, alert in case he needed to step in.

"I did manage a short conversation before Han chopped his head off," Fliss said, and flicked another look at him. "Han waited while I tried to get information out of him, but then the soldier worked out it was Han who was standing behind him, not his friend, and the conversation was over."

"He said his orders were to keep us alive." Han had thought about that a lot.

"I think they need us to clear the raveners. Heldar said he'd lost too many people already, and one died while I was there, poisoned by a tarinac. The soldiers he's using to keep guard did not look like they were feeling particularly loyal to him. If they stick with him, it's so they can get back home, not because of any dedication to the cause."

"So we can try to divide and conquer." Pen tapped her leg. "Any names?"

"Heldar is the leader. The one who died was Evlar." Fliss frowned in concentration. "The woman who was angriest about Evlar's death was Chilm, and the other one who survived was a big man, Delasio's size. His name's Dragmar. Another soldier was with them, a woman called Jardern. She enhaled tarinac poison, and she'll probably still be in a sick bay." She paused, then tightened her lips. Han could tell it was in anger. "There were two others, they were more loyal to Heldar and tried to shoot me when I ran. I didn't hear their names."

"What did they look like?" Han asked.

He would look out for them.

She shook her head. "Big and wearing black. Nothing about them stood out."

"That's not all of them, though?" Delasio asked from behind him.

"No. There didn't seem to be a shortage of them. They sent two air crawlers after us." Han wondered how many could have arrived on Fjern. Five thousand had come on the *Cercatore,* two thousand years ago, but that had been a massive explorer ship.

Even if there were just hundreds, it was a lot of people to fight, especially when they had tech and weapons his Gyr had never encountered before.

Delasio slowed the air crawler and then set them down in an open field beside a dark green forest that followed the curve of the hill.

Taque was already there, waiting for them with his team.

Renardo Gyratta was a little smaller than Vallent's, and they had six Gyr. It looked like they'd left one person behind to hold the line, so there were five, all in full uniform, cutters at the ready.

Delasio obviously knew some of the Renardo team, as he'd once been part of their gyratta. He was warmly met by the group.

Pen also knew one of them, because she embraced the tall, lean man who stepped forward with a smile as she jumped out of the air crawler.

Taque jerked his head, and Han moved off to the side with him.

"You're sure about this?" the burly man asked, his thick, unruly hair dancing in the icy morning breeze. "Aliens, Han?"

"I saw them. I killed two. I ran from them and their tech. It's real, Taque."

Taque gave a curt nod. "Just seems so wild, you know? Unbelievable."

"We always knew we weren't the only ones. In fact, we were the brave outliers, taking the biggest risks. The others who got softer landings, they would have had an advantage in living on planets where everything wasn't trying to kill them all the time. Of course they'd have found a way to travel space again before us."

Taque blew out a breath. "True. But still . . ." He caught sight of Fliss. "Who's that?"

Han didn't know if he could answer that in any way that covered all the complexities that defined Fliss.

His pause was so long, Taque looked over at him. "Han?"

"I think she's my gyrbar," he said at last. "She is the first Gyr-born I've ever met."

Taque sucked in a breath. "How?"

"A Gyr called Ralf Bellini. He ran from Gyr Command and settled on the escarpment. Fliss is his daughter."

"Boss," Pen called out. "We need to show them Fliss's tech magic."

"Tech magic?" Taque murmured as he and Han moved toward the rest of the group.

Fliss looked distinctly uncomfortable at Pen making her the center of attention, and when she pulled out the screen, she handed it to Pen, rather than operating it herself.

"So Fliss and Han were chased by two of the aliens, and after Han killed them, Fliss took their wrist units. They have some tech they use to hunt in the dark, where they can see us by the heat our bodies give off." Pen switched on the screen, and pointed it at Fliss and Ranuk, who were standing together.

"See?"

The Renardo Gyratta team were clearly impressed when Ranuk lifted a hand and waved it.

"How did you graft their tech onto ours?" the man Pen had embraced earlier asked.

"I had to use old tech of ours——it was more compatible with

their circuits than our recent electronics," Fliss said. "Which is interesting in itself."

"That's not all." Ellen gestured to the bag. "Show them the other thing."

Fliss pulled out the remote starter. "I've configured this with the other circuit we took from them, and if I've got it right, I think it will interfere with their tech; reset it, so it shuts down and reboots."

"You think?" one of the other Renardo team, a woman Han thought was called Aurelia, Taque's second-in-command, asked.

Fliss lifted a shoulder. "It's not like I've had anything to test it on, yet. The alien weapon we took doesn't have any circuits to reset——not like the wrist units——so I can't use it. We'll see today if my disruptor works. If it doesn't, we're no worse off, but if it does . . ."

"We can scan to see where they are, and they won't be able to do the same to us." Delasio walked up behind Fliss and stood beside her, lending his support.

"And that? Is that the weapon you're talking about?" Taque asked, pointing to the one Fliss had slung over her shoulder.

"Yes." Fliss held it out. "It doesn't work on raveners, other than to enrage them further, and I think the armor the aliens wear probably shields them mostly from a hit from their own weapons, but if we get hit, it will hurt. A lot."

"Show them what it looks like," Pen urged.

It was just after dawn and there was enough gloom still that the white lightning would be an impressive sight.

Fliss nodded and looked around for a target, eventually aiming at a large rock that stood to one side of the field.

The light bloomed, the buzz, the strange smell of burnt air, the way the light crawled over the rock for a moment before winking out, rendered the Renardo Gyratta team mute for a long moment.

"There really are aliens," Taque finally said.

Han looked over at him, and he raised both hands in surrender.

"Sorry, I still had doubts you were right. It's just such a big stretch to think they landed, didn't introduce themselves and say hello, but instead set up a secret mine and tried to capture two Gyr."

Pen's friend walked up to Fliss. "Can I have a go?"

She handed it to him, and he shot it, almost dropping it in surprise when it sent out its beam of light.

"It hurts, you say?" One of the other women on the Renardo team asked.

"Took me over twelve hours to heal," Fliss said. "And it hurt some of my gyra as well as my body."

Han hadn't known that. "Hurt them, how?" he asked.

"Shut them down for a bit. But they eventually recovered."

"So, where are we going?" Taque asked, looking up at the lightening sky.

He was right, time was wasting.

Han pointed toward the mine. "It's about a half hour run from here. There's a long-hauler from Vallent, Jackson, who may or may not be their prisoner. They shot him, and Fliss doesn't know if he was killed or just injured."

"What was he doing mixed up in this?" Taque asked.

"They stopped him on the road some time ago, persuaded him to buy them supplies," Fliss said.

"We think whoever helped them initially either thought better of it, or fell foul of them and was killed, and they needed another source to bring them food and supplies." Han wondered yet again at the reasons the first Fjerna had helped them. Why had they done it in secret? What could possibly have been in it for them?

"So we rescue him?" Pen's friend asked.

"If we can. He lured Fliss out there, with plans to hand her over to them, so my advice is not to put yourself at risk to do it," Han said.

"What did they want with you?" Taque asked Fliss.

"They're using depth charges, which is stirring up the raveners. Be prepared to come across a lot of angry monsters. They wanted a Gyr to deal with their problem."

"They don't have Gyr of their own, if they're also descended from the Travelers?" Another of the Renardo team, a younger man who looked to Han to be a new recruit, asked.

"They didn't seem to understand what we are," Fliss said. "Maybe some of the Travelers didn't have gyra? Maybe it was just for the explorers going into more dangerous territory?"

Han thought about what Fliss had said as he led the way, jogging through the trees.

According to the records, the Travelers had found planets that were perfect for them to settle, but because of their numbers, it had been decided that some had to push on, move into more uncharted skies.

It made sense that the gyra, rare as they were, would be reserved for those going to places where life might not be as easy.

And if that was so, if these aliens didn't know about the gyra, and didn't have Gyr in their society, they were in for a big, nasty surprise.

26

Han looked back, checking to see where she was often enough as they ran that Fliss could see his behavior was noted by the others.

The Vallent team weren't surprised, but the Renardo Gyr were obviously curious about it.

She let Pen and Delasio go ahead of her, and found herself beside Taque, the leader of Renardo Gyratta, whenever the path widened to allow two abreast.

"You're new to Vallent Gyratta?" Taque asked.

"Just joined yesterday," she said. Whatever he was expecting as an answer, that clearly wasn't it, because the burly man almost lost his footing.

"Yesterday?" He glanced up ahead at Han. "I thought Han had known you longer than that."

"I was with the Fithsu Gyratta before that. I met Han when Dakar died."

"Ah." Taque glanced at her. "And before Fithsu?"

"I was living in the Provinces, up on the escarpment."

"At a gyratta?"

She shook her head. "I was never in a gyratta until Dakar took me to Fithsu. Before then I had never met another Gyr." She thought about it. "Other than my father, that is."

"Han said you are . . . Gyr-born?"

Finally Fliss understood where he was trying to go. "Yes."

There was a noise from behind them, and she glanced back, saw Pen's friend, a Gyr called Jerome, and a muscular woman whose name she hadn't caught yet, staring at her in astonishment.

She faced forward again, uncertain how to take their reaction.

"Can I touch you?" Taque slowed, and she realized he wanted to feel that she was Gyr for himself. The same way he had reserved judgement on the existence of aliens until he'd seen her use their weapon.

She kept jogging, but reached out her hand, and he grasped it.

She felt the buzz of interest from her gyra, felt the response in return from his.

When he pulled back, he was no longer looking at her, but focused up ahead, the hand that had touched hers cradled against his chest, almost as if he were injured.

She lifted her gaze, saw Han had stopped and was watching them.

Suddenly so uncomfortable with the situation she didn't know how to react, she sped up, leaving Taque behind and making straight for Han.

"All right?" he asked, and she stopped beside him, then leaned close.

He pulled her closer, kissed the side of her neck, and whispered: "No time wasting, please."

She smiled, relaxing at last.

Had she ever dreamed of finding someone who would put so much effort into making her happy?

Dreamed, yes, her gyra told her. *Thought we would find it, no.*

Ellen had stepped to the side when Han had stopped, and now she came closer and winked at Fliss, a cheeky gesture that made Fliss smile even more broadly.

"You should not have brought her here." Taque finally joined them, his hand still cradled close to his chest. He was looking at Han, frowning. He nodded to Fliss. "She should not be at risk. She's too precious."

"I am no more precious than anyone else." Fliss felt the shock of his statement shiver through her. "And I know how the alien tech works. I had to come."

"You are the only Gyr-born. We should be shielding you, not putting you in harm's way."

Before she, or anyone else, could respond, the sound of a ravener roaring came from up ahead.

Over the roar, she could just make out shouting.

"We deal with the raveners, disable the aliens fighting them, and move on," Han said, turning away from Taque.

That's the plan he'd outlined earlier if they came across raveners. They'd all agreed.

They couldn't leave monsters running around, in case the raveners came blundering in while the Gyr were trying to take the mine.

They didn't want to kill any aliens they found outside the mine, either, but they couldn't move efficiently with prisoners.

Everyone had multiple sets of slim restraints for immobilizing the soldiers until they could circle back to fetch them.

They all knew the dangers of leaving someone helpless on Fjern, the raveners, even the lesser threats like the waronga, could get them, but it was the best they could do, short of killing the aliens outright.

Han set his pack down and everyone followed suit, piling their things close together beneath a tree.

Then they started to move toward the noise, spreading out, the Vallent Gyratta working like the team they were, silent, in tune with each other.

Fliss kept back, watching them for cues, giving them room to move.

Taque's people were the same, moving to the right flank, also coordinated in a way that Fliss had never seen from non-Gyr.

"It's good you're at the back. Don't take risks," Taque told her as he slid past. She didn't answer him, angry that what he'd got out of touching her was a need to keep her from making her own decisions, in the name of keeping her safe.

Her father had done the same, but to keep *himself* safe.

She pulled out the screen and switched it on. Beyond Han and the others, she could see the massive signatures of two raveners and four smaller blobs of orange.

Han turned back to her, and she held up a hand with two fingers, made a claw, and then four fingers. She pointed to the location of the four figures.

Just to make sure she'd covered everything, she turned east and gasped as a massive bloom of light lit the screen.

"Wait." Her call was low and urgent, and everyone stopped and turned to look at her.

"A spaceship, maybe." She pointed toward it. "Very big."

Han looked torn.

"Four of us can deal with two raveners and four aliens," Pen said.

Han gave a reluctant nod. "Ranuk, Minette and I will go with the Renardo team to check out the ship. The rest of you join us after you've dealt with the raveners." He glanced at Taque, seeking agreement and the Renardo leader gave a nod.

Han caught her eye, eyebrow lifted at her in silent question.

She copied Taque, giving a nod, and then threw Han the remote, so he could use it to neutralize any scan of their heat signature.

Hopefully.

He caught it deftly, his eyes on her as he slid it into a pocket on his jacket.

Then he, Minette and Ranuk ghosted after Taque and his team, and Pen led the rest of them to the left, toward the sound of fighting.

FLISS FOLLOWED right behind the others, stopping when Pen lifted a hand.

They were close to the river here, Fliss could hear it rushing to her left, but over the sound of running water was the buzz of the aliens' weapons, and the shrieks of the raveners in response.

She could see through the trees that it was two largarti, dancing back and forth as the aliens shot at them.

"Can't they see they're not slowing them down, just antagonizing them?" Ellen murmured. "And they're *largarti*. Once they're riled, they keep coming until they're too injured or they're dead. Or you are."

"They don't have anything else to keep the raveners back," Fliss said. "It's that or nothing. And while they probably don't understand much about the largarti, I think they've realized if they stop shooting and run, they're dead."

A crackle of light hit the largarti closest to the line of trees where she was crouched with the others, the bright white of it running up one of its eight legs. It shrieked again, turning away from the source of its torment to face the forest.

"It's seen us," Pen said, as it went still, then lifted its body higher. "Let's draw it away."

Hopefully, the aliens would think they were responsible for driving the largarti off.

Everyone was careful to be silent as they backed away, fanning out in a line.

Fliss made sure she was in the middle, tossing her bag to Pen and the screen to Ellen on either side of her.

She kept the alien weapon, just in case, but it was slung across her back, and wasn't in her way.

"You going to do your thing?" Pen asked. She didn't sound like she objected.

"I'll try."

Delasio, who'd taken the outer edge on Pen's right, made a sound of approval, like he was looking forward to seeing it.

Fliss hoped she didn't disappoint.

The largarti wasn't behaving normally, though. The repeated shots with the white lightning had enraged it beyond sense.

It didn't stalk, it blundered, smashing through bushes, bumping into tree trunks as it came after them, its black carapace gleaming as it raced across the patches of early morning sunlight filtering through the trees.

It was going to be hard to control.

Still, she stepped directly into its path so that it would see her.

As it lunged for her, mandible jaws snapping a hair's breadth from her shoulder, a shot of white lightning hit the monster from the side.

Fliss froze in shock.

There was another alien in the woods with them.

Fliss heard Delasio swear behind her as she lifted the weapon off her back and found a bush to crouch beside.

"Where are they?" she called to Ellen. "Can you see them on the screen?"

"Yes. There's only one of them, right in front of you, behind that tree," Ellen called softly from a few trees over. "I thought it was one of our own crew coming back this way. There must have been five of them, because there are still four in the clearing."

Fliss wondered where the soldier had been hiding that her screen hadn't picked them up the first time.

She needed to work out why later, though.

She finally saw him, edging out from behind the tree as Ellen had said.

She sighted between the enraged largarti's legs and took aim, shooting him as he ran forward in a crouch.

The white light hit him directly in the chest and he staggered back, but didn't go down.

As she suspected, the armor they wore protected them at least partially against their own weapons.

The light distracted the largarti, and it turned toward the alien, pouncing on him, both sets of pincers getting a grip.

She could hear the sound of the soldier's armor groaning under the pressure, and she threw her weapon down, racing for the largarti and jumping high to grab a leg.

She swung up onto its carapace and ran to its head. When she got there, she looked over the top of it, down onto the man suspended in its jaws.

He stared at her, eyes wide with shock and pain.

"Stop," she said, but the largarti didn't want to listen to her.

It was too far gone with panic and rage.

It raced away, still carrying the alien in its jaws, with Fliss riding on the top of it.

At least it was going in the right direction, so Fliss let it be, waiting until it broke free of the trees and began heading down the hill to the more open ground of the valley.

The moment it was out of the confines of the woods, it lowered its body a little, far less stressed.

"Drop." She made the command as forcefully as she could and it did obey this time, dropping the man. "Burrow."

She jumped as it swerved to the left, in the same direction as the burrow she had found when she'd been traveling with Jackson days ago.

There was definitely a nest of them.

She landed in a crouch beside the soldier, who lay sprawled and dazed on the ground where he'd been dropped.

He had lost his weapon, and she could see the largarti's pinchers had pierced his armor. Blood was leaking from the gashes in the black shell, but that wouldn't be the most dangerous part.

The largarti's pinchers were venomous——not enough to kill you, unless you were already too far gone in shock——but enough to make life very miserable.

She used her restraints, tying him up, and then bent to sling him over her shoulder.

He was babbling at her in his strange language, but she ignored him, slowly taking the walk back to the others step by difficult step.

She was stronger than a Fjerna, but this man was a lot bigger than her, and his armor was extremely heavy.

She could leave him, she considered.

That had been the plan, and he was probably no worse off here than in the trees.

She was about to do it when Delasio came racing out of the forest, then slowed at the sight of her.

"All good?" He sounded too casual.

"He's heavy. I was about to dump him here, but he's been bitten."

Delasio plucked him off her shoulder easily. "We can give him some anti-venom where we left the packs."

"What's going on with the others?"

"Still at it." He sent her a sidelong look. "What happened to the largarti?"

"I sent it back to its burrow."

"Good." He shifted the soldier to his other side.

The man had stopped babbling the moment Delasio had come out of the trees, and now he was absolutely still.

Fliss moved around to the back to check on him. "His lips are blue."

Delasio sped up a little, jogging toward where they'd left their equipment.

Fliss already had the anti-venom out before Delasio had set the man down, injecting him in his neck, one of the few areas where she could reach his skin.

"Done." She stepped back. "Back into the fray?"

Delasio grinned. "Naturally."

They ran in the direction of the clearing, and through the trees Fliss could just see Ellen and Pen trying to draw the remaining largarti into the forest.

They were in sight of the aliens, though, forced to move into the open to engage the largarti, and as she and Delasio reached the edge of the trees, Pen went down.

She was shifted, in fighting form, as was Ellen, but as the white light hit her, she shifted back as she fell.

Delasio made a sound beside her, not loud, but intense.

She glanced across at him, saw he was shifting as he ran into the open, his already big presence becoming massive, his cutter out and sparking.

"Ellen." That's all he said, but Ellen obviously knew what he meant, because she grabbed hold of Pen and pulled her out of the way, moving her into the protection of the trees.

Delasio's focus was the aliens, Fliss could see. They had taken Pen down, and he was going to return the favor. Probably with interest.

That still left the largarti.

Out of the corner of her eye, she saw Ellen crouch beside Pen, laying her down. Then she came toward Fliss, still shifted, cutter still activated.

"Help Delasio," Fliss told her.

She could deal with the largarti.

It was easy coming at it from behind, as all its attention was on the aliens, still shooting at it.

She jumped and caught hold of the smooth, hard chitin near the knee joint, avoiding the sharp spikes that were ranged along its shin and its upper thigh. She swung herself up, landing on its back, and she felt it register her presence, shivering a little as if it could shake her off.

White light sizzled overhead and she dropped, lying flat on the hard shell and moving forward using her elbows and knees.

"Retreat."

It didn't, but it was uneasy now, more than enraged. She could tell by the way it was lowering and raising its body, as if it couldn't decide whether it was in attack or defence mode.

Delasio was moving around the edge of the clearing, and Fliss saw the alien soldiers had picked up on his presence.

Two turned their weapons in his direction.

They looked nervous, Fliss thought. The largarti wasn't down, and now they had Delasio to deal with, as well.

Ellen caught up to him, settling into a shoulder to shoulder stance that screamed well-trained and deadly, and they advanced, despite the weapons aimed at them.

"Find cover," Fliss ordered the largarti, and was relieved when it began shuffling backward into the trees.

Largarti never backed down, not that she had ever seen, but they didn't have long memories, and if you could get them out of the fight, you could persuade them to go back to their burrows.

But the alien soldiers weren't going to cooperate with her efforts.

They huddled together, two facing the largarti, two facing Delasio and Ellen, and opened up fire all together, forming a bright onslaught of light.

How did they power their weapons, Fliss wondered? They seemed to have a never-ending stream of energy.

It crackled up the largarti's legs and abdomen, and Fliss felt the uncomfortable prickle as small strands of it touched her where she lay on the largarti's back.

Bad, her gyra said. *Very bad.*

Unable to stand the ferocity of the attack, the largarti threw itself at its tormentors, lunging for them and managing to pierce one with a mandible.

Fliss looked right, checking on Delasio and Ellen, but they had dived out of the way of the lightning, rolling left and right, and then coming back up so fast, they clearly took the aliens by surprise.

With one of their group impaled on the largarti's mandible, the soldiers lost their cohesion, their huddle falling apart.

"Take your prey to your burrow." Fliss couldn't think of any other order that might get through.

The largarti backed up, lifting its mandibles, so she looked right at the woman who had been impaled.

It was Chilm.

She was still conscious, her eyes glassy with shock as she tried to say something to Fliss.

As soon as the largarti reached the treeline it turned to face forward, racing between the trees, and Fliss was torn, wondering what to do about the impaled soldier. There would be no way to pry her off unless the largarti was dead, and she didn't even have a cutter.

She stood, balancing as the largarti scuttled through the forest. Chilm began to struggle, kicking at the largarti's eyes with a boot, and it stopped and tried to scrape her off its mandible against a trunk.

The soldier struggled weakly as the largarti pried her off.

Fliss held still, waiting to see what the ravener would do next.

When it started forward again, she jumped off its back.

It disappeared through the trees, and she knelt beside Chilm.

The alien woman's breathing was a rattling wheeze, and her skin looked bloodless.

She reached out a hand, and Fliss took it.

"This ... fucking ... place," Chilm said. "Monsters."

"I know," Fliss commiserated.

"Evlar. Gone. Now me."

"I'm sorry." There was no way, short of getting her advanced medical help in the next few minutes, that Fliss could see she could survive.

Chilm coughed, blood flecking her lips.

"Where are you from?" Fliss asked her.

"Verdant ..." She pursed her lips, coughed again and then parted her lips to speak, her chest heaving. She turned her head suddenly to the side, then slumped over.

Fliss turned her gently onto her back and Chilm's hand went limp in hers.

Fliss crouched beside her and the silence of the forest settled around her and the dead soldier.

What a waste. What a crying waste.

She heard a sound behind her and whirled. Came face to face with Delasio and Ellen, still in shifted form.

"She's gone."

"So are the other three." The way Delasio said it, Fliss guessed it had been in the form of having their heads separated from their bodies.

"Pen?"

"She's coming round," Ellen said. "She's half-awake, anyway, but not happy."

She began to shift back to normal form, and with a sigh, Delasio did the same.

They walked back to Pen, and Fliss saw she had tried to stand, hadn't quite managed it, and was propping herself up against the tree.

"The largarti's gone?" she croaked.

Fliss nodded. "Back to its burrow." She saw the weapons the aliens had been using were piled nearby. "What now?"

"We should go help the others." Pen tried to straighten again and then gave up. "Well, you should. I'll just rest here a while."

"Wait where we left the equipment," Ellen told her. "Take a pain blocker and see how you feel."

Pen nodded, sank down to the ground. "In a bit."

Delasio crouched beside her. "I'll carry you." He picked her up without waiting for her to agree, and after a moment of stiff resistance, she gave a sigh and leaned her head against his shoulder.

They all walked together, with Fliss finding the screen and her bag along the way, dropped by the others earlier.

She switched the screen on, but it was losing power, so she only did a quick scan of the area. There was no one that she could see, just the bright light in the distance, where the big alien ship was located.

She closed it down and put it away to preserve it.

Delasio laid Pen gently down among the bags, tucked between the large roots of a tree, and handed her her cutter.

"Use your comm if you need help," he grumbled, and she smiled at him, but Fliss could see the effort it cost her.

The soldier they'd left there earlier was still unconscious, but he was tied up, anyway, and no danger to Pen.

They began to follow the route Han had taken with the Renardo team, but they had barely left Pen behind them when a massive boom rattled the branches and made the ground beneath their feet rumble.

Without a word, they began to run.

No matter what had happened, it didn't sound good.

27

THE TINNY SOUND OF METAL BANGING ON METAL SEEMED INCONGRUOUS in the early morning air.

Han crawled on his stomach to the crest of a low hill and looked down at the mine. He couldn't find the source of the faint noise, but it didn't matter.

Something much more interesting caught his attention.

A massive spaceship was now standing in what had been the open area behind the mine's gates.

One of the buildings Han recalled seeing as he flew over the mine, moments before he'd been shot down, had been crushed beneath the back left corner of the immense ship. Han could see bits of fibre swirling around in the wind, and the glitter of window glass on the ground nearby.

"Do you think that was a mistake?" Taque asked as he settled into place beside Han, pointing to the crushed structure.

"Maybe they had no choice." The ship was so big, he couldn't imagine there was anywhere else nearby with enough flat, open space. "After all, they don't need the building anymore, anyway."

"What's that noise?" Minette whispered, pressing up on his right-hand side.

"Repairs?" If they were having mechanical difficulties, that would suit him.

If they were, though, it wasn't stopping them from loading up.

The men and women below were working hard, their focus clear.

A ground crawler, a Fjern-built one, drove up to the rear of the ship, to where a ramp had been lowered down. It was dwarfed by the massive ship, and Han wondered if it was Jackson's long-hauler. If so, it was being used to haul ore.

Soldiers began unloading boxes full of raw ore out of the back of it, and when they were done, the long-hauler drove off behind a long, low building. The soldiers began running the ore up the ramp, into the hold of the big spaceship.

The faint sound of an engine from the east had Han scanning the sky, and finally a smaller ship came into sight, moving slowly.

It had a sling fitted beneath it, and . . .

"Is it carrying . . . your air crawler?" Ranuk had pushed himself between Han and Minette, his head just behind Han's shoulder.

"Yes. They're stealing it." It was interesting to note that the aliens must be as intrigued by Fjern's technology as they were by the aliens' tech.

"How is that big ship even going to take off?" Jerome wondered from Taque's other side.

That was a good point. There were no air blades, and no engines either, that Han could see. But the smaller air crawler seemed to have an engine——he could hear it——he just didn't know where it was.

The engines that were part of the *Cercatore*, the explorer ship that had brought his people to Fjern, were massive. At least fifteen people could stand on each others' shoulders and just reach the top of one. And there were four of them.

He had studied them often, as the ship remained a museum in Nasnere to this day.

This ship, although it traveled through space like the *Cercatore*, did not seem to have any visible means of propulsion.

He had a feeling the smaller ship, the one carrying his own air crawler, was the one that had come after him and Fliss when the other one had been knocked out of the sky, but next to the mothership, it looked tiny.

"They're certainly working fast," Minette said as someone shouted encouragement to the soldiers who were loading ore, and they sped up.

Above them, the smaller spaceship hovered with Han's air crawler swinging below it, seeming to struggle to find a place to set down.

"They know Fliss and I have gone for help and that someone will be back to stop them, so they're grabbing what they can before leaving, and they must have called down the mothership to do it."

"So, how do we do this?" Taque looked down the rise. "There's at least fifty of them, by my count."

Fifty wasn't a lot against eight Gyr, but these people all had weapons that could hurt them and armor that would be difficult to cut through.

"We should take the big ship." Han couldn't see any guards around it. They must be confident everyone in the mine compound was one of theirs. "They can't go anywhere without it."

"Agreed." Taque turned to him, a spark of glee in his eyes.

The Renardo Gyr leader was looking forward to this.

"Six of us go in, two stay outside, out of sight, in case we get into difficulty."

Han chose Ranuk to stay outside, and Taque chose Aurelia, his second-in-command.

Before they began to move down the hill, Han pulled out the remote Fliss had given him. She thought it would disrupt the heat signature tech the aliens had, by resetting it. It meant he would have to push it again at intervals as their systems would reboot. She didn't know what those intervals were.

If it worked at all.

"You going to zap them?" One of the other women on Taque's team, Karla, asked.

"Might as well. It can't hurt to try to blind them to our heat signatures."

Han pointed the device down the hill and pressed the button.

With a sputter, the smaller spaceship's engines died, and it fell from the sky, tilting slightly as it dropped so its side hit the top front edge of the big spaceship.

Han's air crawler, hanging below it, smashed into the big ship and then into the ground, rolling over once.

The smaller ship jerked and then fell after it, landing on top of it, on its other side.

As the small alien ship hit his air crawler, Han heard a low whump of sound, and both vessels went up in flames.

He caught Minette staring at the remote in his hand and then at the burning wreckage.

"Was that supposed to happen?" Taque asked.

Han shook his head, suppressing a laugh of disbelief at how well Fliss's tech had worked. "But let's use it."

They ran, using the distraction to move fast down the grassy slope, without trying to use any trees as cover.

They had deliberately dressed in black, and in the chaos that was happening below, Han hoped if anyone glanced their way, they would look similar enough to the alien soldiers not to raise the alarm.

Before they got to the bottom of the slope, Ranuk raced past him and jumped, grabbing a thick branch of a tree and climbing up to disappear into the foliage. Aurelia joined him, the branches and leaves rattling slightly as she made her way up.

It was a good idea, and should give the two lookouts eyes on the whole area.

Up ahead, soldiers were shouting as they converged on the fire at the front end of the spaceship, and Han realized the panic would be more about saving the big ship from damage so they could leave, rather than the lives of the pilot and crew of the smaller vessel.

He had wanted to take the big ship, but downing the smaller ship might end up having the same result.

The ramp into the mothership was abandoned.

Everyone had rushed to put out the fire, and the team reached it without a single challenge.

Han kept close to the side as he took the ramp, and found himself in a truly massive space, with metal bins full of raw ore lining one side. There were four vehicles that might be the aliens' version of ground crawlers, two of which were seriously damaged.

Raveners, Han guessed.

The space would have been able to swallow his air crawler, no problem.

He moved on and found a double door.

Taque caught up, and they waited for the others, then Han pushed through into a passageway.

It was eerily empty.

Everyone must be outside, initially to help load the ore, and now, to douse the fire.

"Almost too easy," Taque murmured, moving ahead as Han studied the polished metal walls of the corridor.

As he said it, white light hit him in the chest, and the Renardo leader went down.

Han shifted, jumping and extending his claws into the thin metal of the ceiling. He swung his legs back, bracing them against the wall so he hovered above everyone else, face down.

Minette followed his lead, choosing to brace against the opposite wall, and below them, the three remaining Renardo Gyr crouched low, waiting.

A soldier ran from around a corner toward Taque, then started at the sight of the rest of his team.

Jerome, who'd shifted along with everyone else, leaped at him, covering the distance in a moment and taking him down before he could get off another shot.

He had him restrained in moments.

"Wait," Han whispered to Minette when she seemed about to drop down, and she nodded.

They didn't have to wait long.

Two more soldiers ran around the corner, shooting as they came. Jerome took the brunt of both streams and went down.

Han dropped, Minette a half second behind him, landing almost on top of the soldiers' heads.

When they were restrained and Taque and Jerome were settled against the wall, as comfortable as they could make them, Han motioned for silence and listened, trying to hear if anyone else was coming.

There were four of them now, the two remaining members of the Renardo team, Karla and Tyrone——the new recruit——and himself and Minette.

"It seems like this is the whole guard contingent," he said, looking back at the three downed soldiers.

He led the way forward, scanning the corridor to see how their presence had been picked up. Those soldiers had known they were here before they'd even turned the corner.

He saw a few blinking lights set high on the ceiling, and had to assume that the aliens monitored their own corridors and it had given them advance warning.

There were rooms either side of the corridor all the way along, but he was looking for the control room of the ship.

Han guessed that was right at the front, where the smaller ship was burning.

He slowed when he heard voices up ahead, raised and sounding stressed.

"They're worried about the damage," Minette whispered.

Han nodded. He wished he could understand what was being said, but the tone was clear enough.

Panic and fear.

He wouldn't like to be stranded on a planet without a way off, either, especially if the locals had good reason to be hostile.

He was still shifted, his gyra primed and his every sense alert, so he picked up a change in tone from up ahead instantly and put on a sudden burst of speed as the doors up ahead began to slide closed.

They'd been seen——again——Han was sure of it.

He reached the doors before they slammed shut, holding them apart, and then Minette was with him, grabbing one side.

He took the other and they bent the panels inward with a screech of metal. He stepped into what was clearly the command center.

There were only four people inside.

Everyone had turned to stare at him, but none had weapons.

Han could see visible fear on their faces.

"You are the . . . monsters who . . . fight the other monsters?" The woman who spoke struggled with her grasp of Fjerna, each word halting, but understandable enough.

Han studied her.

She was in a dark blue uniform, sleek, with an insignia on the upper arm, not the bulky armor of the soldiers from outside.

Han could see smoke and flames visible from the left of the massive transparent screen that ran along the front of the ship.

"You did this?" The woman asked, gesturing toward it.

Han nodded. "We did."

She made a sound of fury, and one of the two men standing behind her began to shout in their own language, the sound fast and fearful.

He wasn't shouting at the Gyr, though, he was shouting at the woman. He pointed to a screen, and when Han glanced up at it, he could see two blobs of heat coming fast from the north.

He had a sinking feeling he knew what they were.

Air crawlers.

Air crawlers from Nasnere.

The woman turned, horror on her face, and argued back, but the man gesticulated at the image again, and hit a button on the panel beside him.

A voice came through, and another screen nearby flickered to life.

A man appeared, dressed similarly to the woman, and Han had the sense he was standing in a similar control room.

He looked visibly shocked to see Han and the other Gyr.

There was more shouting.

Han knew he was missing something. But while the aliens were distracted with each other, it was a good time to act.

He signaled to Minette, and she moved, taking the woman in blue down and restraining her while she was in the middle of her argument, as if the Gyr were not the biggest threat.

Karla and Tyrone got the idea, and took two more.

Han forced the shouting man to the ground, tightening the restraints.

The figure on the screen gave a final yell and then it went blank.

"We need . . . run. Out of here." The woman looked over at Han. "This . . ." she looked over at the man he had restrained and spat. "This idiot . . . called to destroy . . . this ship. Because we will soon be overrun by your people."

Han got the gist.

The Gyr *weren't* the biggest threat.

The aliens didn't want their tech in Fjerna hands. And if he read the situation correctly, there was another spaceship like this one overhead. And it was about to destroy its companion.

"Let's go." He hauled his captive to his feet and let him run under his own steam out the door. Han waited for the others to do the same and took up the rear.

When he reached Taque and Jerome, Karla was hauling her still unconscious boss up onto her shoulder, and Tyrone was doing the same for Jerome.

Han grabbed the backs of two of the guards' jackets and began dragging them out, and Minette took the third.

When they reached the loading bay and the open ramp, Han saw a few soldiers were milling around below.

The woman in the blue was just ahead of him, and as she ran out, she screamed something at them.

They scattered, racing away.

As soon as he got out, he saw Delasio, Ellen and Fliss were running out of the trees toward them, and he dropped one of the guards for Delasio to take, swinging the other over his shoulder.

"Run."

Delasio scooped the man up, and Ellen helped Minette with her one as they raced back toward cover.

They had just reached the thin, first line of trees at the bottom of the rise when a roaring noise rose up behind them.

To Han, it sounded as if the air itself had cracked in two, and as he looked back, a hot white light shot down from above.

For a moment there was a terrible silence, and then, as if that crack in the air had sucked every bit of oxygen into it, he found he couldn't breathe.

When the air came howling back, it brought dust and debris swirling around them all.

Where the ship had been was now a crater.

The smoldering wreck of the vessel was still there, but it was a blackened ruin.

"What?" Taque croaked from where Karla had dumped him at Han's feet. "What happened?"

"The aliens happened." Han looked up into the sky, but there was no sign of the spaceship that had obliterated its own vessel.

He had thought of the aliens as beatable. And on the ground, soldier against Gyr, they were.

But this was something else.

This was something the Gyr could not defend against.

And if the Gyr couldn't defend against it, no one of Fjern could.

28

THE ALIENS WHO SURVIVED WERE NOT TALKING.

They sat, huddled together, heads down.

Every now and then Fliss saw one look over at the destroyed spaceship, and then quickly away.

The man who Han said had initiated the destruction by letting the other ship circling above know that they were damaged and the Gyr had taken the bridge, was completely shunned. He sat apart from the rest, looking almost catatonic.

The one benefit of the unbelievable power of the strike was that it had frightened even the biggest raveners away.

That was one headache they wouldn't have to contend with for at least another couple of hours.

The sound of air crawlers on the warm midday breeze lifted Fliss's spirits.

It meant Delasio and Karla were approaching with the two vessels they'd left behind that morning.

There was no room for them to land within the gates, so they set down on the road outside.

Pen was still listless. Delasio had carried her out from the woods and she was lying beneath the trees beside Jerome and Taque, with Ellen watching over them.

Of the three injured, Jerome was the worst off. He'd taken two hits simultaneously and he'd only regained consciousness once since he'd been hit.

Still, that one stretch of clarity had buoyed them all.

Fliss, Aurelia and Minette were on guard duty, keeping watch over what was left of the soldiers and crew of the ship. Ranuk had carried over the soldier who'd been left with Pen, and lain him with the others. The anti-venom was working, and he'd started to come round.

Ranuk had told them he'd seen a small group run north when the ship was hit from his lookout position, and given Fliss had yet to see Heldar, she was sure he was among them, unless he'd died in the strike.

She had a feeling he was someone who would always have an escape route, though.

Quite a few of the soldiers who'd scattered when the ship was hit had come back, giving themselves up.

They preferred the relative safety of being prisoners of the Gyr than taking their chances with the raveners.

Han walked across her field of vision, and Fliss watched him as he moved through the debris, looking for information or anything that could be saved.

He looked calm, but he was not.

He was furious.

Every now and then he looked north, waiting for the air crawlers coming from Nasnere to appear.

All the buildings had been damaged in the strike. A few were completely gone, and the two that where left had walls ripped away and roofs partially collapsed.

Whatever was worth finding in them would have to be retrieved now, or it would be blown away or destroyed by the raveners or the weather.

"How big are the air crawlers coming from Nasnere?" Aurelia asked. "Will they fit this many prisoners?"

"Gyr Command's problem if they don't," Minette said.

Fliss wasn't sure that was true.

The sooner they could get rid of the prisoners, the sooner they could thoroughly investigate the site. And go home.

Han called out, waving to her, and she jogged over to where he was standing.

He was looking down at something, and when she got closer, she saw boots sticking out from under a collapsed wall.

"Jackson?" she asked.

"You tell me." Han lifted the wall up, muscles flexing as he did. He flipped it over, away from the body beneath.

She crouched beside the old man, lying on his back, his eyes open. He was covered in white dust, blood smeared down the side of his head and on his arms and legs. He was bound, hand and foot. "It's him."

"He must have been kept prisoner here, and he died in the blow-back after the space strike." Han studied the wreckage of the room. "Looks like it was an office."

Fliss rose to her feet, feeling sick at the thought of Jackson trapped in here, with no chance to save himself.

She did a slow turn. "That might be a map." The corner of a thin, flexible sheet stuck out of the ash, and Fliss pulled it out.

It was a map. It showed the hills and the mine, the routes to Renardo and Vallent.

"They could have put this together themselves," Han said, stepping close to her to study it.

"Depends on how long they were here, but, yes. They could even have gone into Vallent or Renardo in disguise. It would have been impossible to tell them apart from the Fjerna."

Before he could respond, she heard the sound of approaching air crawlers.

Everyone turned to look, and the largest air crawler Fliss had ever seen crested the hill and flew down toward them, with a smaller one flying just behind it.

They hovered over the site, blowing debris and dust, and then moved east, looking for a place to land.

"Do you know who's in them?" Fliss asked, pushing the hair that had blown into her eyes off her forehead.

"Someone from Nasnere Gyr Command, would be my guess." Han sounded grim. "Maybe some Gyr from one of the Nasnere gyratta." He drew in an audible breath. "They didn't even try to contact my comms device to warn us they were close."

"Do you reckon they understand how dangerous it was to arrive without checking we had the site under control?" Delasio asked, walking toward them. "That they could have killed us?"

"Maybe, maybe not." Han's mouth formed a hard line. "This was a fuck you to me. To all of us."

He kept his eyes on the two air crawlers as they hovered over the trees, looking for a clearing big enough to take them both.

He seemed to come to some kind of decision. "This is what we are going to do. Look through the debris for any pieces of tech that look like they might be salvageable and load them into our air crawler. If Gyr Command have decided not to act in our best interests, then I'd like to get as many advantages as possible."

Delasio drew in a quick breath. "You sure this is the time to be adversarial?" he asked. "We've got aliens with superior weapons threatening the whole planet."

"No, I'm not sure." Han's words were short. "But it's time we started acting in our own best interests. I don't know what that looks like, and I'm wary of threatening to withhold our protection, but if they can't see fit to respect us, even when we're all that's standing between them and alien forces, then when will they?"

Delasio shook his head. "Put that way . . ." He sighed, and Fliss could see he was worried.

"I'll go meet them." Han came to a sudden decision, and looked over at her. "Why don't you come?"

She looked down at Jackson and then away. "I'd be more use to Del here, given my gyra's ability with electronics. I could find things that might be useful." Although any place would be better than here for a bit.

Han reached out and rested a hand on her shoulder. "I'm sorry about Jackson."

She blinked back sudden tears at his sympathy. "I didn't know him well, but he didn't understand what he'd gotten into. And at the end, he was trying to get away, and was very sorry for involving me." She turned away. "Why do you want me to come?"

He paused, but Del had already moved off and was starting to sift through the debris. "I always want you with me. But I want to give Del and the others time to find as much as possible. Your presence will be cause for delay."

"Because they'll freak out about a Gyr-born?" She hadn't known how soon she'd be presented to Gyr Command, but if it was going to happen anyway, why not make it count by giving Del and the others more time to get useful tech?

He nodded. "Is that all right with you? I have to believe that Teranimo has already told at least those at the top about you. Teranimo made it clear he knows, which means Gyr Command knows."

Put that way . . .

She gave a sigh. "Then let's go."

They walked in the direction the air crawlers had landed, Han keeping the pace unhurried.

It was also in the same direction as the largarti nest.

She pointed that out to Han as they walked.

He glanced at her, a tiny light of humor in his eyes. "You don't say."

"The largarti are probably all hiding in their burrows after that explosion."

"Maybe."

But largarti had such short memories, they might already have forgotten about the big bang.

It seemed almost inevitable when she heard one scream in rage in the distance.

Both air crawlers rose up out of the trees moments later, moving south east, and found a place to land just up ahead of them.

Han came to a stop and waited, and a few minutes later, four black-clad Gyr and four people Fliss guessed were Fjerna——Gyr Command administrators——emerged from the bush.

"Hannu." The Gyr in the lead moved directly toward Han, her hand out, and the two embraced, hand to elbow, opposite shoulders bumping, in the way Fliss had seen since she'd joined the Fithsu Gyratta.

"Lolia." Han's tightly-held irritation mellowed a little at the sight of someone who was obviously a friend. "I'd heard you'd been made leader of the South Nasnere Gyratta."

"And I'd heard you were babbling about aliens, and was coming over to tease you about it. But shit, Han, you were not exaggerating." As she spoke, she glanced at Fliss, gave a tiny nod in greeting.

Fliss nodded in return, pleased.

"No exaggeration." Han stepped back. "But coming when you did, before I called you in, nearly got us killed." He shot a look at one of the men in formal pants and jacket. "Which is why I told you I'd be in touch when the situation was dealt with."

Lolia looked over at the man as well. "That true, Hedgeworth?"

Hedgeworth straightened a little. "We assumed you would either be done by now, or in need of help."

"You assumed?" Lolia's words were soft.

Fliss saw a change in the demeanor of the other three Gyr with her. They looked over at the Gyr Command group, and subtly moved toward Han and their leader.

"I didn't know that, Hedgeworth." A woman in similar formal wear, who was standing slightly behind the administrator, stepped around him, a frown on her face. "Why would you disregard a direct request from a Gyr leader?"

She glanced at the Gyr and then at her fellow administrators.

Fliss thought she saw worry in the woman's face.

Maybe the divide was becoming clearer to those with eyes to see it.

It was a new world for Fliss, but from what Han had said, Teranimo had been seriously unhappy with the loss of trust, and as far as Fliss could see, he had every right to be worried.

If the Gyr lost faith in Gyr Command, the whole of Fjern would be in a completely new place.

"Because it was *aliens*, Yanno." A second administrator spoke up. "We felt we needed to get here as soon as possible."

"Then you should have let me know, Barilar, so we could have coordinated." Han did not hide his anger as he spoke to the second man. "What if some of my people had been harmed because you couldn't be bothered to respect my wishes?"

There was a moment of silence, and Hedgeworth shifted under the sudden scrutiny.

"I'm sorry, Han," Lolia said. "I didn't know any of this."

Han gave her a nod of understanding, then turned to Hedgeworth. "The aliens destroyed their own ship because during our attack they saw you coming and panicked."

Hedgeworth glanced up, face set, and said nothing.

It was a strange response.

The message Fliss received from his body language was that Han's anger meant nothing to him. He did not seem to care.

An uncomfortable silence stretched out.

"So what can you tell us?" Yanno said, subtly stepping in front of Hedgeworth, putting him in the background. "It looked to us, as we approached, as if a massive bolt of lightning came down."

Han focused on her. "There are at least two alien motherships. The wreck at the mine and one still orbiting Fjern. When the one still above learned we had taken the ship on the ground, and saw your air crawlers approaching, they destroyed it rather than let us get our hands on a working version."

"That was a weapon that we saw? A weapon shot from a spaceship?" The other woman administrator's voice was a little faint.

"Yes." Han's tone was short. "You're lucky one of their smaller air crawlers had just crashed into the bigger ship, making it less likely for them to be able to take off, otherwise they may have chosen to strike your air crawlers, rather than their own."

That seemed to grab everyone's attention.

No one on Fjern could defend against such a weapon.

"Are there many survivors?" Lolia asked.

"We've rounded up about thirty," Han said. "At least five got away, but given the raveners, I don't know how long they'll last."

"Do we know where they're from?" Yanno asked.

"One of them started to tell me, before she died," Fliss said.

Every eye turned to her.

"And you are?"

Hedgeworth was the one asking and Fliss didn't like his tone.

"You first," she said, with a polite smile.

The woman trying to act as mediator made a sound of annoyance. "This is Ric Hedgeworth, my fellow administrator at Gyr Command in Nasnere. I'm Miriam Yanno."

"I'm Fliss Belaire." Fliss kept her attention on Miriam Yanno, ignoring Hedgeworth completely.

"You were saying, about the aliens?" Lolia prompted.

"The one I spoke to said they were from Verdant. I think she was going to say more, but she was already dying, and she couldn't speak any further."

"Dying?" Miriam Yanno asked.

"Largarti," Fliss said. "Impaled."

The Gyr all winced.

"I've never heard of a Gyr called Fliss Belaire," Hedgeworth said.

And here they were.

Fliss guessed this is what Han had wanted.

"My father is Ralf Bellini," Fliss said. "I believe he ran from Gyr Command many years ago."

Her father's name had a definite effect on the administrators.

"I knew Ralf Bellini." The other woman with Miriam Yanno spoke up. "He's still alive?"

"Last I knew," Fliss confirmed.

"You're saying you're his daughter?" Hedgeworth was eyeing her suspiciously. "That would mean . . ."

"She's Gyr-born," Han said.

Lolia gasped. "Truly?" She lifted her arm.

"Truly," Fliss replied, and took the offered hand.

Lolia closed her eyes, and Fliss felt her gyra prickle beneath her skin. They liked Lolia.

"Truly." Lolia's eyes opened with a snap. "Where have you been all this time?"

"My father ran to the escarpment. I've been protecting a small mining community in the Provinces."

"A Gyr-born?" The man behind Hedgeworth, the one Han had addressed as Barilar, stepped closer, eyes wide. "You seem . . ."

Fliss waited for him to finish. When he didn't, she frowned. "Seem?"

"Barilar was going to say normal," Han said, voice soft. "He stopped because he suddenly realized how ill-considered that would be."

"Aliens, and now Gyr-born." Miriam Yanno rubbed a hand over her heart. "This is a day."

"We'll need you to come to Nasnere Gyr Command," Hedgeworth said, his cold gaze on Fliss.

"No." Han's tone was grim. "She will not become another Lucille Defoe."

Miriam Yannon flinched at Lucille's name.

"You have no say here, Kardenian." Hedgeworth's teeth were set.

"You've shown very clearly that you don't think I do," Han agreed. "But you cannot force Fliss to leave with you. And I and my gyratta will protect her with everything we have. If you want a war with the Vallent compound, then you can try to take her by force. And you will lose. Otherwise, you will accept what I have said. She will not go with you."

"The South Nasnere Gyratta will stand with you," Lolia said, and she had a strange, dark glint in her eye. "You will be at war with two gyratta, Hedgeworth." She looked down. "Lucille Defoe was my friend and I will not see the only Gyr-born disappear the same way she did."

"I think we have enough on our hands with an alien invasion, without picking a fight with our own warriors, don't you think, Hedgeworth?" Miriam Yanno's tone was dry, but if Fliss wasn't mistaken, she was coldly furious.

"Either Gyr Commmand directs the Gyr, or it has no function," Hedgeworth said.

There was another silence at that, and Fliss thought that everyone on the administrative team wished that Hedgeworth hadn't said that.

The idea was spoken, now.

She could see Hedgeworth regretted it, as well.

Because they did, in fact, seem to have no function.

"You're right," he said to Yanno. "Let's deal with the aliens."

They turned and began walking to the mine.

But nothing was resolved.

The ugliness of the confrontation lingered in the unspoken tension as Han led the way to the mine.

Fliss had a bad feeling things would only get worse.

29

Han sent a quick message over comms to Del to let him know they were coming, a head's up to make sure everything they'd found was safely stored on the air crawler before Gyr Command arrived.

When they reached the mine, Del was picking through the rubble, and Han noted he'd created a pile of things to one side.

Han guessed it was the things he'd discarded as too damaged.

A few of the prisoners stood as they emerged from the bush.

"We need medical treatment." A woman in a standard black uniform stood beside the woman he'd captured on the ship's bridge, the senior officer in the blue uniform.

It looked to Han as if the woman speaking was acting as interpreter for her boss.

"You're the linguist?" he asked.

She nodded. "I am Kalia. I have studied Fjern more than anyone else, and I will interpret for Captain Linao."

The woman he assumed was Linao spoke to her, the words quick, and as Fliss had put it, twisty. As if he should be able to grasp it, if he only concentrated.

Beside him, he heard Lolia make a sound of interest as the two women spoke. Then she signaled to her team and they spread out, reinforcing Ellen, Minette and Aurelia's positions as guards to the group.

"We need to be returned to our other ship," Kalia said.

"They'd need to contact us for that to happen," Minette said to her. The look she sent both women was one of amused contempt. "And so far, everything about you has been a surprise. From your stealing our ore, to shooting down our air crawler, to hunting our people, to blowing up your own ship. Not a friendly hello has been exchanged once, as far as I'm aware."

The captain looked away.

"We weren't responsible for those decisions." Kalia spoke without her boss giving her anything to interpret.

"Captain Linao looks pretty senior to me," Aurelia said.

Han watched the woman tightened her lips and cross her arms over her chest. So she understood Fjern, at least a little. Perhaps she was using Kalia more as a buffer, as a way to give herself time to respond.

She turned and spoke after a beat, and Kalia nodded.

"We still need medical attention."

"You'll get it." Miriam Yanno walked toward them, her gaze avid as she took the aliens in. "It should be easy enough to do. You don't seem to be physiologically different to us at all."

"We're not." The captain spoke directly to Yanno, her words short, her accent thick. "We from same ancestors."

"And yet, as my friend said, you didn't think to introduce your-selves before you began mining our ore." Han watched her lift a shoulder defensively.

"Where are you from?" Hedgeworth asked.

She hesitated, glanced at Kalia, and spoke quickly.

Kalia lifted her hands. "It won't do you any good to know, you can't get there. Not yet, anyway. Your tech's not advanced enough."

"True. I'm assuming you're from the group of Travelers that got one of the more welcoming planets?" Miriam asked.

Kalia glanced at Linao and was given a nod of permission to proceed.

"The Verdant String, yes." Kalia looked around her. "You have been held back in this place." Her gaze slid to Han and the other Gyr. "Although, in some things . . ."

"Let me guess, you don't have Gyr," Han said. "We got the gyra because we were going to less welcoming places."

Kalia translated what he said to Linao and the woman lifted her shoulders, rattled off a reply.

"We don't know this word, *gyra*. But the changing to monsters . . . that is something we do not have."

"Even for a linguist, your Fjerna is pretty good for someone who's just arrived. How did you learn it?" Evela Carnsworth, the fourth administrator, who Fliss had been introduced to on the walk over from the air crawler, was the one to ask that question.

Captain Linao and Kalia exchanged glances and kept their silence.

"My guess is they were here for some time, circling above, listening in," Ranuk said. "And then they got someone from Fjern to help them."

Kalia's quick glance toward Ranuk told Han they were right about the helper.

"Who?" he asked.

Linao took her time, speaking to Kalia in quick bursts.

The translator's lips thinned, clamped together. Kalia looked uncertain when she turned back to them.

"The captain doesn't know the details about this. Heldar arranged it, not her."

"He's dead, isn't he?" Ellen asked. "Your Fjerna helper?"

There was a long beat, and then Kalia and her boss participated in a long conversation.

Han watched the other aliens in the group as they spoke. Some watched the two women, others looked away or down.

They were troubled. Some shifted their gaze toward the thick bush.

"You left whoever it was out for the raveners?" Han guessed that would have been the easiest way to dispose of a body.

There was a sudden silence.

Everyone could read the body language of the captain.

She snapped something at Kalia.

"This is Heldar again. Captain Linao has nothing to do with it."

"Anyone inexplicably missing?" Han asked Miriam Yanno.

She looked thoughtful. "One of the Gyr Command comms staff disappeared a month ago. Never reported for work, seemed to have never returned to his home." She looked at the captain. "Elias Trovich."

The woman refused to look up from her feet.

"I'd take that as a yes," Han said.

"At least we don't need to worry about a traitor in the ranks," Barilar said. "Sounds like he's met his fate already."

"I just want to say something." Aurelia had been standing quietly to the side as the conversation progressed. "If either my team leader, or my colleague, die because they were attacked with your weapons, that is murder. As it is, I consider what was done to them grievous bodily harm, and as the captain, it had to be under your orders."

"Agreed." Han's gaze flicked to Pen, still lying beside the tree. "My colleague was also attacked, while she was trying to help your people, in fact."

Kalia's eyes were wide as she relayed that to her captain.

Linao's eyes lifted, met his, and then swept around the group. She barked something in response.

"She says you boarded her ship, she was merely defending it."

"You have no rights of defense on this planet, as you have not declared yourselves. You are interlopers. Every act of violence committed could be seen as an act of war."

Linao tightened her arms, which were crossed over her chest, and did not respond.

Kalia spoke to her, and Han could hear a pleading note in her voice.

"We aren't officially from the Verdant String." The man who'd called down the strike on the ship had risen to his feet during the conversation, and had taken a few steps toward them.

Linao turned to him and hissed, like an enraged tarinac.

He responded; a stream of invective. "She says she'll find a way to kill me. Can I ask for your help?" The man hunched his shoulders. "Will you give me sanctuary in exchange for information?"

"I think we can work something out." Miriam Yanno glanced at her colleagues, and they nodded.

"I am Ludig Darvan and I was hired as the navigator for this mission. Despite being from the Verdant String, we are not actually acting for the Verdant String Coalition." At his words, Captain Linao turned her back and he gave a bitter smile.

"You're a private enterprise?" Yanno asked.

He nodded. "Many years back, a few companies found two liveable planets before the Verdant String Coalition did, and they claimed and settled them, mined them." He blew out a breath. "Behaved badly."

A few of the other crew gave tiny nods at that.

"It all came to a bad end nearly a year ago. The Verdant String Coalition found out exactly what was going on, closed them down, and started prosecuting the heads of the companies." He gave a wry twist of his lips. "Some of them managed to grab the ships they'd built," he gestured to the smoking ruin behind them, "and run, looking for a new place to settle and start up again."

"And they think they can settle here?" Hedgeworth asked, outrage vibrating in his voice.

"No." Darvan shook his head. "They thought about it when we first found Fjern, until they saw the monsters. They weren't so keen after that. But scans showed minerals and ores that are worth a lot back home, so they decided to set up for half a year or so, take what they could, and move on."

There was silence for a moment, as everyone considered the implications. They had almost been invaded.

Being robbed seemed like a lesser problem, all things considered.

"Except now you've lost one of your ships," Han said.

"Thanks to him." Captain Linao turned her head to look at Darvan. She shook her head, as if she still couldn't believe it.

Darvan responded to her in their own language and they had another heated exchange.

Han had the feeling she was telling him she didn't care about the rules, she cared about not being stuck on a planet far from home.

"I think we need to get you to Nasnere for that medical help you need." Barilar had said next to nothing, Han had noticed, but now he stepped forward.

His words spurred everyone to movement and soon Lolia was ferrying people back and forth in her air crawler.

When they had all the aliens inside Gyr Command's big transporter, it lifted off, back to Nasnere, with Lolia's team shadowing it in their own air crawler again.

Barilar had stayed behind, and Han wondered why.

There was something he didn't like about the Gyr Command administrator, but he didn't have anything concrete to go on.

He did know that Barilar was sacrificing influence and power by staying back, not arriving triumphant with the aliens safely under guard.

A man like the administrator only allowed others to take the glory if there was a bigger pay-off later.

Han couldn't see what it was yet, but he knew it was there. He just had to find out what it was.

Barilar turned and caught his gaze. He waved his arm in the direction of Nasnere. "Hedgeworth already called for a team from Northern Nasnere Gyratta to help survey the site when we saw the lightning strike from the sky. They can help us here, and then I'm hoping Taque is happy to put them up at Renardo Gyratta tonight and I'll stay in town."

That made sense. There was certainly no safe place to stay out here overnight. Every building was either gone or severely damaged. Nasnere was a four hour air crawler flight from here, so it wasn't practical for Barilar to return to home base.

If Hedgeworth had called North Nasnere Gyratta when he'd seen the strike from space, then the Gyr would be here in under two hours.

Barilar turned away from him and Han watched as he moved over to the pile of damaged electronics and other detritus Delasio had piled to one side, crouching beside it and looking over each item.

Han lifted his gaze, met Delasio's, and his friend gave the tiniest of smiles.

Han kept his face neutral and moved toward Pen, Jerome and Taque, to check on them.

From Delasio's reaction, it looked as if he had managed to find at least some items with potential.

Han wanted to go home now, although it made sense to wait for the North Nasnere Gyratta warriors and speak to them before he and the team left for Vallent.

He wanted Pen to be checked by a medic, although she did seem better. And he didn't like the quick, sly looks Barilar was giving Fliss.

Taque was recovering, but Jerome was still not right, and he thought the Renardo team, at the very least, should go now.

He crouched beside Taque, and Karla and Minette, who were talking softly beside Jerome——an open med kit between them—— turned toward him.

"Time to get back to base," he suggested to Taque.

The Renardo gyratta leader gave a nod. "Yes."

Karla stood in relief, and between her and Minette, they lifted Jerome and carried him toward the air crawler.

Taque got carefully to his feet, and his team moved toward him. Like Karla, there was relief on all their faces.

They were all worried about Jerome.

"Thank you for having our back today," Han said, gripping Taque's arm at the elbow.

Taque nodded, his own grip a little less steady, but he had a grin on his face. "We got them." His gaze slid to Fliss, who was standing with Ranuk, a little way down the hill. "Watch over her, Han. She's too precious to lose."

"Agreed." He said nothing more, but Taque gave a grunt of approval and limped to the air crawler.

Barilar watched them from a distance, standing amidst the smashed buildings. He didn't say anything, or call out, but Han thought he looked put out that the Renardo team was going without requesting permission to do so.

The air crawler took off, Karla in the pilot's seat, and suddenly it was just his team and Barilar left.

He felt a strong urge to follow right behind them, board the air crawler and leave Barilar to his own devices.

There was nothing left here that was of interest, and he wanted to get back to Vallent and start contacting Fjern's gyrattas.

His encounter with Hedgeworth had brought the reality of their position home to him.

Gyr Command was not even trying to play nice anymore.

Or, at least, some of them weren't.

Miriam Yanno seemed to be disturbed by Hedgeworth's behavior, but she was the only one who'd pushed back against it.

It was time the Gyr faced facts. The threads that held the Gyr and Gyr Command together were coming undone.

It was time to forge a new way forward.

30

FLISS WATCHED THE RENARDO TEAM LEAVE WITH A TUG OF ENVY.

She wanted to be gone from this place, too.

She heard Han mention they were waiting to switch off with the North Nasnere Gyratta team, who'd be arriving soon, and in her view, they couldn't come soon enough.

It had been a very long day and there was nothing more they could do here, anyway. The mine was destroyed, and the direct strike to the mothership had made getting inside it impossible.

The heat of the strike had melted some of the exterior, and what had been the open rear ramp was a crumpled, melted mess, with no gap wide enough for even her or Ellen to wriggle through.

Even if they could get inside, there was no guarantee there would be any space to move beyond the small openings.

Barilar was walking around the ship, his face curiously blank, and he stopped to look at the still-smoldering, melded-together wreck that was the smaller alien air crawler——although the Verdant String translator, Kalia, had called it a hover——and Han's ship.

"What happened here?" he called, catching her gaze.

She reluctantly moved a little closer. "I wasn't here when that happened," she said.

"They were carrying Han's air crawler in a harness, bringing it to the mothership to load it up." Ranuk walked toward her, and something in his tone made her think he was lying. "I was lookout and I saw the whole thing. There wasn't a suitable place to land, because the mothership had taken up so much space, and in trying to set down close to the big ship, there was an accident."

Barilar shook his head in disbelief. "Incredible." He looked at burned-out wreck of Han's air crawler. Then at the remains of the mothership. "Their greed was their undoing."

That was the truth.

If they had left when they realized she and Han had gotten away and would be back with support, they would be safely in the skies above right now.

But they'd tried to take as much as they could before they left, and now they were a ship down, with some of their people prisoners.

Ranuk must have been thinking along the same lines, because he tipped his head up and looked at the late afternoon sky. "Do you think they'll negotiate for their people, or just leave?"

Fliss wondered the same. "The one I dealt with, Heldar, I don't think he'll be happy to be left behind. If he still has comms with the ship above, then someone will probably try to come and get him and the people he escaped with. But as for Captain Linao and her people?" She shrugged. "I don't know."

"I remember Kardenian saying some escaped." Barilar had walked closer to them, his gaze on her a little unsettling. "You know who they are?"

Fliss shook her head. "I didn't see them go, Ranuk did, as lookout. But Heldar wasn't with the prisoners, and I don't think he was in the mothership, so I'm guessing he was in the group that ran. He seemed to be in charge of the mine site, and if they're going to risk coming back for anyone, it would be him."

"We need to keep watch in case they do." Barilar glanced up at the sky. "I'll see if the North Nasnere team are in comms range, and tell them to keep a watch for the group."

He moved away, and Fliss noticed he only lifted his wrist unit close to his mouth when he was far enough from them to speak without being overheard.

She and Ranuk turned and walked toward the others.

"Was that story true?" she asked him quietly. "About how the air crawler crashed?"

Ranuk hunched his shoulders a little, then gave a small smile. "No."

They reached the others, Han, Delasio and Ellen standing together, Minette sitting beside Pen against the tree.

"What did happen, then?" she asked. She assumed whatever it was, the Gyr had good reason not to share it with Barilar.

"You happened." Ranuk's smile widened. "Han pushed that button, and their air crawler fell straight out of the sky."

She stared at him, then at the others.

Minette grinned at her from her seat on the ground. "It was . . . quite a surprise."

"I didn't think . . ." She trailed off. She had thought it would reset systems, but she had to admit, she hadn't thought about air crawlers at the time. She had been focused on heat signature systems. But there was no reason why her jammer shouldn't have affected all the aliens' systems, if they were based on similar tech.

Ranuk had been protecting her when he'd lied.

"Do the Renardo team know?" she asked.

Han gave a nod. "I don't think Taque will say anything. He feels protective of you."

That was true. Perhaps too protective, but . . .

"It's just electronics," she said. "Does it matter if Gyr Command knows?"

Han gave a tiny shrug. "I couldn't have made what you did." He looked around the group. "I don't think anyone else here could have, either."

Every gave a nod of agreement.

"So this is an advantage we have over the aliens, and right now, I think it's wise to keep our advantages to ourselves. Especially from

Gyr Command, who have enough interest in you already, without adding this to the mix."

She gave a sigh. This was not how she wanted things to be.

But then again, she had friends who stood up for her, a man who lit her gyra on fire, and a place to stay that was hers by right of who she was, not what she could do.

If she had to deal with Gyr Command, so be it.

She heard the sound of air blades, and everyone looked up and to the north.

Fliss thought she heard more than one set of blades, and sure enough, two air crawlers skimmed toward them over the trees.

One was the same size as their own air crawler, parked outside the gates, the other was a small, two-person vessel, like the one she and Han had taken the other evening to confront the zuby.

While they circled, looking for a place to land, the sound of a carranda's roar carried over the sound of the air blades.

It must be close.

The smaller air crawler banked and headed back over the trees, Fliss assumed to see why the carranda was riled up, and which way it was moving, and the larger crawler landed beside their own.

There was the usual Gyr meeting, which Fliss watched from where she sat beside Pen.

Han and Minette obviously knew the North Nasnere Gyr better than the rest of the Vallent team did.

"Han and Minette trained together with Evan and Isolde in Nasnere," Pen explained, voice a little stronger than it had been before. She had taken the lightning hit direct to her chest, and Fliss worried it had affected her lungs and heart.

Aside from Evan, who was clearly the team leader, and Isolde, there were two others from North Nasnere, one of whom Minette seemed to have met before, and a new Gyr who had to be introduced to everyone.

They had obviously seen the mothership from the air, but they moved toward it, clearly amazed by its existence and size.

Barilar moved from around the side of it to greet them, and Fliss wondered what on earth he'd been doing, lurking at the back.

She guessed he was looking for equipment they could salvage, and suddenly, she snapped her head to Pen.

"Did anyone bring the alien weapons from the clearing?"

Pen's eyes widened, and she tilted her head, thinking. "I don't think so. I can't remember for sure, but I was pretty messed up at the time."

That was true.

"I'll ask Delasio." She stood, moving toward the group, trying to remember the sequence of events.

She had thrown down the weapon she'd brought along after she'd shot the Verdant String soldier, and she remembered seeing four piled to one side after the events in the clearing, but since then, she hadn't been back that way, and had no idea if Ranuk or Delasio had moved them.

The Gyr were standing in a group together with Barilar, and Han's back was to her.

She caught Delasio's eye as she approached and jerked her head to the side.

He stepped out smoothly, but Han looked at her over his shoulder, eyebrow raised, as if he'd somehow known she was coming toward him.

She gave him a quick smile, to show that nothing was wrong, and moved toward Delasio. Han studied her for another beat, then turned back to the conversation as Evan asked him something.

"What is it?" Delasio's voice was soft.

She turned, forcing him to walk back toward Pen with her.

"I just remembered the alien weapons," she said. "The ones you and Ellen stacked near the clearing, and the one I brought with me from the gyratta this morning." She glanced at him. "Did anyone retrieve them?"

"Shiiit." He shook his head as they came to a stop beside Pen. "Well remembered. It's been quite the day, and I forgot about that."

Delasio looked behind him at the group. "I don't think Han would want Barilar to know about them, if possible."

"Why don't I go get them?" she said. "If anyone asks, you can say we left some equipment in the woods, and I've gone to collect it."

He looked uncertain, and she realized he was worried to let her go by herself.

"I'm as Gyr as you, Del."

Pen gave a snort from where she sat, propped up against the tree, but said nothing.

"But I worry," Delasio told her, eyes sparking with humor.

"It's just raveners out there now," she reminded him. "The aliens are all gone."

"True." He looked back at the group again, and she did, too. It looked as if they were all still deep in conversation, and Barilar wasn't paying any attention to her and Del at all.

"It's, what? A ten minute jog from here?"

"About that," Fliss agreed. "Although it'll take me longer to get back if I'm carrying all the weapons."

"Thirty minutes, then, from now. Then I come look for you."

She grinned at him and stepped behind Pen's tree, slipping away without fanfare, and when there was enough cover between her and the mine site, she ran, enjoying stretching her muscles after hours spent standing still on guard duty.

She found the clearing easily enough, and the four weapons, piled neatly together.

She slung two each over her shoulders and then went looking for her own weapon.

She finally found it, hidden beneath a bush, where she'd thrown it after she'd shot the fifth guard and jumped onto the largarti's back.

The fifth guard.

He'd shot the largarti, but when she'd finally got it to drop him, he no longer had his weapon.

So there was one more out here.

She studied the trees, trying to remember the way the largarti had run, and walked the way she thought they had gone, looking for the missing weapon.

She heard a faint sound, a warning that she wasn't alone, just in time to dive away.

The crackle of white light missed her, but it flickered and crawled over the bark of the tree near where she landed, and she had to lean away to avoid it touching her.

Before she could unhook one of the weapons on her shoulder, Heldar was suddenly in front of her, shoving a barrel in her face.

He was injured.

There was a nasty slash across his shoulder, which was still bleeding, and he looked terrible, his eyes were wild and his face was dirt-streaked.

"You're trying to kill me," he said, voice rough and weak, his accent heavy, as if he was struggling to recall how to speak Fjerna. "As if your monsters weren't bad enough."

"It seems you're the one trying to kill *me*." She was still crouched down, and she worked out she might be able to launch upward and flip, kicking him in the chest or face as she did it.

Of course, he might shoot her first, but from the look in his eyes, she didn't have much to lose, either way.

"No. Your people killed Bo and Rick, and the others. Took Bo's *laz*. I only just got away." He looked down at the weapon in his hand. "I couldn't believe my luck when I found this one."

"What people?" Everyone she knew had been within sight of her all day.

"The little hover. It came while we were fighting that monster. The monster got Unger, and then they landed and tried to kill us all."

Was he talking about the North Nasnere air crawler that had gone looking for the carranda?

She stared at him in shock.

"Why would they do that?" she asked. It made no sense. They'd be more likely to save the aliens and take them prisoner, especially as Heldar was the mine site leader.

She knew Barilar had communicated that to them.

Except . . . his injury did look a lot more like a cutter slash than a carranda injury.

Like someone had tried to take his head, and missed.

Her gyra prickled beneath her skin, in the way they sometimes did when another Gyr was close by.

Not Delasio, her gyra told her. Not Han. But someone.

Before she could surge up and flip, Heldar hit her with a stream of light, just a single, quick burst.

She hadn't known the weapons could do that.

She felt the punch of it, but he had set it very low, she realized, lower than when she'd been hit before, and she'd only received a single, small pulse.

She was momentarily incapacitated, but that's all he needed in order to grab her and step behind her, the weapon to her head.

She tried to breathe through the pain, her gyra shivering in shock beneath her skin.

It was quick and light, she told them. *Keep calm.*

"Don't come closer, or I'll kill one of your people," Heldar called out, and when Fliss was able to blink away the pain and focus, she saw a Gyr standing between the trees.

He was holding a cutter in one hand, and an alien weapon in the other.

"One of mine?" the Gyr asked. He studied her. "Vallent Gyratta?"

"Yes," she managed to get out.

"Pity," he responded. And then he lifted the alien weapon, and shot them both.

31

HER GYRA FORCED HER AWAKE.

She could sense their panic, their outrage at the harm they had suffered.

You will recover, she told them.

She had felt them move to her extremities in the brief moment between when the Gyr warrior had lifted the alien weapon he must have taken from Heldar's group, and when the stream of light had hit her chest.

Most of them had avoided a direct hit.

Some might not recover, they told her, and she could feel their fright.

They will, she soothed. *It may take more time.*

We will take his gyra in compensation for any we may have lost, they vowed, and she realized they were talking about the Gyr who had shot her.

She had no problem with that.

She wasn't quite sure why he had shot her, though.

He was Gyr. There were plenty of ways he could have dealt with Heldar which didn't involve hurting her.

And if Heldar was to be believed, and given what had happened, she was coming to the conclusion that on this topic, he could be, someone was trying to kill him, not take him prisoner.

He was probably already dead.

That thought pulled her sharply from the half-conscious musing she was doing, and focused her attention on where she was, and what was happening around her.

She opened her eyes to find she was lying under a tarpaulin, bound by her wrists and ankles. It was completely dark beneath the covering but she could feel hard metal tubes around her.

She tried to think what they could be, and then remembered what she had been carrying when she was shot.

The aliens' weapons.

We should destroy them, her gyra said.

She thought about it, and eventually agreed. While they might be useful if she got free, they could be turned against her just as easily, and neither she nor her gyra were prepared to have that happen again.

She let her gyra have free rein.

The Gyr who shot us also has one, though, she reminded her gyra.

They didn't like to be reminded.

She sensed the white hot anger, the feeling of betrayal.

They expected Gyr to protect Gyr.

She heard voices approaching, and lay very still.

"You'll have to pretend to look for her." Barilar's voice was unmistakeable.

"We could drop her somewhere close to a ravener, cut her to draw them out. That would take care of things." The voice of the warrior who shot her stirred her gyras' anger, as well as her own.

"No. Gyr Command wants her, and this is a perfect way to have her, without rousing the Vallent Gyratta's suspicions." Barilar's voice was soft. "Heldar is dead?"

"Head separated from his body." The Gyr moved, she could hear the rustle of his clothing. "Just in case, because he was almost dead, anyway. I think the weapon was set to a kill level, or close to it."

"What if Kardenian or his team find the body?" Barilar asked.

"I left Reese out there, getting rid of the rest of the group's bodies. He can say he fought a few of the escapees because they tried to shoot him, if anyone finds them before the raveners do."

"That will work. Take the air crawler up, and when it gets too dark, I'll make an excuse why you have to go back to Nasnere. Will she be unconscious that long?"

"No idea." The words were drawled, as if the Gyr was baiting Barilar. "I've never used alien weapons before today. Heldar hit her with a shot first, then me. Even though she's Gyr, she took a lot of damage. But she's restrained, so it doesn't matter, either way."

"All right. You're sure Evan doesn't suspect anything? He thinks you're a loyal Gyr?"

"Yes." The answer was short.

Fliss wondered if his tone was because the warrior felt guilty betraying his team leader.

Her gyra at least were mollified that only two of the North Nasnere warriors were betrayers, although they thought that was two too many.

"Good. Keep it that way." Barilar's voice became harder to hear, as if he'd turned away. "I've told Kardenian that Evan needs to stay here and help me, but you can help search from the air."

"What did you tell them about Reese?"

"That you thought you saw someone in the trees, and Reese's searching on foot, you by air."

"He didn't look happy when you were talking to him."

Barilar barked a laugh. "No. He wanted everyone to help, but he'll take what he can get. Fortunately he was in too much of a hurry to argue. He and his team are all gone, either on foot or by air, looking for her. So tell Reese to watch out for them, and keep out of sight."

The door to what she guessed by now must be the two-person air crawler opened, and the warrior got in.

She could hear a moment of silence before he started the engine.

He'd looked back to see if she'd moved, she guessed.

As he lifted off, something shifted, rolling toward her in what she knew now to be the small rear hold.

The other alien weapon?

He wouldn't have been able to take it out with him, that would have made the Vallent team suspicious.

She lifted the tarpaulin and it rolled up against one of the other weapons.

She carefully lifted her head, and laid her cheek on it, and her gyra gleefully made it a useless metal tube.

The air crawler banked and she thought of Han and the others below, maybe Delasio and Pen in the big air crawler above, all looking for her.

But there was nothing she could do about that now.

She would simply have to survive this, and get back to them.

"I SHOULDN'T HAVE LET her go alone." Delasio sounded sick, and Minette glanced over at Han with a *do-something* look in her eyes.

Han grasped Del's shoulder. "She's Gyr, Del. She was just going to quietly pick up the weapons. There isn't a single Gyr you would have hesitated to send out to do that, and Fliss would not have had it any other way."

Del nodded, his eyes on the ground, looking for any trace of her.

Han was fighting a roaring inferno within, a mix of guilt and rage and fear. Because Gyr Command had her.

He was sure of it.

Not Barilar himself, although the smarmy bastard was involved, Han would bet his gyra on it. He had been in sight of Han the whole time, as had Evan, Isolde and the others from North Nasnere who'd come in the bigger air crawler.

"It was either that shifty Jaco, in the two-seater, or his friend who he dropped off to hunt for the escapees." Minette had taken against Jaco in the brief minutes they'd met the warrior, before he'd gone back to his two-seater to help them look for Fliss.

"Maybe." Han wasn't ruling it out. "But Barilar or Hedgeworth——or Yanno or Carnsworth——I'm not discounting any of them, could have called in others in advance. Any one of them would have known Fliss was out here with us, and also that there was potential to snatch her."

"We're sure it's not a ravener?" Minette asked.

Ranuk made a sound up ahead and Han sprinted over to him, Minette and Del on his heels.

"Something happened here." Ranuk was crouched low.

There was blood on the leaves covering the ground, not enough to signify a death, but plenty for a bad injury.

Han reached out a hand and touched the blood with his fingers, felt the tension in him ease a little.

"Not Fliss's." He leaned back on his haunches. "Who's could it be? It isn't a Gyr's."

"One of the escapees?" Minette guessed. "This Heldar person Fliss spoke about?"

"Maybe." Han studied the surroundings. There had been a fight here, and . . .

"Look." He pointed to a tree and Del moved over to crouch beside it.

"The mark of an alien weapon." The big warrior's fingers brushed the blackened bark.

"You think the aliens shot Fliss and took her?" Ranuk sounded unsure, and Han felt the same way.

He didn't want to let go of his certainty that Gyr Command had her. However . . . "If they have taken her, it's as a bargaining chip. They'll want to get back their own people in exchange for her." Which meant she was alive.

And tracking aliens down and rescuing Fliss would be easier than taking on Gyr Command.

He lifted his wrist unit, letting Pen and Ellen in the air crawler above know what they'd found, and then they spread out, silent and on alert, looking for signs to follow.

Once Del found the path, it was easy.

It looked, strangely, as if two people had been dragged through the trees.

Han wondered if Fliss had injured or killed one before she was taken down, which was more than possible, and would explain the blood.

The path led to an open area in the woods, big enough for an air crawler to land.

Han had a sinking feeling that if Gyr Command were involved, then Fliss was already long gone, flown out to some secret location.

He walked the perimeter, looking for any sign of her, and when he saw more blood, he lifted a hand, but the others were already focused on him, moving his way.

He followed the trail——it was a short one, but by the time he reached the end, the body he found there had been ravaged.

Two waronga were fighting over an arm, which they had almost completely detached from the corpse.

The head was already gone, but cleanly. With a cutter.

"It's not Fliss." Del breathed the words out on a relieved sigh.

"No, it's an alien." Minette eyed the man and the waronga warily. "Why would Reese kill him, not capture him?"

Good question.

Han moved toward the waronga, cutter out and sparking, but they had their prize and they ran, cooperating for once in the face of a larger group of enemies.

He crouched beside the alien, but there was nothing on his body but a long-handled knife, and no clue as to who he'd been.

Except . . . someone had taken a knife from Fliss.

Heldar.

Han turned the hilt over in his hand, looking for a sign it was hers, but there was no way to know.

He slid it into his pack and rose up. There was no sign of Fliss here, and no sign of the rest of the escapees, either.

"She's gone, isn't she?" Del asked as Ellen landed the air crawler in the clearing behind them.

"We'll make absolutely sure, first. But I think so." There would be some sign of her, otherwise.

Han and the others walked back to the clearing, where Ellen was getting out of the air crawler, leaving Pen still lying inside.

"It's almost dark," she said, and held out Fliss's heat signature screen.

Han had forgotten all about it.

He took it, switched it on, and saw it was dangerously close to being out of power. He turned in the direction of the body, moving the screen, and the flash of a heat signature bloomed and then disappeared as he moved past it.

He stopped, and Minette leaned against his side, body as tense as his own, as he slowly aimed the screen back to the right.

It was the usual indistinct shape made of orange light, but Han thought it might be a person.

It was smaller than a ravener, bigger than a waronga. Although it could be a yinalla.

Or even an isilo, drawn by the blood.

The screen went blank, and he handed back to Ellen.

"Dead," he said. "Pity."

He dipped his head close to her ear. "Stay here with Pen, but be ready for anything. And I'm not talking raveners, I'm talking traitorous Gyr."

Ellen gave a nod and drew her cutter as she leaned casually against the side of the air crawler.

The others were already doing what he wanted them to, spreading out and walking between the trees, as was the way of the Gyr, when they were sufficiently bonded as a team, and had been together long enough.

He had never worked out exactly how it happened.

Whether the communication was gyra to gyra, bypassing the conscious mind, or whether it was simply that when you were together enough, and had the same information, warriors had a good sense of what to do next.

He walked directly toward where the heat signature had come from, pretending to study the ground as he went.

Del and Ranuk had taken the flanks, moving fast and quietly on the outer edges.

Minette ambled in a random, zigzag pattern, going where the whim took her, as if she had no agenda, other than to investigate whatever caught her eye.

"Fliss," she suddenly shouted, cupping her hands on either side of her mouth. "Fliss!"

A Gyr stepped out from behind a massive tree, cutter out but by his side, and called a greeting.

Minette had seen him, Han guessed, or had sensed he was close and had given him a good excuse to show himself.

"You're looking for your team member?" He started moving toward them. "I'm Reese, North Nasnere Gyratta. Jaco sent me a comm to keep an eye out for her while I was down here, looking for that group of aliens that got away."

"Hannu Kardenian," Han said, hand out to grasp Reese's elbow, but the man lifted his hand in apology to prevent the usual greeting, to show it was covered in blood.

"Trouble?" Han asked. Minette stepped up beside him. "This is Minette, one of my team."

Reese nodded toward her. "I came across the group we're looking for. Bastards shot at me, and I killed one of them. You might have found the body?"

"We did. I wondered what had happened." Han watched him carefully. He could be telling the truth, but it was harder to tell, Gyr to Gyr.

"They had a few of those weapons on them, attacked me, and I just got out of the way. I had to kill one, but the rest ran off. I've been skulking around, looking for them ever since. Might as well, since Jaco's above, helping you look for your friend."

"Do you think the aliens could have taken Fliss?" Minette asked him. "To trade for the prisoners we took?"

Reese blinked at that. "I hadn't thought of that. I didn't see her, but if they got her with one of their weapons, she could have been lying unconscious somewhere while I fought them." He lifted his shoulders. "Could be."

"You found something, boss?" Del called out, but he was coming up from behind Han, when Han knew damn well he'd been ahead of himself and Minette. Which meant he'd doubled back.

"Reese, from North Nasnere." Han turned to his friend, but Del's face was absolutely unreadable.

Reese waved his blood-slicked hand at Del.

"You need a lift back to the mine site?" Minette asked.

"That would be welcome," Reese said, flashing her a smile. "It's getting dark and I think Jaco will probably meet me there."

He got into step with Minette, and she chatted easily to him as they walked back to the clearing.

Han let them go a little way ahead.

"What did you find?" he asked so softly, it was barely audible.

"Four other bodies," Del murmured. "Up ahead. Heads removed."

"Strange Reese didn't mention that." Han could feel the cold rage rising up, drowning out the fear for a moment. "Or that there was no way they could've taken Fliss, because they were dead. By his hand."

He was glad Del had doubled back, so Reese thought they didn't know about the others. Best to keep him thinking he'd fooled them. "Where's Ranuk?"

"He took some images of the dead, then he was going back to the clearing, to pretend he'd been there all along."

Han decided he wanted to talk to Jaco again. Have a look inside his air crawler.

When they got back to the mine site, that's exactly what he was going to do.

32

Fliss knew the moment they came in to land.

The sound of the air crawler engine changed, although Jaco landed so smoothly, he was shutting down before she was even sure they'd touched the ground.

They were north west of the mine site, and eight hours had passed since Jaco had turned away from the farce of pretending to look for her, and flown off.

He'd gone due north for twenty minutes, pretending to be headed back to Nasnere, and then he'd diverted north west. Her gyra had a sense of direction that was spookily accurate, and she didn't doubt them for a moment.

She had fallen asleep during the long flight, and she guessed Jaco had set the air crawler to autopilot for some of the time as well.

Now, as she heard him move around up front, she kept still and limp. By his own admission, she had taken a lot of damage.

Let him think she was still unconscious.

Until she had a way to free herself from her restraints, she would play almost-dead.

Although the bonds weren't extremely tight, and her gyra were working to ensure her hands and feet didn't swell, she could tell it would hurt when they were removed. She wouldn't be at her fighting best for several minutes afterward.

Her pretence would also force him to carry her. Which meant she would be up close and personal with him. She could take his gyra any time she wanted.

Yes, her gyra said. She could sense their righteous fury.

Jaco eventually climbed out of the front, and something in the long pauses she'd noticed from him told her he didn't want to leave the air crawler. He didn't want to be wherever they were.

Interesting.

And not particularly encouraging.

If even the Gyr betraying her did not like the destination, she had a sinking feeling things were bad.

Finally he came around and opened up the back.

He moved the alien weapons out of the way with a grunt, piling them to one side so he could slide her closer to him.

He flipped the tarpaulin up and away, grunted again at the sight of her.

"Shit, I hope you're not dead," he muttered.

Jaco hauled her close, put a hand against her throat, and blew out a breath.

"Pulse thready, but there. Thank fuck."

The threadiness had to be her gyra, messing with him.

It was quiet wherever he'd taken her. She could hear the sigh of wind in trees, the high-pitched dawn chirping of birds, which was interesting, as there were very few song birds on Fjern.

So, an isolated place in a forest.

There was a fresh, dewy scent to the air, and a slight chill, which made Fliss even more convinced it was shortly before dawn.

Jaco lifted her over his shoulder and started walking, his boots crunching on dried leaves underfoot.

She risked opening her eyes, careful to keep her body completely relaxed.

She wanted to see how many people she was dealing with before she showed her hand, but so far there was no one in the growing light of pre-dawn but Jaco.

She got a close up look at steps as Jaco climbed them, and they were covered in moss, with leaves piled up on each one, as if he was the first person to use them in a while.

If this was the Swathe, the vast forest that lay to the west of Nasnere, then it wouldn't take long for leaves to build up, but even if she was just looking at a few days' worth, that meant there wasn't a lot of traffic coming and going from this place.

Jaco entered a code on the keypad by the door, she could hear the faint ping with each press of his fingers, and then he shuffled forward as it swung open.

We know the code, her gyra told her. *We could hear which buttons he pushed.*

Are his gyra aware they are coming to us? she asked them.

Yes, was the answer. *They understand he is unworthy. They will come.*

Fair enough.

The door thunked closed behind her, the sound heavy and metallic, and she smelled stale air and the faint tang of mustiness.

Disused, or just rarely used?

Jaco walked down a narrow passage and then opened another door, with Fliss trusting her gyra to catch the code for this one, too.

Of course, they told her.

This second section of the building smelled different.

Someone was living here.

She caught the faint scent of food, of tea, and the clean, fresh scent of a shower soap that Fliss herself liked to use.

The sound of bars rattling sent a flash of adrenalin through her, though.

There was a prisoner here.

Jaco flipped her suddenly, laying her down at his feet.

She felt the restraints around her wrists and ankles release as he unshackled her, crouching so close beside her she could feel his boots and knees against her side.

Then he rose up and stepped over her, but stood close enough she could easily reach him.

With him standing in front of her, she opened her eyes again, saw a massive space with a long wall of bars caging off three quarters of it.

On her and Jaco's side, the smaller side, there was a bench, a small kitchen area, a table and chairs, and a couch.

On the prisoner's side, there was more or less the same, except it included a bed and what looked like a bathroom with a privacy screen.

"I brought you a friend," Jaco said.

A woman stood with one slim hand curved around a bar. "Who?" Fliss caught her gaze, saw her repress a flinch of surprise at the realization that Fliss was awake and aware.

"Name of Fliss. You should be thrilled to have her, Lucy. She's like the little one you're growing inside you. Gyr-born."

Lucy sucked in a breath, her eyes going wide, and for the first time, Fliss noticed she was pregnant.

Now is the time, her gyra told her.

She couldn't agree more.

She slid a hand up Jaco's trouser leg, her fingers closing around the skin of his ankle.

He jerked in surprise, looking down at her.

"Please." She fluttered her eyelids, looking up at him, her voice faint. "Where am I? What happened?"

He tried to shake her off, but she tightened her grip, feeling his gyra slide out of him and into her palm, the almost icy-cold buzz as they sank into her body.

As soon as it was done, she released him, rolled and rose to her feet, all pretence at confusion gone.

She shook out her hands, feeling the burn as blood circulated freely for the first time.

Her feet pricked with pins and needles.

"What . . .?" Jaco listed to one side, stumbling until he fetched up against the table, then gripped the edge to steady himself. "Did you . . ." He lifted his gaze to her in horror. "Did you take my *gyra*?"

"How could I do that?" Fliss asked. She wasn't going to admit to anything. "I have no gyra-na." She lifted both hands.

"No," he conceded, "but I feel . . . strange."

"You're capturing and imprisoning your own," Fliss said. "You should feel strange. You should feel a lot more than strange. You should feel ashamed."

"Jaco-boy here wouldn't be Gyr at all without his promise to betray his own, would you?" Lucy leaned against the bars, her face neutral, although Fliss thought she could see tension in the way she gripped the metal poles.

"You were given your gyra on condition you work for Barilar?" Fliss asked, the depth of her shock making her voice rise.

"What's it to you?" Jaco tilted the other way, as if giddy, and then lifted his wrist unit up as if to initiate a comm.

Fliss lunged at him, grabbing his arm.

Her gyra killed the unit a moment before she was forced to step back, arm raised to block the punch he aimed at her face.

"You've done something to me." He lifted his wrist to his mouth again, and this time she let him.

When he realized his comms unit was no longer working, he narrowed his eyes, edging back.

He drew his cutter, but the spark of plasma would not light.

"You *have* taken my gyra." He stared at her, and she could see absolute hatred in his gaze.

"You didn't deserve them." She backed up a little. He wasn't Gyr anymore, but he was armed and she was not.

He struck out, his cutter slashing at her midriff and she jumped back, fetching up against the bars.

He backed away, moving to the door. He tapped in the code, cutter extended to keep her back.

He pulled the door open and slammed it closed behind him, and she could hear him running down the passage.

She went after him, letting her gyra take over as her fingers punched in the code, not allowing herself to look back at Lucy.

At how she would feel at being left inside, locked up.

She had to stop Jaco taking the air crawler.

They were stranded too far from home without it.

But she was too late.

It was already lifting up when she burst through the outside door.

She ran and leaped high, her fingers sparking along the undercarriage, just grazing the metal, and the engine coughed, but it managed to lift higher, wobbling a little.

It wasn't working as it should, though.

She could see Jaco had to fight it as he navigated away, but he managed to keep it going, and it disappeared over the trees.

Damn.

Han would have worked out it was him who'd taken her, though.

When Barilar pulled Jaco off the search for her and sent him off in the direction of Nasnere, he must have figured it out.

Fliss was certain of it.

She'd have preferred the air crawler for herself and Lucy, but maybe Jaco would run into Han when he got back. Be persuaded to talk.

At the very least, his lack of gyra would tell a story.

One that had her fingerprints all over it.

She stared out at trees so tall that they almost blocked the light, thick and dark green.

She turned to look at the building, studying it in the weak, green light filtering through the forest.

It was long and low, the dull gray of prefabricated walls, with a flat roof that had grasses and moss planted on it.

All but invisible from the air, she guessed. Except for the comms booster tower that sat in the far corner, as close to the trees as possible.

It had been painted green, and Fliss guessed it would be hard to see from the air, as well.

Even if Han had worked out who had taken her, he wouldn't know where to look.

And if he did find Jaco and got him to talk, that was eight hours or more in the future, and it would take him at least that long again to fly back.

She couldn't risk staying here, hoping for a rescue.

She was going to have to do the rescuing herself.

She walked back up the stairs, entered the code and jogged back down the passage to Lucy's prison cell.

When she opened the door, she saw Lucy hadn't moved, her gaze catching on Fliss's as she stepped inside.

Fliss walked to the bars, looking for a way in.

The barred door was in the middle, and it was secured with a massive padlock.

"The key is over there." Lucy pointed and Fliss turned to see a cabinet pushed up against the far wall. "They leave it here because there are a few different people who come to check on me, and they never know who might be the one who's free. So they decided to have just the one key, easily accessible."

The cabinet had gouge marks in it, and Fliss turned back to look at Lucy. "String and a knife?" she asked.

"String and a fork." Lucy pulled it from her pocket. "They took the knives a while back." She tossed the fork onto the table near her. "I sometimes thought trying to get that drawer open would drive me mad."

She didn't ask Fliss to hurry, or even ask her if she was going to set her free.

Too many disappointments, Fliss guessed as she opened the drawer and took the key out. She walked over and opened the padlock, lifting it up and opening the door.

Lucy seemed to shudder out a breath.

"We should probably hurry. But we'll need supplies. Jaco got away in the air crawler."

Lucy put out a tentative hand. "Are you really Gyr-born?" Her other hand rested on the curve of her stomach.

"Yes." Fliss let her fingers curl around Lucy's. Her gyra exploded in delight at the feel of another Gyr-born, almost giddy with joy.

She lifted her gaze, locked eyes with Lucy. "Are you Lucille Defoe?"

Lucy nodded. "My baby is so . . . happy to meet you. And so am I." She let her hand drop with reluctance. "Did you really take Jaco's gyra?"

"I did."

"So you're a walking gyra-na." She eyed Fliss and then gave a sudden, delighted grin.

"Not really." Fliss grinned back. "When I take gyra, I don't pass them on. I keep them."

Lucy stilled, took a tiny step back. "How many gyra have you taken?" she asked.

"Three sets, now. Although one of them wasn't me, the gyra came to me on their own." She noticed Lucy's sudden distance. "It has always been in self-defence. I don't go around robbing Gyr of their gyra."

Lucy cleared her throat. "How did you know my name?"

"The Gyr in my gyratta, Vallent, are worried about you. In the South Nasnere Gyratta, too. They'll be very pleased to see you alive and well." She thought of Han, and her heart gave a little leap in her chest. Now he would be worrying about her, as well as Lucy.

And she . . . she worried about him. About what he would do to find her.

She could see no obstacle she would allow to stand if he were in danger. She had a suspicion he would do the same for her.

Nasnere might be burning.

"Lolia's been looking for me?" Lucy asked.

Fliss blinked. Forced herself to nod. "Lolia. Hannu. All their team members. I think they're going to break with Gyr Command over you."

Lucy sucked in a breath. "I know one person is looking for me, one I'm sure of, but I didn't realize the others . . ." She brushed away a tear with the back of her hand. She had moved over to the cupboards while they'd been talking, and now she opened them up. "Supplies."

Fliss stepped close and eyed what they had available.

It wasn't bad, actually.

They wouldn't starve. Not for a few days, anyway.

But they had a long way to go.

33

HAN CROUCHED ON THE ROOF OF THE BUILDING OPPOSITE VALLENT GYR Command, watching.

Teranimo had not come out all morning, but Han had arranged for a message to be delivered, telling the scientist he wanted to meet him privately, and the time of the meeting was near.

Was Teranimo going to ignore him?

That was a possibility, he acknowledged.

If he did, Han would find another way to get to him. And he wouldn't be so polite.

The door to headquarters suddenly opened, and Teranimo stepped out.

He looked disheveled, a look Han had noticed him sporting more and more, lately. Like he hadn't slept and had sat hunched over screens for hours.

No one had come out of the building since Han's message had been delivered, and he'd had no warning from Ranuk——who was watching the back of the building——that anyone had exited that way.

It looked like Teranimo was going to meet him alone, just as Han had requested.

Han dropped down to the balcony below the roof's edge, moving through the empty top floor apartment he'd broken into earlier, and racing down the stairs.

He emerged in a back alley and then moved through a series of short cuts to get to the meeting point ahead of the scientist.

The building he'd chosen was abandoned, an old storage facility that was slated for an upgrade that hadn't yet happened.

He kept to the shadows once he was inside, letting his gyra sift through all the creaks and groans of the old warehouse in case there was anyone here who shouldn't be.

Teranimo, clearly making an effort to be quiet and stealthy, slipped through the half-open door on silent feet.

He came to a stop in a beam of sunlight shining through the windows above the door. Making himself the perfect target.

"Han?" His whisper sounded over-loud in the silence.

Han stepped out of the shadows, and Teranimo's lips thinned into a hard line.

"A bit overdramatic, isn't it? You could have just come to my office at headquarters."

"Could I?" Han asked. "I don't think so."

Teranimo eyed him. "Why do you say that?"

Han moved closer to him, watching his face. "What happened to Lucille Defoe?"

A shutter went down on Teranimo's face, and he finally stepped out of the light, into the darker shadows.

"Just tell me what's going on, Han. Trust me."

Han studied him. Someone was going to have to give here. To find Fliss, he'd do anything, but Teranimo was asking for trust.

We could always kill him after, if he's lying, his gyra said.

That was true.

Han fisted his hands. "Fliss was taken."

Teranimo stiffened, sucking in a breath. "Taken, how?"

"Taken by an air crawler at the mine site."

"What?" The word was shaky. "Who took her?"

Han stared at him. "What do you know about it?"

For a beat, rage sparked in Teranimo's eyes, and Han blinked.

"I know *nothing* about it." Teranimo's voice was shaking. "I want to know. Who. Took. Her?"

"Before I answer that, I want to know what's going on with you. Why did you tell me to hold back making a fuss about Lucille Defoe?"

Han had sensed something was off with the scientist for a while, and he wasn't putting his cards on the table without finding out the cause.

Teranimo leaped forward, grabbing hold of Han's jacket in his fists, jerking him close.

Han let him. There was nothing a Fjerna could do to him that he could not counter.

After a moment, as if recognizing the futility of his actions, Teranimo let him go with a curse, and turned away.

"Lucille Defoe and I were lovers," he said, stopping with his back still turned.

Han felt a tingle at his nape.

He hadn't known that, but it wasn't uncommon for Gyr and Gyr Command staff to form romantic liaisons. They interacted with each other more than most.

"When she couldn't shift, she was removed from her gyratta and came to live in Gyr Command headquarters in Nasnere. I was stationed there at the time, and what started as something casual, grew to mean a lot more." Teranimo sucked in a breath. "She was afraid of the transfer ceremony, but accepting of it. She knew when she was recruited that if she couldn't shift, she'd have to give her gyra back."

He finally turned back to face Han. "But then the gyra-na broke, and her gyra stayed inside her." He rubbed a hand over his hair. "There was a lot of consternation over that, and I was asked to do tests on her to see if there was something different about her that had made her gyra resistant to leaving her."

"And was there?" Han asked.

"Yes." Teranimo looked pale, tired, and ill. "She was pregnant."

"What?" Han stared at him.

"She'd been living at Gyr Command for three weeks before she had to go through the transfer ceremony. In that time we'd . . ." Teranimo cleared his throat. "We saw a lot of each other."

"What happened after the tests?" Han asked.

"Like a fool, like a fucking, clueless fool, I wrote up my findings and published them to the shared Gyr Command system."

Han stood quietly while the silence grew between them.

"They took her?" he said at last.

"Whoever 'they' are. Yes." Teranimo looked around, moved toward an old piece of machinery, and sat on the edge of it, as if his legs wouldn't hold him up anymore. "I loaded the data in the evening. The next morning, she was gone. Vanished as if she had never been there in the first place."

"What was the excuse given?" Han asked.

"There *was* no excuse given. That's just it. Everyone simply professed ignorance. It was: *Maybe she left on her own. Maybe she's on the run. Maybe you're making a fuss about nothing, Teranimo. Let's give you a break and send you to Vallent.*"

Teranimo lifted haunted eyes to his. "I've been searching for her every day since then. And there is no way she wasn't taken. Who by, I really can't say. I have my suspicions, but I haven't managed to get any hard evidence on anyone. So, I'm begging you, Han, if you have an idea of who took Fliss, please tell me. Because it'll be the first headway I've made in seven months."

"Jaco of the North Nasnere Gyratta," Han said.

"A Gyr?" Teranimo seemed stunned. "A Gyr took another Gyr?"

"I'm almost completely sure of it. And his friend, Reese, is in it with him. And I think Pal Barilar, of Nasnere Gyr Command."

"How do you know this?" Teranimo sounded . . . broken, as if he was afraid to trust Han might have found the culprits. "I spend every waking moment I have searching, I've visited every single Gyr Command headquarters on Fjern in the last seven months, inventing any reason I could for going there. Whoever took Lucy must know why I'm doing it, but they just let me go, unhindered. Which tells me she's nowhere I can easily find her."

"So we watch Barilar, and we talk to Jaco and Reese." Han already had both groups covered.

"Do they know you suspect them?" Teranimo asked.

"I don't think Reese does. Barilar might be a little more suspicious."

"And Jaco?"

"Jaco was the one who flew Fliss away in his air crawler." Which had been right there, at the mine site. He must have had Fliss inside, and Han had stood nearby, so focused on finding Fliss in the woods he hadn't given the air crawler or the warrior a second look.

He'd known it for sure when they'd gotten back to the mine after looking for Fliss and Barilar had given some bullshit reason why Jaco had to fly off to Nasnere.

Han hadn't believed him.

Not. At. All.

"I've checked," he told Teranimo, "and Jaco hasn't gone back to his gyratta. He hasn't been seen in Nasnere, either."

"So he's still traveling with her. Or guarding her, wherever he's taken her." Teranimo's voice was soft. Thoughtful.

"That's our best guess."

"Our?" Teranimo raised his head.

"I may have the most to lose here," Han said. "But my gyratta is behind me. Has been from the start."

"Anyone you specifically don't trust?" Teranimo asked.

Han lifted a shoulder. "It pains me, but the whole North Nasnere Gyratta has to be suspect. Even if Evan and Isolde don't know what Jaco and Reese are up to, they may say something to someone who does."

Teranimo nodded. "And South Nasnere?"

Han hesitated. He trusted Lolia. Did not want to think any of her team could be accomplices, but if Jaco could, so could they.

"Lolia is not involved, but team members she trusts could be. So I'm keeping her out of it for now." He was keeping everyone but his own out. It was just safer that way, and he refused to make another mistake when it came to protecting Fliss.

"Why do you say you have the most to lose?" Teranimo frowned suddenly, as if replaying what Han had said in his head.

"Because Fliss is my gyrbar." Han didn't know if he should be telling the scientist this, but the time for secrets was over. "Did you tell Gyr Command that Fliss was Gyr-born?"

"No!" Teranimo looked horrified. "When I worked out she was, I wanted to find out everything I could about her. I am going to be the father of a Gyr-born. I was desperate to speak to her, to study her. But I would never have made the same mistake again."

Secrets.

If he'd known what Teranimo was truly up to, known he hadn't spoken to his bosses at Gyr Command, he would never have put Fliss in their sights. He would have kept quiet about her.

"Your gyrbar?" Teranimo finally spoke up again. "Like the myths?"

"That's just the thing," Han told him. "It's not a myth."

It was as real as things got.

And Gyr Command was about to find that out.

The hard way.

34

"MY BABY WANTS YOU TO TOUCH ME AGAIN," LUCY SAID, STOPPING, HER hands going to her lower back.

She looked tired.

"How long were you locked up?" Fliss asked, reaching for her hand. Because Lucy was Gyr, and should be stronger than this.

She hadn't had the chance to exercise, to move, for months, was Fliss's guess.

"Seven months. Two weeks. One day." Lucy leaned against a tree, and curled her fingers around Fliss's.

They had done this numerous times since they'd started walking.

Fliss and her gyra were as enthusiastic about the contact as Lucy's baby.

"She's so bright and sweet," Fliss said, smiling up at Lucy. "Have you got a name for her yet?"

"Madeleine."

The moment she said the name, Fliss felt the baby react.

She smiled. "She knows it already."

"Yes." Lucy smoothed her hand over her stomach. "Did your mother interact with you like this? Speak to you?"

Fliss shook her head. "You have an advantage. My mother wasn't Gyr, my father was."

"Is it an advantage?" Lucy asked quietly. "Maybe it would be if I was free, if I was living my old life. I'm worried . . ." She bit her lip. "I'm worried my fear, and panic, and . . . rage, have affected her."

Fliss gripped her hand a little tighter, then let it go. "Your baby is Gyr-born. She has gyra to protect her. They would have filtered out anything that would harm her."

Lucy drew in a shuddering breath. "You're sure?"

"I am positive." She gave a lopsided grin. "I should know."

"True." Lucy pushed off. "Okay, I'm ready to keep moving."

"Not yet." Fliss turned, scanning the forest around them. "I want you to climb this tree."

"Shit." Lucy cursed softly. "Raveners?"

"Need a boost?" Fliss asked her, rather than answer.

Lucy gave a snort. "I may be out of shape and pregnant, but I'm still Gyr."

Although she hadn't been a Gyr for long, Fliss knew. Less than two months was all they'd given Lucy before they'd decided to take back her gyra. And since then, they'd had her locked up.

Still, when she turned back, Lucy had already climbed up onto the first branch, and she had her hand down to take the pack with their supplies.

Fliss handed it up and watched her climb higher.

Once she was out of sight, Fliss relaxed a little.

It would help to have Lucy hidden and off the ground, although her scent would still be a giveaway for whatever was coming for them.

She waited, trying to see what it was her gyra had picked up. The sudden flash of an isilo running between the trees caught her attention.

That was . . . not good.

The one she'd dealt with before hadn't exactly been responsive to her orders, and she had a bad feeling there were more of them this time.

They usually ran in packs.

She sighed.

"What is it?" Lucy whispered from above.

"Isilo."

"Shit."

Fliss gave a low chuckle. "Yep."

She eyed the branch above, wondering whether she should simply wait it out with Lucy, but the isilo seemed bold enough to try and get to them, and she would not endanger the baby, no matter the risk to herself.

Another isilo ran between the trees, and then two more approached more cautiously, directly toward her.

So four at least, no . . . she caught sight of a fifth one.

This was not going to be like what happened at the river in Vallent.

She wouldn't be able to ride them all.

Suddenly the two who'd been approaching cautiously exploded into action, racing toward her.

She braced, waiting for her moment to jump over them, when from above her, she heard a screech. A creature she didn't recognize flew out from the branches.

Fliss caught sight of long, sharp claws, a fluffy body, long arms.

Everything on Fjern had some way to rend, claw or bite. No matter how big or small, there was something dangerous about them.

The animal smacked into the side of one of the isilo, who'd gone still at the initial screech, and with a flick and a snap, the isilo caught it in its jaws.

It half-gulped the unexpected snack down, backing away with its prize, then turned tail and ran.

The other isilo chased it for a few steps, then slowed, looking back at Fliss.

"What was that?" Fliss called up softly to Lucy.

"A polantis. They're like the warongas of the trees. It tried to drop down on me."

"I like the way you work." Fliss said. But she doubted there would be more handy polantis for Lucy to throw, and now she had four isilo slowly creeping closer, eyeing each other to see which one would be the first to attack.

There were too many to fight them all, so she would have to touch them each briefly. Alarm them.

And there were two things that alarmed all living creatures on Fjern.

Fire, and carranda.

"Is there a lighter in that pack?" she called up.

"Maybe."

She heard Lucy rummaging through the bag.

"There is."

"Okay, light a leaf and drop it down." Fliss kept her eyes on the approaching isilo, but she began to use her boots to drag the leaves on the forest floor into a pile, moving around to get it as big as she could.

A leaf floated down beside her, smoking, the fire winking out as it coasted on the breeze.

Still, there was a smell of smoke in the air now.

"Keep doing it," she said. And she lunged, giving a crazy screech as she did so, grabbing hold of the closest isilo's head.

"Fire!" she screamed at it.

Then she danced back.

The isilo she'd touched had backed up, head raised, nostrils flaring.

One of the isilo on her left side suddenly darted in, jaws wide, neck extended to take a bite, and she flipped over it, hand out.

"Fire," she hissed as she touched its skull on her way past.

Another leaf floated down, smoldering red at the edges, and as soon as she landed, Fliss jumped again, back over her attacker, plucked the leaf out of the air and set it down on her pile.

Some of the leaves were damp, but others were tinder-dry and they caught straight away with a crackle.

The breeze that had been dancing and gusting all morning helped create a tiny pyre, and the flames licking at the damp leaves helped add to the smoke.

The two isilo she'd touched were both moving away, and the final two seemed confused.

Fliss stood behind the pile. It only came to her shins, but it was burning.

The isilo seemed to regroup a little as the breeze turned the smoke in a new direction, drawing closer again, and Fliss had the sense she'd run out of time.

With a shout, she kicked out at the leaves, and then leaped through the burning embers, starting on her right and moving around the clearing as fast as she could.

She smacked the nose of each isilo she passed, holding the image of a massive fire in her head.

They froze when the burning leaves fluttered around them, and flinched at her quick smack.

Her heart was heaving in her chest, because if one had snapped at her, taken her down, the others would have piled in after.

A burning leaf blew against the side of one of the isilo, and with a screech, it ran.

The others followed, heading deep into the trees and swerving left.

For a moment, she simply let herself draw in smoky air, and waited for her legs feel a little firmer.

Then she walked around the clearing, stomping on burning leaves to put out the fire.

She turned when Lucy dropped from the tree, pack in her hand.

"I have to say, I thought you were going to go down." Lucy shook her head, and Fliss could see her hands were trembling. "What were you doing when you touched them?"

"I have a way of dealing with raveners." Fliss glanced at her. "I had to go out to get rid of them pretty young, and with no cutter, or any weapon, really. So I persuaded them to go away instead."

"And that works?"

"Not always. Sometimes they're too angry, or frightened, or confused, but mostly it does. The isilo are harder, though. We don't have them in the Provinces, and I'm not used to influencing them. But fire is pretty ubiquitous as a fear."

"Is this part of being Gyr-born?" Lucy's gaze searched the trees as they started walking.

"I really don't know." She'd never thought being Gyr-born was unique, and gyra were surely gyra. "I thought it was part of being Gyr. That everyone can do it. You just aren't taught how." She thought about it. "I've got more than twenty-five years of practice when it comes to doing it."

"Fair enough." Lucy glanced at her. "If we get out of this, will you teach my baby how to do it?"

"Sure." Fliss could sense her gyra's delight at the prospect. But even if they got out of the Swathe and made it back to safety, they still had Gyr Command to deal with. "What were Barilar's plans for you? And little Madeleine?"

"I don't think he knew himself." Lucy smoothed a hand over her stomach. "It worried me. Because while at the start Barilar had a med tech come and do some tests, take some blood samples, that stopped maybe a couple of weeks in. I never saw her again, and I wondered . . ."

"If they'd gotten rid of her?" Fliss asked.

"Maybe." Lucy grimaced. "Probably. She was very confronted when she first arrived to take the samples. I don't think she realized I was a prisoner when she accepted the job."

"Surely they'd have chosen someone aligned with them?" Fliss saw a stick and bent to pick it up. It was long and straight. It could be useful.

"I think she was in their camp——the one that says Gyr need to be kept in their place——but visiting me in prison was a little too . . . real for her." Lucy gave a bitter laugh. "After she disappeared, I was just waiting for them to do the same to me. Because I had the feeling each week that I was becoming more of a problem than a useful curiosity."

"Or they planned . . ." Fliss glanced at Lucy's stomach, and kept her mouth shut, just in case the baby could hear.

"Yes," Lucy's gaze was steady. "Take my baby, then take my gyra, then be done with me. I had the same thought." Then she smiled. "But you arrived and got me out."

"There's still a long way to go," Fliss warned her. But anything was better than that room.

And she was Gyr. Lucy was Gyr.

If anyone could make it on foot through the Swathe, it was them.

"I've been meaning to ask you," Lucy said. "How did they get you?"

"I was at the alien mine site——"

"Alien?" Lucy turned to her, eyes wide, but Fliss had a strong sense it wasn't in disbelief, it was in alarm.

"You know something about the aliens?"

Lucy gave a slow nod. "I thought they were messing with me." She gave a low laugh. "I thought they were trying some strange psychological experiment on me, talking about aliens."

"What did they say?" Fliss could hear the scream of a largarti far in the distance. Far enough not to worry about it yet, but she upped the pace a little.

"It was one of the admin people who came to check on me occasionally. Elias." She said the name slowly, and if Fliss was to guess, that's how he'd said Lucy's name. In a slightly mocking tone.

"I've heard that name before," Fliss said. She tried to remember when, and was sure it was the day before, at the mine site.

"He worked in comms at Nasnere headquarters. I thought he was nice, back when I was part of South Nasnere Gyratta and the only problem I had in my life was my inability to shift." Lucy scoffed. "Ah, the good old days, when I was carefree. Back before I broke one of the gyra-na and caused Gyr Command to just about lose their minds."

"I think Miriam Yanno gave Elias's name as someone who'd disappeared from work and never came back. They were speculating on who could have helped the aliens set up the mine site, because whoever it was had died up at the site, either in a ravener attack, or was killed by the aliens."

"Dead? Huh." Lucy didn't sound particularly sad about it. "He didn't help them set up a mine site by himself, though. Barilar was in on it. Elias discussed it with Barilar over comms quite openly while he was checking on me. Whoever came always arrived very late, stayed overnight, and left the next morning. They used their time at the bunker to plan, like they felt they didn't need to watch what they said in my presence. It contributed to my feeling of being disposable.

"It was Elias who picked up an alien transmission on the comms desk by chance and opened a line of communication with them, and then Barilar did the negotiations, although I'm not sure what exactly he was getting out of it."

"And that's why Heldar had to die." Fliss had wondered why Barilar had sent Jaco out to kill the alien leader. But if Heldar had been captured by anyone else and had given up the name of the Fjerna who'd helped him with the mine in exchange for a trip back up to his mothership . . . Barilar would have been done.

"So, you were up at the alien mine when Barilar grabbed you? What were you doing up there?"

Fliss could hear from her breath she was struggling to keep up and slowed her pace, even though the largarti was still audible in the distance.

"We were up there to take the aliens prisoner."

"And did you?" Lucy asked.

"Yes. But not before a second ship demolished the one on the ground, so we couldn't explore it." Fliss recalled the bright light, the feeling of all the air being sucked away. "And they're still up there, circling." She looked up as she spoke, but all she could see was blue skies and the tops of the trees.

"What was Barilar after from them, do you think?" Lucy stopped, hand to her back, and knowing what was coming, Fliss looked around for a good place for her to rest.

"Whatever it was, he either already has it, or it's gone from him forever."

Given what she knew about Barilar now, she would guess it was something to help control the Gyr.

And she could only hope the aliens hadn't trusted him enough to give him his pay-off in advance.

35

The chirp from Han's comms unit was muted, but still loud enough for Gyr ears.

Delasio turned to him. "Yanno again?"

"She's persistent, I'll give her that." Han glanced at the message and focused back on North Nasnere Gyratta.

Yanno was only a short distance away, behind the vast walls of Nasnere. If he were to turn and look over his shoulder, he would be able to see them in the distance.

The tree he and Del were perched in gave a good view back toward the city, as well as the gyratta in front of them.

"Do you think she's an ally?" Del asked.

Han lifted his shoulders. It had seemed so at the mine site, but there was no way he was trusting anyone from Gyr Command until he had Fliss back.

"Air crawler coming." Ellen's comm came moments before Han heard the engine himself.

It sounded wrong.

Like it was struggling.

Han turned west, in the direction it was coming from, toward the orange, red and purple sky of sunset.

It was almost a full day since Fliss had been taken.

Too long, his gyra chanted. *Too long, too long, too long.*

He watched as the two-seater seemed to fight the sky, corner blades jerking.

"He's run into trouble." There was satisfaction in Del's voice.

Han didn't even look over, his focus was on the air crawler as it landed outside the gyratta gates.

He moved fast as soon as it touched down, dropping off the branch he was crouched on, landing on a few more below to slow his descent a little before he hit the ground.

Del followed, the bigger man grunting as he cracked one of the branches on his side of the tree on the way down.

As soon as his feet touched the forest floor, Han sprinted, making it to the air crawler just as Jaco swung out of the pilot's seat.

He slammed the warrior into the side of his air crawler, cutter lifted and sparking.

Jaco's eyes went to the blade, wide and fearful.

"Where is Fliss?"

"Han?"

Evan stood just inside the arch, and when Han lifted his head, he could see shock on his friend's face.

"Let him ask his questions, Evan." Delasio walked toward Han, cutter also out. "Your house is dirty."

That seemed not to shock Evan as much as Han thought it would.

"You know," he said, voice neutral.

"Maybe I suspected." Evan did a slow sweep of the clearing. "Is it just you two?"

"No." Han said. Ellen and Minette were on the other side of the gyratta, keeping watch for air crawlers and traffic from Nasnere.

Teranimo was with them, out of the way for now.

Ranuk and Pen were in Nasnere itself, watching who was coming and going from headquarters.

When that's all he said, Evan gave a quick twist of his lips.

"Fine. At least bring Jaco inside. I have to admit to wanting to know what he's been up to myself."

Han stared at him, and Evan rubbed a hand over his face.

"I may have suspected, but I'm not involved, Han. I really don't know what's going on."

While they'd been talking, Han saw four of Evan's team had come to stand behind him, all of them armed.

"Reese gives up his cutter first," Han said, spotting the Gyr in the group. "He's in this as deep as Jaco."

"Ah." Evan turned, hand out, and reluctantly, Reese handed his cutter over.

They had a brief, low conversation Han couldn't hear.

What he could hear was Jaco's breathing. It was getting harsher, more worked up.

"Let's go," he said, pulling Jaco away from the side of the air crawler and marching him to the entrance.

As they stepped under the arch, Jaco began to scream, a sound so viscerally shocking, Han pulled the warrior back and let go of him.

He collapsed onto the ground.

"I forgot," he panted. "I forgot."

"What did you forget?" Han stood over him, glancing up as Evan joined them, and Delasio stepped up behind him, having his back.

"That she took them! She stole them from me!"

"Fuck me." Delasio said the words long and slow. "She's getting a real reputation."

Han glanced back at him and saw the almost deranged glee on his friend's face.

He had to admit to feeling a similar sense of delight at Jaco's misfortune himself.

"That's what you get for betraying your own, Jaco. Where did you leave her?"

"What's happening?" Evan demanded.

"Jaco here just proved he took Fliss." Han stepped back, studying the man curled at his feet.

"That's why you left the mine site so quickly when you got back? You thought Jaco had taken her?"

"I thought it then. I know it now."

"How can you be so sure?" Reese asked. He was staring at his friend in shock.

"Because Fliss has taken his gyra. He can't enter the gyratta anymore."

There was a moment of stunned silence.

"She has a gyra-na?" Evan asked.

"No. It's a gift she has." Han realized she'd taken three sets now. Each time in self-defence.

He didn't blame her for a single one.

"He really has lost his gyra?" Reese walked forward, taking advantage of the space Han had given Jaco, and crouched beside his friend.

They stared at each other, the stare, in Han's mind, of co-conspirators.

Then Reese stood and ran, and it was only when the dark shadows between the trees swallowed him that Han saw what he'd done.

Jaco choked, his hands around his throat as he tried to draw breath through the deep slit his friend had made across his neck.

"Where is she?" Han knelt beside him.

Jaco looked up, and Han thought he saw bitterness in the ex-Gyr's eyes. Bitterness and resignation. "Swathe." He coughed the word out, his breath rattling, before his gaze went blank.

"What about Reese?" Delasio asked.

There was a shout from between the trees.

"I think Ellen and Minette have got him." Han turned toward the sound.

They did, indeed, have him.

Ellen emerged from the trees, walking behind Reese, arm over his shoulder, cutter to his throat.

Minette walked beside him on the left, and Teranimo took the right.

He had worried about bringing Teranimo here. He'd tried to convince the scientist to watch Barilar in Nasnere, where he could more easily come and go from Gyr Command, but Teranimo had insisted that would only arouse suspicion.

Eventually Han had recognized that Teranimo had as much right to interrogate Jaco as he did.

Maybe more.

That chance was gone, but not without one clue.

"So. The Swathe." Han said as Reese was dragged back. "How many hours from here?"

Reese's eyes darted from Han's face, to Evan's, to his team.

"You're going to let him question me?" he asked Evan, in disbelief.

"I've been suspicious of you and Jaco for a while," Evan said. He turned to Han. "So, they grabbed your team mate in the forest, and took her off somewhere to the Swathe?"

"Yes," Han said.

He didn't tell Evan she was his gyrbar. Her abduction was serious enough on its own merits, without what she was to him.

And he suddenly didn't want Reese to know how desperate he was to get her back.

"Why?"

"She's Gyr-born."

"And she's most likely with Lucille Defoe. Who is pregnant with a Gyr-born." Teranimo spoke for the first time, and Evan turned to look at him.

There was a long silence.

Every Gyr stood silently in shock, some with heads bowed, others with gazes flicking around the group.

"Why would you work against your own?" Evan eventually asked Reese.

The warrior had to sense the growing fury, because he swallowed hard before answering.

"I wouldn't be Gyr without my promise to do Barilar's bidding." His words were stiff. "He came and told me I would get a place, but only if I acted for him. That if I failed him, he'd take my gyra back."

There was another long silence.

There was nothing more corrupt.

Nothing.

Gyr were chosen on merit. There was simply no other way it could be done.

But hadn't Han just been thinking someone like Ralf Bellini should never have become Gyr.

"Mistakes in choosing a recruit are one thing. Every now and then you see a Gyr and think, they did not fulfill the potential they must have shown when they applied. But a deliberate fouling of the system is something else."

"Agreed." Evan's voice was rough. "Where are these Gyr-born, Reese? How deep into the Swathe?"

"I never went to the Swathe." Reese looked down at Jaco's body. "Jaco went often, and a few low-level Fjerna from Gyr Command went out, too. The bunker's about seven hours from here. Jaco said it was impossible to find the first time without the coordinates, but he stopped needing them after a while."

"What did you think he was doing?" Han turned to Evan. "When he took his fourteen hour round trips?"

He saw a flash of temper in the team leader's eyes at the unspoken accusation. "Jaco was the tenth member of the team. I was told I was only allowed nine, but if Gyr Command had the use of him for personal protection occasionally, I could have him the rest of the time."

Oh, that made a sick kind of sense. Barilar setting things up in advance, making sure there was lots of room for him to use his pawns without scrutiny.

"And Reese?" Teranimo eyed the Gyr with disdain.

"Barilar was just setting things up with me, I think." Reese avoided his team mates' eyes. "I was told to keep an ear out for any talk against Gyr Command from the Gyr, that sort of thing. Jaco got his gyra shortly before the Lucille Defoe situation. Barilar thought it would be easier to use the new guy, as no one would have gotten used to having him around yet. There would be less questions."

"He was right," Evan said, grim. "There *were* less questions."

"So what are we thinking, boss?" Minette asked. "Fliss took his gyra, and did something to his air crawler, but he somehow got away?"

"Did something to his air crawler?" Evan asked.

"Didn't you hear it struggling?" Ellen asked.

"I did." Han felt another lift in his chest. Fliss had taken Jaco's gyra, and damaged his air crawler. She had to be all right.

"So what now?" Evan asked.

Han looked west. "Now, we go find our girls."

36

"My gyra asked me, you know?" Lucy said.

"Asked you?"

"If I wanted to be pregnant." Lucy sighed. "I thought it was theoretical, at the time. Turned out not to be."

"The person you said was looking for you." Fliss turned her head toward Lucy in the dark of their hidey hole. "He's the father of your baby?"

Dawn was close, and she decided to stop trying to sleep.

Lucy turned to her with a sigh. "Teranimo, he's a——"

"I know who he is." Fliss hadn't met him yet. Han had made sure of that.

Could he have simply been interested in her because of his impending fatherhood of a Gyr-born all this time?

She swore softly.

"Problem?" Lucy asked.

"Just a bit of miscommunication." She outlined what she knew, and Lucy thunked her head back in frustration.

"He's probably so suspicious, he's afraid to trust anyone." Fliss guessed she couldn't blame him there.

She adjusted one of the sticks she'd jammed into the opening of the carved out mini-chamber high up in the tree, creating a door of sorts.

She had noticed a few of the hollows while they'd walked through the forest earlier, and Lucy told her they were carved out by polantis, like the one she'd thrown at the isilo.

They used their long, sharp claws to dig into the tree trunk and scoop out the wood to create a nest.

The trees were wide enough that the damage usually didn't kill them.

This one had the advantage of being close enough to the ground that Lucy could get to it, but high enough to keep them safe from isilo.

It had also been empty.

Whichever polantis had carved this out was long gone.

She had been able to avoid most of the raveners she'd heard the day before, steering them away whenever one got too close, but she knew she had to find a place off the ground for them to spend the night.

She'd heard of the Swathe.

Who on Fjern hadn't?

But the reality of the massive forest was something that had to be experienced to be believed.

One of the miners had once told her it ran from coast to coast, and was ancient.

She believed him, now. There was something solemn and majestic about this place.

"How did Teranimo look when you last saw him?" Lucy asked.

"I've never met him. Han's so suspicious of him, he kept him far away from me."

"I'm just glad he's still alive." Lucy's voice was soft. "I've never known someone so driven. I *know* he's looking for me. But I was afraid he'd get himself killed doing it, rattling Gyr Command's cage in Nasnere. And I was too afraid to ask Jaco or any of the others who came to watch me about him. I didn't want to bring him to their attention."

"Well, he's not in Nasnere anymore, he's been moved to Vallent, so he probably did make a pest of himself in the capital." Fliss thought about Miriam Yanno, about her clear worry at the growing divide between the Gyr and Gyr Command, and tucked her knees under her chin. "Was Barilar the only senior administrator involved in your abduction?"

Lucy lifted a hand. "I don't know. I only ever heard Jaco and the two admins who came, Elias and Antonio, checking in with him when they got to the bunker."

"Chances are, it's not just him, but it can't be a huge conspiracy, or I don't think you'd be so far from Nasnere, and I don't think there'd only have been three people coming out to check on you, although I know Jaco's team mate, Reese, is also involved."

Outside, a chorus of bird song met the dawn, and Fliss scooted forward, arching her back to get the kinks out. It hadn't been comfortable, but it had been safe.

She crawled through the narrow opening and stood on a branch as wide as she was tall.

She tried to hear over the noise of the birds, the sigh of the trees, but no raveners screamed or called, and she dropped down, flipping forward as she fell and landing in a crouch on ground deeply cushioned with dead leaves.

She waited a beat, listening, then she stood.

"It seems safe."

Lucy grumbled about small bladders and active babies on her more conventional climb down, and Fliss grinned.

She circled their tree, giving Lucy some privacy and checking for any signs of danger.

They had to find water this morning. They only had a few sips left each.

The food situation was better, they had at least another full day's worth.

"We should look for yakkuna trails," she said to Lucy as they started walking. She remembered how the trails had kept leading to water for her and Han up in the hills.

It was worth a try, anyway.

But it wasn't necessary.

Even over the sound of the birds, they could hear water after they'd been going for half an hour.

The quality of the light up ahead also changed.

"There's a big clearing up ahead," Lucy said. "Either that, or something has thinned out the trees."

They moved forward cautiously.

The ground underfoot was spongier, almost boggy, as they got closer to where the trees seemed to end, and Fliss slowed even more, her every sense alert, her gyra buzzing beneath her skin.

When she caught a glimpse of what was through the trees, she blinked in surprise.

They both moved a little faster, now that they knew what had caused the conditions ahead, but stopped just past the treeline.

A river had obviously once run through here, sliding between deep banks, with trees growing close to the edge on either side.

Now it looked as if a massive claw had come and gouged out the trees, the soil, the river banks themselves.

"It was all the rain," Lucy said. "Three months ago, it rained for two weeks straight. Hard, driving rain. Relentless." She carefully stepped onto a splintered tree trunk. It had branches and other debris pushed up against it on the river side, and there was a bad smell of decomposition and river mud.

The river had obviously flooded its banks in a raging torrent, ripping up everything on either side of it before it subsided again.

It still ran fast and dirty, churning up the mud it had displaced.

Fliss climbed up onto a downed tree and ran lightly down the length of it to get closer to the water. She looked up and down the river, trying to see if there was a good place to cross.

She noticed something strange in the water, and moved a little closer, but her gyra made her stop after a few steps.

Danger, they whispered.

A fish leaped from the tumbling, foaming waves, long, with pale green scales, and teeth as long as her fingers.

No way was Lucy going in there.

No way.

Fliss had just started back toward Lucy when she heard the snort.

She stood absolutely still and looked to her right.

A carranda lifted its head up above the smaller trees that lined the newly made clearing.

It had been keeping low, keeping quiet.

It probably caught their scent ten minutes ago.

Sometimes they came straight for you. Sometimes they waited for you to come to them.

She glanced across at Lucy.

Her new friend was standing as still as Fliss was, her head turned in the carranda's direction.

She had seen plenty carranda in her time, but she never got over her wonder at the sight of them.

They were simply massive.

This one's short fur was dappled dark grey and pale yellow, the perfect camouflage to blend in amongst the trees.

It could surely not move easily through the Swathe, the forest was too thick, but she bet the river's rearrangement of its banks, creating a slash of open ground through the width of the Swathe, had attracted it.

"Those eyes are just plain beady," Lucy said, voice low. "And they are studying us." She shivered. "I've never seen one in the flesh."

Fliss had hoped Lucy had faced one before, but of course, she hadn't been able to shift, so Gyr Command would have kept her away from raveners.

"I'm going to walk toward it along the bank," she said, and started doing it. "When I say, start edging back into the forest. Go far enough back to where the trees are very close together."

"We can both do that," Lucy hissed.

"No. It's got our scent." There was no mistaking that. It was totally focused on them.

Once a carranda had your scent, it was singular in its pursuit.

The trick was persuading it to find a different one.

They were the hardest to influence, and she had always been glad there weren't a lot more of them on the escarpment.

Fliss picked her way through the detritus, careful of where she put her feet.

She couldn't afford to fall and hurt herself now.

She came at the carranda at an angle, so he would have to focus on either her, or Lucy. As soon as it had to pick its prey, she would be able to work out a plan.

The carranda snorted again, shaking its massive head, and then turned toward her, its yellow eyes fixed on her.

She felt a wave of relief.

"All right, start edging back," she called softly to Lucy. "Slowly, very slowly. You don't want to give it any reason to turn and look at you."

Lucy's mouth formed a hard, unhappy line, but she stepped back carefully, feeling behind her with her foot before she placed it down, until she was back inside the forest, out of direct line of sight.

It could still follow her scent, but the carranda had Fliss's scent, too, and it shifted again as she kept moving across its field of vision.

She came to a stop when she was directly in front of it, her back to the raging, leaping river.

Too much movement confused them.

She had found that out long ago when one had chased her into a flock of har-hars and then lost its focus when hundreds of birds had lifted off, big wings beating.

The river wasn't quite the distraction that a massive flock of birds could provide, but it was better than nothing.

The carranda took its first direct steps toward her after they stood looking at each other for perhaps a whole minute.

Fliss didn't want to run toward it. The terrain was too unstable.

There was mud, loose rocks, broken and jagged branches and tree trunks, and more than a few animal carcasses as well.

No wonder the whole place stank so much.

She let the carranda come to her. A turnabout to its own strategy earlier.

It remained upright, balancing on its back legs, and it used its arms to part the young tree growth and step through onto the bank.

The movement was almost dainty for such a large creature.

Its limbs always struck Fliss as surprisingly delicate, long and slim, each of its three fingers and toes almost elegant in their tapered shape.

It lost its footing almost straight away, a trunk it stepped on snapping beneath its weight and putting it off balance.

It didn't like that.

It snarled, looking down, and a long strand of glistening saliva plopped down by its feet.

It was hungry.

That was never good.

Fjerna, and Gyr, for that matter, didn't make for much of a meal when it came to carranda, but they'd eat anything when they were hungry. Anything that moved.

It was the reason there wasn't a creature who didn't fear them.

It took another, more careful, step, and then bent again, this time to nuzzle a carcass.

Fliss felt her gorge rise and she had to look away to keep what little she'd eaten this morning down.

A buzzing sound in the distance caught her attention, and it caught the carranda's, as well.

An air crawler.

She wondered if it was friend or foe.

More likely to be foe, given she'd failed to stop Jaco leaving.

And the timing was right.

Even with the damage she'd managed to inflict on the air crawler when he got away, he'd have gotten back last night.

If someone had left to come get her after he got back, they should be getting here around about now.

The carranda lifted its head and gave a roar.

Then it turned to her, gathered its haunches with a little wriggle, and leaped toward her.

37

"REESE SAID THE ROOF WAS FLAT AND COVERED IN GRASS AND MOSS."

Han had started to tune Teranimo out. He'd been muttering to himself almost constantly for the last seven hours.

The scientist had attached a camera to the underside of the air crawler and it was scanning the ground below them, while he studied the images on a screen.

On Teranimo's orders, Delasio was flying as high as the air crawler could above the forest without compromising image quality, and he'd loaded a program he'd created to look for shapes that were too perfect.

Like a rectangular roof made to look like a wild meadow.

"There!" His shout startled everyone onboard.

Which was just Del, Ellen, himself and Teranimo.

If they were bringing Lucille and Fliss back, and either of them were injured, they needed the room.

Del flew lower, and then Han could see it, too.

A bright green rectangle between the darker green of the trees.

They had spoken about whether to land further away, come back on foot in case Fliss and Lucille were still in trouble, and not alone, but given the remote location, whoever was down there would have heard them anyway.

"Just land?" Del said, working it out for himself.

Han nodded, and there it was, an open space just the right size for an air crawler.

The bunker, as Reese had called it, was just that. Low, grim, depressing.

"They wanted to keep comms open," Teranimo said, pointing to the signal booster on the far corner of the roof.

They landed and Han was out before Del switched off the engines, running up the steps to a door that was secured with a keypad lock.

"Too many people coming and going for a more sophisticated locking system," Ellen guessed.

Han slammed his shoulder into the door and felt it give a little.

Del joined him, and after they coordinated three hard kicks, it popped off its hinges and sagged, letting them in.

The passage smelled musty and unpleasant.

They didn't have to kick the door in at the end of it, though. It opened on its own.

"Whoever left would have had to reenter the code on the passage side to lock it," Teranimo said, and Han could hear the hope in his voice.

If Fliss and Lucy had escaped from here, then they certainly wouldn't have bothered.

He stepped into the room, and went still at the sight of the jail cell.

He walked toward it, and he could hear Del swear softly behind him, could hear Ellen gasp. Teranimo was dead silent, and he turned to look at the scientist over his shoulder, saw the blank expression in his eyes.

He wasn't Gyr, but Han would not put extreme violence beyond him now.

A padlock was hanging from a loop in the open cell door, although because of the bars, Han could see in without any difficulty.

"They would come and check on her," Teranimo said, in an eerily calm voice, "and they'd make themselves food in this little kitchen area, watching her, and sleep on this couch, and then they'd go back, and leave her alone again for weeks."

"Yes." From what he could see, that was exactly what had happened.

"This place isn't new," Teranimo said. "It looks at least twenty years old."

Han studied it with more critical eyes. He had to agree.

"Do you think they held Gyr here before?" Ellen's voice vibrated with shock.

"I don't know." Han hoped not, but things did not look good.

"Well, they definitely aren't here." Ellen was edging out the door already, desperate to leave. "So best we go looking for them."

"They'll have had almost a full day on the move, if they escaped at the same time as Jaco left in the air crawler, but with Lucille pregnant, and going on foot, I'm not sure how far they'd have gotten." Han turned his back on the cell to face the others.

No one said that on foot, without the ability to shift, and without a cutter, they were both extremely vulnerable.

"Fliss has her persuasion thing. She makes peace with the raveners, and lets them go on their way." Del sounded a little too hearty. "She'll be careful."

"You want to stay here, in case they come back?" Han asked Teranimo.

The scientist looked around, shaking his head. "There is no way they're coming back here."

Han turned to look over his shoulder at the dark, depressing space.

He had to agree.

"THE OPEN SPACE created by the flood is coming up," Del called.

They had passed it on the way in, and Han had been astonished at how much destruction had been wrought by the river overflowing its banks.

"I don't think they could have gotten much further than here, surely," Ellen said, looking down as they reached the break in the trees.

"I agree, but they could be anywhere along here, have taken any number of routes from the bunker." He considered things. "Follow the river. Let's see if we can see any sign of them."

Maybe they'd have to fly up and down until Fliss reached the river bank and flagged them down.

Or he would get Del to set them down and go hunting on foot.

The problem with that was the vastness of the area.

"Can you work out what would be a straight line on foot from the bunker to here?" he asked Teranimo.

The scientist bent over his screen. "We need to go a bit further north, that would put us directly in line with the bunker."

Fliss would be someone who went straight, Han thought. Because it would be easy to find her that way, and she would surely know he was looking for her.

"Carranda ahead," Del said, as the air crawler moved slowly downstream, following the twists and turns of the river.

"And Fliss." The sight of her made her name almost soundless on Han's lips.

She stood directly in front of the ravener as it approached her.

Carranda always struck him as deeply wrong. Massive, but with long fingers and hands that mirrored the Fjerna. The fact that they had opposable thumbs worried him.

One day, the brain behind those yellow eyes would fire a few more neurons, and they would begin to level up.

As it was, they could reach forward and grab. Their arms were long, and their fangs and claws sharp.

And they were quick and very, very focused.

They were the head of the food chain, and there was no mistake about it. And Fjern had a very violent food chain.

As the sound of the air crawler reached her, Fliss turned briefly toward them.

"Wriggle side to side," Han told Del.

At least he could put her mind at rest that they were friends, not foe.

Del did it, and Fliss turned back to the carranda, but she lifted an arm behind her in greeting.

"Where's Lucy?" Teranimo had unclipped himself and was crouched behind the co-pilot's seat, looking down.

"Maybe Fliss drew the carranda's attention so Lucille could hide." Ellen had joined Teranimo, crowding behind him. "Because she's definitely trying to keep its focus on her."

She had lifted her arms out to her sides, and the carranda, which had been moving forward when Han had spotted it, but had gone still as they buzzed overhead, began to move toward Fliss again.

"Buzz it again," Han told Delasio. "Distract it."

Del turned the crawler, coming back in even lower than before, and the carranda stopped again, raising its head and screaming at them as they flew over it.

Fliss took the distraction they'd given her and moved forward, not to hide, but to go straight at the ravener.

No matter which direction she was going, he thought she'd move faster, but she was slow, as if she had to pick her way carefully.

"The ground has to be treacherous," Teranimo said. "That isn't solid ground down there, it's detritus piled on top of debris."

That would explain it.

She hopped over something, leaped over something else.

Del turned in a tight circle, trying to keep the carranda's attention on the air crawler.

"Is she . . . trying to get killed?" Teranimo asked.

She was definitely risking herself.

Han wanted out of the air crawler, so he could help her below.

She had gotten close enough to the carranda that it could grab her if it turned its attention back to her, and then she hopped, skipped and jumped a little closer and suddenly, she was standing beside its feet.

She disappeared suddenly from sight, and at that same moment the carranda's focus shifted from the air crawler to the ground in front of it.

"What's it doing?" Del lifted up a little and moved back, and suddenly the carranda raised its right foot and shook it.

That's when Han saw Fliss, holding on to its ankle.

It was trying to get her off, but on the unstable ground, hopping on one foot, it overbalanced.

One long limb came out to break the fall, but its paw went straight through the ground, so the carranda ended up on its side up to its shoulder, its arm buried deep in the debris and mud.

It didn't like that.

"It's in a frenzy," Ellen said, voice hushed.

They could hear the screaming over the engines as it thrashed.

It slammed the foot that Fliss was on into the ground, but only once, and Han guessed it had hurt itself doing that.

It suddenly went still.

"She's doing her thing," Del whispered. "Come on now, you fucking monster, listen to the little Gyr."

The carranda slowly rolled onto its stomach, bunching its knees beneath it, and carefully raised itself up, pulling its arm out of the mud.

It shook itself, and Han thought he saw Fliss, covered in mud, near the claws of its toes. Was that her hand, still resting on its foot?

The contrast was ridiculous.

Her hand was tiny in comparison.

It clambered to its feet, unsteady, shook itself again, then moved cautiously toward a section of new growth trees, its short tail down and almost tucked.

It shouldered through the trees and began to move north, keeping to the more solid ground of the forest, and pushing bigger trees over when they were in the way, so it didn't have to step back onto the debris.

As it moved away, Fliss flicked excess mud off her, then picked her way back to the tree line and disappeared.

"Find a place to set down, Del."

There weren't a lot of options, and they eventually had to land a fair way down from where Fliss had disappeared.

Before Han could launch himself out of the door, Teranimo gripped his arm.

"I'm coming."

Han hesitated, but he couldn't turn away from the determination in Teranimo's eyes.

He gave a nod, jumping down and waiting for the scientist to join him.

A largarti screamed in the distance.

"We'll stay here, just in case," Del said, and Han nodded.

They had set down in an open area beside the river that was clear of debris, and Han started on a route that was just within the trees, Teranimo close on his heels.

They had been going for ten minutes when his gyra ran hot beneath his skin, making him stop in surprise.

"They're just ahead," he told Teranimo. "Fliss?"

He ran forward, his gyra setting his feet where they needed to go, and he burst through thick bush to find Fliss standing, fists at her sides, looking at him.

She was covered in muck and mud, and stank.

She saw his reaction, and gave a slow, wide grin, wriggling filthy fingers at him. "Happy to see me?"

He grinned back, reached out and grabbed her close, touched his nose to her very muddy one. "Very."

38

SHE WAS CLEAN, AND RESTED, AND FED.

Fliss leaned back in her chair and reached out her hand below the table, put it over Han's.

He gripped it, curving his fingers around and running his thumb over her skin.

They didn't look at each other.

She couldn't.

She wanted privacy, and him naked, pressed against her, and that wasn't going to happen until they had planned out what to do next.

So while she got through this, she had to focus anywhere but him, though her gyra had worn her down on the touching.

As they sang with joy now, she couldn't regret it, even if it was much more difficult to follow the conversation around her.

Teranimo was talking, and she could still feel how rattled everyone was at his presence.

She had let Teranimo into the gyratta.

It had been simple enough to constrict the flow of the scan, letting it wink out for a moment so he could step through.

No one had reacted well to her doing it, though.

They had thought the arch was sacrosanct. That it couldn't be breached.

She hadn't realized how deep that conviction went until she smashed it.

Not that it wasn't useful for Teranimo to be inside with them. And Lucy wouldn't have come in without him, so no one said anything to her about it.

But her gyra picked up on their unease and she was sorry for it.

"Miriam Yanno called here about ten times," Barnes said. "In the end, I stopped answering."

"Do you think she's an ally?" Ellen asked.

Han shrugged. "Now that everyone's safe, I'll speak to her, see what she has to say."

"What's Evan's plan?" Teranimo asked.

"He says he'll keep Reese locked up and say nothing about Jaco being dead until we can set up a way to out Barilar. And Miriam Yanno might help us with that, if she's actually on our side."

"She might just be calling about the aliens," Minette said.

Fliss closed her eyes. She'd almost forgotten about the aliens. "Lucy heard her guards talking about the aliens with Barilar. He was behind helping them. And that's why he sent Jaco and Reese to kill Heldar. He didn't want Heldar talking to anyone about who'd helped them set up the mine."

"What the hell could he have gotten out of it?" Delasio asked.

"If I was to guess, a way to control us," Fliss said. Her eyes were still closed, and she realized she was about to hit a wall.

People spoke around her, but she no longer heard them, and suddenly she was lifted off her chair and carried away.

The rib she had cracked when the carranda had tried to shake her off its foot had healed, but was still a little tender, and when she winced, Han adjusted his hold to make her more comfortable.

"I didn't know your rib was cracked." He spoke quietly.

She wondered for a moment how he knew, and then realized her gyra had told his.

"It was almost healed by the time you found us," she murmured back.

"Hmm." He nuzzled her neck and she heard her door open and then close behind them. Felt herself being laid gently on her bed.

"Close the curtains," she whispered.

She heard him close them, and lifted her feet up so she could pull off her boots.

"I'll do it."

He undressed her carefully, as if he were taking inventory of her cuts and bruises. He touched her lightly, a brush of his fingers near each of her injuries.

Almost everything would be healed by now, but a few sticks had gouged deep during the skirmish with the carranda.

At least the stinky mud was gone.

"Now you," she told him, voice low, when he had taken every piece of her clothing.

She hadn't opened her eyes while he'd undressed her, but now she forced her eyes open and found him standing at the end of the bed, naked, just like she wanted him.

She sighed in appreciation and anticipation.

"You're wasting time," she whispered.

He moved so fast, he was braced above her before she could blink, face as serious as she'd ever seen it.

And then, suddenly, he wasn't wasting time any more.

Fliss was pulled awake by the chime on Han's comm unit.

It wasn't that late.

Her gyra had an inbuilt sense of time, and she knew she had crashed out early in the evening.

She lay, still naked, limbs twined with Han's, her head resting on his chest.

She lifted her face up to his, and their gazes caught and held.

With a sigh, Han answered the comm.

"Miriam Yanno," he said. "You've found me."

"At last," she said in response. "Where have you been?"

Han hesitated, then shrugged. "I've been rescuing Fliss Belaire and Lucille Defoe from a secret bunker in the Swathe, where Barilar was holding them prisoner."

"I just saw Fliss Belaire with you two days ago," the administrator said, after a pause.

"Yes, and then she disappeared mysteriously from the mine site. That was Barilar's mistake. If you're his ally, you can tell him there were only two people who could have taken her, and I tracked them down."

Yanno drew in a quick breath. "I am not his ally."

When Han said nothing, she made a sound of impatience.

"You're serious, aren't you? You were in the Swathe? And you found Lucille Defoe."

"I did. If you haven't been trying to contact me about that, what do you want to talk to me about?"

"Aliens," she said. "The major issue facing this planet right now, if you remember?"

Han waited a beat before he answered.

"The major issue facing me until earlier today was the abduction of Fliss and Lucille, Administrator. And given Hedgeworth thinks he knows how to deal with the aliens better than the Gyr, why aren't you speaking to him about them?"

She sighed. "I've put in an official complaint about Hedgeworth."

Han scoffed and she made another of those irritated sounds.

"He may have acted like an asshole when you confronted him, but he's alone in his thinking," she said. "We take good relationships with our Gyr seriously at Gyr Command. He broke every tenet of our procedure, and I went to the Nasnere Council and had him suspended for his conduct."

"What is your procedure on kidnapping Gyr and locking them in a bunker for seven months, like Barilar did to Lucille?" Han asked. "Or using an alien weapon on Fliss Belaire and then taking her to the same bunker?"

"Why would Barilar do that?" Yanno asked, voice soft.

"Because Fliss is Gyr-born, and Lucille is pregnant with a Gyr-born."

"Shit." Yanno sounded like she was moving around now, pacing back and forth.

Fliss didn't know if she was trustworthy, but she sounded rattled by what Han had told her.

And upset.

"I want to make this right, Kardenian," she said at last. "Clearly we have a bigger problem than I realized at Gyr Command. I want to find out what's going on. And no way is Barilar acting on his own. I'll make sure he's finished for this, but I want to know who helped him, as well."

"I know one person. Lucille says his name is Antonio. Works with you at Gyr Command."

"I know him. Consider him finished, as well."

"If you want to talk about aliens," Han said, "it seems that Barilar is the one who helped set up that mine. He sent Elias Trovich to meet them, but Elias was also one of the people he sent to check on Lucille Defoe occasionally, to make sure she was alright, alone in her bunker in the Swathe."

"What?" Yanno didn't shout it, but Fliss thought it was only because she was a woman with a great deal of self-control.

"Lucille heard the aliens being discussed between Elias and Barilar."

"Did she hear why Barilar would do something like this?"

"No." Han's answer was short. "I look forward to asking him."

"Leave this to me, Kardenian." Yanno sounded like she was talking through gritted teeth. "I'm having Barilar arrested tonight. Although . . ." Her tone became thoughtful. "Come to Nasnere. I need your testimony." She paused. "Maybe this is the development we needed. The reason I was calling you is because the mothership has made contact. We allowed the captain to have her comm device back, and her people orbiting above spoke to her, but we couldn't understand what they said to each other. We took the device away, and since then, there's been silence."

"We'll come tomorrow," Han said. "We've been running on no sleep for days."

"Fair enough." Yanno sounded pleased, and Fliss guessed she was just relieved Han had agreed to come at all. "Let me know when you're arriving and I'll meet you."

"Don't make me regret it, Administrator." Han cut her off.

"There's going to be trouble, isn't there?" Fliss asked.

"There already was trouble," he said. "Especially if that bunker really has been used any time in the last twenty years."

That was very true.

This wasn't all on her or Lucy. This was long-running.

She relaxed back. "So we have all night?" she asked, innocently.

She saw his mouth curve into a smile. "Why, so we do."

39

HAN WAS GONE WHEN SHE FINISHED IN THE BATHROOM, OFF TO CALL AS many gyratta as he could, and spread the word about the bunker, what had been going on there, and who was behind it.

He was rallying the troops.

She pulled on her battle gear and braided back her hair in quick, efficient movements, but when she reached for her jacket, she went still.

There was something heavy in the pocket.

She lifted it out and stared at it in astonishment.

Her knife.

Her missing knife, that Heldar had taken from her.

She unsheathed it, enjoying its heft and how well the hilt fit her hand.

This was Han's doing.

He had remembered.

She had only mentioned it——and how the loss of it upset her ——once.

She tossed it into the air, flipping it end on end with delight.

Then she slid it into its sheath and centered herself——went inward.

She had come to a decision about the way forward before she'd seen the knife, and she had been fighting an internal battle with her gyra over it.

They guarded her jealously, and did not want to give up any advantage, but she was winning.

Lucy's baby was her secret weapon, and as she stood, eyes closed, communing with them, they eventually conceded the argument.

She stepped out of her room and headed for the kitchen, her stomach a twist of nerves.

She would be breaking many traditions with this.

Traditions she had never participated in, had never experienced.

When she reached the communal area, the whole team was there, sitting around the table, eating, and Fliss drew in a breath to steady herself.

She would get this over with.

She walked to Teranimo, who was seated in front of an empty plate, face drawn and serious. He kept glancing at Lucy, who was making tea at the counter.

Fliss crouched beside him and lifted up her palm.

A single bead of silver rose up out of the center.

It felt . . . strange. And her gyra were still grumpy about it.

Every single person stopped talking. Every piece of cutlery was laid down.

Han stepped into the room at that moment, and she heard his grunt of surprise.

She turned her head to look at him, but all he did was raise his eyebrows and then give a nod.

She was going to do this, no matter what others thought, but to have his approval was a relief.

She focused back on Teranimo.

"It will be very inconvenient to have to be here to let you in and out every time you need to come and go," she said. "And Lucille needs to be in a gyratta. Her baby needs to be in a gyratta."

There were slow nods of agreement all around the table.

Teranimo eyed the silver ball, then lifted his gaze to hers.

"Are you sure?"

"I have accumulated quite a few sets," she said, and then smiled. "And while my gyra prefer to keep what I get, I have persuaded them this is the right thing to do."

Lucille had moved over to them, and she reached out and put a hand on Fliss's shoulder.

When Fliss looked up at her, she saw her friend's eyes were bright with tears.

"Thank you." Lucy only mouthed the words, as if she wasn't able to speak them.

Teranimo turned and looked up at Lucy as well, and she dropped her hand and linked fingers with him.

"I accept." Teranimo's voice was rough.

Fliss raised her hand, placed her fingers just below the hollow of Teranimo's throat, and tilted her palm up.

The ball rolled down and as it touched Teranimo, it sunk into his skin without a trace.

"Who needs a gyra-na?" Minette murmured.

Fliss glanced at her, searching her face for anger or unhappiness. "These were special circumstances."

She checked how Teranimo was taking to his new reality as she stood up.

His eyes were closed, and Lucy was sitting beside him, holding his hand.

"You up to come to Nasnere?" Han asked him.

The scientist lifted his head, eyes snapping open. "Oh, yes."

"Then let's go."

IT SEEMED that while Miriam Yanno had some pull, she hadn't quite been able to put Barilar into custody.

The man himself stood to one side of the councilors, guarded by two officials from the Fjerna security authority.

He looked blank-faced, but Han picked up the way he flexed and bunched his hands, and the tightening of his lips.

Pal Barilar was suppressing some extreme emotions.

Han leaned back in his chair in the council chambers, stretched out his arms, and let his fingers come to rest on the bare skin of Fliss's neck.

He felt her go still beneath his hand and then relax into it.

His gyra hummed in contentment.

She was magnificent.

And infinitely mesmerizing.

The way that Barilar kept flicking his gaze her way made Han wonder if the administrator realized how dangerous she was to his stranglehold on Gyr procedure.

She had usurped Gyr Command's control this morning.

As Minette had said, who needed a gyra-na?

Not the Gyr, any more.

She lifted a hand and curled her fingers around his where they rested against her neck. "Thank you for the knife." She was looking forward, and her voice was quiet enough, only he could hear it.

He had noticed her wearing it when she'd stood after making Teranimo a Gyr.

"My pleasure."

She flicked him a sidelong glance, and his breath caught.

"Hannu Kardenian."

Miriam Yanno calling his name forced his attention back to the front of the room, where the administrator stood with her colleague, Evela Carnsworth, before a full eight-person sitting of the Council.

The doors were closed, though. Besides his team and Barilar, no one else was in the room.

The council had decided to keep this very private, for now.

"Hannu Kardenian, you are called to the carpet." The council speaker, Ophelia Minn, gestured him up.

Han stood and walked down the aisle to the symbolic carpet before the Council. Yanno and Carnsworth shifted to make place for him.

"You accuse Administrator Pal Barilar of kidnap and imprisonment?" Nasnere's head councilor, Neesha Rasmu, asked.

"Two counts of it," Han said. "And perhaps more."

"Perhaps more?" One of the other councilors, a gray-haired woman Han didn't know, asked.

"The bunker where Fliss Belaire was taken to, and where Lucille Defoe was kept for seven months, was not new. It looked as it if had been used for a similar purpose in the past."

"You can give us the coordinates, so we can see this bunker for ourselves?" Lin Evett, who Han had dealt with before, asked.

He had always seemed a fair legislator, but Han no longer trusted any of them.

"Of course." Han let his gaze sweep across the eight members. "But the Gyr will oversee any trip out there, to make sure no evidence is taken or destroyed."

The offence on every face was almost comical.

"There seems to be an issue of trust," Neesha Rasmu said.

Han gave a nod. "There is."

"Do you have good reason for your distrust?" Neesha Rasmu tilted her head. She seemed, for the first time since they'd arrived, rattled.

"Administrator Hedgeworth endangered my team at the alien mine site, without giving a thought to their safety. Administrator Barilar imprisoned two Gyr in a bunker and helped aliens set up an illegal mine——aliens who tried to kill or capture me and my team. Further, when Lucille Defoe disappeared, taken by one of your own, none of you did anything." Han glanced back at Lucille, sitting beside Teranimo. "I made as much noise as I could. Lolia of South Nasnere Gyratta, where Lucille was originally stationed, made noise. Teranimo made so much noise he was demoted to Vallent. And yet, silence." He looked across at Miriam Yanno. "And all that time, she was a prisoner, alone in a bunker in the Swathe."

"We *were* looking for her," Yanno said evenly, but her eyes were flashing with anger. "Or, we thought we were. Administrator Barilar offered to take on the task of finding her. He asked us to pass any questions about her on to him to answer."

Barilar stepped forward, mouth open to speak, but before any sound emerged, the door behind him was thrown open.

Han turned.

"There's a big alien spaceship above the city." The security guard pointed up. "Just hovering over us."

The councilors rose to their feet, one of them shouting instructions to someone on their wrist comm.

"I can speak to them." Barilar's shout cut through the noise.

Every eye turned toward him.

"But I want concessions. Charges dropped."

"No." Every Gyr spoke almost in chorus.

The councilors gaped at them.

"Agreed," Miriam Yanno broke the silence. "Barilar does not get out of any consequences for his actions."

"Then I won't help." He leaned back against the wall, arms crossed.

"I wouldn't trust anything he did, anyway." Han turned away from him to face Yanno. "And I assume you can add the charge of treason to the list?"

"Yes." She looked delighted by the idea.

"The aliens can speak Fjern," Fliss said. "They were here for months before they made contact, and I can't see how they would have known the first person they approached to help them would so happily sell out his own people unless they'd been monitoring Barilar's comms and knew he was already breaking the law."

"Of course," Yanno murmured. "Of course. If they had contacted anyone honest, that person would have come directly to us and the council."

"Which means they can communicate perfectly well with us." Neesha Rasmu gave a nod.

She had risen to her feet when the news had come through, and now she descended the slightly raised dais and moved toward the doors at a stately pace.

"Let's see what they want, shall we?"

40

"I don't trust them." Fliss leaned against the wall beside Pen, watching the captain of the second alien ship on a screen, his translator standing beside him, hands behind her back.

The council had just agreed to allow an air crawler down——a hover, as they called it——to fetch their people.

It would have to be in three trips, as the hover couldn't take everyone at once.

"You have stolen from us, Captain Pim. What restitution do you offer?" Neesha Rasmu's question was soft and yet completely unyielding.

The captain stared at her, then his mouth twisted into a sneer and he spoke sharply to his translator.

"We offer not to destroy this city as we leave," the translator said, face neutral, eyes staring ahead at nothing. "You have no leverage here, and we are not looking for an alliance or any favors from you. Be grateful we are going and have no plans to return."

A frisson of shock seemed to run through the room. And outrage.

"You *are* looking for favors, though," Neesha Rasmu said. "You want your crew returned."

There was a beat of silence.

"Captain Linao ordered the attack of our people, and harmed two of them. We could decide to keep her here to serve out her sentence."

The captain looked at the head councilor, while he spoke softly to his translator.

She cleared her throat. "I wouldn't advise that. Send them up and please make sure Captain Linao is in the first group, or there will be trouble."

Han was standing near the head councilor, and he turned back to look at Fliss as the screen went dark. Her gyra could still feel the pulse of comms from it, though.

"Impressions?" Councilor Rasmu asked.

Fliss moved forward, finger raised to her lips, and the councilor's mouth opened in surprise.

Han bent his head and murmured into the councilor's ear. Her eyes widened and she turned her back to the screen.

Fliss stopped beside Han, went up on tiptoe to reach his ear. "It's still transmitting vision and sound," she whispered. "Someone in the comms room must be helping them. And given Elias Trovich worked here, it's very possible the aliens have another ally here."

He nodded, his gaze scanning the room as she moved toward the screen at an angle, hoping she could stay out of view.

She had taken in the layout of the space when they'd arrived.

She, Pen, and the rest of the team had hung back against the walls on either side of the entrance, while Han had gone deeper inside, accompanying the councilors and the Gyr Command administrators.

There were three communications techs in the room, each sitting at a station with a screen. One had risen when they'd all arrived, and had shown them to a screen which had been set up for them to use to communicate with the aliens above.

Other than the three techs and their equipment, the large room also contained eight screens, stacked in two layers of four, showing wide-angled views outside the Nasnere city wall.

This wasn't just a comms center, it was a ravener watch station.

When she reached the screen, she noticed all three techs had suddenly focused on her. She looked back, and saw not only was Han studying them, but the other members of the team had straightened from the wall, and were watching in quiet readiness.

"What's going on?" Miriam Yanno asked, picking up on the sudden tension.

"This screen is still transmitting. The aliens can see and hear us, even though we can't see them." Fliss rested the fingertips of both hands on the top edge of the screen and her gyra found the transmission hardware and reset it.

The screen flashed as it did, and then went blank for real.

"It's off now," she said.

"So which one of you was enabling that?" Han asked, turning directly toward the techs.

Fliss's own gaze went to Barilar, still standing with his minders in a corner of the room.

He looked unhappy.

Was that because she had foiled the aliens' plans, or because it was now clear there was someone else in the room working with them, and he hadn't known it?

"It wasn't one of us, it was Elias," one of the techs said.

"Elias is dead." Miriam Yanno narrowed her eyes at her. "It's a bit hard to blame a dead man."

"No, she's right," one of the other techs said, standing slowly from her chair. "The comms from the alien ship came through Elias's old station. I thought they'd found it randomly, but obviously not."

That notion sounded better than the possibility of another traitor in their midst, Fliss thought.

Barilar was shaking his head, his gaze flicking over the comms techs.

"Got anything to say, Barilar?" Delasio had obviously been watching him, too.

Barilar sneered at him. "They won't like having their listening post destroyed." He flicked his gaze at the screen and then at Fliss.

"We should have simply let them in on our private discussions?" Neesha Rasmu lifted her chin in disgust.

Barilar waved a hand, as if to dismiss her, his lips in a tight line.

He must have offered his help to the aliens in exchange for something, and from his demeanor, Fliss guessed he hadn't received it, and now knew he never would.

"What's happening?" one of the techs called out. She was pointing to the screens that focused on what was happening beyond the city walls.

White lightning was discernible in the distance, moving evenly and methodically in a circle around the city.

"The mothership is shooting at something." Fliss moved closer to the screens to get a better look, and then worked it out. "Shooting raveners."

The first carranda came into sight.

There was no sound, but she could see it was shrieking as it ran. A long welt ran down its left flank, and it was headed straight for Nasnere.

"Largarti," Pen murmured, pointing to another screen.

"Zuby and . . . is that an irham?" Del asked.

Fliss glanced at where he was looking. She had only ever encountered a handful of irham.

Sure enough, one had been flushed out. She shivered at the sight of it, all stick-like limbs.

They were very hard to kill.

"They're flushing out every ravener near the city, forcing them to come this way." Neesha Rasmu sounded astonished. "Why would they do that when they're about to send down an air crawler to get their people?"

"Why don't you ask the prisoners?" Fliss said. "Captain Linao will probably know."

IF LINAO DID KNOW, she wasn't talking.

The prisoners had been brought out onto the lush green grass of the courtyard at the heart of the city hall; Fliss assumed to get them out of whatever small rooms they'd been kept in.

Nasnere Gyr Command was probably unable to cope with receiving over thirty new prisoners at once.

Fjerna security officers stood watch, about ten of them spaced around an area with chairs and a few tables that had been roped off.

At the far end of the courtyard was the entrance to the old Traveler ship, now a museum.

Fliss had glanced at it a few times, very interested in having a look around, but that would have to wait.

There had been no further communication from the alien ship above, and Linao claimed she had no idea what her colleagues were doing. Even though the courtyard was open to the sky, the captain did not so much as glance upward as she spoke through her translator.

Ludig Darvan, the one prisoner who had been more open with them in exchange for staying on Fjern, had also claimed to be at a loss.

"Maybe they want to overwhelm you with danger so there are no tricks when you let the prisoners go. They could be trying to divide your attention to keep you too busy to cause them any trouble." He lifted his shoulders as if that was the best he could do.

Fliss watched Captain Linao closely during Darvan's exchange with the council, looking for any reaction from her, but she could see none.

She stood beside Han, her gyra soothed by his presence, even with raveners closing in on the city.

The North and South Nasnere Gyratta would be racing to intercept them.

The alien ship had only done one circuit around the city, firing almost continuously as they riled up the raveners, but once was enough.

Some of the monsters would veer off, or fight each other, rather than head for the walls, but enough would head for the noise and activity of Nasnere.

Certainly far more than usual.

"Darvan is right. They've forced us to split our attention," Han said, looking up at the empty blue sky. "Maybe so that we don't have as many guards on the prisoners."

Fliss wondered what difference that would make.

All but one of the prisoners wanted to go home, she was sure of that. There was no reason for them to escape, no real need for them to be managed.

"Maybe they don't understand that only the Gyr will go out to deal with the raveners. That we can leave the prisoners to Fjerna security." Fliss was sure the aliens didn't really understand how things worked here, but still, that explanation seemed too simple.

"Our team need to go outside to help," Han said, shading his eyes as he continued to scan the sky. "There are too many raveners, even for two fully staffed gyratta."

Fliss had guessed as much. "Pity my reset remote won't reach high enough to drop them out the sky, in case they do it again." Fliss leaned against Han a little as she looked up.

The ship was still nowhere in sight.

Han looked down at her, expression thoughtful. "Why not try?" he asked.

She nodded. "I'll have to fetch it from the air crawler, but at least I could have it in case they try something with the hover they send down for the prisoners." She didn't know what they would try, or why, but it couldn't hurt.

"Agreed." Han touched her, a light brush of his fingers against her cheek.

"Kardenian." Miriam Yanno cleared her throat behind him. "Both Nasnere gyratta have called for your support. There are simply too many raveners headed this way."

Han nodded, lifted a hand above his head, and the team suddenly crowded around them both.

"We're going?" Del asked.

"Yes." Han nodded toward Yanno and they jogged away, a smooth unit, moving in sync in that way that thrilled Fliss. She had been a Gyr alone for so long, and this felt *right*. Right and good.

They headed through the open arch at the opposite side to the museum, toward Gyr Command Headquarters, where they'd set their air crawler down earlier.

"Fliss, I want you to get the remote and go back to the Hall. There has to be a reason they've tried to overwhelm us with a ravener attack while still relying on us to give their people back, and the answer is in the courtyard."

"Agreed," Minette reached out and touched Fliss's shoulder as they ran. "Bring those fuckers down again if you have to. There's something very off about this."

Fliss . . . or rather, her gyra . . . knew some of this was a diversion.

They wanted to protect her. Keep her away from the mass ravener attack.

But it wasn't only that.

Han did want someone watching the prisoner transfer. Because there really was something else going on.

She sighed. "I know what you're doing." She looked around as they jogged together, but no one would look her in the eye. "And even so, I agree, one of us needs to be watching when they send down their air crawler. It might as well be me as anyone."

Even though they knew she had developed ways around it, some of this attitude was because she couldn't shift, she was sure. They had spent too long seeing that as a weakness.

She and her gyra both noticed everyone relax at her acceptance.

"We don't think you're weak. We think you're precious," Pen said at last, when they'd reached the air crawler and had to stop, had to look at her.

"I'm no more precious than you." She hadn't liked it when Taque said it. She liked it even less coming from her own team.

"We'll have to agree to disagree." Del was already inside the air crawler and he leaned out and handed her her pack.

She opened it and did a quick check that the remote was still inside.

It was, and she slid it into the side pocket in her pants, ready to use if she had to.

"Well, you're precious to me, too. Please be careful." They were climbing in, and she didn't like the sudden lurch she felt at the thought of them going into so much danger.

Han went last, as Del started the engine and the others settled in their seats.

Fliss gripped the front of his jacket.

She could see the Shift was just beneath the surface of his skin already, his gyra priming for the fight.

"Be safe," she whispered to him.

He kissed her, saying nothing——which was right, because there were no guarantees when you fought, especially more than one ravener at a time.

The kiss was hard and urgent and then he wrenched himself away, locking eyes with her for a moment before he climbed in.

Del lifted off before he even got the doors closed.

She watched the air crawler turn west, and as she followed them her gaze caught movement high up in the sky, almost directly above her. Another ship, headed down.

She turned and raced back toward the courtyard.

The aliens were coming. The transfer was about to begin.

41

When Fliss reached the courtyard, it seemed that no one had noticed the approaching hover yet.

She looked over at the prisoners, and felt a frisson of shock when she saw Captain Linao was muttering to herself.

She had separated herself slightly from the rest of the group, and was turned away, hunched over a little, and Fliss could see her lips were moving.

They had been played.

The captain must have had a way to contact the ship above all along. Some kind of small comms device they didn't know to look for, most likely.

Fliss moved back until she stood beside one of the pillars that surrounded the courtyard.

She watched the captain closely as she pulled out the remote and pointed it in Linao's direction.

She pressed the button.

Linao tapped her ear, tapped it again.

It looked like the disruptor had worked again.

Linao turned back at her fellow prisoners and then tilted her head up to the sky.

Moments later, the sound of a ship descending became clear.

There was a palpable tension in both the Fjerna and the prisoners as the hover came into view.

Fliss stayed where she was, under the cover of the veranda.

The hover was small enough that it could land comfortably in the courtyard itself, although everyone had to move back around the edges to give it room.

Fliss studied it as it came down, interested all over again in the lack of blades, at how quietly it ran.

When it touched down, the pilot did not switch off the power, and there was a moment where no one moved, until the door opened and a man dressed like one of the soldiers Fliss had first encountered at the mine site stepped out. He held his big weapon pointed downward, but all he would need to do was lift it up to shoot.

The Fjerna security officers had divided the prisoners into groups, and they ushered the first lot forward.

"Where is Captain Linao?" The soldier scanned the crowd.

"Captain Linao goes last," Miriam Yanno said.

"No. She's first." The soldier's accent was thick, and he lifted his hand toward Linao and made a *come here* gesture.

"You endangered this whole city with your actions earlier, riling up our raveners." Yanno stepped forward, placing herself in front of the prisoners. "Our Gyr are in significant danger because of it. I'm not inclined to agree to anything you ask for, which you should have considered before you acted as you did. You do not dictate the order of evacuation. A captain always leaves last, to make sure all her people are safe first. This is how it is done on Fjern."

The soldier stared at Yanno for a long moment.

Fliss almost thought she could see some kind of respect on his face at her words.

"No. The captain comes now."

Yanno sighed, and shook her head. "Proceed with the first group," she said to the security officer.

The prisoners moved forward, slightly nervous now, as if they didn't know how to proceed.

It was a strange standoff.

The soldier blocked the way to the hover until the last moment, then stepped aside, allowing his fellow invaders past him and into the hover.

As the last one past him, he raised his weapon and pointed it at Miriam Yanno, then moved it across to Neesha Rasmu.

He could only know who the head of council was through inside information, or through what Captain Linao had told her friends above earlier.

There was a shocked moment of disbelief.

"Captain Linao. Now."

Fliss leaned against the pillar, slid her hand into her trouser pocket and grabbed the remote. She pressed the button through the thick fabric, just to see if it would work, and the hover's power source cut out.

The sudden silence was a shock, and the soldier's weapon dipped downward as he turned his head toward the open door.

The pilot emerged. "Something cut off the power," she said, looking around the courtyard. "The whole system reset."

"You did this?" The soldier turned back to face Yanno and Neesha Rasmu.

"We did." Fliss stepped forward, noting the jerk of surprise from Yanno.

The administrator had clearly not noticed that Fliss had returned. "Undo it."

"No. This is a warning. At any time, we can reset your hover, and bring you crashing down. You do not give the orders here." She tilted her head. "How do you think we brought your hover down at the mine site?"

Linao made a sound, and the soldier turned to her.

"She's right. They did bring down our hover at the mine site. I didn't know if it was deliberate or some kind of accident."

"How long will it take to reset?" the soldier asked the pilot.

"Another few minutes," the pilot answered. "If someone doesn't do whatever it was they did again."

"I could shoot you," the soldier said to Fliss. He had his weapon raised directly at her.

She lifted both her hands, showing they were empty, pretending complete calm while her gyra panicked at the thought of another hit. "You could, but as you can see, I'm not the one resetting your hover. Even if I was, I assume you plan to eventually take off. So what good would harming me do other than make us more inclined to wait until you're nice and high, and reset it again?"

She gave a low whistle, and then smacked her fist into her palm. "Boom."

He stared at her, and she stared straight back.

She knew she'd won when his shoulders slumped a little.

"Fine." He climbed into the hover and shut the door, and after a few minutes, the power coughed back to life.

Fliss glanced over at Linao, saw her lips moving. Her comms were working again, just like the hover, but there was nothing Fliss could do about it unless she wanted to bring down the hover, and despite her theatrics with the soldier, she did not.

She half-closed her eyes against the rush of air as the hover rose up, and stood, head tipped back, to watch it disappear into the blue.

They left much faster than they arrived.

"Well played." Yanno had moved up to stand next to her. "How did you do it?"

"Gyr secret," Fliss said.

"Gyr have no secrets from Gyr Command."

Fliss didn't think this was the time to tell her she did not feel obligated to Gyr Command. "Why do you think they wanted Captain Linao up first?"

Yanno didn't look inclined to drop the topic of how Fliss had cut off the hover's engines, but she turned to look at the captain.

Linao was turned away, now, huddled with her translator and a few others, talking in low voices.

"You think they wanted to take her in the first batch and then go? Leave the others here?" Yanno asked.

"Maybe." Fliss thought about why that would be. "Could be they don't have enough space or supplies up there for everyone. There are a lot of them."

"You think it's a logistics problem?" Yanno sounded thoughtful. "That's possible. Especially if they're far from home."

"So they want Linao, because she'll have information for them, plus she's got the most experience and would be harder to replace. Everyone else? Maybe they're disposable." Although Fliss had noticed at the mine site that the captain was angry about having her ship blown up by her colleagues, and having her life endangered by them.

"We've ruined that plan, between us," Miriam Yanno said.

Fliss shrugged. "It still doesn't explain why they riled up the raveners." She felt the sick tug of worry at the thought of Han, and the others, fighting outside the walls.

She glanced across at Captain Linao, saw she was watching her and Yanno, and she didn't look friendly.

Fliss wondered if she should tell Yanno about the captain's secret comms device in her ear.

She didn't think it would help the situation at the moment, but if Linao ended up a prisoner here once this was over, she would mention it. Right now, it was more useful to watch her while she thought no one knew what she was doing.

As they stared at each other, she saw Linao's expression change, and the captain turned away, head bowed.

If she were to guess, she'd say Linao was getting another message.

Fliss slid her hand into her pocket and engaged her disruptor again.

Linao spun to face her almost immediately, eyes narrowed.

Fliss sent her a sweet smile in return.

She knew how long the disruptor worked for, now, given the pilot of the hover had tried to power up continually after the reset.

It was ten minutes for the hover. Maybe less for the comms device, but probably not by much.

Yanno had moved off to talk to Neesha Rasmu, Fliss guessed to pass on their speculation about what the aliens were up to, and Fliss took the chance to head back into the building.

If they were simply waiting around for the hover to return, she would prefer to go check on the screens inside the comms room, see what was happening with the raveners.

There was one comms tech in the room when she got there, and the woman ignored Fliss when she walked toward the screens, her head bent over her work.

It looked deceptively quiet beyond the walls to the west and south.

There was a largarti, lying dead or wounded, crumpled close to the wall on the west side, a zuby was crashing through the trees in the south, running away.

But east and north . . . she stared in horror.

There were two carranda, so many largarti that a whole nest must have been disturbed, and a tarinac, and they were all enraged.

Gyr worked in teams, trying to bring them down, cutters sparking.

She could see Han, fighting to hold back one of the carranda.

There was something in the way he moved that had her eye focusing on him immediately, and she held her breath as he leaped high, cutter out as he took a swipe at the carranda's flank.

"You will come with me. Now." The woman's voice behind her was cold, but not as cold as the touch of the alien weapon against the back of her neck before it was lifted away.

The comms tech.

The one who'd pointed the finger at Elias earlier.

"Or?" Fliss kept her voice steady as the woman pulled her pack off her shoulder, although her gyra were in panic.

"Or I'll kill you right now. You know what this weapon can do. I got it out of Hedgeworth's office. He was very interested in what was taken from the soldiers at the mine site before he was suspended by Miriam Yanno. I've placed it on the highest setting, which I'm guessing means it can kill. The aliens want you alive, but their immediate problems will go away if you die now, so I don't think they'll be too upset about it."

"What problems will go away?" Fliss asked.

"They know it's you resetting their systems. You're the only Gyr left in the city, and there were only Gyr at the mine site when that other crash happened. You have to be the one doing it."

Fliss had to admit she had set herself up for that during her confrontation with the soldier earlier. She should have realized they'd be able to put two and two together.

"And why do they want me?"

"They don't want you, specifically," the comms tech pulled her back by the collar of her jacket and pointed her at the door. "Any Gyr would do. They wanted two at first, non-negotiable, just in case one of you dies, but they're settling for one now." She gave Fliss a little shove. "Barilar wanted to hand you and that other Gyr he was holding out in the Swathe over because neither of you could shift. No use wasting a good protector if he didn't have to. The aliens were supposed to land near that bunker and get you, but you were rescued before that could happen."

Fliss shivered at the thought. "How were they going to get a Gyr this time? They didn't know I'd be coming back to the courtyard."

"Well, here's the thing." The woman's smile was clear in her voice. "They thought they could get one of you by themselves. I was shut out of helping, and therefore profiting, because they decided to shoot up the raveners and force them toward the city. They were going to try and grab a Gyr when you lot raced out to protect Nasnere."

"That doesn't sound like a particularly good plan," Fliss said.

The woman gave a laugh. "No. How they thought they'd grab a Gyr who was busy fighting a ravener, I have no idea. But when you came back to the courtyard, Linao told them she had one in hand, so to speak, and I got the call to go out and grab you. You can't believe my surprise when you came to me."

The comms tech forced her out into the corridor and pressed the weapon briefly into the middle of Fliss' back. "Hands on your shoulders. Keep them there or I shoot."

Fliss complied, trying to see into each room they passed.

There was no one around.

She guessed everyone was outside, watching for the hover to return to fetch the next group of prisoners.

It was an exciting, once-in-a-lifetime occurrence, after all.

"Why?"

The woman didn't pretend not to understand the question.

"Because they have tech that enabled them to do a full scan of Fjern when they got here, looking for precious minerals. It was Barilar's deal at first, I was just helping him for a lump sum, but with Barilar out of things, they'll give me the whole scan in exchange for you."

They had reached the end of the corridor, and Fliss pushed open the door.

"You're going to use the map to enrich yourself?" She saw they were on the far side of the building to Gyr Command, in a narrow lane that ran beside city hall.

"It'll show me where to buy up land and dig."

She hadn't paid attention to what it meant at the time, but Fliss remembered that at the mine site, Ludig Darvan had said that his people had scanned the planet when they arrived, that they hadn't wanted to stay because of the raveners but had decided to grab useful minerals before they left.

They could only grab them if they knew where they were.

That must have been Barilar's motivation for dealing with them.

When the aliens had arrived, he'd seen an opportunity to profit, but when the mine site was discovered, he'd had to scramble for another way to benefit.

Lucy said that she'd begun to worry that she'd become more of a problem than an asset to Barilar. He hadn't known what to do with her.

Selling her to the aliens was a way to get rid of her and make himself rich into the bargain.

All he had to do was grab another Gyr in addition to Lucy, and he was back on track to get the list of ore bodies.

The comms tech pushed Fliss toward the end of the lane.

High above them she heard the hover return, but the comms tech wasn't looking to her right, where the ship was descending into the courtyard.

She was looking left.

A small hover, just like the one Han had brought down at the mine site, came at them from an angle over the roofs, low enough it wouldn't be seen from within the high walls of the courtyard.

It landed in front of them.

"They're quiet," the comms tech said with admiration.

Fliss saw a few people peering out of their upper-story windows at them, and there were a couple more further down the street who'd stopped and were staring.

None of them could save her.

They wouldn't even know what was going on.

A soldier jumped out of the small ship, and the comms tech clutched Fliss closer to her. "First the map, then you can have her."

"Here." The soldier pulled a thick roll of parchment out of his jacket pocket. The comms tech reached out, took it, and opened it one-handed. Fliss guessed she was still pointing the weapon at her back with the other.

"What's this?"

"A list." The soldier's accent was strong. "All deposits and their locations."

The tech studied it for a beat, but she must have been satisfied, because she pushed Fliss forward.

"You found what is resetting our systems?" The soldier grabbed Fliss, putting his own weapon near her head.

We could disable the weapon like we did on the way to the bunker, she told her gyra, more to calm them down than because she could currently do it.

No weapon was pressed against her skin at the moment, but as soon as one was . . .

"Here's her pack." The comms tech held it up. "I couldn't get her here on time and search her."

"Search it now," the soldier ordered, struggling to pronounce the Fjerna words correctly. He began patting Fliss down. He made a hum

306

of interest as he felt the remote in her pocket, but when he pulled it out, he pulled a face. "Too low tech. Do you recognize?"

The comms tech glanced up from the pile of stuff she had tipped onto the ground. "Looks like an air crawler remote."

The soldier tossed it to the side and it cracked as it hit the pavement.

Damn. Even if she got it back, it probably wouldn't work.

"This might be it." The woman lifted the heat signature screen.

"More promising." The soldier took it, threw it hard onto the ground and smashed it with his boot.

"I think our business is concluded." The comms tech straightened up, patted her roll of parchment, and walked away without another word.

"In." The soldier jerked the barrel of his weapon in the direction of the open hover door, and Fliss considered her options.

Her gyra did not want her to get in, but they did not want her to die.

Always a chance to escape later, they eventually opined.

She had to agree.

She climbed inside, and the soldier jumped in after her and closed the door.

The space was very small, with two forward-facing seats in the front for the pilot and co-pilot, two seats facing each other in the back, and a small area for supplies.

"Sit." The soldier pointed to the floor and sat down in one of the back seats, his weapon steady on her.

The pilot lifted off, but her sense was he didn't go high, instead skimming low again over the rooftops.

Fliss put her hands down on the smooth, hard surface beneath her and let her gyra explore.

They found the mysterious engine in moments.

Only, it didn't feel *that* mysterious. Her gyra recognized the foundational tech. It was similar to the tech that had created *them*.

Cut it off, she said.

They were still low, she could feel it.

She would have a chance this way.

If they got any higher, she might never see Fjern and Han again.

Unacceptable, her gyra agreed.

The engine shut off.

The pilot screamed something as he looked back at her for the briefest of moments, before he hunched forward, fighting the hover as it cleared the city wall and fell.

"Undo it." The soldier pushed off his chair to crouch beside her, his face a snarl, his weapon in her face, pressed into her cheek.

Dead, her gyra sang. *The weapon is dead!*

"It's not me," she shouted at him, as if panicked herself, and he said a word she was sure was deeply rude, and rose to his feet, leaning over the co-pilot's seat.

Fliss followed behind him, throwing herself onto the chair behind the pilot and strapping herself in.

The soldier tried to do the same, landing in the chair opposite, one arm sliding into a strap.

Fliss glanced over the pilot's shoulder, saw they were about to land in the middle of a ravener attack, and curled in on herself as the hover smashed into the ground.

She was jerked inside the straps, the burn as they cut into her shoulders nothing to the pain of her side hitting the back of the pilot's chair.

As if from far away she heard a carranda roar in fury and pain as the hover jarred, then flipped.

The soldier in the back with her was flung to the side as they went airborne, and then the hover bounced, rolled twice in a way that rattled her teeth and seemed to reach in and squeeze her stomach, before it came to a stop.

She was dizzy. Sick.

But it was nothing compared to the fear.

Part of the roof had been torn open in the crash, and a carranda leaned in, hooked its teeth into the hole, and ripped.

42

HAN HEARD THE FAINT SOUND OF AN ENGINE AND TOOK A PRECIOUS second to look toward the city wall.

He had sliced the carranda's back leg, and it had paused its attack while it processed the pain, giving him the moment he needed.

Minette was on the carranda's other side, and she darted in, swiping her cutter at its right leg, but he only caught her movement out of the corner of his eye, his attention on the alien ship flying toward him.

As it cleared the walls, it went suddenly silent, the engine cutting off.

He danced further from the carranda's reach as the ship pitched straight down.

It smashed into the ground and then bounced.

The carranda had started running toward it the moment the ship had cleared the wall, attracted as ever to anything that moved fast. Its curiosity put it right in the air crawler's path as it tumbled through the air.

The ship clipped the carranda's side, and the ravener roared with pain, spinning toward the vessel as it rolled to a stop.

It sprinted to the ship, ripping back the roof with its teeth, and a man scrambled out, arm clutched close to his chest as if broken.

"Careful!" Minette's shout was lost in the carranda's scream of outrage and triumph as it reached out, lightning fast, and grabbed the man up with long-fingered paws.

Han moved slowly, keeping out of the carranda's line of sight as he circled the alien ship.

The door facing away from where the carranda was ripping into the alien it had caught was partially open, crumpled inward in the crash.

Han stared in shock at what he saw inside.

"What is it?" Minette called softly from his left.

"It's . . ." He felt a strange feeling of weightlessness.

It was Fliss——hanging limp from straps around her arms.

Another man lay at her feet, his head at a strange angle.

"What?" Minette hissed.

He ignored her, running toward the door, his gaze flicking between the carranda and the ship.

The carranda lost its grip on the man and dropped him, then went into a rage at the loss, scrabbling at the ground to pick him up again.

That was good. That gave him some time.

As long as the ravener was focused elsewhere, he could get Fliss out.

He pulled himself into the ship, felt it wobble a little as his weight shifted its center of gravity.

It had landed more or less the right way up, but its legs had been severed in the crash, and the ground it had ended up on was not completely flat.

"Fliss." He whispered her name, and she tried to lift her chin, her eyelids fluttering a little.

He unclipped the harness, careful not to jostle her.

He could see a massive bruise forming on the side of her face, and when he brushed his fingers over it, he could feel a lump above her ear.

He lifted her out of the seat, careful not to stand on the body lying on the floor, and backed out.

Even in full shift, which he was, he was forced to set her down in order to jump out.

Minette had come around the side, and her eyes went wide with shock at the sight of Fliss.

Han turned and reached in to get her.

As he lifted her out, the alien ship rocked, and when he raised his head, he saw the carranda leaning over the roof.

Its gaze was fixed on him.

He took a step back, tucking Fliss close to his chest.

She made a sound, and he risked a quick glance down.

Her eyes were open, but not focused.

The aliens had been taking her, he realized. Taking her up to the mothership.

Taking her away from Fjern. From him.

The suddenly quick fire of rage that swept over him left him shaking.

The carranda's claws scraped over the roof in a high-pitched shriek, and it began to climb over the top of the ship.

It stopped on the roof, balancing in a squat, and Han backed away as it reached through the hole it had made with its teeth earlier to pull out the dead soldier.

It couldn't get him through the gap, and grunted in frustration as it tried.

Han kept backing away.

The carranda tried to force the body through the space a final time and overbalanced, falling backward.

Han turned and ran toward the wall, holding Fliss as firmly against him as he could.

Minette joined him, keeping pace, her head turned to look behind them.

Han heard the carranda scramble to its feet, and for a moment, as he glanced back, he thought it was equal odds whether it would try again to get the body out the ship or chase after him and Minette.

He stopped, and Minette stopped with him.

They waited, Han willing the carranda to go back to its unfinished task.

But, while it glanced at the ship, it ended up turning to face them, yellow eyes interested.

"Shit." Minette breathed.

"Take her." Han held Fliss over to Minette, who in shifted form was easily able to carry her.

She took her reluctantly.

"I'll distract it. You get to the closest entrance."

Minette gave a tiny nod.

"When I say go, you go." Han moved forward, cutter out, although he didn't initiate the spark yet. He moved slowly, every step smooth, his eyes on the carranda.

It eyed him right back.

"Go!" He ran straight for it, and it hopped forward in delight, its back legs still injured, although it seemed to have forgotten it was hurt.

Its long razor-clawed paws reached out, trying to grab him, and he dived under them, sparking his cutter and severing a digit.

It lifted its paw to its mouth with a cry of shock, and Han came up right beside its legs, slid through them and jumped up to grab the spur at the back of its knee.

He swung, one-handed, and lifted his cutter with the other, slicing at the soft skin to get at its tendon.

It bellowed as his cutter dug in, and fell forward, both front paws on the ground, kicking out with its back leg to dislodge him.

He caught a glimpse of Minette as he held on.

She had just reached the city wall, and was running along it to get to the closest hatch——the narrow, low openings built at intervals along the wall, put there just in case Fjerna got caught outside, and had a ravener coming at them, with no Gyr available.

He hacked at the back leg again, and with a howl, the carranda lifted both hind legs and kicked.

Han flew through the air, landing hard.

He lay, winded for a moment, head turned to see what the carranda was doing.

It wasn't spinning around to find him, though, it was crouched down, staring at Minette as she moved along the wall——coiled in on itself, as if ready to spring.

No.

No. No. No.

As Han forced himself up on his knees, it tried to leap forward, but he had succeeded in damaging its hamstring, and its right leg collapsed beneath it.

It didn't stop, though.

It keep moving forward, dragging its leg behind it.

Han staggered to his feet, his gyra humming beneath his skin, repairing his injuries.

They were as determined as him to take the carranda down.

He sprinted toward it.

Even though it was dragging its leg, it was moving fast, its focus on Minette and Fliss complete.

He reached it, ran up the back of its injured leg and onto its back.

Minette had seen it by now and had slowed her pace, hoping it would lose interest.

He saw Fliss stir in her arms, and Minette crouched down, setting her on the ground.

They spoke, heads bent together, and then Minette helped Fliss to her feet, arm beneath her shoulder, as Han reached the top of the carranda's neck.

He'd killed a few carranda in his time, and the kill blow had always been to the eye or severing an artery.

But a bleed-out would still give it time to reach Minette and Fliss, so the eye it was.

He jumped, arms spread wide, onto the top of its head, and swung his cutter down, stabbing at its eye.

It jerked its head upward as it caught the movement and his cutter hit the corner of its eye, rather than the center.

It spun right, head still thrown back. The short fur covering its skull was smooth and slick, and Han hooked his fingers into its nostril to hang on.

He swung wide, to the left, as it shook its head, and then stabbed again as he came into reach of its left eye.

It shrieked as he got it dead center, and lifted a paw to fling Han away before it collapsed on the ground.

Han landed hard against a rock near the wall and blinked back double vision as he saw the carranda drag itself toward Minette and Fliss.

He rolled onto his side, pushed himself back up, in time to see Minette dart forward, cutter sparking.

She got in a swipe across its nose, but it flicked her away, slamming her into the city wall.

Then it went still.

He managed to start walking, his balance off, his gyra hot beneath his skin, against his skull, as they tried to fix what was wrong.

Fliss lay on the ground, hand outstretched, touching the carranda's cheek.

It lay quietly, breathing in quick, shallow breaths, as blood seeped slowly from its eye and nose.

"Shh," Fliss whispered as he approached, and he stopped where he was, gaze going to Minette, who was using the wall to sit upright.

Slowly, the carranda's breathing slowed and then finally cut off completely.

Minette slumped back in relief, and Han staggered forward, falling beside Fliss and drawing her close.

"They were taking you," he said.

"I didn't let them," she whispered back.

43

"Do you think the aliens are gone?" Fliss lay tucked up against Han's side, stretching out the last of her stiffness from the day before.

"Miriam Yanno says they're watching the sky, and I think that's going to be someone's full time job from now on, but it seems they have gone."

"I suppose they lost a lot of their hovers, as well as a mothership and quite a few people. And they left empty-handed."

Han reached out and tucked her close as she said that.

It was incomprehensible that they could have left with her.

"My gyra would have found a way," she said quietly. "They would have worked out how to take over the ship, and flown us back."

He brushed back her hair as he turned on his side to face her. "I believe you. But still . . ."

Something in his eyes, some resonance from his gyra, told her he would have been in a dark place until she returned.

"They were lucky Miriam Yanno didn't know what had happened to me. That they had the nerve to send their hover down a third time to fetch Captain Linao, hoping to get her before someone noticed what was happening over the wall, was truly brazen."

"Captain Linao was obviously much more important to them than we knew." Han ran a finger along her temple, where the last of her bruises were fading away. "Miriam Yanno said they came down very fast the third time, grabbed Linao and those left with her, and went just as quickly."

They had been banking on no one in the comms room alerting the council to what was happening beyond the walls. Jana Rush, the comms tech, had returned to her post as if she hadn't just sold Fliss for a list of mine sites, but when she'd seen the crash on screen, she'd run.

Her plan was over if Fliss was alive to tell the council what she knew.

The comms tech would be in hiding for the rest of her life, although Fliss was confident the Gyr would find her. Everyone had taken great offence that Rush had tried to sell a Gyr.

The sound of someone walking past their guest suite had Han tensing beneath her, and Fliss kissed his bare shoulder. "You don't trust Evan or his team?"

Evan had welcomed them into his gyratta last night as guests, and Fliss thought he and his team had been welcoming and hospitable.

"I want to trust him, but he had Jaco and Reese under his roof for a long time."

The taint of suspicion would linger, especially toward any Gyr who had anything to do with Barilar, and anyone nominated after Jaco, as well as anyone in Gyr Command who was Barilar's ally.

"What's happened with Hedgeworth?"

Han stirred, yawned, and pulled her closer. "Miriam said last night that they've found comms between him, Barilar and some other administrators on how to curb the Gyr's influence. Hedgeworth's claiming it was just talk, that he never knew about Lucille's imprisonment, or about what Barilar had planned for you, but he's done. The council have stood him down permanently and they'll do the same for anyone on that list. At the very least they never spoke up about what Barilar was doing, and that condemns them."

A light knock at their door brought them both upright.

"It's me, boss," Delasio called softly.

Fliss slipped out of the bed, leaving Han to answer, and went into the bathroom to shower.

When she came out, Del had gone, and Han was pulling on his clothes.

"We have to go?" She saw the bruise on his side was fading, but it was still visible, and she walked over to run her fingers along his skin.

He sighed, feathered his own fingers into her hair. "A final meeting with the council before we leave for Vallent."

She dressed in clothes Evan's team had lent her, and walked with Han to wait outside the gyratta next to the air crawlers for everyone to join them.

"Something is different about the arch." Evan stood beneath it, eyes closed. He was still limping from the ravener battle the day before, and there was a deep cut on his cheek that was taking time to heal.

He tilted his head up so the scan would play across his face.

"I recalibrated it," Fliss said. "It was off-kilter."

Evan opened his eyes and stared at her in surprise. "My gyra say that you are right."

"What does that mean?" Isolde, Evan's lieutenant, asked.

"When the oscillation is off like that, it damages your gyra."

Isolde walked back under the arch to see, lifted both arms and tipped back her head. "This is good."

"You should go to South Nasnere Gyratta, make sure their arch is right, too." Evan moved toward the air crawlers.

Fliss had planned to go to South Nasnere anyway, to say goodbye to Lucy and Teranimo, who'd decided to settle there. It had been Lucy's original gyratta before she was taken by Barilar.

"I will."

"You should probably go to all the gyratta on Fjern. Because there hasn't been one that you've encountered that was right so far, has there?" Delasio asked as they climbed into the air crawler.

"No." That should have occurred to her earlier. Not a single one was correctly calibrated. "Who is responsible for maintaining them?"

"Gyr Command." Han looked thoughtful as he said it. "It's something else to raise today."

As the air crawlers lifted up, a convoy of two, Fliss simply hoped they could get through the day without any more treachery.

"I CHALLENGE your witness to say that I was ever at that bunker." Han could see Pal Barilar was sweating, standing on the accused side of the chamber. His legal representative had allowed him to answer in his own defense.

Han was sorry he couldn't simply separate the man's head from his body.

Still, it was satisfying that every Gyr who was able to get to Nasnere in time for the hearing had come. For one day, the Fjerna would have to deal with the raveners on their own, because no one had stayed behind today.

Han had gotten the message out to everyone he could, got Jayna and Barnes to travel to Nasnere from Vallent, and Gyr from North and South Nasnere Gyratta, Renardo, as well as two smaller gyratta from the east were all here.

And they were angry.

The fixed stares were putting Barilar off his stride.

"I never said you were there." Lucy was calm as she stood on the accuser side. "I said you were behind my kidnap, you are the one who directed Jaco, Antonio and Elias to transport me to the bunker, and I heard you on comms calls to them numerous times while they were checking on me. Calls during which my imprisonment, and how I was doing, was discussed."

"We only have your word on that," Barilar's representative broke in. "There is no evidence Administrator Barilar was behind what happened."

"There is," Miriam Yanno said. "I call Oliver Reese."

There was a murmur among the Gyr at that.

He was Gyr, and some would have heard he was complicit in what had happened.

Since yesterday he had been under guard in the capital, and Han wondered what would be done with him.

He guessed Miriam Yanno would use the gyra-na to take his gyra.

It looked like he knew it, too.

He kept his head down and did not greet his fellow Gyr.

Barilar's face told everyone present what a blow Reese's appearance was to him.

He clenched his hands together and stared straight ahead, making no eye contact with anyone.

"Do you testify that Pal Barilar made you a Gyr on condition you spied on your fellow Gyr for him?" Miriam Yanno asked Reese. "That he did the same with Louis Jaco and used Jaco to kidnap and check on Lucille Defoe? That you were involved in conversations with both Barilar and Jaco about this, and that Lucille Defoe's testimony is accurate?"

"Yes." Reese looked over at Barilar. "You offered me what I wanted, and then destroyed any pride I had in becoming Gyr." He turned to the Gyr in the room. "I'm sorry for betraying you. I suspect that by the end of the day, I will no longer be among your ranks."

Barilar was shaking his head, but Han thought it was more a matter that he was refusing to accept that he had no place left to hide, than denying he had done what was alleged.

"Anyone have any more evidence?" Yanno asked.

When there was silence, she signaled to the security officers and they led Barilar away.

"She'll be the end of you! Both her and that baby will." Barilar shouted out the accusation just as he reached the door. "Their kind will taint your gyra and you'll get weaker and weaker. In a few years you'll see I'm right, and it'll be too late."

He was hustled out, and there was a moment of silence.

"What is he talking about?" Yasmin Ren, leader of the Naloo Gyratta to the east of Nasnere, asked.

"I'm Gyr-born," Fliss said. "I think he's warning you not to have children."

"We *can't* have children." Evan stood from his seat. "I still don't understand how you can exist."

"I can." Pen stood, and Han noticed Delasio was standing behind her, face set in stone, as if he were tamping down on massive emotions. "This morning my gyra asked me if I wanted to conceive. If I want to, I could be pregnant right away."

"Explain how." Lolia shoved to her feet.

"Del and I . . ." She glanced back at Del, and he took a step closer to her, for support. "Well, we have been together for a while now. Except this morning, my gyra told me for the first time that they could make sure I was or wasn't pregnant, according to my feelings on the matter." She paused. "This is because of you, Fliss."

Fliss blinked in surprised, frowned, and then gave a slow nod. "The arch scans?"

"The arch scans," Pen agreed. "They oscillate properly now."

"What are you talking about?" The full council had been watching and listening in silence, as had Miriam Yanno and a number of other administrators. Now Neesha Rasmu stood to ask the question.

"We're talking about the arch scan at the entrance of our gyratta actively harming us. We don't know for how long. We are talking about the scan being set right, and now, we have the ability to conceive, if we so wish." Han had intended to raise the matter of the arch scan anyway, but now, with Pen's revelation, it was the perfect time.

That their sterility wasn't a built-in feature of being a Gyr, but a consequence of the arch scan, was beyond enraging.

"How was it set right?" Miriam Yanno asked.

"I set it right," Fliss said. "It was off-kilter, and my gyra know how to fix it."

"What was being done whenever a tech from Gyr Command came to maintain the arch scan?" Taque asked into the silence.

The administrator took a small step back. "I am going to confess something to you. It may sound self-serving to hear my excuse, but truly, I was told I was upholding a two-thousand year tradition to keep the Fjerna safe." She looked over at her fellow administrators and then at the councilors. "We were told this by whoever came before us. And I have told it myself to the new administrators coming up behind me. It was the truth as I knew it."

Han thought the silence from the Gyr was probably more frightening to the Fjerna in the room than a loud protest.

Miriam Yanno cleared her throat. "When I was sworn in as a senior administrator, I was told there was a decision . . ." She drew in a breath and looked across as her colleagues. "A decision to prevent the Gyr from having children."

There was a sudden murmur. It whispered through the room and then faded, but Han could feel the beat of shock and anger coming from every Gyr. Their gyra were resonating in concert with each other.

Miriam straightened up, pushed back her shoulders. "I was told that early on, after we landed on Fjern, there was genuine worry amongst the Fjerna that the Gyr would be able to rise up to be some kind of ruling class. And if they were able to have children, expand their number, then that would make the scenario even more likely."

Han wasn't surprised by the revelation. He even understood the logic behind it.

It was the lies he didn't accept . . .

"While onboard the *Cercatore*, everyone used contraceptives, as the mothership could only support so many people, but when we landed . . ." Miriam drew up her shoulders. "It was up to individuals whether to have children or not. And a decision was made to alter the scan in the gyratta arches to take the choice away from the Gyr, and then to tell them their infertility was because of their gyra." She rubbed her sternum in agitation. "We were told it wasn't permanent, the Gyr could have children if they gave up their gyra, which meant a good flow of young warriors to protect us."

"So our whole system is built on lies?" Han asked softly.

Miriam slowly nodded. "Yes. It has never sat comfortably with me, and it's why I am being honest about it now. I have wanted to speak out many times in the past, and my understanding is a few other administrators who wanted to do the same conveniently disappeared or were killed in ravener attacks before they could talk. Those disappearances kept people silent."

"So the arches were maintained to perpetuate infertility for the last two thousand years?" Teranimo asked.

Miriam nodded.

Han stared at her for a long beat, then at the council behind her and the other members of Gyr Command in the room. Some were obviously shocked, clearly hearing this for the first time.

Others——very few, but some——he could see they had known.

He turned, putting out a hand for Fliss to take, and they walked out.

Every Gyr followed them.

They did it in silence, and Han could hear a rising babble of voices from the council behind him.

He headed for the museum, to the *Cercatore*, the mothership that had brought them to this planet, because he knew it had a gyratta inside it, a place where the Gyr could be alone and safe.

The others worked out where he was going, and he could feel their approval, their gyra transmitting agreement.

They walked past the museum's welcome desk, past an astonished curator, and through the dull gray passageways, until they came to the only arched door on the ship.

He picked up Fliss' excitement at visiting the ship, and looked across at her, smiling, despite his feelings of betrayal, at her enthusiasm.

He had been inside the *Cercatore* before.

The novelty of visiting the first gyratta had drawn him as a child, had inspired him to put himself forward as a recruit, and when he'd become Gyr at the age of seventeen, he had made his way to this room on his first free afternoon just so he could finally step through and see inside.

It was set up for ten groups of ten, and the Gyr with him could easily fit into the space.

Before they entered, though, he held up a hand to stop anyone stepping under the arch, motioned to Fliss, and understanding, she stepped through and stood beneath it, eyes closed.

She opened them, nodded that it was now correctly calibrated, and Han led the way inside.

He could see that Pen and Del were standing close together, murmuring softly to each other, and he felt a lift of happiness at the sight of them.

His gyra were intrigued by the prospect of a child in the gyratta.

About the prospect of all of them having the choice.

"What do we do, Han?" Evan was the first to speak. "I will not let this go."

"I cannot see myself submitting to Gyr Command's instructions ever again." Lolia's voice was grim. "First they kidnap Lucille, then this . . ." She turned to Teranimo. "You really didn't know about it?"

Teranimo shook his head. "I was never an administrator, I was hired as a scientist."

Lolia seemed to relax at that, gave a nod.

"Can you come to our gyratta and recalibrate our arch?" Jasmin asked Fliss.

She nodded. "I had planned to visit all the gyratta on Fjern, because, as Del mentioned this morning, none of the arches I've encountered have worked properly. Not a single one so far."

"What did Barilar mean, about you tainting our gyra and making us weak?" Jerome, from the Renardo Gyratta, asked.

Taque gave him a hard look. "Do not talk to the Gyr-born that way."

"Being Gyr-born doesn't make her untouchable," Jerome answered back. "I have a right to ask questions, to try to understand what Barilar meant."

"You'd trust the word of a man who tried to sell two Gyr to aliens in exchange for wealth?" Lolia asked with contempt. "A man who imprisoned a Gyr who was pregnant to find ways to hurt us?"

There was silence.

"Jerome is right." Fliss spoke up, and every eye turned her way. "I am not special. I am Gyr, just like you. But unlike you, when I'm in danger, when my gyra think it's my life or the life of my attacker, and that attacker is Gyr, I am able to take their gyra." She shifted self-consciously and Han moved to stand behind her. He put a hand on her shoulder, and looked out at his fellow Gyr.

He saw shock on some faces. Others, who knew what Fliss could do, were calm and keeping a watchful eye on the others.

"However, Barilar didn't know that about me, I don't think." She tugged nervously at her jacket. "I think he meant if a Gyr-born has gyra, by logical conclusion, those gyra have to have come from their Gyr parents. That it will weaken those Gyr parents. That each generation of Gyr-born will dilute the concentration of gyra bit by bit, until we are the same as the Fjerna."

It was nothing the Gyr hadn't considered before, but that had been theoretical, because they had always thought they couldn't have children.

"Are you saying that Barilar is wrong?" Evan asked.

"I don't know. What he's warning about is the opposite of the fears the Fjerna had about us taking over because we would be powerful and many. So, either the original administrators and scientists knew something Barilar doesn't, or he is lying to make us afraid."

"Or they were wrong," Jerome said. "Paranoid."

Fliss nodded. "Maybe they were. They wanted strong Gyr to protect them, but not too many of them that they could take over. My own guess is the process of creating a child shows the gyra how to multiply themselves. I don't think my father had less gyra after I was born."

"Well, we could ask him," Jerome said.

Fliss shook her head. "I'm afraid he was one of the people my gyra saw as my enemy. I took his gyra from him when I was three years old."

There was an almost physical recoil from amongst the Gyr.

"It is good to understand that Gyr-born babies will not understand what they are doing," Lolia murmured.

"I understood," Fliss corrected her. "My father was abusive. My gyra knew that he was able to hurt me more as a Gyr than as a Fjerna, and so they took his gyra. That made him weaker, and me stronger, and it was a perfectly logical step, in their mind."

Han felt the anger rising in him once again at what Ralf Bellini had done to Fliss. He saw the same sentiment on the faces of a number of others in the room, and felt himself relax a little.

"Will all Gyr-born be able to do that?" Del asked.

Fliss shrugged. "I just don't know."

"There is a lot we don't know." Han could feel Fliss's discomfort at being the center of attention, and sought to move the conversation away from her and her abilities. "It sounds from what Pen and Del have experienced that our gyra will give us the choice about children. No one will be forced into a situation they do not want. We can see how this plays out over time."

That seemed to lower the tension, as everyone considered the options.

"So, what do we do now?" Taque looked around the group. "Because I am not bowing to Gyr Command any more."

"Now we set up our own Gyr Command, run by Gyr." Han had been thinking of this for a very long time. "Now we become autonomous."

44

BEFORE THEY LEFT THE *CERCATORE*, FLISS WANTED TO FIND OUT WHERE the pulse was coming from.

Han hesitated, surprised when she went deeper into the ship, rather than leave with the other Gyr to confront the council, but he followed her.

She glanced back at him. "Can you feel it?"

He shook his head. "Feel what?"

She thumped her fist on her chest twice. "That."

He frowned. "No."

"It's coming from here." She stepped into the room at the front of the ship, with chairs facing a large screen that took up the whole front two thirds of the wall. Control panels lined the sides.

"This is the bridge. Where the captain and navigators sat." Han stepped in with her.

"Here." She walked to one of the control panels. Tapped it.

"The mysterious flashing light." Han lifted the flap that had been fashioned to sit over the light, added long after the spaceship had been forced to land here. "I used to love lifting the flap to see it, when I was little."

"Can't you feel the resonance?" she asked. "It's trying to say something. I just can't understand what."

"A beacon." Han crouched beside the light, and stared at her, eyes alight with excitement. "That's how the aliens found us in such a big galaxy. They followed the beacon."

Fliss's breath caught. "It led them to us. The Ancestors set it as a cry for help to their fellow Travelers."

"But we didn't get help." Han studied the blinking light.

"Should I shut it off?" Fliss asked. Her gyra could do it, she was sure about that.

He shook his head. "I think that's something we have to discuss with everyone. But I'd say no. We know they're out there, now, and if Ludig Darvan is right, the Verdant String Coalition is not a bad organization. We weren't dealing with its citizens, we were dealing with criminals on the run from them. Hopefully Darvan can tell us what to expect and how to prepare."

He lowered the flap and rose.

"Time to upend the natural order?" she asked, sliding a hand into his.

He tugged her out of the room. "The way things were wasn't the natural order. I think that's why I've always had so much trouble with it."

She wasn't sure what the answer was. What the right balance was to strike. But what they had now was not working, Han was right about that.

"What will happen to Gyr Command?"

"I don't care right now," Han said. "Maybe I'll care in a few days when the reality of this settles, but I will not have faceless administrators threatening my gyrbar."

She stopped at the entrance to the museum, which was set at the double doors at the bottom of the *Cercatore's* loading bay. "We can punish those who meant us harm, but there are many who appreciate us and will be just as angry on our behalf about what's gone on here." She thought of Enid, of the gratitude of the people she'd saved in Vallent.

He gave a slow nod and she looked out into the courtyard where the rest of the Gyr were waiting for her and Han to join them.

Waiting to confront the council and Gyr Command together.

She had hoped for a new life when she'd left the escarpment with Dakar, she had hoped to meet more Gyr and find some personal freedom.

She had gotten everything she'd wished for.

She looked up at Han.

And more.

So much more.

ALSO BY MICHELLE DIENER

Science Fiction Novels

Verdant String series:

Interference & Insurgency Box Set

Breakaway

Breakeven

Trailblazer

High Flyer

Wave Rider

Peace Maker

Sky Raiders series:

Intended (Short Story Prequel Available Free to Newsletter Subscribers)

Sky Raiders

Calling the Change

Shadow Warrior

Class 5 series:

Dark Horse

Dark Deeds

Dark Minds

Dark Matters

Dark Ambitions: A Class 5 Novella

Dark Class

Dark Class Epilogue: Free on newsletter signup

Fantasy Novels by Michelle Diener

The Rising Wave series:

The Rising Wave (Prequel novella to THE TURNCOAT KING)

The Turncoat King

The Threadbare Queen

Fate's Arrow (Coming late 2022)

Mistress of the Wind

The Dark Forest series:

The Golden Apple

The Silver Pear

Historical Fiction Novels

Regency London series:

The Emperor's Conspiracy

Banquet of Lies

A Dangerous Madness

Other historical novels:

Daughter of the Sky

Short Paranormal Fiction

Breaking Out: Part I (Short story)

Breaking Out: Part II (Novella)

To receive notification when a new book is released, sign up at michellediener.com.

ABOUT THE AUTHOR

Michelle Diener is an award winning author of historical fiction, science fiction and fantasy.

Michelle was born in London and currently lives in Australia with her husband and children.

Connect with Michelle
www.michellediener.com

ACKNOWLEDGMENTS

Thank you so much to Claire, Jo and Justin for your eagle eyes and great suggestions as always. Thank you also to Christine B., Tania H., Jess W. and Diane J. from my reader team.

Thank you to MiblArt for the wonderful cover.